Serendipity in Berkeley

Kay C. Beerman

This book is a work of fiction. All characters in this book have no existence outside the imagination of the author and have no relation whatsoever to anyone bearing the same name or names. All incidents are pure invention.

Cover design by Kelly A. Martin of
KAM Design

ISBN: 978-1-7004-47982

THE BAY AREA BLUES: BOOK 4

The Bay Area Blues Series:

To serve and protect the public.
Law enforcement has the ultimate purpose.

If the protectors don't protect,
who'd stand between good and evil?

Odes to law enforcement wearing blue
with honor and integrity in the Bay Area.

CONTENTS

ACKNOWLEDGMENTS

As I stated prior, this book is a work of fiction. None of the persons or occurrences in the story exist in reality.

However, so as to make my story more fun, I inserted some song titles and quotes from movies in the story, and I hope for people to reach out to the original works.

Below I listed such prior art that appears in my story (Alphabetical order).

Song Titles (artist, year of the song recorded or released):

Calling All Angels (Train, 2003)

Hotel California (Eagles, 1976)

Love is in the air (John Paul Young, 1977)

Sister Golden Hair (America, 1975)

Movies and TV Shows, (year, quotes I used)

An Affair to Remember (1957, *I was looking up…it was the nearest thing to heaven. You were there…*)

Bram Stoker's Dracula (1992, *I have crossed oceans of time to find you.*)

Casablanca (1942, *Here's looking at you kid, Kiss me. Kiss me as if it were the last time, Round up the usual suspects.*)

The English Patient (1996, *I promise I'll come back for you. I promise I'll never leave you.*)

Finding Nemo (2003, *I look at you…and I'm home…*)

Jerry Maguire (1996, *You had me at hello.*)

Star Trek, Season 3, Episode 9: The Tholian Web (1968 TV, *In critical moments, men sometimes see exactly what they wish to see.*)

Serendipity (2001, *If we're meant to meet again, then we'll meet again.*)

Star Wars, Episode IV: A New Hope (1977, *You're my only hope.*), *Episode V: The Empire Strikes Back* (1980, *Impressive. Most impressive. Obi-Wan has taught you well.*), *Episode VI: Return of the Jedi* (1983, *Your insight serves you well.*)

The Three Musketeers (1993, *One for all, and all for one.*)

You've Got Mail (1998, *I wanted it to be you, I wanted it to be you so badly.*)

007, Goldfinger (1964, *Shaken, not stirred*), *SPECTRE* (2015, *Well it's all a matter of perspective*)

I am profoundly grateful and revere each artwork as a miracle of human history. Thank you.

Kay C. Beerman

CHAPTER 1

Berkeley Police Department Detective Bureau, Berkeley, CA

Early Saturday morning, mid-April

The Detective Bureau was rather quiet during weekends when there weren't any major crimes in the city.

Although the detectives were typically on call on weekends, they often took turns to work at the office. This morning, Sgt. Sam Crawford and his partner on the force Detective Carter Halls were at their desks, finishing up paperwork.

Carter's dark blond hair desperately needed combing, but he was a lot more awake than a couple of hours ago after a dose of coffee. His hazel eyes had finally enough power to decipher what exactly he was looking at in front of him.

It was only Carter's duty day today, but Sam had decided to join his buddy so that he could keep him company and finish up his own paperwork too. The truth was he had nothing to do except either go to the gym or run. He played shortstop on one of the police/fire ball teams, but he'd injured his right shoulder last season. He wasn't quite ready to even 'play catch' yet until his doctor would deem him good to go. At his age…although he'd be only thirty-three this year, he shouldn't have slid into home colliding with a younger and bigger catcher.

The telephone on Carter's desk rang. "Detective Halls…"

Sam, sitting next to him, looked up.

"Wait a sec," he said to the receiver and asked him, "From the dispatcher. Wanna hear?"

"Sure."

He switched to speaker. "Go ahead, Susie."

"Okay, we got a call from a few good Samaritans reporting kind of a traffic accident at the intersection of University Avenue and Fourth Street…"

Carter frowned. "Kind of?"

"Well, people said…it's like um…a guy from the sky landed on a truck…"

"Er…what?" They looked at each other, grimacing.

"Yeah, that's what I said too. Nobody seemed to know what exactly happened. Anyways we got a fatality. Either of you can go?"

"Sure, which side?" Sam asked.

"North. Thanks." She hung up.

He got to his feet, picking up his jacket. "'K, laters."

"Clear the scene ASAP, or people gonna kill us. It's damn Saturday."

"No shit."

Berkeley in Alameda County was the city on the east side of San Francisco Bay and home to University of California (UC) Berkeley. It was an academic town, relatively quieter than neighboring cities, but Fourth Street was one long stretch of road with many stores. If the police cordoned off the area long, it would create a huge traffic jam. Very inconvenient for shoppers. They might not kill him but certainly curse at him. Dammit.

When he arrived at the scene, the yellow tapes were fluttering in the wind, and a few uniforms and CSI were already at work.

He parked his unmarked black Charger at the tail of the police cars.

The accident looked…weird: The vehicle involved was a Ford F-250 with a raised suspension in the middle of the intersection, just below the University Avenue overpass. It had some construction materials and equipment on the truck bed. The male victim was still on the partially smashed hood, face up. His age could be forties, but he had bald spots on his head. Could be older. His skin was sickly pale, unnatural just for his demise. And the victim was also thin. He might've been sick or a drug addict. His clothes were a tired cotton shirt and sweatpants. And no shoes… Wait, no shoes? Then where the hell had he come from? Sam took a mental note.

He then looked up at the University Avenue overpass and spotted a couple of their CSI were also working there, dusting the handrails that stood at the edge of the curb. He'd climbed over them? Suicide? But to commit suicide, the overpass around Fourth wasn't high enough to kill. What exactly had happened?

"Hey Sarge, you working on Saturdays now?" one of the uniforms greeted, lifting a part of the yellow tape up for him.

"So are you, Jack, long time no see," he replied.

"Since that friggin' jewelry larceny case."

"Ah, right, that damn fraud case." The unfinished business still made his mouth bitter, the case that he'd had to stop investigating for the time being due to lack of evidence. He shook his head once as if it'd help him forget the acrid memory. "Thanks." He went under the tape, approaching the truck.

One of the medical examiners was at work on the victim, using a medical thermometer probe to take the body temperature. Although he was tall, he had to stay on the step to reach the correct position of the liver since the truck sat high. Then, he deftly put a small paper bag on the victim's hands assisted by a seasoned CSI Sgt. Oscar Silva, so that they could preserve his fingers and hands in case they'd have potential evidence. Sam recognized the doctor right away when he'd spotted him.

Dr. Barry Taylor. The legendary chief medical examiner/forensic pathologist at the Alameda County Coroner's Bureau. His iconic long silver hair was tied at his back with a purple scrunchie. Sam saw part of his clothes, Levi's with fringed trimmings underneath his white lab coat and leather flip-flops. He might be wearing a pale pink T with a peace symbol. Sam grinned surreptitiously.

This doctor played the guitar in a veterans' band *EZ Poppas* that performed rock 'n' roll once a week at his café of the same name downtown.

When Sam had become a sworn police officer about ten years ago, the doctor had been working as a pathology specialist at University of California San Francisco (UCSF) General Hospital and Trauma Center where Sam had been airlifted for his burn trauma. He'd helped treat his burns as a former ER doctor and later he'd been hired by Alameda County Coroner's.

"Hey, Doc Taylor."

"Oh, hey Sam." Barry turned around to face him, his distinctive blue eyes sparkling. "You're on call too?"

"I was at the office. Need to finish friggin' paperwork."

"Damn." He shook his head. "Wherever we go, why in the hell is there always paperwork waiting for us?"

Sam snorted. "Tell me about it."

"You're too young to be buried under 6 feet of friggin' papers. It's pathetic. Where's your date?"

"No date."

"No kidding. Young, good-looking dapper like you?"

"Aw, thanks, Doc, please tell that to all the women in the world."

"Huh…" He stood there with his hand on his hip, staring at him.

Sam was tall and handsome, light brown hair with splashes of blond and eyes of aged bourbon color; he'd played ball in school, including college, still played shortstop so his body was toned but not heavy. A good cop, better man.

"Don't look at me like you wanna date me, Doc."

"Well hell, I wish I could. Unfortunately I like women. But why don't you come to my café tomorrow when I play? Many girls will be there. You could hook up with one of them."

"No time for a date, but I like to listen to your music though."

"Every Sunday evening at 7. Come tomorrow evening."

"Sure, thanks. Okay, Doc, about the vic. Can you give me your initial assessment? I heard he'd fallen from the sky." He took out his notebook.

"Yup, that's what I heard too, though he didn't have vestiges of angel wings on his back." And Barry pointed out one stocky guy standing outside the yellow cordon tape, who was talking to the uniform. "That's the driver and owner of the truck. He repeated the story to me and to the cops too."

"Ah, okay. We'll interview him later. So ETD is?" He asked him the victim's estimated time of death.

"About forty minutes ago, so…around 8:20am, according to the liver temp."

"He died from the fall, then," taking notes, he muttered.

"Timewise, yeah, that's the logical understanding, right? But then there are quite many inconsistencies."

"Like?" His brow furrowed. Could be hard to find COD – the cause of death?

"Well, I need to cut him open to really know what happened, but if he died from the fall, the body condition is too good. I mean, look, all his bones are intact. Possibly a little cracked finger or two, but I don't think he died from the fall. And where the hell did he come from? Did you notice he's barefoot?"

"Yup, I'm puzzled too."

"Feet were a bit dirty so he must've walked without

shoes."

"Okay…oh, what about the skull? Maybe a skull fracture?"

"Negative. No severe blunt force trauma. Well, I need X-rays to give you an accurate evaluation, but it's beautifully intact."

"Huh…" He wrote the doctor's words in his notebook.

"He might've suffered from a hemorrhage like cerebral or any internal or might've had acute heart failure, but if you'd die or suffer from those friggin' traumas, your body displays at least part of the symptoms. He has none of those, let alone a fall accident. Look, the truck's windshield is also intact, just a little tiny crack and its front hood nicely crushed to cushion him."

"Yeah…okay, anything else?"

"Instead, he might've been ill."

His pen stopped. "Very pale, isn't he?"

"Hmm, I'm suspecting our victim could've been poisoned."

"Whoa."

"Like I said, I need an autopsy and to check his blood and urine, but he has those curious bald spots, and his fingernails have leukonychia striata, a.k.a. Mees' lines."

"Mees'…oh, you mean white lines across the nails?" Even he knew what it meant. "So, he was exposed to poison recently."

"Possible. Either arsenic or any heavy metal for a time. But there's also another possibility. He could be a chemotherapy patient. Pale, thin, Mees' lines, bald spots, and all. We must check his internal condition."

"I see." He nodded. "I'll get his fingerprints and check the database. But like you said, I can also imagine the case that he could've been a cancer patient at a hospital and came here directly from there."

"Right," Barry agreed. "His brain was confused from his chemo and he wandered out of the hospital without shoes, took a taxi, walked or something and fell off the rail of the overpass… Still, bizarre, though."

"Yeah, we gotta search for witnesses, but so far, I like the chemo scenario best," Sam said, "but your initial assessment won't tell us COD, right?"

"Need an autopsy and all sorts of lab tests. Anyway, do fingerprints, okay?" And he started to walk to his van, pulling the latex gloves off his hands, throwing them in the transport personnel's trash bag.

"Doc, can you perform an autopsy on him now if you go back to the Coroner's Bureau?"

"No can do, Sam. Remember I'm on call today? I'm going to San Leandro and Hayward after this."

"But I need to know COD. This is too bizarre."

"Hell, if I could stay in the autopsy room, I'd love to do that for you, and actually I really want to know COD too. But I possess only one head and one body and four extremities, although some people believe I have more than two sets of them. Anyway, must go now. But you're welcome to escort the transport vehicle to the Bureau and get his fingerprints if you want to do it yourself. No assistants there today."

"Any medical examiners available?"

"It's Saturday, Sam. Only I'm on call and…" Then Barry remembered something. "Oh wait, there could be another medical examiner there."

"Seriously?"

"Yeah, should be working to catch up on goddamn paperwork today, like you…"

Sam rolled his eyes. "No one can get away from friggin' paperwork, huh?"

"Precisely. Nothing is certain but death and taxes and paperwork."

He grinned at the doc's tweaked quote. Yeah, he liked Dr. Barry very much.

"Hope papers can wait. I just gotta know COD, ASAP."

"I got you, just a sec." Barry took out his phone and swiftly made a call. "Hey," he greeted someone on the other side casually. "Do me a favor. I'll be sending you one male body right now. It's a case for the Berkeley Police and they're in a hurry to know COD. I'll send my initial assessment electronically after this phone call. And the BPD detective is escorting the transporter. Um…Sgt. Sam Crawford. Yeah…I know. Okay, thanks, I owe you one." And he laughed lightly at the phone. "Yeah, tell that to the detective coming along with the body. He thinks paperwork could wait. Anyway, appreciate it. See you on Monday." He hung up.

"So, another doc will help me then," Sam said with relief.

"Yeah, this doctor's very new there."

He remembered now. A few months ago, the Coroner's Bureau had hired a new female medical examiner/forensic pathologist. He hadn't paid any attention to the bulletin, as he knew they were all excellent. So, he had no idea who she was.

"Sorry, Doc, I don't know her yet."

"Oh, no worries. She's several years younger than you are, but she's very good, more than good, meticulous and exceptional, to be precise."

"Whoa, my expectation is rising, Dr. Taylor."

"She won't disappoint you. In fact, she graduated and got degrees early and awards for excellent performance in the industry in Europe. Don't underestimate her. Treat her right or you'll get burned."

He didn't get what he meant, but he replied, snickering, "I don't wanna get burned ever again. Been there, done that." That drew a light laugh from Barry.

"What's her name again?" He really should've read the internal news.

"Alexandra Wallace, M.D., but all of us call her Dr. Alex. She used to work with live patients but changed."

"Huh, just like you, then, Doc." Now he vaguely recalled he'd heard the name several times and seen it on the autopsy reports. "So, she's European."

"I don't know if you can call her a European when she

was born and raised in Berkeley and a US citizen."

"She's local?"

"It's obvious you don't read any internal newspaper, Sam." Barry laughed.

"I'll try to read more from now on." He smirked wryly. "Thanks, Doc."

"Hey, Sam, drive safe, so you won't add yourself to my work." He waved and walked toward his van.

Sam shook his head again, chuckling. He first gave Carter a ring to take a statement from the truck driver coming with a uniform. Then, he slid into his car.

*****

Sam Crawford. Sam Brayden Crawford.

Wow. It'd been ten years already.

After the chief coroner had hung up the phone, Alex mused.

He was now a detective. And Sergeant. Taking care of major cases. Talk about time flying.

She'd been eighteen years old, a pre-med at UC Berkeley. She wasn't sure how old he'd been then, but she knew he'd been a rookie.

One spring Saturday night, on her way back home from a small theater in San Francisco – she'd been asked to play Ophelia in *Hamlet* in her BFF Rachel's experimental production for junior high kids – some speeding asshole in his pickup truck chased by the police had hit her little VW Bug hard from behind on Interstate 80…

Her car was pushed off the highway after a couple of spins, rolls, and landed in the ditch on the shoulder. The crash was extensive with the front airbag deploying that caused her chest to whoosh all the air out of her lungs, suffocating her with unbelievable pain. She had no idea if she was upside down or right side up. She was trapped in the driver's seat, half-unconscious in the totaled car.

Feeling like dreaming with pain…

She was losing consciousness, thinking about her family, BFFs, and her future, hazily listening to sirens.

Then she heard the voice that assailed her blurry mind, waking her up. "Wake up, don't go sleep, baby! Rescue is coming, just hang in there."

The windows were all shattered so she perceived the voice wasn't just her dream. Suddenly a warm touch on her face.

And he asked her, "What's your name?" "Connie." "Okay, Connie, hang in there."

It was her middle name, but she was using it as her first name. Also due to her mother's status at that time as a single mom, Alex's first driver's license had her middle name *Connie* as the first name and her mother's maiden name *Morgan* as her surname, until her mother got married to Alex's biological father a couple of years later.

She was in shock and her body temperature dropping drastically.

She exerted all her power to look back at him, still feeling fading away. Then his voice: *Connie, stay with me. Don't sleep.* And she felt another touch. She opened her eyes again to gaze at him.

She saw the police officer in uniform encouraging her.

He touched her cheek and hair, his bourbon hued eyes staring at her.

Huh…warm but strong eyes. Sending her care, affection and passion. Maybe she was close to heaven.

She dimly thought, *I was looking up…it was the nearest thing to heaven. You were there…*

It was just a quote from a movie that old movie buffs she and Rae had watched together a few days before.

An Affair to Remember. An old movie but a good one. She'd liked the quote so much.

Staring at his eyes, looking at heaven, she tried to stay awake. He smiled and nodded. Then, the firefighters began ripping her car door off.

Soon, she was out of the car and on a stretcher on the ground. Her neck and body were immobilized. And the EMTs started assessing her injury, telling her it wasn't too bad for this type of accident. You were lucky, they said. She mulled if she'd be really lucky, she wouldn't have been hit by the douchebag. Later she'd found she'd fractured only one rib, a humerus and her clavicle. Yes, they'd been right about her being lucky…

But bad things came in multiples.

At one point, the firefighters and EMTs were briefly back to their own trucks, and she was alone on the stretcher. Suddenly her VW's engine exploded and began shooting flames. She wasn't directly hit by the first explosion, but she heard a huge sound and felt a jolt, and the next moment, embers were flying all over. And she couldn't move on the stretcher.

The firefighters started to extinguish the fire, but leaked gasoline from the car ignited, creating more explosions that forced the firefighters to retreat for a while. Now she could see the falling embers were like part of a meteor shower aiming for her. Her dress would soon be melting and start a fire. She'd be burned to death. She thought it was the end of her life.

"Sam!" someone shouted.

The next moment, he threw himself over her and covered her body with his. She felt the whole stretch of his hard body on her, his elbows on both sides of her to support him not to crush her.

He looked at her so warmly and murmured in a gentle tone, "Hello, Connie. I'm Sam. Nice to meet you. No worries. I'll protect you."

He said *hello*… She looked up at him and found he was gazing back on her with his eyes now calm sepia color shielding her from flames glowing behind him. It was definitely heaven in his eyes, mesmerizing her and something more as their eyes locked. Intense attraction. Strong chemistry. It was also emanating from her, making her hot inside, such feelings that she didn't know she had in her.

He said hello… He got her right there. *You had me at hello.* Just like the movie, *Jerry Maguire.*

Then she gasped when the realization had reached her sense. He was guarding her from the falling embers! She saw a couple of tiny embers landing on his back. But then who'd protect him from those embers?

"What about you, Sam?" She couldn't help but start weeping. "Sam! What about *you*?"

"We'll be fine," he replied, smiling, but he turned his face away from her.

"No!"

Abruptly one firefighter blasted the fire extinguisher on him. "C'mon Sam!"

She was sobbing. "I'm fine; we're all fine," he said just before he left with the EMT.

"My god, rookie, you got balls." Quite a few cops, firefighters and EMTs gathered around him, while she was tended by the other EMTs. "Kevlar saved your life, but it doesn't look good, Crawford."

He didn't go to the same hospital as hers, and she even hadn't known he'd been airlifted.

Afterward, she'd never seen him again, even when she wanted to say *thank you.* Eventually she'd written a thank-you card and sent it to the Berkeley Police. No response from him. She had no way of knowing if he'd ever received her card…

The aftermath of the accident had given her much physical pain and PTSD like fear of fire and entrapment, and nightmares.

She'd had bad dreams often for a long time until recently. She'd had to relive the accident repeatedly every time she'd had one. Nowadays she seemed to be better, but still have them occasionally, rarely but more than once in a blue moon. Every time she had the nightmare, he had to sacrifice himself for her over and over again and that gave her more pain.

As she'd suffered from nightmares like that, it wasn't hard to guess how many nights he'd had his own nightmares along with his physical pain from the incident.

She'd never forgotten his heroic act, always grateful.

Soon after the accident, she'd moved to the East Coast and then flown to Europe, where her parents had been working for many years.

Later the Alameda County Coroner's Bureau had hired her uncle as the chief medical examiner. The Bureau also covered Berkeley, so naturally he'd often reported to her about Sam. Her yearning for him had intensified.

Recently the Coroner's Bureau had looked for a medical examiner/forensic pathologist. So she'd jumped at the chance to see him again.

It hadn't happened.

She'd never met him at work when she'd seen many other detectives and deputies visit them on a daily basis. But not Sam Crawford.

She'd romantically thought every star and planet had lined up to have sent her away from Europe to Berkeley; their paths seemed to be finally colliding like interacting galaxies in the universe…

Um…nope. That was just fantasy. They hadn't met again anywhere, not even in the town, not even at the Coroner's.

They weren't meant to meet again. The incident ten years ago was just one of those isolated local traffic accidents with a heroic cop. And the flowing emotions and special bond that she'd felt between them were merely figments of her imagination due to the accident injuries and silly wishful thinking.

Reality wasn't like movies.

Then, on such an ordinary Saturday, out of the blue, with the least expected timing, her then-hero would be back in her life. With three glitches.

He might've been already married or had a girlfriend or

become a ladies' man who didn't do keeps.

You got to be friggin' kidding me.

This was the first phrase Sam had thought after meeting Dr. Alexandra 'Alex' Wallace.

When he saw her face for the first time, he had some tingling sensations in his skin.

And when he shook hands with her, the hair on the nape of his neck stood, followed by all the hair on his body.

Not only his hair but something else south on his body woke up.

She was so damn beautiful.

She was petite in stature. She had blond wavy hair below her shoulders. It looked so soft that he had to make an immense effort not to touch it. She had amazingly striking blue eyes, generous kissable lips in her cute oval face, and her body, even clad in a casual cotton blouse and jeans, was still inviting him to guess underneath the clothes.

This all-American beauty would cut open stiffs. Weigh each organ including the brain. Saw bones. An expert on forensic pathology.

And he wanted to sleep with her already.

He got aroused by the coroner he'd never met before.

He tried to make sense of it. Possibly because she was gorgeous, but mainly because he hadn't had any sexual encounter with a woman recently; thus, hard-on.

She was just staring at him after introducing each other. Her eyes were glowing in blue.

He wondered what kind of blue it was. Azure? Cyanine blue? Almost the color of glaciers, cool, sophisticated. And it stirred up his memory.

Connie. His forever dream girl. She'd had incredibly unique blue eyes like Dr. Alex did, but brunette hair.

As her face had been drastically affected by the accident, he didn't remember exactly what she'd looked like. Her marvelous eyes and brunette straight hair had only been clear in his fuzzy memories.

That had been one warm spring…one weekend night…

After a brazen speeding 20 over the limit and running a red light on MLK – Martin Luther King Jr. Way, a pickup truck had gotten on I-80, chased by the BPD and CHP along with their chopper, it hit a small car from behind at 90.

He'd seen the victim's VW Bug had literally flown off the road, rolling as if it had been carried away by a tornado. He stayed at the scene since he witnessed the batshit crazy hit-and-run, while some were following the suspect to catch him.

When he caught a glimpse of her, the hair of his neck rose, followed by a shudder causing his body hair to stand. The accident had given the victim bruises, lacerations and swelling on her face. But her eyes. The color of blue that he'd never seen before, cool translucent glaciers. He was shaken by some unknown force in his sternum.

When he covered her body with his to shield her from the falling embers, all he could say was *hello* and assurance that she'd be okay, hoping to convey his hidden feelings for her through her sensual blue eyes. And he felt her emotions crashing back on him. Their chemistry was sparking. The image of her beneath him in bed emerged in his mind, surprising him, still feeling right about it…

He'd never met her again after all. She'd sent him a handwritten thank-you card later at the BPD, worrying about his condition. But when he'd finally got hold of it at work, four months had passed since the fateful night, even though his burns had been healing rather quickly after a couple of skin grafts and a month of rehab.

He'd searched for her at first with his college buddies, Jason the cop and Tom the journalist, despite the fact that he'd only remembered her eye and hair color. They'd pulled out the accident report and found: *The victim, Connie Morgan, 18, a resident of Berkeley, a student at UC Berkeley.*

And her driver's license at the DMV site.

But that was about it. She hadn't lived at the address on the plastic by the time they'd checked.

It had turned out that he couldn't find her anywhere after that. She'd never renewed her California driver's license. She'd looked as if she'd vanished from the face of the earth.

"If we're meant to meet again, then we'll meet again." It was a quote from the movie *Serendipity*. A movie buff, Sam had often watched old movies and remembered some. But he'd doubted such a thing as serendipity had existed. In his opinion, it was just how a person was prepared to react to something significant to him even not then but later. On the other hand, there might be something humans couldn't comprehend why and how it had occurred. Just like that evening…

The precursor to the incident had started when one of the officers had to take his kid to the hospital for an unexpected fever. As a rookie, Sam volunteered to do his graveyard. And he wasn't assigned to patrol that evening, but when he came to clock in, he found himself in the patrol squad on the duty roster. Plus, his boss asked him to patrol on MLK just before he drove off in his police cruiser, instead of the different area in the schedule…

If all those queer changes hadn't happened, he wouldn't have been there for her, or met her.

Or it had never left an impact on his whole life in amazing ways: To be a strong and compassionate cop, a better man, had been his everyday purpose of life so that he'd stand proudly in front of her as a grown man when he'd meet her again. Even though he didn't really believe he'd meet her again. A voice in him had always said if they were meant to be, he'd already met her again.

Still, yearning for her had stayed in his heart, and every time his old wounds had given him pain, he'd been forced to remember the night and the girl.

More than ten damn long years. And his eyes still looked for her in crowds from time to time.

The emotions that he'd tried to bury deep inside were bubbling up to surface now.

By a new forensic medical examiner.

Why was she attracting him so much just like Connie had? She didn't look like her at all…except her eyes, although he hadn't really known her real face either.

He was carefully observing her.

Alex didn't feel they were doing some romantic *meet-again!* or *it's you!* kind of scene from *An Affair to Remember* or *Serendipity* or *You've Got Mail* or whatever. Rather, they were examining each other as if two predators were sniffing around.

And then, her hero of ten years finally opened his mouth, "Er…I think Dr. Taylor called you?"

Okay, just as she'd thought. His words were far from romantic and proof positive that he didn't recognize her. So no *We meet again!* romance movie scene. All he wanted was her to perform an autopsy on his vic. Oh wait, that was her job to conduct a perfect autopsy to find the cause of death. That was what she'd been hired for. Duh.

And it seemed her uncle Dr. Barry Taylor must've never told him they were related, either. Good for him to keep the promise with her, especially when she didn't like anyone to think she was here by nepotism.

Her then-hero turned out to be forgetful. And the chemistry she'd felt at the incident had definitely been her imagination. Could've been some female hormone thingy. Reality sucked. Dammit.

"Yes, Dr. Taylor called me," she replied indifferently.

"Sorry to make you work more."

"No problem."

"But it's Saturday."

"Right back at you." She tilted her head and asked him, "Where's your date?"

He laughed, "Dr. Taylor just asked me the same thing."

"Oh." Uncle had also wanted to know it for her?

"No date, just paperwork to date with." He smirked. "Besides, not many women like major crime detectives who work irregularly."

"Really?" Two findings here, she thought. He wasn't married. And he had no girlfriend or at least no committed relationship. But could be the third glitch on her list, a ladies' man.

"What 'bout you?" Abruptly his voice changed a tone. "No date?"

She swallowed and blinked for an instant and smiled at him. "No date whatsoever. Besides, not many men like coroners who work irregularly."

At that, as if it was a cue, he relaxed and chuckled.

"Alright, let's get goin'." She moved into the autopsy prep room, swiftly putting her hair up with a pencil.

Wow… He'd never seen any woman do that, but it was awfully sexy and now he could see the nape of her neck with loose golden hair, enticing him to drop a kiss there.

"Er…um…is that natural blond?"

"Yes." She grimaced. Strange question in the prep room.

"Um…can…can I see my vic now too?" he quickly said before his emotions ran away.

"Sure. There's an extra lab coat or scrubs and latex, etcetera. I think you know all if you'd come here often enough."

"Yeah, thanks. I usually come in with Dr. Taylor. This is the first time with you."

She froze. *This is the first time with you.* As if they were going to make love for the first time.

Of course, he meant an autopsy. Hello? She was the only person who could feel the sexual notion from that phrase. Yep, clearly a female hormone thingy.

Slip of the tongue. He just couldn't shake off his feeling that he wanted to make love to her.

He should think well from now on before he'd open his damn mouth.

The victim had been transferred to the autopsy table by the transporting officers. As their CSI had taken his clothes to analyze, the victim was under a white cloth.

"Okay, so, let me test his blood and urine ASAP," after she finished wearing scrubs and gloves, she imparted.

"Got it." Also clad in a lab coat, he nodded and followed her into the autopsy room.

He couldn't take his eyes off her. And she noticed he was observing her with curious eyes, almost scrutinizing. This detective must not trust her, she figured and frowned. "What? You've never seen someone extracting blood and urine from a deceased?" Then she noticed. "Oh…urine."

"Whoa," so did he. "Greenish…never seen that before."

"I have," she calmly stated and put the tube in the rack.

"Um, you didn't put the sample tubes in the rack to the lab." He pointed out the rack that had a sign said, *To County Lab ASAP*. Empty.

"I don't need to," she answered casually. "I have all the gadgets and means to deal with them myself, so no need to send the specimen to the county's, especially today is Saturday, so…"

She could see plenty of question marks filling inside his fine cerebral cortex.

"Come along; I'll show you, Sgt. Crawford." Carrying the tubes in the rack, she directed him to follow her.

"Sam, want you to call me Sam."

"Okay, Sam." Then she added after a heartbeat, "You can call me Alex, then."

"Alright, Dr. Alex,"

She turned to face him, laughing. "Just Alex is fine. I like a reciprocal relationship."

Her laugh stopped. His eyes darkened. "Say that again?"

She was stupid. *Think before you speak*. She quickly

explained, "I meant equality."

"Ah, okay." He smiled, with a bit of disappointment. "Alex."

The automatic door of her lab opened when she looked up at the face recognition system, and she let him in first. "This is my lab to help CSI and the county lab."

"Holy shit…um…excuse my language."

There were several machines sitting humming low in an ample space. He'd seen some before, only in big labs or research centers.

"That looks like one heck of a gas chromatograph–mass spectrometer." He pointed at one machine.

"Oh, you recognize it?"

"My major at college was criminology, and I studied a little chemistry used in forensic science."

"I see." Okay, so when he'd been called a rookie ten years ago, he'd graduated from college and the police academy, which meant he must've been twenty-two or three then. So…he was four or five years older than she was. Finally she'd found out what she'd wanted to know about him. Odd. Ten years had passed and she'd discovered his age.

"Alex," his voice pulled her out of contemplation. "What's that?" He pointed at another machine.

"That's…um…in short, blood/DNA analyzer, and attached is its specific computer."

"And…that?" he asked, pointing at a bit larger machine.

"That's atomic absorption spectroscopy."

"Jeezus."

"Let me start analyzing these and on to an autopsy, okay?"

"Okay, but I have a question."

"Go ahead." She already started to prepare the specimen but didn't seem to mind him asking questions. She was a multitasker.

"Where did you get the money to buy all those machines? They're enormously expensive."

"Alameda County had budget."

"BS."

"It's true, but some philanthropist donated a lot of money." He didn't need to know the money had been from her research projects for the pharmaceutical companies.

"Sam, how much time do you have?" She inserted the question to stop him mulling over the money.

"You mean to wait for the autopsy to finish?"

"Yes." She nodded, working on the tube and pipette meticulously, skillfully.

Damn, she was good, he thought. She must've worked in the lab for quite a long time.

"As long as you'd want," he said gently. Almost too gently, as if he'd say to his lover in the middle of sex.

She turned her face to gaze at him with those stunning glacial blue eyes.

Immediately the hair on his body stood up. Also somewhere else too. Uh-oh. He cleared his throat, walking up to one machine pretending to study it so that his lower limbs from his waist down would be hidden behind it. "Well, I mean, since it's Saturday, I have time. I just want to know how he died. Please give me the result."

"I'll do my best."

In the autopsy room, they stood across the body on the table.

Her eyes were so idiosyncratically beautiful, especially since she was wearing a surgical mask.

His memory of that Saturday night on 80 had been unexpectedly stirred by the sight of her eyes as if a gust of wind had swept him. The brunette girl with amazing eyes. Phenomenal chemistry they'd shared…

And she passed one of the surgical masks to him. So much for the sensual nostalgia. Back to reality.

"Thanks." This shut down the odor of death quite a bit.

With a clipboard by her side, she started examining the outside of the body.

He looked at his vic again. Under the autopsy room lights, he looked much paler and awfully thin. But he didn't look too old. She was carefully studying the body, pulling its arms and trying to flip him. He helped her flip the body halfway to prone so that she could see his back.

"Hmm," she mumbled, "this is odd. Look over. Can you see?" She pointed at the victim's back from the upper portion to his thighs. "Abnormal discoloration in the postmortem lividity," referring to the unusual change of colors under the skin after death.

It wasn't regular purplish red pigmentation. More like... "Green..." He scowled. "Never seen it. What does that mean?"

"I can guess, but I need to open him."

"Can you give me your educated guess?"

"Poison."

"Ah...of course. His urine was green too. What kind of poison?"

She quickly repeated, "Let me open and check everything, okay? I just don't like too much guessing. Lab test will give us some results too."

So, she wasn't one of those who was prone to do guesswork. He liked her attitude.

While she was performing the autopsy, he waited on the bench, just outside of the autopsy room, contemplating the meaning of this encounter...with her, wickedly sexy, smart medical examiner.

Basically, after that night, he hadn't been able to keep a long-term or even a short-term relationship with any woman, because, first, he'd always sought extraordinary mutual attraction like the one he'd had with Connie, and second, some women had considered his scars gross, which meant they'd rejected even going to the damn beach with him much less making out or sex. He must admit that his burn scars weren't exactly something to be displayed like a painting in the museum, rather a bit nasty especially over the ripples of his muscles.

Since this medical examiner seemed to emanate the same chemistry with him as Connie had, he should ask her out. He'd already lost the chance of asking the real Connie out, so he should try every woman he felt right.

Let's start with a baby step. Let's start with lunch first and then dinner, dance, then to his domain. She could be the one who wouldn't be so scared of his scars. She was an M.D. and a coroner, for fuck's sake.

The phone on the wall near the door rang. He picked it up, looking into the window, and found her signaling him to come inside, saying, "Sam, you ready?"

"Yeah, thanks." *Duty calls.*

He put on his scrubs, gloves and mask, hurriedly stepping into the autopsy room.

"What'd you find, Doc?"

"Very intriguing."

CHAPTER 2

In the autopsy room, he first realized that she'd already taken X-rays on his victim. The photos were on the display box in the corner. She noticed he was eyeing them, "Not even drastic bone fractures… Well, two of his fingers were broken. But that's all. No skull or spine fracture, either."

"Actually, Doc Taylor said he couldn't find any fractured bones."

"He was right," she said and then added, "By the way, his fingerprints are over there." She indicated the other side of the corner that had a small office space with a desk, computer and printer. On the edge of the desk, he saw a few strips of paper for latent fingerprints. Also a little paper bag.

"Ah, thanks." He retrieved them in a plastic evidence bag and into his pants pocket. "What's in this bag?"

"That's his fingernails. Give them to CSI. I don't have time to deal with them."

"Thanks. I should've damn well thought of clipping them myself."

She was not only meticulous but also kind. She certainly hadn't needed to do that but had done it since no one else was working today. In retrospect, she'd done an autopsy even without her assistant. Even though her boss had ordered her to do it, she could've said no. It was Saturday.

"Um…hello?" she asked. "Did I miss something?"

He'd been not moving in the middle of storing the evidence in his pocket. "Oh, no." He quickly came around. "So, what'd you find?"

His victim had already been nicely stitched up except his head. But in fact, he was okay with an open body since he could learn a lot of things from it. So he said, "Doc, next time around, can I see the body open? I know I can learn a lot from it along with your explanation."

"Oh, okay. If there's such a case, I'll invite you in."

"Thanks." Oh yeah, there would be cases. From now on, he'd try to visit the Coroner's Bureau more often to see her…and her autopsies.

"But don't be sad, Detective. I have parts of some organs left outside so that you can observe. I thought you might like to see."

"Aw…how nice of you." He laughed. "No, wait, don't show them to me yet. First things first. COD? I absolutely, desperately wanna know that."

"Yeah, I know. Dr. Taylor even told me on the phone." She laughed, too. It was muffled by the mask, but he liked her laugh. He wanted to hear it without a mask. Later. She went on, "I'll send you the report in detail later. First of all, his ETD is just about when he'd fallen as Dr. Taylor's assessment said and his stomach was empty. Obviously he hadn't had any dinner or breakfast. And your victim died of poisoning."

"Hmm…I kinda felt it," he confessed. "He looks too pale, and no physical damage from the fall and green urine and green livor mortis."

"And his brain and part of an organ are green too."

"What? So, he's like dyed green inside?"

"Kind of. Unless he's *the Incredible Hulk*."

He blinked. Twice. "Um…you just joked?"

"Never mind. It's not even funny." She turned around

and pointed him to the victim's brain on the scale. "Look."

"Whoa." He was stunned. "It's green."

"I told you; unless he's…" But she stopped and rolled her eyes at herself.

"Hulk," he said it for her, his lips curving under the mask. Her glittering blue eyes were dancing with amusement, captivating him again. The smile in her eyes suddenly disappearing, she was just staring back at his eyes. They must be looking at their own images in each other's eyes. He noticed she sighed softly under the mask. Jeezus, she was hot. Too hot. Sizzling hot that he wanted her right now. The chemistry between them was exceedingly high, arousing him even though they were clad in gloves, scrubs and masks. Wasn't it because the room was too warm? Oh wait, this was the autopsy room and temperature was set low…

Looking up at him, she cleared her throat and stated, "You're very strange, Detective."

"So are you, Doc," he added, grinning. He'd known the only doctor who could joke around during an autopsy was Doc Taylor, but now he must add Doc Alex to his list. The Alameda County Coroner's Bureau must be becoming a more and more wonderful place to visit.

She lightly coughed again and continued, "Anyway, part of the other organ was also greenish, and I have the lab results of his blood and urine test."

"That's quick."

"Thanks to state-of-the-art machines," she said nonchalantly and started reading the results on the computer screen. "Okay…so, this is intriguing, like I said. Here's the thing: the organ discoloration is from hydrogen sulfide gas…"

"Hydrogen sulfide… ? That rotten egg odor thing?"

"Correct, but I don't think it's direct COD."

"But you said COD was poison."

"It's a bit more complicated than that." She raised her index finger and continued, "Be patient, Detective."

"Sam."

"Sam, okay," she resumed unaffectedly. "He was exposed to hydrogen sulfide of very low concentration like 2ppm for a certain period of time. That made his organs and livor mortis greenish."

"Ah, okay, green urine too?"

"No, that was actually from thallium poisoning."

"Whoa, I never had a thallium poisoning vic before."

"Congratulations on your first case," she said in a not so much congratulatory tone.

"Wow. So that's COD?"

"Yes. Did you notice he has white horizontal lines on his nails?" She held up one of the victim's hands and showed him his fingertips.

"Ah, right. Mees' lines."

"Oh, you know about Mees' lines?" and she added quietly, "Impressive. Most impressive. Dr. Taylor has taught you well."

He narrowed his eyes. Had she…? "*Star Wars*."

She stared at him without a word. So he pressed, "You just quoted from *Star Wars*, didn't you?"

She hadn't known her former hero was a movie buff. She couldn't take it back now. She cleared her throat, "*Episode V*." Oh, why should she have needed to say that? She regretted right away as soon as she'd said it.

"I know. That's one of the famous Vader quotes. Dr. Taylor's part is Obi-Wan. Well, yeah, Doc is Obi-Wan to me." And his eyes were laughing. She hated his competitive guts. Yeah, she shouldn't have said any of them at all from the get-go but he should've let it go, right? Crap.

"Those Mees' lines are also from thallium." She went on as if nothing had happened.

"No arsenic?" He seemed to have decided to let it go.

"No, not at all. Only hydrogen sulfide and thallium. And thallium in his system is outrageously high. That's his COD."

"It wasn't from chemotherapy, even his bald spots."

"Nope, he had no chemo drugs in his system, and I couldn't find any carcinoma or even tumor in his organs. And thallium poisoning can also result in hair loss, for the record."

"I see. So the point is how, right? It's gonna be either homicide, suicide or accident."

"Sam, he has Mees' lines," she pointed out for him.

"True. Accumulation. Rarely suicide." Those who'd want to commit suicide usually wouldn't kill themselves little by little.

"That's correct, statistically. Either accident or homicide, that's your job to find out now."

"Got it," he said, "Thanks."

"No problem." Taking off her mask first, she discarded it along with the gloves and scrubs. He followed suit and threw his into the bin. She put her lab coat back on. Then, after releasing the stoppers on the wheels of the table, she started pushing it toward the body refrigerator. Abruptly his arms came around over her, brushing her hair and shoulders, his hands holding the bar by her hands as if he was enfolding her whole body from behind with his imposing stature.

Her heart almost ceased working. "What're you doing?" she said under her breath.

"Helping," he replied in a low tone. She could hear him breathing. Both, in silence, moved the table and pushed it into one of the empty lockers of the fridge. She closed the door and signed off. She knew he was still standing behind her so close, casting his shadow on her back and the face of the fridge, that she could feel his exhalation. She turned around hoping he'd move away, but he was fully trapping her in his personal space and he was in hers. She looked up at him. He put his left arm on the fridge above her, leaning against it, which made him closer to her.

"Wanna kiss you," he whispered, lowering his head gradually. He was giving her time to say no if she didn't want to.

He was staring at her eyes intensely, enthralling her. His eyes had exactly the same hues as ten years ago, aged bourbon color as oak, bronze, amber, a touch of gold; in this close proximity, the surge of emotions from them took her breath away.

Déjà vu.

His strong yearning had just thrown her into the scene when she'd looked up at his eyes and thought of the quote from the movie *An Affair to Remember*, amid the accident. And now she was thinking of exactly the same quote. Like in many movies, even when they'd been apart for ten years, they'd met again. And once more their passion sparked just like before, crossing place and time. Although she knew he could be just another playboy bachelor who liked to try kissing any woman he met, since he didn't remember who she was, how could she say no when her hero asked for a kiss?

He must see the affirmation in her eyes. His right hand pulled the pencil out of the bun; her gorgeous blond hair loosened and cascaded down her shoulders very slow, silky threads looking so soft and smooth almost like golden gossamers. He reached into her amazing hair; the feeling was outstandingly pleasurable, giving him ecstasy. Holding her at the back of her head to the nape with his big hand, he kissed her on her luscious lips. The electric sensations came to both as endless waves. All of his body hair rose with ripples of exhilaration. He touched the corner of her lips with the tip of his tongue, urging her to open them for him. She granted his wish. His tongue freely entered her mouth.

He just couldn't stop kissing her. He pushed her onto the fridge, he held her with the full length of his body. She could feel he was hard, hard muscles and hard…bulge. She was almost flattened between him and the stainless steel lockers. Both were hard but he was blazing hot and fridge cool. It seemed like she was standing facing a bonfire in cold weather. And he was holding her so tight as if he wanted to fuse himself to her body.

She obscurely resolved that even though he didn't remember her, even if he'd kiss all women who happened to arouse him when he met them, it would be awesome if he'd ask her out tonight and eventually…

Because she…

And her phone rang with vibration in her jeans pocket. She jumped, separating their lips. "Sorry. It's my work phone. Gotta answer."

"Go right ahead." He stepped back a bit to give her some space.

She eyed her phone at a glance first and answered, "Hi, Dr. Taylor."

Oh shit, that was her boss. He briefly closed his eyes. Was kissing one of his staff problematic? Er…in the workplace?

"Sam, it's Dr. Taylor and he'd like me to use speaker so he can talk to you too."

"Okay." He seriously hoped Doc didn't possess x-ray vision.

She switched on speaker, and he said, "Hey Sam. I hope you're helping Dr. Alex."

"Trying, Doc." And he glanced at her and found her looking utterly disheveled, eyes dreamy, lips puffy from his passionate kiss. God, he wanted to make love to her now.

"So, what did you two find? Poison?" Dr. Taylor asked.

Passion, he wanted to report to him.

But Barry continued, "At the scene, he didn't have livor mortis, but probably by the time you examined him, he had a good amount of discoloration, no?"

He pushed the phone lightly toward her, touching her hand, keeping his lingering finger there. And their lust and need flared again. He let his breath out slow to calm himself down, thinking of quotes from Mr. Spock of *Star Trek* so that his boner should subside. "*In critical moments, men sometimes see exactly what they wish to see.*"

"Dr. Taylor," Alex reported, "COD's thallium

poisoning, but also we found a low concentration of hydrogen sulfide."

"Fascinating. I'm looking forward to reading your report. Okay, thank you for your service, Dr. Alex. Why don't you go home now? If your paperwork can wait, so to speak. It's Saturday, for Pete's sake."

"Okay, I will, thanks."

And he hung up. Putting the phone back in her pocket, she said, "Like I said, I'll electronically send the report to the department…"

"Alex," he said, lightly touching her arm, "when can I see you again?"

"Um…I…I'm not sure…" she almost murmured.

"I wanna buy you coffee."

"What for?" she asked, hoping he'd say it's a date, or something romantic, but he said, "Well, cuz you did an autopsy for me on Saturday, so I owe you."

She was gaping at him. He wanted to buy her coffee *cuz he'd owed her for the Saturday autopsy.* Nothing romantic about that. So what was that sensual kiss just a few minutes ago? Why did he say such a stupid thing after such a gorgeous kiss?

Oh, she got it; her kiss hadn't been good enough for him…like, worth a cup of coffee.

"You owe me nothing. This is my job, in case you forget," she said flatly. "I'll send you the report within 48 hours. I'll go back to work. Thank you for helping me, Sgt. Have a good day."

And she walked away out of the autopsy room into the hallway and into her lab. He saw her through the windows on the door, already seated in the back of the room.

He was left alone in the autopsy room full of the odor of blood and death. He hadn't noticed that kind of smell when he'd been with her. He shivered and walked out of the room also. He acutely sensed the change of her mood. She'd been so hot and willingly responsive to his kiss, but then suddenly she'd become icy.

But he knew damn well why her mood had changed.

He'd been afraid of her rejection if he asked her out seriously. So, he'd tried to sound lighter, using the fucking lame coffee stunt. And backfired colossally.

Why he'd wanted it to sound lighter was beyond him because he didn't feel like he should take or treat it light.

He wasn't quite sure yet, but he felt like this wasn't the first time he'd met Dr. Alex. He had feelings of intimacy and familiar chemistry for her, especially after their hot foreplay-ish kiss.

More to the reasons he should've asked her out straight and seriously.

Hadn't he contemplated enough outside the autopsy room? Baby step and all?

What the fuck was he really afraid of?

He knew they'd end up in bed on the first date for their enormous chemistry. And he was terrified she might think his scars gross like other women had done. He could hear a whisper in his mind that she might not mind performing an autopsy on scarred corpses but would damn mind if the scars were on a live human for her to make love to.

He'd been such an audacious man who'd considered choosing a woman as hit or miss, even though it'd been due to his scar problem. But recently he coveted someone who'd be his true mate if she'd even exist. Then he'd just met someone who might be and now ruined it all by himself. Okay, baby step. Back to square one.

First, he must apologize to her properly and if she'd forgive him, ask her out again.

When he was out of the Bureau's building, the sun was high. It was almost noon. The inside of his Charger was hot under the midday sun. He turned the engine on and blasted the A/C. Next, he called Carter at the office. "Hey."

"What Sister Golden Hair at the Coroner's said?" he asked without missing a beat.

"Sister Golden Hair?" Sam asked back, knowing he

meant Alex. *Sister Golden Hair.* The name of the song by *America* but it was such a suitable moniker for her. Suddenly his heart was beating fast with the core of his body burning. Only a short encounter with her, memories flooded in his mind. She was not only unforgettable but also had the power to seize him.

"Found COD of our vic, John Doe, a.k.a. Fallen-from-the-sky guy," Sam imparted rather calmly.

*****

"Your hero kissed you passionately, even though he didn't remember you, and you are depressed?" Rachel "Rae" Cooper, one of Alex's two BFFs since freshman year, now working as a theatrical director for junior high audiences in San Francisco, asked her.

She wore her caramel brown hair in a bob and had merciful hazel eyes. She was also very tall and slim. She'd played basketball during junior high and high school. Alex had always envied her stature and said, *Gee, Rae, wish you could give me even three inches of your height.*

"Depressed? No." Alex put her forehead on the table. "Yes," Rae heard her say in a muffled voice.

"Oh, hon, I'm so sorry." She hugged her shoulders.

They were sitting together in the cozy corner of the café *EZ Poppas* downtown. The café was still closed at this time on Saturdays.

Dr. Barry Taylor, who lived upstairs of his venue, was also sitting with them, holding a tray on his lap, looking awfully worried. He was wearing an apron with plenty of strawberries printed along with a logo, *Strawberry Fields Forever, California Strawberry Growers Association.*

In Barry's eyes, Sam had fallen from being a hero to have become just another shameless horny ding-dong who'd kiss, measure and screw any unsuspecting innocent woman. But in fact, he still kept a little faith in him as he'd known he'd been a good man.

"You know, Alex, dear," he began, "you got hurt very badly in the accident. Your face was swollen and bloody; cuts and bruises all over. You didn't look like you look now. Even I couldn't believe how bad you looked at that time. So, I surmise he didn't really remember what you looked like. Okay, even though he might've found your driver's license and looked at your photo. It'd just confuse him. I don't believe he really knew your face. Besides, your hair color and style were different even in your driver's license."

"Er…that's my fault." Rae raised her hand. "I dyed her hair and used a hair iron to straighten when she'd played Ophelia of *Hamlet* in my college production. I made her brunette for several months till the production ended. I'm sorry."

"Maybe you should tell him you're the one he saved ten years ago, hon," Uncle suggested.

"No." Alex immediately shook her head, still her forehead on the table.

"Why not?" Rae had to ask. "I think Uncle Barry's right. He hadn't known your face. You see, you saw him not injured on his face, but he saw you badly injured. And your hair…sorry. And you practically vanished from California discarding your driver's license."

"I moved to the East Coast; I needed a new driver's license."

"Um…okay, and to Europe…but why on earth don't you want to tell him all about it?" She was bewildered.

Alex finally raised her head up to meet their eyes. "I don't want him to think I want to date him just because I got hero-worship syndrome or sympathy or charity or simple curiosity. The truth is even before I got hero-worship syndrome, I knew I'd love him."

"What do you mean, sweetheart?" Barry grimaced, trying hard to understand her. "You knew you'd love him before the incident had happened? But you didn't know him yet."

"No, I mean, when he tried to stop me slipping into

blackout. When I saw his face…his very warm eyes… I still remember…" Then she asked Rae, "Do you remember we'd watched *An Affair to Remember* several times?"

Movie freak Rae instantly noticed, "Oh, yes." And she nodded with Barry. He was the original movie mentor who had taught them good old movies and known many quotes.

"I saw heaven in his eyes…and then when he placed his body to shield me from the falling embers, at that moment, he said hello and I fell for him."

"Omigod. *'You had me at hello.' Jerry Maguire*, then. Why didn't you tell me?"

"It's personal…I mean…only between him and me. I'm sure he felt the same. Almost like instant sparks. In that second, we shared a special bond."

"So, the chemistry between you two was there even ten years ago. My god." Rae's eyes were dreamy now.

"And you still don't want to tell that to him?" Barry asked.

"I don't think so. If he forgot about it already, which in fact he did, what's it worth telling him? He might think I'm telling him just to get his attention. It's pathetic." She put her head back on the table.

"But he didn't know your real face, Alex, sweetheart," Barry said. "Why don't you give him a chance?"

She didn't answer.

"Chemistry thingy aside, your beautiful memory aside, what he did today is far from heroic." Then Rae, turning her face to him, continued, "It seemed to me, Uncle Barry, he stole a kiss from her, tryin' tasting her, if she was up to go to bed with him, then decided her kiss was worth a cup of coffee. I'm livid for that."

"If you put it that way…" Barry had to admit, "I'm disappointed in him too." When it came to Alex, he couldn't stand by him anymore. He loved his niece so much. "He kissed her deep like foreplay, goddammit."

Alex's parents having almost always been overseas, he'd practically offered them to raise her. He'd long been a bachelor with music as his love and life, so he'd had much slack to take care of her.

No one knew why he'd kept himself single, but the town's speculation was Operation Desert Shield and Desert Storm, the Gulf War, might've given him some kind of PTSD. The birth of Alex and establishing his *Café EZ Poppas* and his band had been right around when he'd returned home. Taking care of the baby and his café must've been part of the cure to save his soul.

She'd rented her place from Barry on the outskirts of town since she'd moved back to Berkeley from Europe, but she daily visited him to have some of her meals here, because she didn't cook and he wanted to see her.

"That's okay, Uncle." Alex raised her head. Her golden hair falling down all over on her face, he had to pick up the strands over her eyes that looked very sad. He thought his niece was the prettiest thing in the world. And Crawford had hurt her like hell. He could think of every swear word for Sam friggin' Crawford from his vast vocabulary of a war veteran and great pathologist and rock 'n' roller.

"It's already ten years ago. He doesn't remember me, and my kiss wasn't good enough. That's all."

*****

After he hung up the phone call with his boss Lt. Dan Montfort, reporting what the coroner had found and talking about what they should do next, he called Sgt. Jason Rivera at the Oakland Police Department. Oakland was the largest city in Alameda County, sitting next to Berkeley, so naturally their PDs often assisted each other.

Jason was the closest thing to him as he'd known him since high school. They'd attended UC Berkeley together and both had studied criminology, but he was much taller and played basketball in high school and college. He was still playing it on one of the police/fire teams and coaching for a kids' team. He had dirty blond hair, sometimes wearing a little man bun and light brown eyes like mead or honey whiskey with tanned color skin. He, like Sam, was a bachelor for a long time. They both didn't have any committed relationships but the reasons were totally different. Jason was simply a ladies' man who didn't do keeps. They actually lived next to each other in the apartment complex set up by the local governments for those who were single and working for the public. And that made it easier for them to see each other often even on a weekday just to have a beer or two.

"Yo, 'sup?" Sam greeted. "Heard you give Carter a buzz."

"Didn't know you were working. We need to talk. Meet me at my place?"

"Sure. What talk?"

"Not on the damn phone," Jason said, "Come see me."

"'K, Jase. Be out in an hour. Gonna drop by."

"Thanks, homie."

"Laters."

So, as he'd promised, Sam dropped by Jason's place…well, next door.

As soon as he opened the door, he quickly pulled him in and passed him a bottle of beer.

"Hey, what's going on, man?" frowning, Sam asked, a bit worried. Jason didn't answer but walked back into the kitchen and sat on the barstool at the counter. He followed him.

"What's going on, Jase? Hope nothing serious." Sitting next to him, he cocked his head to observe his friend's expression.

"No, not serious…okay, maybe it is. Ask you a favor," Jason sounded polite.

Sam laughed. "As if I never do."

"Well duh," Jason said. "Come see *EZ Poppas* perform tomorrow. Meet my new date, okay?"

"Sure, what's so big deal?" Sam grinned. "Besides, Doc

Taylor just invited me."

"Er…well, she gonna bring her friend and you gonna meet both. Kinda double date? I told her I gonna look around and bring a decent guy."

"Okay, time?" He didn't give much thought to it. He'd done a double date numerous times already.

"Sunday performance starts at 7. Let's have some bites before heading to the café. We gonna meet them there 7-ish."

"Okay, cool. And her name?"

"Rachel Cooper. Rae. Rae Cooper."

"Nice."

"Oh, she's nice and sexy. Um…she's a bit different. We dated like four times so far and…"

"Whoa. *You*, dated the same woman four times already? What happened, Ladies' Man? You never dated one woman twice."

"I said she's different. I should go slow with her."

"Hey, you sound a bit chicken…" he started teasing him, but Jason didn't buy it.

"Shut your damn face, Sammy. I just feel like I should go slow. Ammite meet someone special."

He fell silent. Jason might've finally met the real deal for him? He studied his best friend closely and sensed his sincerity and seriousness for this woman. Yep, this was it for him. He knew. But it wasn't his call; Jason had to decide.

On the other hand, he felt he had to tell him about Alex, encouraged by his friend's own conviction. "Jase, I met someone special today too."

But he was skeptical, knowing Sam's obsession for Connie and recent track record. "Not another blue-eyed brunette?"

"Er… Blue eyes, yeah, but blond… You know the new coroner at the Alameda, right?"

"Wut, Sister Golden Hair?" And he gestured making curls with his fingers on both sides of his face.

"Yeah," he nodded. "I just met her, but I got the same vibe as I'd got with Connie."

"Whoa." Jason was completely taken aback. "Fucking Connie thing again?"

"Nope, Jason, Connie's way in the past. I want Alex cuz she's tangible and we have chemistry."

Then Jason grinned wide. "In that case, wanna hear everything from top to bottom, homie."

CHAPTER 3

On Sunday, around 5pm, Alex and Rae came to Uncle Barry's café to work for him. This had been their custom for a long time. His café was closed every Sunday, but he played music with his band in the evening when complimentary drinks were served to audiences, so he needed help.

While both were behind the bar counter, Rae broke the news, "You're my pal to meet a guy in my double date."

"Excuse me?" Drying glassware with a dish towel, Alex frowned. "You don't do double dates."

"Well, tonight is special."

"Okay, Rae, that's enough." Putting down the towel, she demanded, "Fess up. Why are we doing a double date?"

"I want you to meet my date. And I want you to tell me it's okay to be serious cuz he's a good guy."

Alex grimaced, not quite grasping what she'd said.

"Okay, listen." Rae started explaining, "Well, I met this guy at the basketball game. My junior high audience often play sports and I'm sometimes invited by their parents. So, I went one game and he was the coach for the kids and…we dated four times…"

Alex's mouth fell open. "You? Never dated one man

more than twice, dated four times?"

"Hon, in my defense, I never met one single decent male soul before."

"Um…that's true," she agreed, recalling a couple of disastrous dates that Rae had.

"So, it's obvious my track record of dating isn't really glorious. I wasn't so much the dating kind…"

"You and me both." Alex rolled her eyes. "Then, what makes you think he's worth four time dating?"

"Um…you see, he's a bit different. He seems good. I mean, attentive, insightful, kind and very handsome…; not many men I know are like that. Well, that's why he's called a ladies' man."

Alex's eyes grew twice in size. "And you're okay with that?"

"Yeah, so far, no harm done, besides I don't know the whole story. And to me, as long as he's not a pain in my…rear." Rae's affirmative and more or less affectionate reply about that man surprised her. Where did that kind of man come from to step into her life all of a sudden?

"Okay his name?"

"Jason…and I'm not so certain what I'm feeling for this guy is from my sound mind, so please check him if he's really worth dating."

"You always say I'm forever trapped in the past with my then-hero so I cannot date any other man. And now you're asking me to judge your date. What's the change in my qualifications now?"

"Don't be sarcastic, love. I trust your judgment cuz your brain is astonishing. So, please?"

She caved. "Okay, sure, my dear. For you, anything."

"Thank you, hon!" Rae hugged her, relieved.

"Do you know who's coming to the double date with your Jason?" Alex asked.

"I have no idea." She shook her head. "He said he'd need to look around for someone decent. I told him if he couldn't find a good one, don't bother bringing. He agreed on that. So he may not be bringing anyone."

Alex snickered. "Ah, okay." Her Jason sounded very sincere trying to listen to her, Alex thought.

Then, her mind jumped to her ex-hero. She'd finally met him and kissed him but everything had ended up toppling over. And she'd heard his reputation at her work too. Sam was known as a one-night stand policy guy. Not an ideal dating kind, dammit.

She sighed. "Rae, why do we often love someone who doesn't love us back?"

"Ah...that's actually a very profound question, hon," she said, premixing tonight's drinks. "Why's love often one-way?"

"Exactly. When you feel like you find someone by chance and start loving that person with a once-in-a-lifetime kind of feeling, there's no guarantee that person would love you back."

"I'm sorry Alex, but you know you should move on, right?"

She nodded, grudgingly. Her sound brain that Rae had always praised believed she should move on before she'd destroy herself from the inside by loving her ex-hero too much without any tangible return.

Uncle approached them working inside the bar. "Thanks ladies, for your help."

"No problem, Uncle Barry," they said simultaneously.

"Hey, tonight's my performance night so I'm Dr. Barry or Dr. Taylor, while you guys are working. Who knows, someone we know might come in today, if you still want to keep it secret, hon."

"Okay," said Alex.

"Dinner's ready in the kitchen. When you have time, get in there to have some food in your stomach. I don't want you to be starving while we perform. Tummy growling ain't exactly the same as percussion."

*****

EZ Poppas' Sunday evening performance had started as usual and no problems with the sound systems. Their wonderful performance evoked reminiscence in Alex as her uncle had sung her lullabies when she was small.

His band could play a vast variety of genres, and songs were often in eclectic order and collections, but mainly they played good oldies that most people had heard of. Today he and his band had started with *Hotel California* by the *Eagles.*

Alex and Rae were behind the counter, serving pre-mixed drinks, washing glasses, listening to the music.

"This is the best job I ever had," Rae said. Actually, she'd always said that, and it had probably been the ten millionth time. "Comes with your uncle's care and music."

"I know, right?" Alex nodded, distributing mixed nuts in the small bowls.

"Ah." Rae raised her finger and closed her eyes. "Listen. *Calling All Angels. Train.* My mom was crazy about *Train.* Now one of my favorite bands… Gee, your uncle can sing gooooooood."

"Dr. Barry or Dr. Taylor."

Rae opened her eyes. "Oh, ah, right. Dr. Barry." And she giggled. "Don't you feel like we're in some theater production named, *playing conspiracy*?"

Alex laughed. "I once played Hamlet's Ophelia for you, but I don't remember playing a spy. And Ophelia is certainly not a spy, either."

"Ophelia, a spy? Oh no way, hon. To be a spy, you need brain. Ophelia was a bit air-headed. Listen, she committed suicide just for what? She believed her lover was a nutjob? Oh, c'mon. She should've used more brainpower to really comprehend his situations and shouldn't have wasted her life."

Alex couldn't stop chuckling. "You studied Shakespeare seriously and you're practically trashin' him."

"Yeah duh. My First. Freedom of Speech."

At that moment, they spotted two customers coming through the door.

It wasn't exactly too dark in late spring around 7:15pm in the San Francisco Bay Area. The sky was still casting the warm veil of twilight over every street, building, car and person a good half an hour before sunset. Inside the café was a little dark, so Alex and Rae had only seen the tall shadowy figures first and after they'd stepped inside completely, they'd finally recognized the faces.

"Ah finally. Alex, that's…" Then both women were petrified behind the counter, staring at those two tall men.

"Why's he here?" Alex got back her voice first and whispered to her, "That…is…Sam."

"No idea…and where's Jason's pal? Maybe he couldn't find a good man?"

"That…is…Jason, you're talking about?" Another surprise shook her good. "That's Jason Rivera, a homicide detective at the Oakland Police. That's your Jason?"

"You know him?"

"He's Sam's best friend."

"What?" Rae felt she got a heart attack. "How do you know?"

"I'm working at the Alameda County Coroner's, hello?" she kept her voice low. "You know Oakland is obviously part of Alameda County, right? And Oakland Police are one of our primary customers and he's a homicide detective and I'm a coroner. Do the math, for god's sake."

"Oops." Sam Jackass Crawford who'd hurt her BFF was Jason's pal for the double date? "Oh hon, I'm so sorry. Stay here. I'll talk to him."

Rae walked out from behind the counter to greet the two men standing near the door. They were casually dressed in polos and jeans with Nike for Jason and leather loafers for Sam. In fact, they were tall; of course, Jason was a lot taller, but Sam must be around 6'2" and both had toned muscles under the cotton polos. They looked very fine, standout figures among the crowd, any crowds. Several women sitting at a table near the door just couldn't take their eyes off them.

"Hey." Rae smiled at Jason . "Thanks for coming."

Jason's eyes suddenly warmed, looking down at her. She was tall for a woman, but he'd played men's basketball all his life. She felt well protected when standing with him.

"My pleasure." He smiled back at her showing his white teeth, short-circuiting part of her nervous system. Then he touched her arm lightly. "Rae, this is Sam. Sam Crawford. A detective of the Berkeley Police. My best friend and my double date pal."

"Hi Sam, Rachel Cooper. You can call me Rae." She was trying very hard not to punch his face.

"Hi Rae."

"Er…will you excuse us for a sec?" She smiled at Sam and pulled Jason's polo to one corner. When he was out of earshot, she asked Jason with a soft voice, "Why's he here? I mean, why'd you choose him?"

"Um…he's my best friend since high school and very handsome, credible and decent so I thought it's good to bring him to…" Rachel had to stop him. "Jason, we have a situation."

The tone in her voice turned him serious. "What situation?"

"I didn't know you'd bring Sam tonight, so I brought my BFF too."

"Something wrong?"

"Very much."

Rachel figured if Jason was Sam's best friend, he'd already heard of a huge screwup Sam had done to Alex. Asking her out for coffee for her autopsy reward after a passionate kiss.

"Tell me." He bent more to get closer to her face. She stopped talking and stared up at him. His gaze darker, it dropped on her mouth. She could hear her own heart beating crazily. He lowered his head more. But she was a good friend first, and she was the one who'd screwed up.

So she lightly placed her hands on his chest whispering, "Jason, I want you to hear me out, cuz we have a problem."

He laughed softly, "I like your attitude... Being responsible and a good friend makes me like you more."

Her body temperature shot up at his words and some part of her got warm and started pulsating. She didn't remember she had such feelings in her. When was the last time she...

She cleared her throat. "Jason, I didn't know you'd bring Sam, so I brought my bestie. Don't turn around to see her behind the counter, just listen."

"Okay. So your BFF is here for our double date and the problem is...?"

"My bestie is Dr. Alex Wallace and she's here helping at the bar tonight with me."

"What?" And his mouth made the word, *Uh-oh.*

"You're Sam's best friend, so I hope you heard about something that had happened between them yesterday?"

"Yup." He nodded. "Damn."

"I think you know her well?"

"Of course. She's a great medical examiner and kind lady we all respect. I'm in homicide so I meet her regularly even for unknown deaths. But I didn't know you two are close."

"I didn't know you and Sam are close either."

"True."

"What shall I do? I don't think she'd like to see him after his...um..."

"Kiss and coffee crash?" He wanted to say 'crash and burn' but refrained from that, since the *burn* part was too real for him and Sam.

"Yeah, that." She seemed to be okay with that.

Then Jason said, "Wait, Rae, this could be a good opportunity."

Her brows shot up. "What good opportunity? No opportunity here. He hurt her badly and I don't want anyone to hurt her again."

Jason studied her face for a short time. "You're a truly kind and good friend."

"Aw…um…thanks but we don't want to take chances."

"Actually Sam told me he wanted to apologize to her. He said he wanted to ask her out not for the decorum but just cuz he wanted; then he said something stupid that he didn't mean cuz he was scared of her rejection."

"Rejection? Why would she do that after that kind of a kiss?"

Yeah, that was probably what most of the population of the world would think. After all the rejections from women due to his scars, he'd become like a scared ten-year-old girl.

"Anyway, could you just give him one more chance? Would you at least give him a chance to apologize to her?"

Rae was silently pondering. So, Jason added, "Please? I want my friend out of misery."

She sighed and said, "You know I'm not her parent or guardian or have custody, right?"

"Yeah, but every BFF has the right to reject every jackass's stupidity, right?"

Rae started laughing. He also smiled with twinkles in his eyes. She quickly sent a text to Alex telling her Sam wanted to apologize to her for his blunder. She also strongly suggested that she let him have a chance.

And then Rae and Jason brought Sam to the bar. Behind the counter, Alex stood motionless, looking blank. Sam had spotted her there as soon as he'd entered the café, but he'd been waiting for his friend to lead the way since it was their date night in fact.

Jason stepped in first. "Hey Doc, I started dating your BFF. Hope you wouldn't mind."

"Of course not," she replied but her eyes never averted from Sam.

Well, this is awkward, Sam thought, but he didn't back down. "Alex, can I talk to you for a sec?"

Rae said to Jason, "There's a table for you," and said to his pal, "Sam, afterwards, you can come to the table with

Alex, if you'd like."

Sam nodded and he slid onto the barstool. She gave him a complimentary margarita and a small bowl of nuts.

Her hair ponytailed, she looked relaxed with her strawberry apron over her T and jeans. She was wearing yellow gold loop earrings that were the only accessories she had on. After he observed how attractive she was, the hair on the nape of his neck immediately stood up happily followed by all the hair on his body, his dick stirring, exactly the same throbbing he'd felt yesterday when he'd met her for the first time.

"Um…I'm so sorry for yesterday," Sam started, ignoring all of his physical changes.

"If that's about the kiss," she started to say, but he cut in, "No. Not about the kiss, cuz that was the best kiss I've ever had." Even now, thinking about it turned him on.

She blinked and fell silent, staring down at her hands on the counter.

"I wanted to apologize to you for my awkward pathetic excuse to ask you out." Okay it didn't come out precisely the way he'd liked. "I asked if I could take you out for coffee…"

"Yeah, I remember, cuz you thought you owe me for a Saturday autopsy."

"That was not true."

She was baffled, then frowned.

"No that's not true either. I do appreciate you did an autopsy on Saturday without any assistants. And I do feel I owe you."

"Like I said, you owe me nothing," she repeated the words again. "So if that's all about it, then…"

"No, Alex." He stretched his hand out to hold hers on the counter. He felt her tremble. "Alex, I wanted to ask you out personally not for doing an autopsy, but…well, cuz I wanted to. But it didn't come out right yesterday. I was a coward. I figured you might decline. I'm worried about that."

"After that kiss? I'd decline?" She looked at him dumbfounded. "Seriously?"

They both knew they had strong chemistry going on between them and why was he concerned about her rejection? Scared of rejection from women. And actually that was only half the story. He couldn't tell her about the scars yet.

"I'm so sorry. You see, I'm not so much of a lover and I had quite bad experiences so…"

"Sam, please," she implored, ignoring all of his lame excuses or even the rumor that he was a one-night-stand policy guy, with one powerful reasoning, "Don't compare me with other women you know. I'm not them."

It hit him. She was right; she wasn't them. Just because he'd had bad experiences with some women, it didn't necessarily mean Alex was the same kind in the line. "I'm so sorry, Alex. I'll remember that from now on. And you'd go out with me? Maybe some dinner?"

"Yes, I'd love to." She finally smiled brilliantly.

"Thank you." Finally he could breathe. Her generosity and forgiveness had saved him. "I'll check my roster and call you tonight."

"Be waiting."

He took her hand and placed it to his lips, caressing it with them, the shudder running through his spine into his groin. She must feel the same; her eyes wide open, she looked like a deer in the headlights and then gradually closed her eyes as if she was savoring his touch. Yeah, surely a great amount of chemistry and magnetism existed between them.

"Can you come around and sit with me?" he politely asked her when she wasn't busy behind the counter.

"Sure." When she walked to him, he saw her wearing white sandals. Her toes with red pedicures were awfully sexy. It seems she struck every sensual point in his body and touched his heart.

Her eyes were sparkling in blue. Piercing blue. Glacier

blue. Very rare color. And he experienced again feelings of déjà vu along with lightheadedness. Her eyes were the same as of his long lost girl Connie. Exact colors, shades and impression, to be precise.

No, no, no. He shook his head mentally. *Don't go there. Won't go there.* He didn't want to go back there. He'd already left there for good. It was a good experience and great memories but just like another dream that wouldn't repeat. Even though the impacts that he'd felt from two different girls in different times were the same, it was still not right to think about that. Remember Alex said: *Sam, please, don't compare me with other women you know. I'm not them.*

He held her hand reservedly and touched her palm and inside her wrist with his thumb, sending her a shiver. It was almost like foreplay. She decided to forget how she'd felt insulted by him yesterday and enjoy the encounter with her then-hero again. If he'd still act like an idiot, it would be time for her to really leave her past and restart her life again.

He noticed the song that Dr. Taylor and his band were playing now. *Sister Golden Hair.* He smiled at her, knowing her nickname, wondering if she knew she was called by the moniker.

"Like this song?" tilting her head, she asked.

"Yeah," he honestly admitted it. "I do too," she followed.

At that exact moment, the strangest thought occurred to him. He knew one more human being who had exactly the same color eyes as Alex: Dr. Taylor. And he had long silver hair now but when he was a lot younger, would it have been blond? Possibly. And they had the same nose and full mouth on an oval-shaped face. Slim. Long legs… And both witty. The resemblance between Dr. Taylor and Alex was uncanny. Were they actually related? Could be siblings, cousins, or uncle and niece? And if so, why didn't they mention it? Was there a good reason why they kept it secret? Maybe there was. In any case, he shouldn't say anything about it unless he'd consult Dr. Taylor. But it didn't matter whether they were related or not; both were excellent medical examiners.

"Dr. Taylor can really sing. He's awesome," he said.

"I heard he's been playing since high school and even during deployment to the Gulf War in the 90s. He said music saved him."

"Ah… He's semi-pro, then." No wonder he was so good. And music saved him…yeah, war must always be the toughest thing to face. He heard many stories of war from his relatives who had served in the military. It was difficult for them to have gotten over, he'd often heard. They hung onto anything as long as it kept their sanity.

After the performance, the happily satisfied customers and the band members had left; Alex, Rae and their dates helped Dr. Taylor close the café for tonight.

"Thanks for the help," Barry said and gave them a man hug. They'd mostly cleaned up around the sound system including moving a heavy amplifier, mics and spotlights into the downstairs storage. Luckily, the four band members owned each instrument, drums, keyboards, other guitars and brought them in and took them all back home after each session, so all Barry needed to clean up was his three guitars, two acoustic, one electric upstairs in his residence.

"Sam, did you enjoy it?" Barry asked curiously.

"Oh yeah, thanks for great performance. You sing awesome. I should've come earlier. Now I'm a big fan and gonna visit every Sunday."

Barry laughed proudly. "Happy to hear that."

When they went back inside, Alex and Rae were wiping the counter and tables.

But before they got closer to the seating area, Barry stopped Sam. "Hey, you and Alex, reconciled? I heard you guys had some clash."

He mumbled, "Um…yeah…we did reconcile…"

"Oh good. So now what?" Barry asked, still a bit concerned.

"I asked her out honestly."

"And?"

"She accepted."

"Oooh, nice!" He waggled his brows.

"We'll talk about it in detail later…cuz I'm not sure of my work schedule right now."

"Alrighty. No wonder you two looked cozy tonight." Barry laughed again.

"Er…you saw us?"

"Oh, you're good, don't worry," Barry said, "but if someone asks about you two, tell them you guys are dating. Just don't hide or lie."

"I agree," Jason chipped in. "Hiding and lying create trouble. Been there, done that."

Sam's mood lightened. "Thanks, man."

Then finally Barry called out, "Alex, Rae, they'll take you home. Just no hanky-panky tonight. Tomorrow is Monday and I want all of you to report to work on time. So, kick the boys in the butt to send 'em back home as soon as you two get to your front door."

CHAPTER 4

On Monday, in the gray of the morning, Jason was awakened by his phone buzzing on the nightstand.

He drowsily stretched his hand out to grab the phone, noticing it was from his detective partner, Max Reyes of the Oakland Police Homicide Team, and it was 4:30am.

Oh shit; it's already 4:30?

Until around 3am, he hadn't fallen asleep for thinking about the tall, long-legged sexy woman named Rae; every image of her had been so sensual that he couldn't have stopped imagining her naked long legs wrapping around his hips. Jeezus.

"Rivera. Yo Max," he answered the phone in a gruff voice.

"Sorry for waking you up, man," he said apologetically.

"Nah, 'bout time to get up. Go on."

"Early-bird fishing aficionados found a body in Lake Merritt."

"Shit." Not again. He immediately recalled a murder-accident case at Lake Merritt a few years ago.

Lake Merritt, a brackish lake and tidal lagoon, was called the Crown Jewel of Oakland and residents had a lot of pride and love for the place. They often jogged or walked around it or just sat and enjoyed the day or boating, yeah, some fishing.

"Their line caught the stiff, not fish. Scared the shit out of 'em. And OP Divers and Fire pulled it outta the water."

"Know the gender?"

"A female vic, wearing dress and undies but no shoes; could be washed away though the Lake never has a strong current. No obvious trauma found so far. CSI took fingerprints but only one or two readable, if lucky."

"Uh-huh." Fingerprints of drowned victims were usually very hard to read even by a high-resolution computer or extremely experienced fingerprint analysts. "Check the missing person reports. Ask neighbor PDs in Alameda too."

"Ah yeah, got it. Ain't sure it's accident, suicide or homicide at this point."

"What did the coroner say?"

"Deputy Coroner Eric came and said he can't tell COD aside from obvious possible drowning and he wanna wait after the autopsy but the vic looked in the water 24 hours at most considering the temp of the water. Anyways, medical examiner is standing by at the Bureau."

"Okay, goin' at the scene in twenty."

"Hey, the funny thing is CSI said the medical examiner requested to transport a fresh sample of Lake water ASAP, and one of 'em is on his way."

He smirked. "That's totally Sister Golden Hair."

"How'd you know?" Max's voice contained bafflement.

"Well, if something you wonder why, it's usually Dr. Alex thinkin' outside the box to determine COD."

"Huh."

"Anyways, thanks."

"Sure. Bobby and Tammy are gonna start interviewing the witnesses."

"Okay, brother. See ya laters."

"Laters, Jase."

*****

Alex had three office spaces in the Coroner's Bureau. The spaces in the autopsy room and the lab were small, only a desk and chair literally in the corner of each room. The last one was actually her official office, a very good size room that she could store many books, a special incubator for her research, sideboard, chairs, a couch and coffee table to welcome guests.

After the autopsy of the victim, she'd started writing the report in the official office, and wondered about a few peculiar issues in this case. Of course, she'd need to wait until all the lab results would return. And also she was waiting for a phone call from another BFF, an aquatic environmental microbiologist, Dr. Nora Reed. She was also her college buddy like Rae. She was a pretty woman with gorgeous dark brown hair and mysterious sea-green eyes. Her life had been dedicated to her work and running. Alex was grateful that a friend like her would lend a hand anytime she'd need help.

What struck her the most was the victim was young and pretty, even after being submerged in the murky water of Lake Merritt. Her dress was a high-end brand and so were her bra and panties. They were made in France. She must've had a good job or been from a good family. Her family and friends were looking for her right now, at this moment not knowing her fate. So sad.

Then she heard a knock at the door. She looked up and saw a very tall man was standing in the frame of the open door.

"Hey Doc,"

"Jason." She smiled. "Good timing." He knew when to visit her.

She pointed to the chair in front of her desk. He came in and sat on the chair. He wore a three-piece suit and a tie as usual, his signature outfit. He was one of the most handsome cops in town…well, except Sam, but that would be refutable in the eyes of Rae. She just couldn't stop talking about this detective. Alex would suspect Jason could be the one for her BFF as she'd never talked about a man like that before. And it seemed Jason was able to do keeps after all.

"So, you said good timing," Jason said. "Got the COD? ETD?" He took out his notebook.

She cleared her throat, "Well, first of all, ETD was about 24, 25 hours ago, around Sunday midnight to 1am according to the temperature of the water."

"Alright." He started scribbling.

"Her stomach contained very little food but looked she might've had a small dinner of a ham sandwich."

He nodded, keeping writing. And then looking up at her, he asked, "COD?"

"Well, I couldn't find any drastic trauma outside her body, but water *did* exist in her lungs, pleural cavities, stomach, ergo, basically it's wet drowning."

"Oh, so she did drown in the Lake." Jason leaned toward her, thrilled to have found the cause of death.

"Um…Jase, it's not that easy."

"Don't get it. I thought it's quite straightforward."

"I just said her system has water and thus wet drowning, but we don't know if she drowned in the Lake yet. Let me start over. First of all, she had a couple of drugs, cocaine and fentanyl."

"Whoa, heavy duty." He wrote the names of the drugs. "A lot?"

"I'd say, it could've knocked her out. But not killed her. And those drugs looked administered intravenously. I found a tiny puncture mark into her vein on her right arm. Also, for wet drowning, water in her system looked low compared with usual wet drowning cases."

"Um…" His eyes flying from the notebook to her, he asked, "meaning?"

"If she drowned in the Lake as wet drowning, she should have more water in her system, that's what it means."

"I know you don't guess, but is there any possible way

that she had less water in her body? Was it the drugs that had hindered her from swallowing or breathing in water?"

"Well, the shortest explanation is she died before more water got into her."

"Oh, ah, right."

"I've sent the result of my lab test to an aquatic environmental microbiologist. And I'm awaiting her call."

"Aquatic environmental microbiologist…?"

"Study of micro-organisms and diatoms in water surrounding us."

"Which of your lab tests you're talkin' about?" Jason asked.

"Well, don't you want to know whether she really drowned in the Lake or not?"

He stopped writing, his pen in mid-air. "Wait, you mean she might've drowned somewhere else?"

"I don't know yet."

He started laughing. "Alex, you really don't do guesses."

"Nope." She showed him a small smile.

Then, it hit him. "Ah, so the reason you asked for the water sample was cuz you wanted to compare the water in the vic to the sample from the Lake."

"Exactly."

Wow. She was good. Really good. As a homicide detective, this was very important to know whether or not she'd drowned in the Lake. If her lungs and organs contained other than Lake water, then she'd become a homicide or body dumping victim, cuz her dead body would never move itself to Lake Merritt.

"You need to know what kind of water she had internally."

"Yes, ma'am. I think we agree on that part." Jason grinned like he got a perfect three-point shot.

Then her phone started buzzing. She eyed the screen and informed, "It's Sam."

Jason whistled and waggled his brows.

She turned on the speaker. "Hey Sam, you're on the

speaker. Jason's here for an autopsy result."

"Hey, 'sup?" Jason greeted with a little amusement in his voice.

"Hey, actually I'm glad you're there with her." He sounded quite serious.

"Okay, Sarge, I'm listening." Jason too toned it down.

"Your vic could be one of *our* missing persons. We got the request from your PD to check our missing persons cases. And we did go through, and one missing woman seems a very close match. Her parents filed the report on Sunday evening when she didn't show up at the family dinner. They couldn't find her anywhere at the time. They even went to her apartment, but nothing suspicious."

"Oy." Jason put his fingers on his chin, tapping.

He continued, "In fact, our missing persons officer told them to file the report 48 hours later cuz she's a twenty-two-year-old adult female. But she kept her memo in the report just in case. That's why we found her."

"Thanks to your officer."

"Your vic worked at Berkeley Bank downtown as a teller. She had to work that Saturday till 6pm. Parents said they'd talked to her on the phone in the morning just before her shift and at that time she was her usual self. She'd said she'd go to the supermarket after work. And that was the last time the parents talked to her. The clothes your vic's wearing match their description she'd said she was wearing before she went to work on Saturday. Jase, her parents want to see her."

"What's her name and age?" Jason asked, holding the pen in his notebook.

"Evalyn Roberts, twenty-two, a resident of Berkeley. But her parents live in Piedmont."

Nevertheless, Jason said cautiously, "Just similar clothes won't fly, you know that. Anything specific?"

"Yeah, she's supposed to have a tattoo on the small of her back and it's a rosebud with a little red heart next to it. About the size of a half-dollar coin."

She closed her eyes once and sighed. "That's highly likely her. I'll also check her DNA, ASAP."

"Good. We have a DNA sample from her parents. Will bring it in. Can they see her?" Sam asked politely.

Jason looked at her. So she replied, "Yes. They can ID her. She looked fine for being in the water."

"Guess, was only 24 hours since her death and water is chilly…," Jason added.

"'K. I'll talk to them and I'll let you two know when we're coming in. Thanks." He hung up.

"Well hell, that was such professional, impersonal, methodical, unromantic, outrageously grammatically correct English speaking sonofabitch-y, douche Sam." He'd called her personal phone and talked to her the way he had? That was unacceptable for Jason. "Be nice to your own woman should be the number one thing. He didn't even use endearments. Seriously?"

She laughed. "Nice enough to me. And he's at work, so are we."

"Yeah, right." Unconvinced, he didn't stop beating him. "But he could use a bit softer words to you. He called you on your personal phone."

She wanted to say something but her phone on the desk buzzed again. He could see the screen showing a woman's name.

Dr. Nora Reed, UC Berkeley, California

She turned the speaker on again so that he could hear what she'd say, but as soon as it clicked, Dr. Reed greeted with a bubbly voice, "Hey, girl, long time no see, okay, about a month? Are you still enjoying life sans a man? Your hero-worship syndrome still stuck in the tushie?"

"Dr. Reed!" Desperately she raised her voice to stop her BFF's talking, while he was smirking wide. "You're on the speaker and a homicide detective from the Oakland PD is with me, listening to you."

"Oops," immediately they heard her say. "Sorry for my runny mouth."

He let out a little burst of laughter.

"Um, sorry," Nora said. "Didn't know we have an audience."

"Dr. Reed, this is Sgt. Jason Rivera at the Oakland PD. Thank you for your help," he introduced himself.

Jason Rivera? Aha, Rae's serious date! Maybe she could talk to him some other time. Nora snickered secretly. "Sgt. Rivera, glad I can help. And please forget what I said in the beginning."

"No problem." But he was thinking he would never be able to forget her humorous trait.

"Dr. Reed, I believe you called me about the result of the test of the water." Alex took a very formal way of talking.

"Yes, Dr. Wallace, yes indeed." So did she. He was amused with their kaleidoscopic ways of communication, acknowledging Rae was definitely one of them.

"Dr. Reed, do proceed."

"Yes, Dr. Wallace, thank you." So she began, with a more serious tone in her voice, "Your victim had Lake Merritt water in her system." Then she added, "Mostly."

"Mostly?" he questioned, utterly confounded. "Dr. Reed, I'm not a scientist. Please explain in layman's terms."

"Surely. Let me try; hope I can do better, Sgt. Rivera. The water composition including a hydrogen ion exponent…um, acidity, salinity, species and distribution of micro-organisms and diatoms, etcetera, everything matches the water of Lake Merritt. But there are inconsistencies." She took breaths.

"Which are?" He was eager to know, taking a note.

Dr. Nora Reed mildly challenged. "Sgt. Rivera, if water contains chlorine, fluorine, and a tiny bit of lead and copper and freshwater algae in minuscule quantities, what kind of water do you think it is?"

"Er…water of Lake Merritt is brackish…so…your description sounds a lot like our local water district's tap water."

"Congratulations, you're our kind of guy. You can be an assistant microbiologist anytime."

"Nora." Alex rolled her eyes.

"Wait, wait, it doesn't make any sense," he refuted. "My vic had both tap water and Lake Merritt's salty water in her system at the same time when she drowned?"

"Correct, all the numbers matched," Dr. Reed concurred. "Now you have an answer."

"Oh no, no way, Doc, not even. Why did she have the mixture?"

"That's not my job to find, but yours, Detective," Dr. Reed said. "It's your turn to work your tushie off to solve the case."

"Nora, hon, thanks," Alex said.

"You're welcome. Talk to you later, sweetie." They hung up.

"So, she didn't simply drown in the Lake, then," he said after consideration. "More like she died somewhere else, somewhere she could be exposed to two different waters and dumped in the Lake."

"Highly likely, yes," she agreed. "That's the best interpretation so far. Besides, like I said, just drowning in the Lake, she had too little Lake water for wet drowning."

"Okay." He kept taking notes. "Either accident, suicide, or homicide, and then body dump."

"Yes," she said, "and our original question was what kind of water in her system, right? At least now you know that fact."

"Yeah…" He narrowed his eyes. "The question is…what is your *hero-worship syndrome* that Dr. Reed had mentioned at first?"

She was almost petrified, as if she was struck by a lightning bolt, but she answered, laughing, "It's when I was a lot younger and dreamed of a knight in shining armor kinda thing. You know, very girly, mushy stuff?"

He gave her a long look. She squirmed mentally, afraid that he might see the truth.

Then his phone vibed in his pocket. "Excuse me."

Saved by the bell, literally. Relieved, she printed out the report and made several copies for the police.

"Okay, Sam and a uniform are bringing the vic's parents in thirty. You'll be ready?" holding the phone on his ear, he asked her.

"Yes, she'll be ready." She stood up quickly. "I'll go back to the autopsy room to get her ready."

He signaled to her with his hand waving. She nodded and stepped out of her office.

She'd said, *get her ready*… Not Dr. Alex herself but to get his vic ready to meet her parents. He repeated in his mind. This coroner was really different. He'd thought he'd known her well enough, but he hadn't. Not quite yet.

She cared. Cared about his victim and her parents. Sam should know. He should know what kind of woman he was dating.

*****

IDing one's own child was probably the hardest thing to do. Alex was thankful that Sam and Jason were both present when she had to show the body of their daughter on the autopsy table under the white cloth.

After the saddest part had passed and Jason had promised them to find what really had happened to her, the parents were escorted out by him and the uniformed officer.

The Police Departments of Berkeley and Oakland had treated this case as a joint investigation since her body had been found in Oakland, but she'd been a resident of Berkeley.

The plan was to begin with each end of the timeline. The BPD detectives would investigate her personal life while the OPD would scrutinize her death starting from Lake Merritt, considering the case one long string of a timeline, so that they should find the reason why she'd met an untimely death somewhere on the string.

Also, one more case was heavy on Sam's mind. The thallium poisoned victim, John Doe, a.k.a. their fallen-from-the-sky guy. No one had come forward to claim his body even with help from the media, and the police hadn't found anyone matched to his fingerprints in AFIS, the Automated Fingerprint Identification System.

Where had he come from and what exactly had happened to him? Sam and Carter had been canvassing the area, checking the evidence and planning how to investigate this odd case. All they'd known was the victim had been exposed to two poisons, hydrogen sulfide and thallium, and finding the place with those two together wasn't easy either.

Before he was leaving for the PD, he knocked on her office door frame. "Hey."

"Hey back." She raised her head from her laptop and smiled at him, instantaneously melting him inside and outside. "Are you going back to the PD now?" she asked; hopefully he remembered they were supposed to go out tonight.

"Yeah." He nodded, still standing near the door.

"What is it?"

"About tonight."

She noticed his awkward and apologetic tone. Ah. She immediately knew he must be too busy to go out tonight. And she knew all the major crime detectives were leading a case-oriented life and often going home was just to get some short sleep and take a shower and change.

"I understand," she said, still smiling.

"You do?"

"Yes." She nodded. "You have two odd cases you have a responsibility to. Don't worry about it. We can postpone."

"Okay, thanks." Sam just kept his eyes on her.

"Yes? Anything else?"

"I'll make it up to you as soon as the cases close." He smiled, totally causing a power surge in her brain and spine, suddenly her body temperature shooting up.

"Thanks, but no worries. I'll always be here. You can

visit me anytime. Just take good care of yourself while you're working on your case. Eat well…"

He chuckled softly. "You sound like my mother."

"What!" She half stood, getting annoyed. When she got angry, she was awfully cute. He quickly entered her office with only three long strides to reach her, grabbing her arms and kissed her hard. Immediately his body hair rose again at the moment his lips touched hers, getting him hard.

They were standing across her desk, but she was still enclosed by him, the heat from him transferring to her, almost motionless just receiving his kiss and his heat.

His kiss was the same as the first day in the autopsy room. Hot and sincere but insanely good. Again, the tip of his tongue traced her lips and his tongue came into her mouth without hesitation. She sucked his tongue and she felt he shuddered. His hand came into her hair, jolting her, to hold the back of her head, deepening his kiss. He heard himself groan in his throat.

This wasn't just a kiss. This was a precursor to making love.

Then…she heard his phone buzz.

"Oh shit." He swore under his breath, then said, "Sorry for my language."

He took out his buzzing phone and saw the caller ID, *Jason Rivera*. "I'd definitely kill him," he mumbled. She looked so vulnerable like the first day after he'd kissed her, turning him on more. He grudgingly let her go. "Last time was your phone; today is mine. We're absolutely, positively cursed with bad juju," he said, shaking his head, smirking, making her chuckle. Bad juju?

"Jase, 'sup?" Then he inhaled. She figured something must've come up. "Okay, be right there. Yeah, okay." And he hung up.

"Sorry, Alex, gotta go," he remorsefully said, but his heart and body were aching for her. He faced her again and held her face gently with both his hands and kissed. A quick peck. And he placed his forehead on hers. "Oh…Alex…"

he whispered her name. His small utterance seeped into her heart too. She wished she could cuddle up to him, but she knew she'd have to let him go.

Keeping his forehead glued to hers, he looked into her eyes. She saw in his warm eyes that he was concerned about the state of her mind, so, she reassured him, "Nope, I don't have any fever, though your kiss was quite hot and contagious." He found her eyes were smiling. He beamed at her. "I love your fun attitude."

She froze for an instant, but quickly recovered and said to him, "Drive safe; and if you say I sound like your mother again, I'll kill you."

He laughed, in a low rumbling sound that made her hotter in some part of her body. He yanked himself from her and left her office as quick as he'd come in, with the same three long strides.

She just kept standing in the same place, holding on to the desk. She'd taken his words "I love your fun attitude" in the totally wrong denotation. She heard him say 'I love you…' the first part, first and only, and '-r fun attitude' had come rather slow. *Stupid.* She shouldn't be crying for the moon.

"Jase, thanks," as soon as he got out of his Charger, he called out at the tall detective standing by his SUV in the parking lot of the BPD.

"Here." He handed him a folder. Sam opened it and found a stack of paper inside. He suggested, "Read the summary, homie. The first several paragraphs. Concisely composed for us when we ain't get 'nuff time to read all."

Sam looked down at it and noticed it was Alex's autopsy and examination report on Evalyn Roberts, their victim, including the fact that she'd consulted Dr. Reed at UC Berkeley. The paper had been created to submit to the Oakland Police. "Thanks for sharing, Jase."

"You might get it to your office later, but gotta read it right away. Hey, her parents really appreciated you, Sam.

They said you promptly contacted them to notify and picked them up and consoled them. You're a good cop, man."

"Just doin' my job." He kept his eyes on the paper, reading the summary written by her, a concise but detailed enough outline to understand their victim's condition. Only facts. Not even a scintilla of her conjecture. Very much her. He felt almost like tasting her between the lines in her report. After they'd surrendered to each other, her report had suddenly become much more meaningful, as if it was her personal message to him that she was encouraging him to seize the day by pursuing the truth of the case. She'd given him power.

"Okay, so what's your plan, Jason?" he eagerly asked.

"We gonna meet up with Carter and CSI at her apartment in South Berkeley. She was found 24 hours after her death, so it's still within 48 hours. Could be some evidence left there. I gonna leave my truck here and ride with you."

"Got it. Oh, when you took her parents back home, did they mention anything about her relationships?"

"Nope," Jason answered, "no husband, no boyfriend."

"Okay."

"And you and Carter gonna see her boss at the bank later. I gotta go back to Lake Merritt after checking her apartment."

"Roger that."

"Why're you so fucking docile now, Sam? I ain't your boss."

"Ain't it actually your case? She's your vic. I'm just assisting the lead detective, bro."

"Aw…you're nice." He grabbed his head and crumpled his hair. "Hey, watch it!" Sam quickly escaped from his almost chokehold. But both were grinning.

CHAPTER 5

When Sam and Jason arrived at their victim, Evalyn Roberts' apartment, CSI had already been working for a while, led by Detective Carter Halls.

"Hey, man, long time no see," he teased his supposed-to-be supervisor, Sam. "Where've you been at? Hiding?"

"Yo, Carter, behaving yourself?" Jason greeted him while he gave him a man hug.

"Tryin'," he replied snickering. "You still doin' ladies thing?"

"Nah, behaving recently."

"You?" Carter stared at his face amusingly. "No shit?"

"No shit," he asserted, thinking about Rae. "Getting old, bro. Guess time to settle down."

That got the attention of both detectives from the Berkeley PD. "*You* settle down?"

"Don't you?" Jason hit back at Sam, pointing his finger on his chest. "Won't you?" He clearly meant Alex.

"Yeah, I heard you're seriously seeing Sister Golden Hair." Carter smirked.

Sam rolled his eyes. "What's your source of info? Where you get the intel so damn quick?"

"So, it's true, then."

"Shit," Sam swore under his breath. But he reconsidered the situation with her. If she'd hear the rumor that he denied seeing her, it would hurt her. So, he decided to be a man. "Yeah, Amma seriously seeing her. We're too damn busy to go on a date but try spending much time together"

"Huh." Carter sighed, staring at his partner for a good few seconds. He'd never seen Sam declare dating one woman openly before. Yowzah. And then he cracked a smile. "Congrats, to you both, it's high time, right? You guys are already thirty-five…"

"Thirty-two!" both Sam and Jason protested but Carter didn't give a damn about it. He was still in his twenties. Dammit.

"So, Carter, you had uniforms canvass the area including other residents of the apartment?" Jason went back to the case.

"Initial area canvassing is Investigation 101, man."

"Right." Jason's lips curved a bit at his remark. He remembered when Carter had just become a rookie detective a few years ago.

"Randy said he'd do it again later with his team." Carter pointed to the other major crime team.

"Found anything in here?" Sam urged him.

"Nope, Sarge." And he stretched upwards. "We're searching all over but we didn't find fucking anything relevant to her drowning case at all. I mean, *at all.* None. Nada. Oh by the way this is one of those one-bedroom apartments where a young woman first started livin' at," Carter informed them somberly. "CSI's tryin' their best but no damn obvious criminal shit had taken place here. We think we need fresh sets of eyes. You guys might find somethin'. We didn't touch her personal effects yet cuz I thought you wanna see 'em yourselves first. We gonna collect 'em as you proceed."

"Alrighty," Jason said, "I'ma start from living room and kitchen. What 'bout you?"

Sam answered, "Bedroom first."

"Good choice." Jason liked Sam's detective instinct. "Meet you laters."

The two detectives, pulling a pair of latex gloves out of their jacket pockets, walked down the hallway, led by Carter and the uniform.

Sam entered her bedroom. Generally a bedroom was the most personal space in any home and often a treasure trove for the detectives. But he'd just learned this apartment didn't have any distinctive evidence or proof that it'd been used for apparent criminal acts. No special chemical odor, especially bleach smell, when he'd first stepped in the apartment. And it didn't look like right after cleaning; in fact, it looked a bit dusty.

Her dresser-vanity with a huge mirror attached on top, and a jewelry box, figurines, lamps, etcetera on the furniture had already collected a very thin even layer of dust on the surface, which meant no one had touched those for a while. It looked like Evalyn hadn't cleaned the house for some time before she'd gone missing. CSI's black fingerprint powder on certain spots like the handle of the dresser and part of the mirror didn't help to make the room look clean, either.

He walked around observing the overall condition of the room. Not much.

Her parents had said they'd talked to her on her landline every Saturday morning before her work shift. Last Saturday, after the phone call, she'd gone to work all day at the bank and finished at 6pm and it'd been checked and supported by the bank managers, coworkers and their surveillance cameras. According to her parents, she'd said she'd go to the supermarket after work. She'd been seen leaving the bank parking lot in her vehicle, the silver Toyota Camry handed down from her parents, and that was the last time anyone had seen her. The police had already issued a BOLO for her vehicle but they hadn't received any report yet. They had practically nothing in hand right now to track her trail for that day, not to mention solving the case. Jeezus.

He first opened the drawers of the dresser-vanity. Her intimate wear, Ts, blouses, and more casual clothes like sweats, etcetera, were in the two small top and two big drawers below, stored orderly. Nothing stood out.

He moved on to a nightstand by her bed. There was only a lamp and a photo of Yosemite El Capitan in a thin delicate glass frame with silver edges.

Where the hell was her phone charger? He wondered. Didn't most people keep their phone charger on a nightstand or somewhere in the bedroom? The nightstand didn't have any drawers but one shelf under. He found a bible. That was all. He opened the pages of the bible hoping to find something, but nothing at all. No note, bookmarks, or even handwriting. Just a nicely clean bible as if it was part of a staging by a realtor when they'd had an open house.

Then he walked to the closet in the corner of the room and opened both of the bi-fold doors. It was just a regular closet. Her clothes, mostly suits and dresses, were on the clothes hangers creating a row of colorful waterfall. He scanned each of those hanging clothes. Something could be between the dresses. But again nothing. And look at all those neatly hung clothes. The spaces between them had been almost exactly the same before he touched them.

He moved on to a few old looking purses hanging on the wall behind the clothes and a couple of pairs of shoes in boxes on the rack near the ceiling. He checked inside the shoe boxes and purses in case something in them. Only some small items left in the purses, which many women would also leave in there, like a small piece of paper, pen with the bank logo, etcetera, but not much.

And he found she didn't have a laundry hamper in the bedroom.

Every single day except her days off, she'd gotten up, taken a shower, changed clothes, put on her shoes, picked up her purse and off she'd gone to work…

Carter stuck his head in the room behind the open door. "Hey, anything new?"

Facing him, Sam asked, "You checked her laundry?"

"Yeah. No dirty clothes in the washer or cleaned in the dryer."

"She even did her own laundry?"

"I think so, cuz there's newer bottles of detergent and softener half used."

"Hmm…did you find a laundry hamper? Dirty clothes?"

"Negative."

"Huh… Weird."

She really lived here? That question had been popping up in his mind repeatedly.

"Did you find her purse in here? We got the details from her coworker, right? She'd always carried the Louis Vuitton Monogram bucket style, right?" he asked.

"Correct, Sarge, but negative. Not in the apartment. We figured if she'd gone missing with her vehicle, it should've been in there."

"That's true. So it might still be in her Camry. But where the hell were other purses at?"

"They're in the closet. They're hanging on the wall."

"But those're damn old ones. Most young women own quite a few purses and shoes, don't they?"

"Now that you said that, it sounds damn unusual. My mom and Judy have tons of purses and shoes. I believe they're centipedes." Judy was his younger sister. Sam chuckled at his comment. Carter went on, "They know they shouldn't have bought a shitload of 'em. Dad and I always told 'em stop doing such unproductive shit. It's like Dad buying thirty sets of his power tools in just different color cases."

"Well, but he can't wear power tools or tool cases."

"That's silly." Sneering, Carter punched his arm lightly.

"Alright …" A serious expression back to his face, Sam

walked back to the bed. "This bed doesn't look made recently either." He was looking around the hem of the sheets. "Look," squatting down on one knee, he picked a small cleaner's tag on the sheet. Carter also ducked to see it. "I missed that."

Tilting his head, Sam said, still eyeing it, "She must've forgot to have taken it off. But the date here is a month ago. You don't sleep on the same sheet without changing it for a month."

"Not anymore," Carter said, scaring the shit out of Sam. "I said, not anymore. But when you were young like a frat boy, you forget about your sheets unless you and your girl made a mess."

Sam shook his head and said, "Write down the name of the cleaner. *Berkeley Sun-Shine Cleaner*…address is…"

"No need, Sam, I know the place. It's downtown. Near the bank she'd worked. I gonna bring Randy to the cleaner with a photo of her and interview 'em, when you're at the bank."

"Okay." Sam stood up and walked back to the dresser-vanity and started to open the jewelry box. He found no earrings on the earring puff pad, a couple of tiny gold chains and pearl necklace, and two rings. Not so much extravagant items. Then, he recalled her parents had mentioned she'd had a minor metal allergy, so she'd worn limited items. That did make sense. He now saw consistency he liked to see.

And then he took out a dark blue velvet pouch. The sack had a silver-colored swan printed.

"That's an Austrian crystal maker's logo," Carter informed him, standing nearby.

Sam looked at him over his shoulder and said, "I hope you don't lack damn balls."

"It's Judy's thing. She often buys stuff from them. They don't use real gold or platinum or diamond what not, but they use silver and plated metal with their crystals."

Sam gave him a long look and cocked his head. "Thank you, Ms. Carter." But he was punched in the shoulder as soon as he uttered it. "Ow."

"Shut the fuck up and open it, bro," Carter ordered him.

"Yes, sir." And he opened it and emptied the sack gingerly.

There were loose crystals in various colors, red, pink, blue, green, yellow, along with just transparent noncolored ones. "Beautiful," Carter murmured.

"They are," Sam agreed. Next moment, he found a pair of earrings among them too. "Odd," he cautiously uttered. "Those earrings." He picked them up in his palm. "Look, our vic hardly wore earrings."

"Ah, right, they might well be gifts for someone?"

"Or from someone... Don't look like the others, though."

"The crystal maker makes accessories, earrings too. Judy has tons."

"You said the maker doesn't use real gems but just crystals."

"Yup, so, noncolor crystals are used on accessories like the ones you're holding."

"Those ain't crystals," Sam muttered.

"How'd ya know?" Carter looked into the earrings in Sam's hand, frowning. "Look like crystal to me."

He picked up a few loose crystals. "Give me your hands." Carter held out both his palms to him. He put several loose crystals in one palm; and the earrings in the other. "Whoa."

"See? How different?" Sam said.

"Yeah...whoa, the earrings...much heavier."

"I think those are real diamonds."

"Huh...so she was hiding 'em in the crystals?"

He knew about gems a little more than Carter did, since he'd done some work on a jewelry larceny case in Berkeley in the past six months. In the end, Sam and his special team had found it had turned out to be a jewelry-related insurance fraud, and all the main players had been gone by the time search and arrest warrants had been issued due to some awkward glitches somewhere, except for two idiots who had stolen the goods, asked by the owner to commit robbery for a couple of thousand dollars.

"Nowadays many reputable jewelers carry diamonds with serial numbers. If we could find them on those diamonds, we'd be able to figure out where the hell they came from. I guess many people who don't have a good safe in the house, usually try every unconventional secret hiding place to hide their assets."

"True," Carter agreed. "We found money in the freezer a couple of times and I think fridges are already kinda damn old style." And he hurriedly gathered the earrings and loose crystals and every personal effect on the dresser into individual evidence bags.

"I feel strange, though. Did she really live here?" Sam mumbled, scowling. "She didn't use her bed, dusty dresser…"

"And no damn food in the fridge." Jason walked in, hands in the air. "What the hell she was eating, air?"

"No trace of ham sandwich?" Sam asked.

"Ham sandwi…? Ah," Jason remembered what Alex had said. Evalyn's last meal had been a ham sandwich for dinner. "Nope. No food in the fridge, no trash or garbage in the trash bin or wastebasket or anything. She really lived here?" Then, he eyed them, near the dresser. "What the hell?"

"I gonna explain to you in the car. Time for you to go back to the OPD, no?"

"Oy, right." Checking the time, Jason said, exchanging fist bumps with Carter. "'K, brother, behave yourself."

"Right back atcha."

*****

Carter and Randy had gone to the cleaner before it closed for today.

Some workers at the cleaner had remembered Evalyn

very well. She'd regularly used their service for her bedsheets as well as expensive suits and dresses. But they'd had no idea that she was deceased. And they'd never seen anyone else with her before. The only useful information was she'd stopped coming to their shop a month ago after she'd retrieved her sheets. That was the exact date on the cleaner's receipt tag that Sam had discovered on her sheet. But after that, Team Carter had hit rock bottom.

Sam and his boss Lt. Montfort had visited the bank and met the branch manager. However, they didn't find anything special or relevant to the case either. She'd been a good employee and coworker, well-liked by many customers. Team Sam had also hit the end of it.

He'd called her parents again to make sure she hadn't had a boyfriend or any other places to live aside from her apartment. The parents had repeated she'd lived there, since they had always talked every Saturday morning before her shift and sometimes even visited her there. He'd subpoenaed her phone record from her carrier, but he'd have to wait for the results. Since she'd told the parents she'd go to the supermarket after work, he'd requested the security footage on Saturday from the several neighborhood supermarkets. They might find her in the footage with someone or an important scene if they were lucky.

By the evening, the CDs and flash drives had started piling up on Sam's desk. It would definitely take him the whole night and more to scrutinize all of the CCTV footage. Good thing that he hadn't promised Alex to take her out for dinner tonight. At the same time, he wanted to see her, talk to her, kiss her, and…

Each supermarket had provided the footage of the entrance, interior, above the cashiers and parking lot. He started to watch enormous volumes of recordings, remembering what she'd been wearing.

Around dinnertime, Carter brought him a sandwich and coffee. He ate it but he didn't even notice what kind of sandwich it was. His eyes glued to the monitor, his hand controlling the keyboard, some places fast-forward, others slo-mo, he was looking for Evalyn or her vehicle.

When he looked around, the office was dark and only the hallway lights and his desk lamp were on like some kind of beacon. Huh… What time was it now? He looked at the computer monitor. 12:00am. Whoa.

He vaguely remembered everyone including Carter and Lt had said good night to him sometime around 9pm. They'd also been watching the footage helping him, but they'd decided to call it a day.

He stretched his back and sank in the chair, massaging his temple and between the eyes. He needed a bit of a break.

He took out his personal phone. He thought for a while, hesitating. Then he decisively began typing a text message to Alex. "*You up?*" And he rolled his eyes. Such a cliché. Everyone used *you up?* to start a text in the middle of night. The problem was his brain was so exhausted that it refused to be creative. So, he just sent it. He didn't actually expect her to send him back a text. It was already past midnight.

When he turned around, he was just like in a dark ocean floating all by himself, no land or other ships near him. Or he was a lighthouse with his faithful desk lamp and computer monitor lit. And no sounds around him either. The only sounds were again his computer quietly humming.

Being a major crime detective was a fight in solitude but it was worth doing it, since the efforts often led to close cases. The most important mission was of course solving cases. It would give a victim's family some kind of resolution. Complete closure wouldn't be possible because they couldn't bring their victim's life back, but at least they could feel they had done as much as humble human beings could do.

Ding.

He almost jumped. It was a text message back from her. "*Yup. Where you?*"

"*BPD.*" Sent.

"*Evalyn?*"

"*Yup. Checking security footage.*" Sent.

"*Did you have dinner?*" Reading it, Sam grinned. She began sounding like his mother again. Well, she cared about him, which gave him warm feelings.

"*At desk. Sandwich.*" Sent.

"*Sorry.*"

"*Not your fault. At least I ate.*" Sent.

"*Can you finish soon?*"

"*Not sure.*" Sent.

"*You need sleep.*"

The fact was he needed her the most. If he'd sleep, he'd want to sleep with her.

"*Can I come over?*" Sent.

And he regretted right away. "*Sorry, never mind.*" Sent.

"*Bring me soft pretzel from* West Side Story *if still open.*"

He couldn't believe what she'd sent to him. So, it was okay for her he'd visit *now*?

And she liked pretzels from *West Side Story*? Good to know. The bar was located a couple blocks northwest from the BPD, the west side of Berkeley, hence their name, *West Side Story*.

"*Sure. Open until 2am, FYI.*" Sent.

And he was already standing, logging off the computer. He could come back to the office after seeing her.

"*Any beer?*" Sent. He added, thinking of when they'd eat pretzels. Putting on his jacket, he kept his eyes on the phone.

His coroner girl replied, "*No thanks. Some in my fridge. I don't keep body in there cuz it ain't cool enough*, *FYI.*"

He threw back his head and laughed. She was awesome.

"*On my way.*" Sent.

Sam knew where she lived. Well, he did now, since he'd taken her home Sunday night after the *EZ Poppas* gig. But he hadn't gotten inside her house that night, respecting Dr. Taylor's order. He still wasn't sure that she would let him in this time either. He'd just said *can I come over now* in the text.

Her house was in the Berkeley Hills district, one of those amazing places where many expensive good looking houses stood. She'd said she was renting it. According to their inside newsletter, she was one of the world-top researchers who could sell her research and its results for tens of millions of bucks that he couldn't even imagine what it looked like and she'd given money to a local county. So that was where the money had come from for her lab equipment. And she was living in a rental property? She'd surely been capable of buying her own expensive home.

But she didn't look like the kind of spoiled rich woman that he'd dated a couple of times. Alex was driving a white Nissan Leaf; it was pre-owned by her friend. On the other hand, she was wearing a men's Rolex Oyster-Perpetual and her favorite work purse which was steady and big enough to store her laptop was made in France. However, those items looked very much worn and well taken care of. They might've been handed down. She might be a member of some old, affluent yet modest family. It was possible since she'd lived and worked in Europe for a long time. She seemed to be full of surprises and secrets and contradictions that he could peel layer by layer off of her until he'd find just her being, a notion that also turned him on.

It was already past 1:00am when he pulled over to the curb in front of her house. He got out of the Charger with a box of pretzels in his hand and turned around only to meet with amazing views of the town. "Whoa." He hadn't seen it last time as he hadn't paid any attention.

Between the houses and trees below, there was almost a flood of lights. Her house must be positioned on quite a high mound. If the weather would allow, he might be able to see the Bay Bridge and lights of San Francisco in the distance.

Tonight, the fog had started forming, a low murky haze covering the town near the Bay. The part of the fog reflecting moonlight from above and city lights from below generated an image as if it was some sort of a surreal phenomenon. He shuddered, feeling that it would be extremely ideal if he could stay in a lover's bed in such misty weather.

"Hey," She opened the door just before he knocked on it. She must've been observing the security camera image near the front door. She was wearing a casual T and shorts and barefoot. Her straight legs with smooth skin were begging him to caress them thoroughly.

"I just came to deliver your pretzels," he said, showing her a box, hoping she'd let him in.

She accepted the box with gratitude, then added, "Don't be ridiculous." And she stepped back to make room for him.

"Thanks."

He strode inside and realized he was in the foyer connected to the living room. From outside, it looked like a regular Californian stucco house and not so new, but the inside was renovated in a remarkably modern and lucid style almost like Italian Modern. More straight line shapes than organic curves. Less colors, simple but ubiquitous. It looked closer to minimalism and perhaps more masculine than feminine. But that kind of simplicity and cleanness were very much like Alex, succinct, straightforward, no-frills, just facts and truths, but somehow, warm, kind, compassionate. Her sexy feminine look was deceiving. Her appearance had nothing to do with her exceptional talent and character. He not only adored her but also revered her for all that she had.

He followed her to the kitchen. Clean monotone places that he'd love to stay there all day long. It looked easily maneuverable; whoever had designed this kitchen knew how to cook and how to maximally utilize the kitchen and nook.

She took out two bottles of beer from the fridge. Then, she placed the pretzels on a baking sheet and threw it into the oven to warm up.

He hung his jacket on the back of one of the chairs, waiting for her to sit. They clinked their bottles to toast, and he couldn't help but say, "*Here's looking at you, kid.*"

"*Casablanca*…nice." She smiled.

"Yup." He nodded and started drinking beer. It was a simple human act to consume liquid. But her eyes glued to his unconscious movement of drinking beer. His jaws moved, so did his throat muscles and Adam's apple. Fascinating. All male subjects that she dealt with were long gone on the autopsy table and she didn't remember the last time she'd watched a living male doing something at this close distance.

"What?" He noticed she was observing him drink beer. He was baffled but smirked, "Never seen a man drink beer?"

"I haven't seen any men still alive drink anything for a long time, come to think of it. All of my male specimens were motionless in the autopsy room," she replied and was rewarded by his hearty laugh.

"What 'bout your boyfriend? He surely did drink something."

She contemplated for a second and shook her head. "I cannot even remember when I had a boyfriend."

He stopped drinking and dropped his gaze on her. "No kiddin'." This all-American beauty? She couldn't remember when she'd had a boyfriend? Seriously? He was doubtful but she hadn't sounded like she was telling him a lie. And there was no reason to tell him a lie anyway.

"Nope, really. I have to 'fess up, Detective. I'm a complete workaholic. No time for men or myself."

"Huh… Then I should probably collect a fee for my performances. You know, like a stripper?" And he waggled his brows.

She chuckled, and again started studying him when he restarted drinking beer.

He smiled and said, "*Round up the usual suspects.*"

"Another *Casablanca* quote, and…okay, I'm the usual

suspect then, Sarge." She rolled her eyes.

"Yeah, cuz you are."

So, she leaned over toward him, staring at him with those mysterious eyes, and said, "*Kiss me. Kiss me as if it were the last time.*"

His bottle stopped at his lips. That was also a quote from the movie. But had she meant she'd really wanted him to kiss her?

Putting down the bottle on the table, he watched her face closely. Her eyes serious, she tilted her head, as if she was ready to receive a kiss. Suddenly the temperature of the room rose or his body temperature was rising, the prolonged lust for her punching him in the gut. He grabbed her hand and pulled her in over the table, placing the other hand under her chin and raised it until their eyes met, the flames of desire colliding in midair. He lightly placed his lips on hers first to see how she'd react. He saw her close her eyes, her lips slightly apart. Sexy as hell. He then kissed her again, this time more seriously, intensity increasing as it was said, *as if it were the last time.* He was hoping this wouldn't be the last time but the beginning of their relationship.

"Alex, I want you," he murmured on her lips, the sensual motion tingling each other's mouths calling for more intimate connection and mutual gratification.

"Come." She stood up from the chair. The sudden detachment from her warmth gave him a shiver. So, he took her hand immediately. "Where we goin'?"

"My bedroom," leading him, she said it almost inaudibly over her shoulder.

He swallowed, hoping she didn't hear it. He was so elated that he felt like he'd almost come at that spot. He possessively put his arm around her waist.

"Oh, just a sec." On their way out of the kitchen, she turned off the oven. "Always safety first." She beamed at him, making him dizzy. Oh wait, maybe he forgot to breathe and his brain lacked oxygen? So, he breathed. "I like safety first." And he pulled her in to him a little more to drop a kiss on top of her head.

She shrugged, her mouth touching a smile. "I once experienced a bad fire; it'd happened exactly like bad things come in threes…or maybe more in terms of the graveness of it."

"What do you mean?" Somewhere in his mind, something stirred in the memories.

"Um…" She peeked at his face, looking up and saw him staring back at her with his affectionate brown eyes containing shadowy shades. No, no. She mentally kicked herself. "Well, you should know I burn water. I'm terrible at cooking. The reason why the kitchen is clean is because I hardly use it."

"Ah." He seemed to let it go. Thank heavens. "I cook."

"You do?"

"Yeah, I do."

"I thought you cops only eat takeout and donuts."

He laughed. "Yeah, right. But whenever I have time, I try to cook at home. Not fancy but I try to eat healthy."

She looked up at him. "Wow… I've never thought that I could ever hear the word *healthy* from a cop's mouth."

"Gee, thanks." He squeezed her. "But if I don't eat right, I lose my muscles. That, I got to avoid."

"I see." She remembered he played baseball even now quite seriously.

She led him to the second floor where a few rooms and bathrooms were located.

When she opened the French door, an amazing view leaped into his eyes.

His jaw almost dropped. "Whoa."

The bedroom was so huge that he figured his whole apartment unit could fit in here.

Over the California King, high and wide windows were installed across the entire two sides of the bedroom facing the slope of the Berkeley Hills, boasting astonishing night views including the moon and stars in front of him. And the fog. As if the waves were encroaching on the coast, the fog he'd seen outside became thicker and permeated deep into the town, almost shrouding all. It would soon run up the Hills too.

The tall street lamps and the moon had enough brightness without any light in the bedroom.

"Holy…the view… What is this, the Fairmont suite?"

It attracted her attention with a little surprise. "You stayed in that hotel suite before?"

"Well, yeah," he responded nonchalantly, still looking outside through the window. His profile was so handsome that she couldn't take her eyes off him. But her curiosity got the better of her and she asked him, "By yourself?" Well, hello, Alex, what kind of question was that? Of course not by himself.

"Uh-uh," he answered honestly, "with a girl." He responded simply as she'd expected, and he gave her a meaningful sidelong look.

Frowning, she pressed, "What happened?"

"Do I look like I have a girlfriend and trying to cheat on her tonight?" He faced her completely, placing a hand on his hip.

"No. So you dumped her."

"No, she dumped me."

"What? My god, I cannot believe she dumped you. She's stupid." Her blue eyes widened. He could see every detailed hue in them.

"You sound like you know me well, but how do you know then? We just met on Saturday."

She was almost startled by his notion. She should be careful not to disclose she'd known him since ten years ago, by following him from the intel source named Uncle Barry. But this time, she had a good egress to escape from his trained-detective's doubt and pursuit. There was another CI for her now. "Well, I have a wonderful intel source with me in the Bureau."

"You talk like a cop and why do I feel like I know your CI?" He snickered, knowing it must be Jason.

Yup. Bingo. So she said, "*Your insight serves you well.*"

That made him laugh. Oh she loved to hear him laugh as it produced some kind of feeling of bliss in her.

"*Return of the Jedi*, now, huh? Obi-Wan?" Then he walked away from the window to the California King.

"Come here, babe," he sat on the bed and called her, motioning next to him.

She approached and sat by him. She looked so calm but in fact her heartbeat was as fast as possibly a human being's heart could be.

He started, "I really want to make love to you right now, and I think the feelings are mutual. Well, I hope."

Nice of him. He wanted to make sure she'd still be on board with him. "Yeah," she answered honestly, "that's right."

"Okay, then. But before we proceed, I need to talk about something very important."

"Well, hello? Do we need to talk now?" She raised both her arms. "Let's talk later; act now."

Sam smiled at her reaction. Yeah, chemistry was mutual. But about *this*, he had to talk with her. No matter how deep they felt that they had the strongest sexual attraction, he had an obligation to his woman to tell the truth.

"Hear me out, Alex. It's very important."

"Okay." She shut up and looked at him. Her glacier-in-the-ocean-like eyes were now so calm and sincere. He wanted to be submerged in that serene blue.

He sighed. Jeezus, he'd still need guts to talk about this even after many times.

He decisively began taking his shirt off. She wanted to say something but decided to keep quiet as his move was somehow reverential and admirable. And when his shirt slid down on his shoulders to puddle around his waist, she sucked in her breath and understood why he wanted to talk.

He heard her draw breath sharply. He closed his eyes. Had he judged her wrong? Was she also one who couldn't take his flaw? Well, it was true it looked bad.

He'd wanted to talk about his scars. Of course. Why hadn't she thought of it?

And the scars were telling eloquently without words how badly he'd been burned even with the Kevlar.

To shield her from those embers.

Through the eyes of an M.D., she could say it was in fact not too bad and it seemed much better compared to some other burn scars she'd seen on live patients. It was just mostly uneven skin textures depending on the underlying muscles, uneven colors and some lines, but it had been ten years. The scars looked partially healing and fading. The skin grafting must've been performed successfully.

No, she dumped me, he'd said about the Fairmont girl. This could've been the reason?

It was plausible that his scars might trigger some women's innate aversions for something unusual and gross. She'd heard that some of Uncle's veteran friends who had come back from the war wounded had had a hard time keeping a relationship.

And his scars must've weighed heavily on him, especially when he'd been twenty-two or three, at the golden age of his life to attract women, and his twenties and thirties should've been the peak of his life, strong, savvy, feeling of invincibility. Nonetheless, this had happened just because he'd protected her.

"Oh…Sam…" her voice trembled. She felt like crying but no, not in front of him since he was the one who had been suffering and struggling to make sense out of it.

"Gross, isn't it?" He must've been repeating the same drill to tell all the women he'd wanted to sleep with. As if he'd needed forgiveness or permission that even with his scars it would be okay to make love to her.

"Gross? No. Not at all," she told his back. But he didn't turn around to face her, keeping his head slightly down.

"Does it still hurt?"

"Nah, not really." Then he remembered she was an

M.D. "Sometimes. Like with sudden jerking."

"I'm sorry."

"Not your fault, Alex. Did you hear the story about this?"

"Sorta. It was on the news and in the papers. I read your bulletproof vest under your uniform saved your life."

"Yeah… I was lucky."

"The girl saved by you must be grateful even now."

"I don't know. It's been ten years," he said over his shoulder.

She wanted to ask if he'd been regretting having done it or say something more to make him feel better, but she didn't want him to know she was the one he'd saved that night now.

She was afraid he might get mad at her being the cause of his pain and would stop making love to her. And his realization that she was that girl he'd saved might ruin their newly forming relationship that was hanging in a delicate balance. She still didn't want him to think she would like to have a relationship with him for whatever the ridiculous reasons but love.

"So, are you still up to doing it?" he softly uttered.

"Sam…" She touched his shoulders gently. He didn't figure what she was trying to do at first and it almost confused him. Then, she warily lowered herself, her hands touching him and kissed his back, trailing his scar lines with her lips and the tip of her tongue.

He sucked in his breath; his body hardened and then shuddered.

His back tasted salty, proving a day of hard work. She believed he must've tasted salty if she could've licked him ten years ago, for he'd been working hard at that time as a rookie officer and that fact had actually saved her life. Thankful for his service then and now, grateful that she'd finally met him again to love him more.

CHAPTER 6

"God…Alex…" he breathed her name. He couldn't impart anything to her anymore, but eyes shut, he was just enjoying her touch. How long had he waited for a woman like her, who didn't get scared or feel disgusted about his scars? He felt his dignity and confidence had just fallen back into his soul galvanizing inside. He swiftly turned around to hold her on his bare chest, falling on the bed; he saw her golden hair softly float in the air, stroking his face.

He pinned her, kissing her first, while she was taking her clothes and undies off followed by the rest of his clothes. She was as eager as he was to get closer to each other's bare skin. She knew what she wanted and she wasn't shy about it and he liked it very much.

She was honest. She was straightforward about anything, everything, and always tried to be truthful, sincere. If he'd ask the right question, she'd give him the right answer. He liked that too. And her appearance…that was one of the mysteries she held. She was like a photogenic icon of a high school or college homecoming queen with blond hair, blue eyes and dazzling smile and all, but the familiarity of her was almost a miracle from the beginning when he'd met her on Saturday. He'd been regretting ever since that he hadn't seen her long before.

He had to stare down at her for a while, admiring how beautiful and sensual she was in her birthday suit. Her golden hair fanned out over the pillow, her petite figure was covered with gorgeous soft skin, appropriately sized round breasts with pink nipples that he wanted to touch and taste, flat belly and womanly round hips, thighs and long straight legs he admired and imagining pushing them open to settle himself between them almost drove him off the cliff.

"Are we just looking at each other doing nothing?" she asked, smirking.

Moving some strands of her unruly hair from her forehead, he softly laughed, reverberating in his throat and ribcage that unexpectedly made her hot inside.

"Be patient, darlin'. Making love is just like eating an exquisite dish. You have to enjoy with your eyes first before starting to taste it."

"I like your analogy, but just looking at it isn't making your stomach full, is it?"

He laughed again. "Alright, then." He kissed her lips first. She opened her mouth for him, hugging his body with her arms around him fully confidently. She didn't mind touching his scars at all… The confirmed revelation hit him, huge relief invigorating his virility.

His tongue intruded into her mouth, enjoying tasting every bit of it. Then she returned the favor. Sucking his tongue thoroughly. He heard himself groan a few times. He pushed her hair back and kissed her neck where her pulse beat. As soon as his lips touched there, his hair rose starting from the nape of his neck to all over his body, and he felt like some unknown force struck him from inside. He moved his kisses from her neck to her breasts and with his hands kneading them, he licked and sucked each nipple taking ample time. She whimpered and arched her back, the sounds made him harder.

His lips were crawling down on her body, tasting her, until he reached the area with curly golden hair. She eased her legs to give him more access. He pushed her thighs up, then began exploring her most secret place hidden behind the veil. He found the little bud and he gave the area one long stroke of a lick, hovering on her clit for a while to taste it. Her moan louder, his dick harder, his mind was concentrating on her pleasure now. He inserted one finger in her and realized she was wet for him. That notion had almost given him vertigo. Next, he tried two fingers and that affected not only her whimper but also himself since he felt her wall inside squeeze his fingers.

"Sam, my god, no," she was almost crying

"Say yes, babe." He held her thighs with his shoulders and arms preventing her from closing them while he kept licking her, his fingers still in her almost simulating making love.

She came hard under his watch. She hadn't had sex for a long time ever since she'd decided to move back to the Bay Area. It was true that she'd dated in Europe, hoping to have discovered her partner rather than dreaming of Sam. However, this had been the first time she'd slept with her then-hero, who had really stolen her heart ten years ago. That had given her a crazier climax. Her mind was wandering around somewhere whiteout-bright, her ears ringing, but none were unpleasant to her senses with euphoria and giddiness behind her brain, just her heart pounding like hell, breathing difficult.

"Shh, shh, babe, it's okay. It's okay," she finally heard him say.

She gradually opened her eyes. "Hey Gorgeous," he whispered.

She had to clear her throat to find her voice. "Hey…" Still it came out hoarse.

"Enjoyed?"

"That's not even close."

"Cool." He quickly wore a condom and lowered himself on her. Naturally she held him, her arms around him again, touching his scars. Felt so good.

He knew he had a massive erection, so he told her, "Let's go slow. If I give you any pain, just let me know. I don't want to hurt you." Then, he started inserting himself cautiously, but the inside of her was warm, wet, tight, giving him tingles along with his hair standing phenomenon. Again. Was it some kind of sign? Of what?

"You okay?" he asked her a few times and she nodded, "Fine."

The last couple of inches weren't so difficult since her vagina was accustomed to his size. He smoothly slid in the whole length of it. His arousal expanded her vaginal wall but it felt so right to her.

When he sheathed himself in her, holding her close as if nothing would be between them, once again his hair rising with elation, suddenly he saw in his mind's eye the time when chaos was unfolding on I-80, yet feeling urged to shield the girl from the falling embers and he'd laid himself on her, overwhelmed by exhilaration.

My god… He'd never forgotten, and he'd never forget the feeling on her, Connie. He remembered it with every fiber of his being, because it'd been a once-in-a-lifetime encounter for him.

Oh my lord… Instantly, he knew. He just knew it was something that he'd stopped looking for, but he'd unexpectedly found that something, the most precious thing, *her*.

The memories of ten years ago had been pain and joy to protect her. But the truth was the time ten years ago was not important anymore at this very instant, for this was the final integration of his past and present, and his future would be promised as long as she was with him. His epiphany had come when he'd least expected. The girl had also come into his life when he hadn't anticipated. Nonetheless, while he'd endeavored to be a better man, as if the right moment had just landed on him, he'd found his love that he'd once lost.

"You alright?" She was concerned, her beautiful brow

furrowing. "Everything okay?"

"Oh yeah, everything is just so perfect." He looked down at her very tenderly and caressed her cheeks.

Then he clasped both of her wrists together with his right hand, placing them above her head, he instructed her to wrap around his hips with her legs, his left hand holding her butt tight. He slightly put his weight on her so the penetration deepened. And he started moving. It felt incredible. He kissed her and sucked her nipple hard, drawing her moan again. She wasn't reluctant either. She moved along with him; her motion swallowed his shaft when he thrust in, driving him insane.

He abruptly felt her profound unsaid feeling for him. Why he was feeling it wasn't certain, but it was there, right there in her. It felt almost like an old friend had come back from a long journey. The notion amazed him. Making love to her was not just an act itself, but something more. He undeniably touched her bottom line.

He'd determined that the resolution of his lifetime now was to be a faithful, honorable, trustworthy man to revere her, cherish her, love her.

He stroked her bud with his left thumb while he was mindlessly moving in her. Soon, she came again and this time, she also stole his sanity as her vagina had spasms. He reached orgasm right after her. They called out each other's names. And then he collapsed on the bed next to her, taking her with him.

His heartbeat rapid almost out of its normal range, chest heaving for air, ears ringing, eyes seeing bright light and colors, he'd never had such a powerful and rapturous orgasm before. But it didn't stop there; euphoria that had been left by the orgasm was prolonging the duration of afterglow and he felt like he was sailing smoothly on still water. With her. The world around him was only occupied by her presence. The most unimaginably peaceful moment in his life. Ever.

She seemed to be floating in the air, all over her body

still sensitive, after being struck by a paroxysm of orgasm that had lasted for quite a long time. This was the first time she'd made love to someone she loved.

When she came back to earth, she cuddled up to his side. He kissed her on her head. He was so sated and content. Making love with Alex was such a mind-blowing experience she'd practically erased awful memories of every single woman who'd given him a bad taste of so-called *love.* And he felt very lucky that he'd stayed an available bachelor when Alex had stepped back into his life.

She was sleeping peacefully holding on to him. He couldn't let her go and would never let her go. He must talk to her when they were up about an important part of a relationship, making a commitment and starting to live together and eventually having a family. Life with her would be so much fun and contentment, he could imagine, if she'd accept him as her life-long partner.

When he looked over the windows, he noticed the fog had reached the Berkeley Hills and enveloped everything around them. Still, the white fog easily reflected any lights creating halo-like phenomena. It almost blanketed them shutting them off from the outside world keeping them safe and private. He was feeling whole again. The woman who'd always made him grow to be a better man was now all tangible and final, and he knew he'd been head over heels in love with her.

*****

He must've dozed off with her. When he woke up, the fog was gone and the world was in twilight, almost sunrise. He looked up at his phone on the nightstand. 6:00am.

At least he'd had a couple of hours of sleep. Good. Now he'd just detach himself from this warm, soft, beautiful naked body and get up. Well, at least his dick had already gotten up. Nope, not now. He must go back to the BPD to continue watching the security camera footage. He had to remember the police were now her voiceless voice.

He felt a stir next to his body. Alex was watching him with those stunning eyes full of emotions in them.

"Hey…" she whispered.

"Didn't mean to wake you up."

"No worries. I know you have to go back to the PD."

"How 'bout you?"

"I have to go to the office by 10 today, cuz I worked on Saturday."

He kissed her lightly and got up. "I wanna take a shower. Can I use your bathroom?"

"Of course. Towels are folded in the shelves."

"I really wanna ask you to join me in the shower," he hopefully asked her.

"Well, I wish I could, but you're on your way to work."

"True." Oh boy. His woman was very rational and logical and she thrilled him more.

"You know, I'll tell you what I can do instead, Sam. While you're in the shower, I'll quickly run the speed cycle on my washer and dryer for your underwear and shirt."

Had he heard right? Had she just offered to do the laundry for him while he was taking a shower?

"Okay? And I can make some coffee. I burn water but luckily my coffee maker never burns coffee."

He laughed, "Thanks. I appreciate that." He kissed her again on her lips, but this time lingering on the lower lip tugging a little. She sighed contentedly. He wanted her again.

"Sam."

"I know, I know." He got off the bed.

"I just wanted to ask you how you'd like your coffee." That stopped him walking away.

"Ah, well, *Shaken, not stirred*." He grinned, showing his perfect white teeth, electrocuting millions of her brain cells. Damn him.

"Mr. Bond, I cannot give you *a martini* in the morning."

"*Well it's all a matter of perspective*." And her gorgeous

James Bond strode naked laughing, disappearing in the master bathroom.

"Hey, thanks, for the laundry and wiping my shoes." He came to the kitchen, nicely cleaned and wearing freshly washed clothes, and sat on a barstool at the island.

"No problem." He smelled of soap. Good thing that she had neutral soap and shampoo. She didn't believe fragrance of either coconut, vanilla or orchids would suit him. But she didn't have any shaving kit for men so he'd skipped doing it.

"Um…sorry about no men's shaving kit."

"Nah, I have an electric shaver at the office. I'll do it later. Well, it's good to know no man's in your life; otherwise, I'd die in flames of jealousy."

She gazed at him to see if he'd been teasing her or serious. He was smiling wide…okay he was teasing her. Ugh.

She was wearing a new T and sweatpants. She must've taken a shower too. This house seemed to have like three hundred bathrooms.

"Coffee?" she casually asked pointing at her coffee machine.

"Please."

She poured it in a big mug and placed it in front of him. And she came around with her cup in her hand and sat next to him.

"Black?" he asked.

"Mm-hmm." She nodded.

"How'd you know?" He looked purely surprised.

"Well, you cited a quote from *007*, *Shaken, not stirred,* when I asked about your coffee. So, I figured you don't put anything in it. You got to stir it if you put sugar or milk in it."

My god, she was his kind of girl. "You good." And he sipped, followed by an immediate, "Ahhhhh…"

She smiled. "It suits you, huh?"

"Mm-hmm, thanks," and he said, "um…Alex, before I go to work, we need to talk."

"About what?" She didn't like the seriousness in his tone. She was racking her brains what she'd done wrong or not right by him. Could be, cuz dating wasn't exactly her expertise or in her lab manual.

He stretched out his hand and held hers. Uh-oh…she was half in panic. He might be thinking how to break to her that he'd made the big mistake of making love to her. It was the best thing that had ever happened to her and she was really hoping he would make love to her again…well, sometime…someday…okay, maybe never.

"Alex, do you have anyone you're dating other than me?"

Disappointment and sorrow were gradually overhanging her mind. "No."

"Would you like to date other people more?"

Ah, okay so this had been a one-night stand and he'd like to tell her but he couldn't find the way. Still, if she'd have someone she'd want to date, he could casually say, *hey, I let you do that. No problem. No strings attached. We're not ready to keep seeing one person anyway…* She didn't need that kind of crap. She'd want him to speak frankly, concisely.

"Sam, why asking those questions? What do you want to say? Say it forthrightly."

"Um, alright, I just wanna say…er…I'm not telling you what to do or not to do, and you know, you're still free to do whatever you wanna do. So, if you still wanna date other men, that's okay."

She breathed, almost a resigned sigh. Still not succinct but she could take a hint. Yeah, she was right; she was let go cuz it'd been a one-night stand and this was his way of dumping her. Gee, he should've told her it'd be a one-night thing so she hadn't had any expectations. Or she'd been an idiot not to get a clue when she'd known the rumor he was a guy with a one-night-stand policy.

"Ah, I get it. Okay, I understand, Sam. It's been fun.

But we're still friends, right? Maybe shake hands will do?"

His face went blank.

Okay, he didn't even like to shake hands. So much for their chemistry. "Um, okay, then, well, I've had a good time with you…" She needed somewhere to hide and lick her wounds and cry for two years at least. For a starter, she should take some vacay to go back to Europe or the East Coast…

She was about to stand up from the stool and leave, melancholy clouding her features.

Realization struck him. "No, Alex, sit back, hear me out. You're misunderstanding me."

"Misunderstanding you? How?" She glared at him with utter disappointment.

"I think I confused you." He held her hand tightly not to let her go. "I don't wanna make you a one-night stand or fling date; on the other hand, I just don't want to restrict you if you have someone you wanna date. Well, but I'm already done with that, and I'm actually looking for a long-term relationship to start a life with. Do you know what I mean? If you have no one specifically, will I be yours?"

It took her a good two minutes to comprehend what he'd meant. "Oh…"

He was grinning, observing her expression changing like bay breakers. And he finally said again, "So, you get it? What d'you say?"

"You want to be mine."

"Yes. If not now, maybe in the future? But I really, really wanna be yours and I want you to be mine."

He pulled her onto his lap. She didn't resist it. A good sign, he thought.

Holding her, he went on, "Alex, I'd like to take a chance with you. But you're still young; you may like to look around more."

"No, Sam, I've done my fair share of dating, including online. And I don't think I want to look around more. I'm ready for a relationship too. And I want you to be mine."

You've been in my heart for more than ten years, Sam.

He embraced her, whispering into her hair, "I'm glad." And he gave her a passionate kiss. Under her thighs, she felt something stirring. "Guess I wanna go back to bed again…"

She was hanging on to his neck, inhaling his smell. Soap and his own scent. He felt her breath with his own name on his neck. His hair again stood up. Now he was sure that was the sign when he was sexually aroused by her. Only her.

"Darlin', I wanna hear you scream my name again and again now in bed."

She looked at him. "Sam." Now her tone contained a little admonishment, exciting him more, imagining she'd be a great wife and mother of his children since she wasn't afraid of scolding him, which meant she could fight for what she believed was right; she could fight for love, fight for them, or for their children when she'd need to.

"Alright, I can wait." And he cleared his throat. He placed his forehead on hers. "Alex, can I come back here tonight?"

"Of course."

"Um…I mean, wanna bring my clothes, shaving kit…you know…" he meekly added. "I may not be able to come back to you every night but I'll try my best and we can try to…"

Ah, he wanted to live together. Actually she liked that idea. "Sure, let's try to stay in my house. I'd like the idea very much. I know you cannot come back every night since you're a detective, hope you remember that." She grinned at him.

"Tryin'." He kissed her. "If I stay at your home longer, I'd pay half of the rent."

"Oh no, Sam," she interrupted him, but he didn't budge. "Alex, I don't want to take advantage of you."

"Well, thank you. Let's talk about it later when you really start occupying my house, cuz we aren't sure of anything yet. I mean, you might stay at your home more since it's closer to the Police."

"Alright. And don't forget to notify your landlord about me."

"Okay." She smiled. "You're a good citizen."

"Just tryin' to live lawfully."

She slid down from his lap. "You should go, you know that, right?"

But his hand just couldn't let hers go. He enveloped hers with both his hands and then placed it on his lips, kissing it. She enjoyed his kiss so much, but also she didn't want him to be late. "I thought you needed to go to the office sooner than later."

"Yes, ma'am." He smirked. He thought for a second and asked, "Alex, tell me one thing. When did you decide you can be mine?"

She tilted her head and replied, "*You had me at hello.*"

He stared at her face almost fiercely, making her a bit nervous, but soon his face broke into a great smile. "Did I?"

Relieved, she smiled back at him. "Yeah you did."

"The quote from *Jerry Maguire.*"

"Uh-huh."

"Ah…"

Then he wanted to make sure she understood his terms and conditions. "Anyway, no flirt with other men no mo'. You're mine. Remember that, Girl."

"Okay, bossy pants," she said, scowling at him.

She wasn't really modest about kicking an idiot in the ass, was she? Yup, she was cool.

"Alex, you're right and I was wrong. I was too bossy. Didn't mean. I'm sorry," he had to admit bravely as he'd still want to be a better man by her. He'd been trying to do just that for more than ten years. He wouldn't stop now.

His work phone on the island suddenly buzzed. As it was made of granite, the sound became louder for it reverberated on the counter, startling them. It was the sound calling from the reality that he must face as a major crime detective. He just couldn't stay in a sheltered world with Alex forever. He'd sworn to serve and to protect the public. He'd chosen to be in blue.

He eyed the phone. It was from Carter. "So much for romance or man's idiocy." He picked it up while she took both mugs to the kitchen sink.

"'Sup?"

"Yo bro, patrol found Evalyn Roberts' Camry. You coming?"

"Where?"

"Eastshore state park. Near University avenue and Frontage. Uniforms are already there and cordoned."

"Did someone notify the OPD?"

"Jason's on his way."

He was already standing up, holding the phone between his ear and shoulder still in conversation with Carter, attaching his golden badge and installing his service gun where they were supposed to be. Watching his moves, a hot flash went through her core, exciting her, giving her a shiver. Omigod. She was crazily in love with him. What would happen if he'd decide to leave her? How would she be supposed to live without him again?

A couple of important details descended into her mind.

First and foremost, he hadn't said he loved her yet, had he? But they were supposed to have met just a few days ago. Only in her time span, she'd known him for ten years, not his. Hence, no one would say the Love words at this point. So this would be his trial period with her if she was suitable for him. She shouldn't really be ecstatic about everything yet, then. The possibility of him leaving her wasn't zero at all.

Second, the way he'd talked was not the way she talked. He hadn't made his point directly but first tiptoed around the important point in the belief he wouldn't hurt her, possibly due to his considerate trait. Like when he'd apologized for his kiss and coffee fiasco and his declaration of their relationship just now. Huh. She'd have to remember that to avoid any further misunderstanding between them.

"Hey gotta go." He came around to stand near her in the kitchen. The heat was radiating from him warming her. He pulled her into his embrace. Then, looking down at her, he said, "We might see each other somewhere today at work, but if we don't, stay safe. Looking forward to seeing you tonight."

"In case I'm late, I should give you my digital door lock number," she said. He now remembered she had that gadget on her front door. "Call me when you're coming." Then she presented a big thermos to him. "Take this." The graphite black thermos had a big yellow smiley on it.

His mouth twitched. "Coffee?"

"Mm-hmm. The fog dissipated but still chilly in the morning. Okay, it's a smiley face but better than poo emoji. Oh just take it, for god's sake."

He finally chuckled. "Thanks." He dropped a kiss one more time.

"Drive safe."

"Always."

She was seeing him off until his car turned the corner, beyond her eyesight.

"Wait, what? Why the hell your ETA is that late? It's less than ten minutes from your complex, right? Jason lives next door and he said he'd be like ten. Why yours twenty to thirty considering a possible morning traffic jam. Where the goddamn hell exactly are you at?" Carter asked him exasperatedly when he'd reported his ETA from his car.

"Cuz I'm coming from the Berkeley Hills, okay?" he said honestly. He knew Carter would find out sooner or later.

"Berkeley Hills?" He could see Carter's baffled face and he was thinking of all sorts of reasons why he was coming from there. He wondered if he knew Alex lived there. Well, he was a poster boy of gossip. So, he might. But he had no intention to hide the relationship with her, since his mind had been already set on her.

His partner didn't pursue him with that issue. He must have had a lot to do at the scene. "Okay, then."

All the way to the scene, in the light of the early morning sun, he was thinking of her.

No wonder he'd felt the same chemistry with her as with Connie.

And he remembered how she'd reacted to each of his words, actions…and given away the proof she was the girl from ten years ago, unknowingly. He grinned. She'd said he'd had her at *hello*. Yup.

All the thoughts brought up a question: Why hadn't she told him she was the one? There must be a reason on her account why she hadn't. But in fact, it wasn't important to him at all.

God Alex. He missed her already. She was an amazing woman. She'd touched and filled his every feeling, need, and more. Out of bed and in bed. Especially in bed. Holding each other naked. And…okay, that was a friggin' stupid idea to imagine their lovemaking now to create himself a boner and he'd have to get out of the car with that? No way. Practically all the homicide male detectives including Jason plus uniforms were well aware of what a boner looked like and possibly some female officers who had a male partner were, too. Everyone would notice even his half hard-on. Now he had to remember the top players at every number in major-league history, 1 through 99, to pacify his damn stick downstairs, like #1: Ozzie Smith, #2: Derek Jeter, #3: Babe Ruth, #4: Lou Gehrig, #5: Albert Pujols…

It had taken him more than thirty minutes from her home to the scene. The traffic had been worse than ever, with a couple of fender-benders on the roads.

"Dammit, Sammy, what the fucking hell were you doing in the Berkeley Hills? Sightseeing at the vista point? And we had the damn thick fog all night long." As soon as he parked and got out, Jason came by and started, but he suddenly fell silent and gazed at him for at least a couple of minutes and eyed his Charger, still damp with a thin layer of the fog residue. He must've parked his car outside in the Hills overnight.

Carter also came and grimaced. "What the hell happened to your face? Decided to grow a damn beard?"

"C'mon, let me work." He ignored those friends for the time being and walked under the cordon tape. They had to follow him.

"What we got so far?" he asked them, taking his notebook from the pocket.

"Not much." Carter opened his. "Confirmed it's her vehicle. The tag number and VIN number on the dashboard matched with the DMV record."

Evalyn's silver Camry looked very different from the photo provided by her parents and the bank. It was very dirty under the morning sun.

"How long the vehicle was sitting here?" Sam made a face at the appearance of her car.

"Not long. Patrol said it wasn't here last night before the fog," Carter reported from his notebook. "I think the fog helped whoever dumped the vehicle here. Anyways, we decided to haul it on a flatbed to the garage. And we're waiting for the truck."

Sam was scrutinizing the outside of the car. "Hey, did you know her car got a dent?"

"What dent?" Carter came up.

"Look, the bottom of the passenger door," Sam indicated.

"Huh, didn't know that." Carter wrote it in his notebook. "No one mentioned that."

"Hell, no one knew," Jason added. "This is the first time. Her parents didn't tell us that either. Besides, her car was just returned from service at Toyota."

"It happened after she passed," Carter said, suggesting possibilities, "like someone took her vehicle hit something or hit by another?"

"Could be. We should ask our vehicle specialist," looking around her Camry, Sam replied. "Might give us one more piece of evidence. And I believe the driver who drove her vehicle here has an accomplice; unless he walked back to…wherever…that's quite unlikely at that time and the shitty fog. So, someone was waiting in another vehicle." Then Sam added, "And at least a tall male. The driver's seat is set all the way back."

"Two bastards and one damn unknown vehicle," Jason said.

"Yup, and her vehicle is too dirty for just being driven around town. I see kinda changing of hands. Evalyn had kept her car clean according to her friends and colleagues."

At Sam's words, Jason and Carter started examining the car again. "Ah, yeah, bug splats on the windshield too," Jason said at the front of the car, "which usually means you drove the car on the highway or a long stretch of road mostly, at a high speed during the dry season in California. Now, for instance."

"Grasses, trees and flat land. But not desert," Carter added.

"Yup," ducking, Sam said, "the vehicle could've been through somewhere grassy, dusty, dirty…possibly after it was taken." His attention moved to one part of the trunk. He cautiously touched it with his gloved hands. "Yeah, guess we should bring this babe ASAP."

Jason bent his back with him. "What you found?"

"Look close over here," he fingered the place where the trunk lid met the rim.

"What?" Carter also came around and checked it again. "I ain't seen nothin'," Carter admitted.

"Look close, like really close, Carter," Sam instructed him. He needed to learn more from him for sure. Jason was already aware what he meant. "Whoa," he muttered and called one CSI, who he knew well. "Hey Oscar,"

"Yeah?" He came to them.

"You still got some phenol swabs left?" Jason asked him. "Sam found somethin' suspicious."

"'Course. Let me see." Taking out a little kit from his waist pack, he came to near Sam and gazed at him. "Hey, you decided to grow a beard?" Carter and Jason cracked up while Sam rolled his eyes. Oscar took out a phenol swab which could tell whether the stain was blood or not.

"It looks like a transfer bloodstain or smear to me," Sam said.

Oscar looked into the place he was pointing at, just below the trunk. "Did I miss this? Yeah, looks like dried blood." He snapped a shot and wiped with a swab with Phenolphthalein cocktail. The tip of the swab changed color from reddish brown to bright pink. "Yeah, that's blood," he confirmed.

"I gotta bad feeling about this shit," Carter mumbled with dismay.

"Thing's getting nasty, ain't it? Evalyn's case may not be what it seems, Jase." Sam rubbed his jaw, unshaven stubble reminding him of his love, missing her already.

Jason was closely watching his best friend; Sam was unconsciously self-conscious about his stubble. He'd never had such a drastic diversion before. Basically both Sam and Jason were creatures of habit. They hadn't easily changed their daily routine both personally and professionally. And Sam had been known as one of the clean-cut, dapper dudes since high school.

He'd noticed Sam hadn't come home last night, and now he'd come to the scene from the Berkeley Hills without shaving and the same suit, shirt, tie, socks as his yesterday's outfit. *That ain't cool*, as far as the usual Sam was concerned. What had made him change in one night?

But then the shirt looked clean, shoes shining, and he smelled of a new soap and his hair was clean and combed to boot. Yet, no shaving.

There was the only reason that Jason could think why all of the above had happened to him simultaneously: He'd stayed overnight at a new woman's house in the Berkeley Hills, who hadn't had a man in her place before him, and it'd been unplanned; thus, no shaving kit at her place for him. He'd probably thought he could shave at work since most of them kept an electric shaver in their drawer at the office. But he'd had to come straight to the scene from the woman's place, so no time for him to use his shaver at the office, unless she liked a man with a beard and insisted to him to grow one.

They must've run the laundry to clean his shirt and whatnot before he'd come here; stronger proof that the overnight stay hadn't been planned ahead. Oh and his coffee thermos in his Charger. He knew Sam didn't own that kind of silly smiley thermos. It must belong to the woman. And she must be nice to have given him hot coffee in the cool early morning on his way to work just because they'd slept together one night. Hmm…

Wait a minute. He'd wanted to date a new coroner, Sister Golden Hair. Jason had known they'd had to postpone their date since Evalyn's case had occurred. So, what the hell exactly had happened behind his back? He'd have to grill him good later, but sooner than later.

"I feel we're missing something important." Sam turned to him.

Jason gave a sidelong glance at him but agreed, "Yeah, I think she lived not in her apartment but somewhere else."

"At least for a month," Sam added. "We don't know why the hell but someone must've provided her a place to live, cuz no evidence that she rented another unit or stayed at some hotel or something somewhere other than the one we know."

"Romantically involved," Jason suggested. "Or threatened."

"We treated her as an ordinary drowning victim but we should investigate her background closer now," Sam, again touching his jaw, said, drawing attention from Jason. "We got to examine her vehicle good at the garage."

"K, amma gonna talk to CSI. 'Bout time the wrecker arrives." Carter walked away to the front of the cordoned line.

"Yo, Sam, ain't like your new look?" Jason had to tease him.

"Huh?"

"You ain't realize you're doin' it?"

"Doin' what?" His mocking met with his total confusion.

"Touchin' your damn stubble?"

His eyes widened, he looked at Jason. "I was?"

"Jeezus, Sam, you're batshit crazy in love," he lowered his voice so that the other cops or even Carter wouldn't hear him say, "You keep on touchin' your damn stubble you never grew. She got no shaving kit for you? Or she insisted to have you grow a beard? Which is it?"

"Ask me again later," Sam said mutedly.

"'K." He had no plan to push him in front of many, especially when the story had nothing to do with the case.

"Here comes our tow truck," Carter announced to the two in back.

Both detectives quickly ran up to Evalyn's vehicle.

"Hey, watch it, we ain't sure what's in the trunk," Jason warned the driver who was working on the metal chains and stoppers to secure the vehicle before pulling it up onto the flatbed.

"Okay, extra slow," the driver said.

"Jase, look." Sam pointed at the rear part of the underbody of the Camry, little by little moving up on the flatbed.

"Shit," he swore aloud.

Clearly they saw a tiny amount of blood droplets drip on the ground from where the trunk and the back seats shared the partition. It could be due to the change in the angle as the vehicle was pulled onto the flatbed. Everyone believed they had a surprise in the trunk.

The dawn of Tuesday had broken a couple of hours ago

and another workday had started for the people of Berkeley. Yet, the cops at the scene felt the darkness of long before the dawn, looking at the blood droplets dripping very slow at regular intervals on the ground as if they were signposts on an invisible road.

CHAPTER 7

The Berkeley Police's evidence garage was located behind the main building across the parking lot.

The driver and operator of the flatbed truck gradually but steadily lowered Evalyn's Camry in the parking lot and the cops and CSI carefully pushed it into the garage. The vehicle had no more blood droplets dripping, but CSI once more checked the car inside and outside, vacuuming the seat and floor, administering Bluestar to find if there was any blood trace in the car, and once again, checking fingerprints to make sure they hadn't missed anything. Except for the trunk.

"I think the coroner arrived," one of the cops said.

When Sam saw the van with the logo "*Alameda County Coroner's Bureau*" coming into the BPD's parking lot, his heartbeat started pounding faster like he was running, and he just couldn't stop grinning, causing Jason to snort at him.

However, he was really disappointed the coroner who stepped into the garage wasn't Alex but Dr. Barry Taylor.

Barry with a well-known sharp sense quickly realized his face didn't look happy. So he asked him, raising one brow, "Hey, what's the long face, Sam?"

"Oh nothing, Doc." He quickly smiled at him.

"I think he was expecting Sister Golden Hair to step out of the van," Jason explained instead.

"Jase," Sam tried to warn him.

"Is that so?" Barry's lips curved amusingly. "That's too bad, cuz today she was in the on-call van. Not in the coroner's office. So even if you wanna visit her, unlikely to see her. She cannot do an autopsy for you either."

Sam wanted to say something but couldn't come up with good wording.

Carter waved his hand at him. "Give it up, man. Everyone knows you're serious about her."

"Carter."

"No, I'm not the one who told about you to everyone." And he pointed at Barry. "I heard he was the one."

"Dr. Taylor?" Sam's jaw dropped. But other cops including their CSI were grinning too. Oscar was actually throwing his head back laughing. It seemed like everyone knew about it but Sam.

"I didn't say anything special." Barry held up his hands defensively.

Jason patted his best friend's shoulder, comforting. "Dude, Doc just said you and Sister Golden Hair had an awesome time at his café on Sunday and everyone else took the hint. Anyway why hide? We're happy for you."

"You talk like a dad," Carter mocked Jason.

"Ah, excuse me for interrupting the fun party, guys, but I just popped open the trunk and you gotta see this," one CSI had to butt in. As soon as he'd spoken, they caught a whiff of blood and a faint note of the early stage of decomposition.

Led by Barry, three homicide detectives, CSI and other cops who were there gathered around the Camry's trunk, the lid open.

"Let me see." Barry stepped in and looked into the trunk and started assessing. "Alright, a male victim."

It seemed a young man with gray sweatshirt and pants, shoved in the not-so-wide trunk of the Camry along with a bunch of clothes as if they'd been meant for space fillers and cushions so the body wouldn't move around.

Barry retrieved the clothes piece by piece very cautiously, some of which were soaked in blood, passing each to a CSI who placed it in an individual evidence bag. The series of the same procedures was conducted as if it was some kind of ritual, lending a sacred, slow, private ambience. When the body was exposed, they saw the floor of the trunk was smeared with blood apparently from the victim.

Barry took out the liver temperature thermometer.

"Let's see…last night was cool with the fog but inside the trunk wasn't too bad…so…ETD is around 11pm last night."

"COD?" Jason asked.

Barry examined the body and said, "Aha, okay, that's no mystery. One GSW to his left temple."

"Gunshot wound." This was Carter, his eyes on note writing.

"Apparently. But no casing or exit hole…the bullet must be inside."

"Can you tell the caliber?" Jason hoped he could answer that too.

"Jason, you're kidding right?"

"But you're such a great forensic pathologist, so…"

"Aw, thank you. And I may be a good forensic pathologist, but not that good. I'm a scientist not a fortune-teller. I gotta dig this dude's skull and brain to take out the bullet. Better yet, I can take X-rays or CT and calculate the size of the bullet. Either way, let's hope the bullet's still fully intact."

"Can you at least guess the caliber?" Jason persisted.

"Hey, didn't you hear what I just said, Jase? That being said, let me see what I can do…hmm…from this entry wound, I'd say 9mm. And probably at close range, but not contact, though."

"Ouch." Carter touched his own head.

"Anything else? Anything relevant to the owner of the

vehicle?" Sam asked, hoping for something that could connect to Evalyn.

Barry looked around in the trunk. "Not really…and he might be either drug addict or victim. See the injection marks on his arm?" The detectives stuck their heads in the trunk and saw what Barry was showing. "The problem is so many people self-inject with not only drugs but insulin and what not. Anyway I need to bring him back and perform an autopsy first, gents."

Barry signaled two officers who'd been patiently waiting in the corner of the garage. "Let's go back, Officers. This one is urgent."

They'd found who was the victim in Evalyn's trunk, rather fast. His fingerprints were in their database. *Declan Kosarek, male, age 19, resident of South Berkeley.*

In fact, the name was well-known in the BPD. Obviously he'd been an A-list criminal in the East Bay. He'd been arrested numerous times and become a B-list felon, out on parole for a year. And ended up shot dead, a D-list.

However, the detectives just couldn't wrap their heads around why his body had been in Evalyn's car trunk. When Declan was killed, Evalyn had been long gone. Were these two connected incidents or completely independent?

Way past 3pm, Sam and Carter had finally had time to have lunch. Jason had still stayed in the BPD for Evalyn Roberts' vehicle, so naturally he'd joined them.

They came to an eatery near the PD, *Blue Café Berkeley*, a couple of blocks northeast of the department. One of the co-owners was a retired captain of the Berkeley Police, so everyone knew why it was called *Blue Café*, and quite a few of the police population were enjoying meals there. Sam and Carter were regulars here, and Jason also came here with them often enough. It was an ideal diner or more accurately a godsend for major crime detectives who worked irregular hours when they opened almost 24/7.

Sam and his friends were seated in the very far corner where the table was isolated from other parts of the café, so they could talk about important or private matters.

"You mean just gossip," Sam said, rubbing his smooth jawline where he'd just shaved at the office. "Anyways, all you wanna hear me talk about is my private business," he clarified. "You bastards are guilty as charged."

"It ain't private. You gotta share your love life with us," Carter said, biting his hamburger.

"Oh yeah? Since when?" Sam protested.

"Since Sister Golden Hair," the two replied at the same time.

"Unbelievable." He shook his head and started eating his BLT.

Stealing Sam's French fries from his plate, Jason asked, "So, how far you guys' gone already?"

"Jase, it's only Tuesday and this guy," Carter pointed at Sam and said to him, "met her on Saturday at the Bureau and kinda dated on Sunday at *EZ Poppas*. And how could they go far? What intel I ain't got?"

"Don't point at people, Carter," brushing his finger, Sam said to him.

"Sorry, Mother."

Munching on his steak wrap and swallowing it, Jason replied to Carter, "Guess how far."

"Sex," he replied quickly. "Hey," Sam slapped him upside the back of his head.

"Ow!" He stroked there.

Jason laughed out loud, "Love your quick thinking, Carter."

"You gonna make a bald patch in there, Sam. I ain't my grandpa's backyard lawn."

"You spent last night with her," Jason stated. "So, Carter's guess ain't far-fetched."

"I thought so!" His eyes sparkling, Carter pointed out, "You gave away too much evidence, bro."

"Or, he ain't trying to hide," Jason guessed right.

"Well, I don't tell the world but no need to hide. Besides, I damn well ain't against any code of ethics or conduct of the BPD."

"Okay." Jason nodded. "Basically you ain't deny it; that's what you say."

"Exactly."

"Huh." Carter realized, with pure wonder on his face. "Sam, you're already committed to her."

Jason flinched at his remark and stared at his best friend's face, studying. "Are you?"

"Yeah, 'bout time," he effortlessly replied.

"Considering it's really about time for you, how the hell'd you know she's the one in such a short time?" Carter asked.

"When you meet the real deal, you know."

"How?"

"Um…you just know."

"Don't get it." Carter got another bite.

"You're probably still young and not ready."

On the other hand, Jason understood since he felt something significant with Rae. In fact, they were on to the sixth date tomorrow night and everything seemed to be working very well. He was ready to go exclusive or even have a relationship with her, but he didn't know how she felt about it. They'd need to talk.

"Detectives, like more tea?" Tony Novato, one of the co-owners of the diner and a daytime manager, a retired vet and also friend of Dr. Barry Taylor came to their table carrying a big pitcher of iced tea. Sam and Jason pushed their empty glasses toward him.

"Can I have a diet coke?" Carter asked him. "Sure, one diet coke coming up." He poured tea in their glasses and left for the coke.

"Yo," after Carter's coke came, Jason nudged Sam, his tone lower, "You think shithead Declan and Evalyn's case are connected, right?"

"Possible," he also dropped his voice. "We gotta wait

for the autopsy result and CSI lab analysis, though."

"Well, at least we got COD," Jason said and drank up his iced tea.

"Yeah, but we don't know anything else."

"Let's see..." Thinking through the timeline, Carter started writing on a paper napkin, mumbling, "Evalyn expired around...1am and was dumped in Lake Merritt around 3am...both on Sunday morning, ...and you dudes," he pointed at Jason with his pen, "OPD pulled her out of the Lake around 3:30am...that's Monday morning...then today...Tuesday morning, around 7 her vehicle was found. And Declan Kosarek in the trunk was killed around 11pm, which falls on Monday night. So, Evalyn, died, dumped on early Sunday, Declan shot dead on Monday night. Yeah, it seems sequential. Very hard to think about each case as independent, cuz look, there ain't 'nuff slack to insert another vehicle-related incident or irrelevant crime in the timeline."

"Right," Sam agreed with his partner.

"We're sure that she actually got in her Camry and drove after work on Saturday, right?" Jason asked.

"Yeah, the bank camera in the parking lot showed she left in her own vehicle. No passenger, just her," Sam confirmed.

"Huh... So, her Camry was stolen after she'd used it and not by anyone but someone relevant. It's natural to think her killer had taken her vehicle. Checking all security cameras of the possible stores and towns?"

"Yeah, Carter and I are still on it. Too much fucking footage to cover. Hey, help us watch 'em."

"Okay," Jason agreed to lend a hand for them. After all, he was the lead detective of her case.

"Let's talk to Doc Taylor about Declan's body. Wanna come to the Coroner's Bureau?" Sam asked the two friends.

Jason raised his hand.

"I gotta finish up writing the report on him and continue watching the footage. I'ma wait 'til you guys come back at the office," Carter said.

"Okay, let you know the result," Sam said, taking cash out of his pocket for his share of the bill. And he left while whistling the song, *Sister Golden Hair.*

Jason's both brows shot up, eyes wide, shocked. Carter's jaw dropped looking like an idiot.

"Love's in the air…" Tony came back and collected the cash and cleaned the table, humming, "*Love is in the air…*" Apparently he'd already heard about the romance between Sam and Alex.

"Is it a song?" Carter, who hadn't even been born in the 1980s, asked.

"Yup, a nice soft disco song by *John Paul Young*. Hey, 'tis the season… It's spring."

"I think it's already past spring."

"It's late spring. Better yet," Tony insisted.

Carter, deciding to show respect to Tony, agreed, "Okay, I got you." Then he also quickly threaded his way through the tables up to the front door chasing Sam. "Wait up!"

Tony chuckled at Jason. "Make love, not war."

"You speak like my aunt. You must've sipped the water in the Flower Power City."

"Oh yeah, peace and love."

"That, I cannot dispute." Jason laughed and left the diner.

*****

Alex was in her formal office at the Bureau, eating a very late, late lunch, more like early dinner, since it was around five, while she was reading some reports on her laptop. They'd called ahead telling her they were on their way so she could wait for them. However, they hadn't thought it'd taken so much time to get to the Bureau.

Sam and Jason knocked on the doorframe as usual since the door was always open. "Hey Doc. Sorry to make you wait. Traffic jam again."

Her hair was tied with a blue scrunchie, little white pearls on it. Her usual uniform, a white lab coat, was hiding most of her clothes. But Sam could see her bare legs under the coat, reminding him of their lovemaking.

"Did you wait too long?" worried, Sam asked.

"Hi guys, no, not really. I had something I had to finish." And she noticed, "Sam, you shaved."

"Yeah, at the office."

"Very nice." She smiled at them dazzlingly, melting Sam like butter under the sun. He was helpless every time she smiled.

Jason wanted to roll his eyes a million times but instead he said, "Oh, Doc, don't bother, please eat," as he saw she was cleaning up her food half-eaten. "That's okay. I know you want to hear about the result of the autopsy ASAP."

"I thought Doc Taylor did it?" Jason asked, bewildered. "He told us you were riding in the on-call van today."

"Yes, I was. But Dr. Taylor wanted me to perform that autopsy and he also had me analyze the vehicle. So, I asked CSI to bring some samples."

"What did Doc Taylor ask you to check?" Jason wondered.

"Trunk carpet and tires…more precisely the soil and some dry grasses in the tread. I'm sure the CSI lab is capable of analyzing them, but I don't have a huge backlog right now at lab, so I've decided to do it."

She directed them to two chairs in front of her desk, "Gentlemen, please have a seat."

Watching those two good looking detectives pulling the chairs, she couldn't help but wonder sometimes God had given multiple fortes per person.

"First of all, your victim Declan Kosarek, nineteen years old, died around 11 last night, Monday, as Dr. Taylor had initially assessed. One 9mm GSW to his left temple is COD also as in Dr. Taylor's assessment. I've already sent the bullet to your CSI lab. Although they couldn't find any casing, with this spent bullet, I hope they'd have some kind of match that the gun might've been used in a past crime or something."

"Or hope the weapon's at least registered, if we could identify it in our records of land and groove impressions," Jason said, crossing his fingers.

"Yes, that too," she agreed.

"How's the distance, hon?" Sam asked, startling both Jason and Alex for his use of an endearment to her at work. "What?" Sam grimaced.

"Nothing." Jason grinned, and looked at her. "Doc Taylor said it wasn't a contact wound but close."

"Correct. Not contact, but close like intermediate. I found stippling on the skin. No burns. It's a 9mm handgun so I'd say the distance is about 10 centimeters…4 inches."

"Okay." Jason and Sam were scribbling down the information in their notebook.

"Can you tell where Declan got shot? I mean, I know we didn't have a casing in the trunk but if the suspect used a revolver, it's possible, right? Or is there any evidence he was shot outside?"

"Jase, please, let me explain step by step."

"Sorry, go ahead."

"First of all, as for his body, he had no signs of struggle."

"He was likely already incapacitated when he got shot?" Jason's pen stopped, looking up at her. "Either drugged or he was sleeping?"

"Drugged, I suppose. He must've been unconscious before his death. He had a very high level of fentanyl and cocaine in his system before being killed. Very lethal combination but not the amount that killed him."

"Wait, that combination is…" His brows drawing together, Sam glanced at Jason sitting next to him.

"Yeah, that's also the same drugs in Evalyn's body."

"And the concoction in both cases seemed to be exactly the same," she added, eyeing the result of her lab test. "Yes, chemically the same variant."

"Shi… Crap." Jason had to glance upward to see her.

"Er…so, that could be a connection between her and Declan."

"Plausible. Statistically speaking, the drugs on the street are often personally concocted depending on drug dealers; thus, the same variant and the same concoction mean the same drugs were mixed, delivered from the same hand. And in this case, both victims had it intravenously. Jase, is Evalyn right-handed or left-handed?"

"Right-handed, the parents said so."

"How about Declan Kosarek?" she asked Sam since she knew Declan had been in the BPD's system for a long time.

"He's right-handed too. I saw him holding his gun in his right hand on Facebook including at the shooting range videos."

"Okay so right-handed like Evalyn, then." She typed in the information on her laptop.

"What's that all about?" Sam cocked his head.

"Their injection marks are all on their right arms." She placed some close-up photos of their arms in front of them. Both detectives picked them up, staring down at them.

"Foul play," Sam muttered.

"Someone injected them with the lethal cocktail," Jason affirmed.

"In short, Declan was drugged and moved into the trunk and shot?" Sam stopped writing, looking up at her.

"The trunk's carpet absorbed a substantial amount of blood and has some biological matter like skin cells and tiny bone fragments embedded. So, he was likely to be shot when he was lying in the trunk. CSI also found blood spatter patterns on the trunk lid and frame after they sprayed luminol. And yes, that's Declan's blood."

"Huh, someone tried to clean up the blood," Sam grumbled disdainfully.

"What about the bloodstain just outside the lid of the trunk and its frame?" Jason inquired. "Hope it contains fingerprints or palmprints."

"Um…" She pulled out the paper from a stack on her

desk and ran her eyes on it. "It is Declan's blood. It's a smear from something but CSI said they cannot tell anything specific yet. Now, I do have very interesting findings you might like to hear."

"Alright," both leaned forward.

"First, all the clothes stuffed in the trunk with Declan were from the thrift store on University Avenue. I found the tags on each of them. Tags are in the evidence bag back to your CSI. You should call the store. They might remember something."

"Okay, that's good to know." Sam smiled at her, sending sizzles into her core. She had to sit straight again. Damn him. She coughed lightly and went on, "Most interesting thing…at least to me is Declan's system had a very minute amount of hydrogen sulfide and thallium, apparently, he must've been exposed to them when he was alive."

She noticed they wanted to talk so she raised her hand and said, "Let me finish." The two nodded. "I also found a sample of the carpet in the trunk was contaminated by hydrogen sulfide and thallium. The dirt and dried grass in the tread were also contaminated by those same chemicals."

"Evalyn's vehicle was somewhere the ground was contaminated by both hydrogen sulfide and thallium?" Sam concluded, hoping he was right.

"Very likely. But we don't know exactly when and where Declan had exposure to those poisons. Just the same combination doesn't mean those were the same chemicals from the same source. I need to check their variants if they're the same chemicals. Anyway, I sent the tread soil and grass samples to the UCSF geology department. Let you guys know when I get something back from them."

"Thanks, Doc," Jason said. "Okay, so far, we know he was barely alive when he was thrown into the trunk."

"Yes, in other words, first he was drugged, placed somewhere he'd been exposed to hydrogen sulfide gas and thallium in low amount, and got shot in the trunk," she said.

Belatedly it dawned on Sam. "My Saturday's vic, the fallen-from-the-sky guy? John Doe, still yet, died of thallium poisoning and he had a small intake of hydrogen sulfide gas too."

"What?" Jason shot his eyes at him. "Which vic are you talking about? Who the hell was the fallen-from-the-sky John Doe?"

Some paper was immediately presented to him by their forensic pathologist.

"Well, thanks." He read the summary. "Huh…this is…interesting."

"It's Berkeley's local case so you didn't know it yet." Sam said.

"Alright, maybe it was on the bulletin that I should've paid attention to. Anyway, Doc, do you think this poisoned John Doe case and Declan's case are connected?" Jason asked her.

"I don't guess, Jase. Let me check if the variants of those chemicals are the same. If so, then the chemicals are likely from the same source. I'll also check John Doe's body and clothes one more time along with Evalyn and Declan, if there is any similarity or connection among all three, tonight and tomorrow. I think I'll ask help from Dr. Taylor."

"Alrighty, thanks, Doc," Jason stood up and shook hands with her. And he turned to Sam. "Meet you in the parking lot." And he trotted out leaving them alone.

He came around her desk and pulled her up from the chair and hauled her into his arms.

Familiar senses of physical connection sent them bursts of yearning for each other's proximity. They embraced tightly as close as possible, as if they wanted to meld together. He'd never had such a strong urge to make love to a woman all the time before. She'd never felt she wanted to belong to someone. He held the back of her head and kissed her intensely, never loosening the other arm around her. His hard body gluing to her soft one, he pressed his hard ridge on her, whispering into her ear, breathing heavily,

"Alex, I wish I could make love to you now." And his lips traced her jawline and onto the soft neck. "Sam…" she murmured his name, music to his ears, dazzling his mind with euphoria that caused him to arouse more.

And of course, his phone buzzed in his pants pocket. Yup, bad juju. And she started laughing, her head thrown back. He kissed her right there, vulnerably exposed, holding her tighter, pressing his arousal on her harder.

But the phone didn't stop buzzing. He exhaled and answered even didn't read the caller ID. "Yeah."

"You dickhead, leave her alone and come back to the vehicle. We gotta back to the office, you fucking idiot!"

Even without speaker, they could hear Jason yelling at him. She started laughing again, almost doubling over. He must be the one that possessed x-ray vision.

"Alright, alright, on my way. Sheesh." Then, he pretended to hurl his phone into the trash bin. He stopped in the middle of pitching.

"Are you going to play baseball this season too?" when her laughter subsided, she asked casually.

"When my shoulder gets better."

"What happened?"

"Nah, just pretending being young and slid home. Collided with the big catcher."

"Ouch."

"Yeah, tell me about it." And he rolled his right shoulder.

"Does it hurt?" she asked.

"No, just waiting for my doc to clear me."

"You must've really slid home hard." She grimaced as if she could feel it.

"I'd hurt it long before when I was in the SRT …"

"You were in the Special Response Team?" She'd never guessed that. And Uncle Barry hadn't told her about that, either.

"Yeah, long time ago. After the burn accident, a few years of being in uniform, I decided to get in. Before I joined the Detective Bureau."

"Wow..." She could only imagine how difficult and challenging it'd been for him to train and become a member of the SRT after such burns. The burn trauma and scars must've bothered him even a few years later, affecting his lifestyle overall. Still, he'd challenged how far he could go. Probably he'd needed something demanding to assert he'd survived the burns or measure how far he could push himself with his trauma. He'd saved her life and still tried to save others while daring to drive his limit. One of his awesome traits, marvelous determination must've helped him crawl out of the dungeon of burn stigma and soar.

And he wanted to have a serious relationship with her. Her. The cause of his burn and pain and everything that he'd been hindered from doing as a young person. Was it fair not to tell him she was the one who had caused his scars? In fact, what if he hated the girl who had ruined many precious months in the life of the young promising rookie officer?

Wait...he was about to say something when he'd gotten hurt in the SRT. "You got injured when you were in the SRT?"

"Um...yeah, a little scratch."

"What kind of scratch?" She narrowed her eyes. She was a doctor. He couldn't just get away by telling her something ambiguous.

He sighed resignedly. "Got grazed by a bullet." Two in the torso, one that had escaped the vest, to be precise. But she didn't need to hear that.

"Oh, Sam..." At that moment, she clearly fathomed that she was in love with the man who could easily lay his own life down to protect others. He'd done that for her. He'd almost lost his life to protect her from the embers. She'd be forever afraid of losing him from now on more than ever.

"You pushed your limit to save others. That's very admirable," she softly uttered.

"I didn't give much thought about saving lives, sweetheart," he replied. "I always wanna be a better man, honorable man for…" He stopped there. *For you ever since I'd met you on 80.* "Anyways, I'm still tryin'."

"Sam, you've been a good man." She smiled. He gazed on her intensely for a short moment.

"Hon, tell you what." He pulled her closer again. "I'll come to get you here after work."

"Um…but I have my own car."

"I know. I'll escort you back to your house. My Charger has stronger headlights so I'll lead you on the road."

"Er…I appreciate your thoughtfulness, but not necessary. I've been driving myself back home late at night, more than often."

"But now you have me. You can use me. Let me lead you home."

Let me lead you home… She closed her eyes for a brief moment. It was such a precious and profound phrase that she'd love to hear over and over again for the rest of her life, if he'd stick with her.

"Okay, hon?" He cocked his head and placed his forehead to hers again. "Yes." She smiled at him, thankful.

He kissed her and whispered on her lips, "*I look at you…and I'm home…*"

"That's nice… Which movie is that?"

"*Finding Nemo.*" He grinned.

"Oh wow, you cover a broad field of movies. Right, you're a shortstop." Her eyes sparkled with laughter.

"When Jason and I had to babysit his cousin's kids. But I like the quote."

"Me too."

He couldn't help kissing her again, and then he had to tear himself off her lips. "Hey, text me when you think you can go home, will you? Usually takes 20 minutes from the BPD to here."

"Alright, I'll let you know in advance. But think around 9pm cuz I'd like to take a look at all three bodies with Dr.

Taylor."

"Okay. And thanks for working."

"It's my job."

"But still, thanks."

"You're welcome."

She tiptoed and kissed his chin. "Oh, sweetheart, please don't torture me." He kissed her on top of her head and caressed her cheeks. "See you soon, babe."

CHAPTER 8

Wednesday Morning

"Hey Carter, you contacted the thrift store on University? What'd they say about the robbery?" Sam asked.

The detectives had found that the thrift store had been robbed early in the morning a month ago. They'd had some clothes stolen and that had interested them.

Sam and Carter had still been staring at the footage from the supermarkets, seeking Evalyn, but they'd decided to expand the search specifically for her Camry and started gathering the footage from the gas stations nearby. The new images had just arrived at the BPD this morning and piled up on their desk, but from today on they had a helping hand. Nick Montoya, a typical handsome California boy with dark brown hair and light brown eyes, had moved up to become one of the detectives and joined the Detective Bureau a few weeks ago. He'd been assigned to join Sam's team, under Carter; he'd felt ecstatic at first since he'd never had his own tangible team member before, but he'd soon realized he also had a responsibility to educate and encourage Nick to be a better detective. Now he knew how Sam had attended on him for those years. He was lucky to have him as his boss and friend.

"Yeah, I called 'em first thing in the morning; there's three employees on the morning shift, but they're part-timers so they only remember they watched the news the store had some sort of police activity. And they said their manager might remember more and she comes around 11am so I asked them to have her call us."

"Okay."

Carter spotted Sam was nursing his coffee in that silly looking thermos with a big smiley on it.

He smirked. "You guys look so surefire."

"Huh?" Concentration on the monitor cut, he paused the video and faced his buddy, frowning. "What?"

Carter jerked his chin up to his thermos. "Either just using hers behind her back or stayin' together. And I bet my truck on the latter."

"Lucky you ain't lose it today," he simpered.

"So…how's it with her?"

"Well…ain't tell you in detail…"

"Oh, c'mon, don't be shy, dude."

"Er…you wanna hear my *sexual conduct*?" He gave him a sidelong look, lips curving.

"Um…no." Carter decided. "Okay, so not in detail then."

"Everything's phenomenal, bro."

"It's just a few days since you guys met, you know that, right? But you are still sure of this?"

"Like I said, when you find the one, you know it."

"That kind of feeling is mutual?" Concerned about his friend, he wanted to make sure.

"Well hell, I fucking hope so cuz we're stayin' together."

"I don't want you to get burned or shot at."

"No shit; I don't wanna get burned or shot either."

"Then, careful. Make sure she's trustworthy."

"Thanks; I got you," he said so, since he honored his friend's concern.

However, he was certain she was in love with him. He was confident love had no space or time. Ten years ago was now; now was ten years ago. Wherever he'd been then, wherever he was now, love had found him. Not once but twice. Carter was sincerely worried about him as his friend since he didn't know the truth about Alex.

"Oops, phone." Carter reached for his phone ringing on the desk. "Ah, the thrift store."

Sam pushed his chair rolling back to his desk and resumed screening the footage.

He even didn't remember how many hours of footage he'd been staring down at just to hope he could find Evalyn or her Camry.

"Yo, the manager said exactly what she'd said in the police report. No change or waver whatsoever," the police report in his hand, Carter said.

"So she was alone at that time up front early in the morning and heard the sound in back. And the two guys stole a total of a dozen sweats hanging in the racks near the back door," Sam read her original statement in the police record on his laptop.

"Yup. And no surveillance camera. And one of the other employees came in and saw the suspects were driving a white pickup but no tag number, no model. Just white pickup truck."

"Not much to go on, but damn interesting. Remember it was about six pairs of adult male sweats in the Camry with Declan's body, right? Where are the rest?"

"Ah, right. Declan wasn't murdered one month ago. The killer didn't even need the filler," Carter agreed.

"Yup, who the hell stole the friggin' clothes in the first place? And why? The killer just so happened to find the six pairs somewhere later and use as fillers?"

"Carter, Sarge," Nick called them both, standing over the partition from his desk across the floor. "I think you should take a look at this."

Sam and Carter brought their chairs to crowd Nick's

desk.

"Look." Nick pointed at the image, using a slo-mo function.

"Wait, rewind it and stop the image and zoom in," Sam ordered.

"Okay." He nodded and did what he was asked to do.

"Is this…oh, *Power 24 on MLK*, the gas station?" Carter asked.

"Yeah, and this vehicle in the background…it's just passing it. Timestamp is…Sunday afternoon." Nick pointed at the silver sedan in the image that he was halting at. The car was driven from the north to south, from left to right on their monitor, on MLK and the view was clearly captured by one of the HD security cameras of the gas station.

"That sure looks like Evalyn's Camry to me," Carter said. "Look, the dent here. The bottom of the passenger door?"

"And look at the vehicle," Sam said touching the monitor image. "Still clean. The bright sunlight is shining on it. Can tell squeaky clean."

"Damn," Carter mumbled. "The Camry going somewhere for a fucking long joyride before the dump, huh?"

"Likely." Sam folded his arms. "Whoever's driving it went somewhere dirty, grassy, dry but not desert."

"Yeah, bug splats and dry weeds." Carter nodded.

Nick started playing the footage again. But Sam stopped him right away. "Nick, stop and rewind and go slo-mo."

"Okay." He looked bewildered.

The slo-mo image soon revealed what had attracted Sam's attention.

"Holy shit, the white pickup," Carter spat out. "A white pickup was seen in the thrift store robbery too. Well, could be pure coincidence. Let's look for other footage."

"Yup, on MLK and from overlook I-80, I-580 and Highway 24, if this pickup is really following the Camry,"

Sam suggested.

"Why highways?" Nick asked.

"Cuz," Carter replied instead of him, "the Camry ended up dirty like it went some countryside for a long distance."

"Ah," Nick got it right away. "The vehicle got out of the cities."

"Uh-huh," Carter patted the rookie's shoulder.

Sam's phone buzzed. It was from their CSI. He pressed the speaker and answered, "Hey Oscar, any good news?"

"I'm at the evidence garage and talked with our vehicle specialist. First, remember the dent we found? Got some white paint there and we sent it to the Fed's lab. May take a while but they'll know the type of paint."

The three detectives looked at each other. "White paint…" Suddenly their skin got goosebumps. They didn't know the reason yet, but was it possible somehow the white pickup had run into the Camry? They should really look for more footage from all over the towns.

"Next…, er…you know what, let our vehicle specialist talk, cuz it's important. He's an engineering prof from UC Berkeley. Doctor, please. The detectives are listening on the other side of the phone."

"I'm Doctor Abe. I'd like to talk about the Camry's odometer and Toyota's record discrepancy."

"Odometer…" Sam murmured.

"I talked to Berkeley Toyota where she did scheduled service regularly, and the vehicle was just returned to the customer, Ms. Evalyn Roberts, around 4pm from the dealer. Long story short, the Camry gained more than 300 miles within three days after the service."

"300… What the…" Carter swallowed the last word.

"I learned the victim had passed away on Sunday," Professor went on. "She went to work in her Camry on Saturday and considering that fact, the odometer should gain only about 10 miles at most from her commute. However, the odometer shows about 340 miles more, a total of about 350 miles gain. From the look of the vehicle and the place it was found, I suspect it'd been driven at least 150 miles somewhere with dry land with sparse vegetation. Did you talk to an entomologist? There are bugs on the windshield and also some sucked in the air filter and near the radiator."

"Oh, I'll tell that to our boss, Doc," Oscar assured the professor.

"Okay good. Also about the dent. It's not a significant one. It's more like someone opened the door near the Camry, and their door hit the door."

"Huh." Carter looked at Sam.

"Thank you, Professor." They turned off the phone and eyed each other. Nick rubbed his arm, flinching. "Wow, goosebumps all over again."

"It's part of the deliciousness of being a homicide detective, catch my drift, dude?" Carter said.

"Wow…" Nick sighed with astonishment.

"Someone's friggin' philosophical today." Sam elbowed his partner and friend. Then he suggested, "Hey maybe we should give Jason a jingle?"

"Oh yeah." Carter reached for his phone.

*****

Meanwhile, Alex and Barry had decided to take a look at three bodies, the poisoned vic John Doe, drowned vic Evalyn Roberts, and gunshot vic Declan Kosarek, once again, afraid they might've missed something in a short recheck last night.

They took all three bodies out of the lockers.

"Alex, darling, you really think we have more to do?" he asked.

She started laughing. "I'm trying to do my best, Uncle. That's what you taught me."

"Damn, I forgot already." That made her chuckle more.

"Uncle, I'd like you to help me check my lists if I missed something."

"Alright, let's start with our Saturday vic, the poisoned John Doe, a.k.a. our fallen-from-the-sky guy."

She started reading her report, "His primary route of exposure of hydrogen sulfide was mostly inhalation. And as for thallium, this one was his COD, he was exposed both through inhalation and dermal absorption and he had enough time to create Mees' lines."

"Sweetie, which compound was his thallium?" he asked, remembering something.

"Thallium (I) sulfate."

"It used to be in rodenticide, formicide and pesticide. I mean before 1975-ish."

"Yes, it's prohibited in vermin poison. Oh so, if we found an old pesticide factory…"

"I don't think so, Alex. We have no old factory sites at all. They've been cleaned up long before. I checked it. But some household might still have old bags of rodenticide. Some people don't know thallium is poison."

"Ah…I see."

"Also, as for hydrogen sulfide, it could be from an ordinary septic tank or sewage or drainage. Think about it. We saw the dirt and dry grasses in the tread. I'm sure they drove up to somewhere inland very rural, 160 miles from us."

"I strongly concur," she said. "Do you think our John Doe lived in a rural area where he was exposed to both chemicals inadvertently too?"

"Possible, if he lived in an old house and they still had thallium-containing pesticide or an insufficient septic tank. And how did he get to Berkeley from those areas? Still a few mysteries. Okay, let's move to Evalyn, sweetie."

"She likely died not in the Lake before being dumped in the Lake," she started, "but it's very difficult to figure out how in the world did she die in the way both Lake water and tap water got into her. She drowned where and how?" She frowned.

"I agree."

"The problem is the evidence doesn't quite add up. She was unconscious from the drug cocktail before she drowned. We're missing something."

"You're right. Very mysterious lady. Did her body show any sexual assault?"

"I'm not sure about that either. I do have evidence she had some sexual activities previously, but she was submerged in the Lake for 24 hours. Very hard to reach a conclusion. And of course no semen found."

"Okay, move on to Declan. His case puzzled me the most." He scowled. "Look, he's young, he's tall, he's powerful enough to prevent anyone from bullying him. Without scuffling, he was subdued? How did it happen?"

"Well, he was injected with fentanyl and cocaine."

"Alex, for someone to inject you with the concoction, either you're willing to let him inject you, or you're subdued already."

"Oh my god, that's true."

"When he was injected on his right arm, he was either unconscious already or at least drowsy."

"Uncle, let me recheck his body. I have an idea. I need to turn him over."

"Let me help."

They turned his body to a prone position. She started examining around the back of his neck. He realized what she was searching for. She extended a movable magnifying glass over the neck of Declan. "Uncle, look,"

He looked into the powerful glass. "Ah…" There was a tiny hole in the nape of his neck. "I did see this at the first autopsy, but I hadn't thought it was an injection mark. Looks more like a bug bite or just his skin tone. Anyway, I'll swab it and see if I can find any chemical. If I go deeper than the epidermis, maybe subcutis, I may find something."

"Good thinking." He nodded approvingly.

"I'd like to check the variants of hydrogen sulfide and thallium in all cases relevant. If the variants are the same, the cases must be connected."

"Wonderful." She was growing fast. Not his little girl anymore.

*****

Three sets of eyes were better than one set or two, especially when those three sets belonged to trained detectives who were relentless and would never give up on anything.

Six eyes with three different monitors had finally found possibly Evalyn's Camry and a white pickup truck together getting on I-580 East, captured by one of the surveillance cameras at the MacArthur BART, *Bay Area Rapid Transit,* station. When they'd found the image of the two vehicles one after another driven on 580, they'd also realized the truck looked like an older model Chevrolet Colorado. The three detectives high-fived.

Now all they had to do was find more of those images and locate their destination. Yeah, right.

"Okay, it took us like…a couple of fucking trillion hours to find this…I'd be dead buried if we keep on doin' this. Where are they goin'? What's their destination? I bet it's a damn hideout to cool down the killin'." Carter raised his arms exaggeratedly.

After contemplation, Sam said, "How far from here to Mariposa County?"

Carter frowned. "Why Mariposa?"

"That county has Yosemite, right? If they or either of the drivers would've had a connection with Evalyn, he or they might've gone to Yosemite with her before," Sam alluded to a possibility.

It dawned on Carter. "Oh the photo of El Capitan on her nightstand."

"Uh-huh," Sam nodded. "It ain't a postcard; it really is a photo someone'd taken. You don't put a photo on your nightstand if it ain't significant to you."

"Huh." Utterly convinced, Nick opened Google Maps

on his laptop and started checking the distance between the BPD and Yosemite. "Whoa…it is around 160 to 180 depending on which route you'd take."

But Sam sat deep in the chair, chewing over what he'd just said further. "Yosemite is abundant in green. And quite many private homes are in Yosemite. I cannot think of a place that you get contaminated dry grasses and dust particles in your tire tread like her Camry's."

The other two detectives were staring at him and then moved their eyes to Google Maps. The color on the maps of the Yosemite area was a vast sea of dark green and even the satellite image was no different.

"Unless…" Sam leaned forward to Nick's laptop. "Let's say they do have their hideout 160 miles away from us. What if it's actually near Yosemite but not quite in the Yosemite area? Look, to the west of it, there is a wide plain that looks very dry."

"Yup, after the towns like Merced or Planada, nature looks totally different." Carter fingered it on the display.

Nick saw the problem in the area. "It's so friggin' empty. No structures. That means, no surveillance cameras. How do we know they went to that area? Or find the hideout?"

"Hmm…" Sam cocked his head, thinking.

"We cannot just drive around randomly, right?" Nick asked Carter.

"'Course not, dude. Besides, we have no guarantee their hideout or whatever shit was there."

Suddenly Sam stood up. "Where the hell you think you're goin'?" Carter called out.

"I need to talk to Lt."

"What for?" His brow furrowed, Carter also stood up.

"I think we need help from outside the law and believe it might work." Waving his hand, he was walking down to Lt's office.

After Lt and Capt. Spinnar of the Investigations Division had given Sam a 'go,' he came back to his desk and made a call to his friend, Abby Stevens working at Google Maps, who'd once been an instructor for the BPD to teach them about Internet technology and information.

His idea was to use their satellite imaging technology to find any structure in the middle of nowhere in Mariposa and Merced County, west of Yosemite. But Abby told him Google satellite imaging is not always live. She said the images were updated or refreshed depending on the popularity of places as a result of the number of Google Searches. So, if the place was too remote without any attractions, the images wouldn't be popular enough to be refreshed often. The place Sam had wanted to see was...not popular enough to have a frequent refresh treatment. However, Abby had a secret weapon. Her boyfriend worked for the FBI and he might be able to help Sam. She told him she'd have him call him.

He and his team were hoping her boyfriend would give them a hand to boost their investigation.

CHAPTER 9

When Sam and Carter went downstairs to the CSI lab, they met Jason, talking to Oscar.

"Yo, didn't have time to call ya. Came to meet him directly."

"That's fine and for what, Evalyn's vehicle?" Sam asked.

"And her clothes. Oscar said CSI found a couple of tiny fibers on her dress and sent them to UC Berkeley's fiber scientist."

"Really?" He faced Oscar.

"Mm-hmm." He nodded, smiling. The usual smile of his, giving everyone slack amid the harsh reality of the cases. "Tiny fibers. Very hard to see with our naked eyes; that's why we'd missed them at first."

"It's a miracle that water and wave didn't wash 'em off," Jason said.

"They're almost embedded. Figured that she was pressed hard on some gray something and also brown something, possibly carpets."

"Well done, Sgt. Oscar Silva."

"Tell that to your Sister Golden Hair, Sam. She was the one who told us to reexamine her clothes. Without her calling me, we'd have missed finding 'em."

Her name had come out, sending him hot shock inside. Gosh, he missed her so much. Odd that they'd been living together, breathing in each other, but he still missed her so damn much if she wasn't in his vicinity, as if part of him had been snatched away. He'd never felt such emotional deprivation in his life before.

"I…I'll tell her." He barely squeezed his words out, giving Jason one heck of a frowning face.

"Anything else?" Carter jumped in. "You guys got all the clothes not only Jason's vic's, right?"

"Yeah, John Doe's, Declan's and ones from the thrift shop shoved in the trunk. Checkin' 'em all." Oscar flipped his clipboard. "We collected dust particles, grasses and…oh, yeah, bugs. We found bugs on Declan's clothes and from Evalyn's vehicle. Anyways, all of them are in the hands of the specialist outside the lab."

"What 'bout other things like latent prints and firearms, and DNA?" Sam looked at him. "Hope you can make us happy campers."

Oh, he woke up, Jason thought, glancing at him from the corner of his eyes. Every time someone mentioned Sister Golden Hair or Alex, he seemed to slip into somewhere, probably in his dreamland with her.

When it came to her, Sam became powerless. It was true that he'd finally met a perfect woman for him, and she obviously didn't consider his scars gross. But he'd already chosen her as his permanent partner, a.k.a. his future wife. Seriously? What the hell was with him suddenly?

Jason was just concerned it had happened in a very short time not even in a week. Had it been enough time to get to know each other? Was it just some kind of infatuation?

Unless…was there something special between them, which Jason hadn't known? What about Sister Golden Hair's hero-worship syndrome story? It had stuck in his mind, but he hadn't really dug up anything about her yet. Maybe he should, so that he might be able to save his homie's sorry ass from a disastrous love delusion, in case she was not serious about him.

Oscar replied, checking his data, "Er…well, no fingerprints that stand out. Da ya remember we took fingerprints from the handrails of the overpass? Those came back as John Doe's and random people, that's no surprise. Prints on the Camry belong to Evalyn and her parents. As for the bullet, all we know so far was the caliber. 9mm. That's all. And we're combing through the police firearm record if there's any match. If it was used in some crime in the past, we won't miss. As for DNA, we practically got nothing."

"Okay." Sam cocked his head, with his usual keen eyes. "What about the diamond earrings?"

"That's actually us," Jason responded instead. "We consulted the GIA, Gemological Institute of America. Those earrings don't get no serial numbers on them so they cannot tell us anything right away."

"That's too bad," Carter mumbled.

"GIA said they might find some data cuz they're good diamonds. But they need time."

"Alright, and Jase, you should come with us," Sam said on their way back upstairs. "We might have some fun stuff."

"What fun stuff?"

"You remember the Google lady, Abby Stevens, right?"

"Oh yeah, yeah, redhead beauty. What about her?"

"We found Eva's vehicle and a white pickup truck in footage heading east, possibly for 'bout 150 miles of joyride."

Jason grabbed his arm. "No shit?"

"No shit. And we figured they might own a hideout in the remote dry area before Yosemite. Only reason to go off-road. To find a structure from the damn huge area, we consulted Abby. And she said she'd introduce us to her honey, a Fed to help us, cuz Google satellite imaging ain't necessarily live."

"Huh," intrigued, Jason said, "Gotta see." And he

walked along with Sam.

As soon as they reached the office, Sam got a text message from Abby.

"*He's calling you within 15.*"

"*Thanks,*" sent.

"*No problem.*"

And not a long wait later, his phone buzzed. All the heads gathered over the phone, cramming his space. "Oh hell, back off a bit, will ya?" Sam ordered and they retreated. A little bit. Like an inch.

He sighed and read the caller ID on his phone. *FBI San Francisco Office*

"Oooh!" Nick and Carter were so ecstatic to receive a call from the federal agency that they sounded like kids opening a birthday present. "Shh, shut the hell up kiddos," Jason scolded them, feeling like a den mother for cub scouts, with a bad Jason-mouth.

"This is Sgt. Sam Crawford of the Berkeley Police Department Detective Bureau."

"I'm Asst. Director of the FBI West Coast Division, David Harp. Nice to speak to you, Sarge."

A very calm and low voice came out of the phone. Definitely an adult voice.

"Er… Thank you for calling, Asst. Director," Sam responded carefully.

Nick mouthed *Wow…* Not only Nick but all of them hadn't expected such a high-ranking person at the FBI to be calling them.

But AD laughed, "David is fine. The title is too damn long."

The detectives looked at each other, pleasantly surprised, grinning. They liked this Fed guy already.

"Um…I think Ms. Abby Stevens talked to you already?"

"Yeah, you'd wish to access NSA's satellite live images."

"I know we can't, of course not, but if we could get some…"

"Sarge,"

"Sam."

"Okay, Sam, since you're Abby's good friend, I'll try my best to get you what you need."

"Really?"

"Yeah, it's our pleasure to help local law enforcement catch criminals. As long as you and I both follow our protocol, all good. Give me some time…let's see…from a couple of weeks to a month."

"Is that all? Not like three months?"

"I wish I could give it to you within a week, but there are rules when they can release which images for national security reasons and steps I must take."

"No problem, sir…David. Thank you," Sam humbly answered.

"Tell me the timeline that images are needed. The dates. If possible, preferably longer than a pinpoint date and time, cuz we don't know which satellite was observing which area right now, and the coordinates, of course. You can tell me from Google Maps…"

After the phone call with David, Sam had another flash in his mind. "Yosemite, we still gotta check that place."

"Why's that?" Nick was baffled by his statement. "We thought Yosemite was too green and moist to leave dry grasses and dust particles in the tread?"

"Not in that sense, Nick," he went on, "coming back to Evalyn's photo of El Capitan, we have another angle to investigate."

"Yeah, it oddly stuck out," Jason said. "That's the only non-human photo of her few frames, and her parents confirmed they'd never been there with her."

"Carter, call CSI about the photo and ask if they can pinpoint where the photo had been taken."

"Okay, boss."

"Good idea, man," Jason said. "If we get to know the location, we can canvass there, and…" but his eyes spotted a visitor coming into the office. "Hey, that's Sister Golden

Hair." And he slugged his face mentally after he'd said something he shouldn't have said. Of course, Sam would go total meltdown without any delay. But everybody would understand why she was his soft spot.

She was friggin' gorgeous. With her abundant golden hair, pure translucent blue eyes, yet in a modest navy blue suit covering small stature that made men wonder how it looked under those layers of fabric, her appearance would knock the wind out of any man who was warm-blooded.

As soon as she walked in, the office had suddenly become as if having its own sun. And everyone here had already known the best part wasn't her features but her caring, kind, sweet nature. Most of them were standing up from their chairs waving at her. And she was smiling and wiggling her fingers back at them. They were smiling, snickering, knowing she was dating Sam…or more like he was commuting from her house.

Sam kicked his chair out, making a dash at her. Jason became horrified he might knock her over on the floor to start making out with her. Yeah, it didn't happen, much to his relief, but he'd almost given him a heart attack or two, for his absolute endless passion for her.

However, he wasn't that stupid, or smarter than Jason had imagined. He hadn't hauled her into his embrace to give her French kisses. Jason sighed, sitting back in his chair. He'd never seen Sam so passionate before. He'd always been cool, reserved, observing. Alex must be really different from other women.

"Hey." He caught up with her in the hallway. His hands cupping her elbow, he looked down at her.

"Hey back."

"To what do I owe the pleasure of the visit?"

She chuckled at his old-fashioned way of greeting. He instantly softened, amazed how much she could relax and soothe him.

He picked up a wild strand of hair from her cheek and tucked it behind her ear and stroked her hair. Touching her hair like that was now his habitual gesture that she loved a lot. His touch gentle, a series of his moves sent thrilling sensations into her. His eyes tenderly sparkling, she felt like she was soaking in warm liquid. She closed her eyes briefly, wanting to snuggle up to him now. They were sure that their sexual hunger blazed instantaneously almost into glowing flames. No one was around them. He could kiss her until her brain power would fly out of the window. Except… The door behind them suddenly opened.

"Oh, welcome to my office, Dr. Wallace, come in. Sorry Sam, gonna steal her."

She waved at him and entered the office. The door was gently closed leaving him alone in the hallway.

Gee, it was his Captain Spinnar, the head of the Investigations Division, Lt's boss. He looked at the door. Yeah, the plaque on the door clearly said his name and rank. Thank goodness, he hadn't kissed her mindlessly. Or Captain would've shot him. He'd been lucky today. Phew.

Alex came out of the Captain's office about half an hour later. She dropped by Sam's team to say hello and passed on what conversation they'd had.

"So, he asked me to do a familial DNA search on the fallen-from-the-sky John Doe to find if anyone related would be in CODIS or your records."

"Familial DNA…was it the one used to have found the *Golden State Killer*?" Nick asked.

"Yes, that's right. Quite many cold cases were solved by this new technique."

"Wait, so you have to do all the work by yourself?" concerned, Sam asked. "It'd take many days to find out, right?"

"No worries. The technologies in the field…any field have been progressing rapidly every day, every minute. We have a good program profiling DNA in genealogy to find familial DNA rather quickly and I do have that program installed on my computer. Your Captain knew it, so he called me." Then she stood up. "Gotta go. Oh, I almost forgot..." And she took out another thermos from her purse and exchanged it with the one on Sam's desk. It was still the same thermos, graphite black with a yellow smiley. "You have two of those?" Sam didn't know.

"Several," she replied. "I thought you might've finished the coffee already. We have a mean coffee machine at the Bureau so I brought the beans you like and brewed it. It should keep you awake."

"Whoa..." the three amigos of Sam's muttered to him. "Lucky you."

"My god, thank you, hon."

"I had time and I was called by the Captain, so..." Then she took out a box from the big paper bag that she'd kept in the locker in the hallway. "And these are for everyone here. They taste amazing."

"That's *Uncle Berk's*." Nick almost jumped. "I thought I smelled pastries."

"Yup." She opened the box and presented it. "I wasn't sure what everyone here likes."

"Well, we eat anything," Carter assured her.

There were many different pastries from sweet to savory packed in the box. "Please share and you included, of course." She patted Jason's arm.

"Thank you, Doc," he said, while Carter and Nick brought the box to their breakroom...a little corner in the office where there were a coffeemaker, fridge, microwave, tables and chairs set inside a doorframe to separate it from other sections. "Hey, from Doc Alex. Pastries from *Uncle Berk's*," Carter announced and was responded by *Ooh* from all the detectives and they were quickly gathering at the corner, thanking her. She waved at them.

"Anyway, Sam, really gotta go."

"Thank you for everything," he said, walking her out of the office. "No need to escort me to elevator or front door. I'm not a kid. Go back to work, Detective," she laughed. He had to kiss her. A very light quick peck. Still enough to send them both a shiver.

"I'll come and get you after work," he said. "I'll text you," said she, holding his arms to support herself since his little kiss created quite a bit of dizziness in her. "Stay safe, baby."

*****

On the weekend, Alex and her two best friends met at Uncle Barry's café, sitting at their usual round table. Sam and Jason had to work extra hours on the cases so they'd decided to do a girls' brunch.

This time, their topic wasn't about Alex and Sam, but Rae and Jason, since she announced he'd want to have a relationship with her, in other words, he was making a commitment to her.

Jason said what?

Alex was about to bite her chicken on the fork. Nora was sipping her pink lemonade. And both froze in the middle of consuming the food. The little piece of chicken fell back onto the plate from her fork, but she was still petrified with her mouth open and the fork in midair. Then Nora suddenly started coughing. The lemonade must've gotten somewhere it shouldn't have. Rae had to rub her back until the choking sounds subsided.

"My word, never seen suicide by lemonade. Don't choke." Barry ran to Nora, gave her a back rub with Rae and a clean towel and water, then he wiped the table for her. "I don't want to perform an autopsy on any of you."

"Oh, Uncle Barry." Alex came back too, frowning at him.

"Sorry." He didn't look really sorry and left with some towels.

"You okay?"

"Yeah, thank you," Nora said, still her voice hoarse, but she turned to Rae with her sparkling sea-green eyes, mouthing *Wow*.

"You never done it so quickly before or ever. What made you think differently this time?" Alex asked.

"Says the woman who's living with the guy she's known only for a couple of days," Rae sassed her.

"Touché." Nora snickered.

"Traitor." Alex nudged her.

"Ow. I still love you." Nora smiled at her.

"Aw…I love you too." And she faced Rae. "Anyway, it's not about me and Sam today. It's about you and Jason."

"Right," Nora agreed. "Isn't it too quick for you?"

"It's not so quick, compared to them," Rae stated, thumbing toward Alex. "I dated him like…er…seven times so far."

"Seven? With one guy?" Nora needed to clarify. "That's your first, isn't it?" Rae nodded once.

Barry came through the French door by the bar separating the kitchen and the dining area, and joined the girls.

"So, he wants commitment." He got that. Jason must really like her…or be already in love with her?

"Yes." Rae said, putting down her fork by her salmon salad.

"You want it too? What'd *you* want?" Nora asked.

"Well…don't know."

"Did he say he loves you?"

"No. Tell you the truth, that's one thing that makes me hesitate," Rae confessed, her shoulders sagging.

That, actually Alex wanted to know too. It seemed that Sam and she were having a great relationship. And he'd declared to her and his friends that he'd been committed to her. But he still hadn't told her he loved her. Shouldn't he have said he loved her by this point since they were having a relationship and started living together? Wasn't that kind of commitment one step before engagement if they'd stick together? Or was she wrong? Maybe still too short a time for him, then? Still the trial time, then. Bummer.

Barry suspected both Sam and Jason had been looking

for an opportunity to end their freewheeling lives and settle down to have a family. So, if it wasn't an infatuation, it would stay long. To him, both men were very careful about dealing with women. Both had been burned by some women before…well, figuratively. So, if they'd said they were ready for commitment, they really were. The women could trust both men. However, not telling Rae *I love you* was also disheartening. Jason had to say the words if he wanted to keep his woman.

"Well, Sam's been her hero for a long time and being with him is her dream." Rae was envious.

"That's true," Alex had to admit that assertion. "I'm living in my dreamworld, yes, but like I said, just because he used to be my hero didn't mean we're the best match. I'm still walking on a tightrope everyday cuz he didn't even tell me he loves me."

"He didn't, either?" the three said in unison.

"Nope."

"Huh…" Barry was very disappointed. No wonder Alex had been a little antsy even after she'd got Sam and started staying together. Since Sam had already publicly declared his commitment to her, he'd imagined they'd already declared love for each other. What was he waiting for? Was he afraid of something? Rejection? From Alex? Gotta be friggin' kidding, right?

"Alright," Barry said standing up. "I must bring something for bounce, then. Would you like to have my original homemade vanilla ice cream with espresso, making it Affogato?"

Three hands shot up. "Three Affogato coming up." Barry left to the kitchen.

"Now," Rae faced Nora, "it's your turn to be grilled."

"Wait, wait, you cannot do that."

"Why not?" Alex asked innocently. Her appearance had a definite advantage when she wanted to look innocent.

"Well, first of all, I have no romance anywhere near me," Nora explained. "Whether I like it or not, I don't have anybody. But have no fear, my friends, I've just joined some online dating thing, so you'll see."

Barry came back from the kitchen just in time with ice cream and espresso.

"Haven't had Affogato for ages!" Nora picked up spoons distributing them while Alex did the napkins. Rae cleaned up the plates.

Barry placed them on the table including his and sat on the chair. The four comrades holding each spoon raising it like before a sword fight of the three…four musketeers, Aramis, Athos, Porthos, and D'Artagnan of *EZ Poppas*.

Barry called out, "*One for all, and all for one*!"

The three girls repeated, "*One for all, and all for one*!" "*Un pour tous, tous pour un*!"

And then they dug into their Affogatos.

CHAPTER 10

A few weeks later, one morning, when Jason walked into the BPD Detective Bureau, the three amigos of the Bureau, Sam, Carter and Nick were still staring down at the monitors trying to find those two cars.

"Yo," in such a short greeting, Sam had heard a touch of amusement or bliss in the tone.

He looked up to see his face. Huh…his lips were curving…like a stupid hyena. Well, but for a hyena, he was awfully good-looking. He was always stylishly dressed in his three-piece suit, clean and well-groomed. His toned body was elaborately shrouded by suit and tie. He was the epitome of a handsome, taut, sexy guy.

So…what the hell exactly was the difference in him today? He could imagine one thing, though.

But before even he said anything, Carter opened his mouth, "What the fuck's with you?"

"You're what the fuck is." Jason said challengingly.

"No shit, Sarge, your face." Coming around pushing his rolling chair, Nick supported Carter.

"What the hell's wrong with you?" Carter asked him, restating, not letting him go easily.

Jason sighed. "You ain't gonna let it go, huh?" He

wanted to be done with him by swearing, but thought twice about it. Better tell the truth than let Carter go on his merry way. Besides, he wanted the relationship with Rae official just like Sam had done with Alex. "We moved up to a relationship."

"Whoa." Nick and Carter stood up. "Congrats, man." And they gave him a man hug.

Sam grinned. "Congrats, homie." And he granted him a big man hug. "I knew it."

"Thanks Sammy," he said, sitting next to him. "You knew?"

"Duh." He beamed. "Alex told me already."

"You got the best CI." Jason laughed.

Sam elbowed him. "Hey, you didn't come here just to declare the relationship with Rae, right?"

"No shit. I came here with some info." Jason grinned. "Here, open it." He took out his flash drive and passed it to Sam.

"'K." He inserted it in a USB port.

"Look for the file named *Yosemite lodges*."

Carter and Nick gathered standing behind them.

"Evalyn's El Capitan photo," Jason explained. "We asked CSI to locate the place where she might've taken that photo at, right? But CSI couldn't really pinpoint where? There's a theatrical photographer in San Fran and he knows some awesome techniques. He got the possible lodges in Yosemite for me."

The three sets of eyes were staring down at him. "Wut?" Jason grimaced.

"Theatrical photographer? I see Rachel's name all over this file," Sam said pointing at it on the monitor.

"Yeah, my lady helped me."

"Your lady..." Carter mumbled. "That sounds so historical, man."

"Zip it Carter. Gonna thwack you."

"No, thanks."

"Here we go." Sam opened the file.

There were three lodges in Jason's file. Their names, phone numbers, locations were in it.

"I know which one already. That one. *El Capitan Lodge*." Jason fingered one of them on the monitor.

"How?" Sam looked at his friend. "You psychic?"

"I gone there on the past weekend. And took several photos of El Capitan. The photographer advised me how to take a photo exactly like Evalyn's photo. She seemed to have taken it from the balcony on the third floor. Will bring in my print if you need."

"Oh wait, you took Rae."

"Yeah, just a weekend getaway."

"Good for you." Sam smiled, thinking he could do the same for Alex, anywhere she'd like to go.

"Okay, Carter, give 'em a call," Sam instructed the young detective. "Ask about Evalyn and her partner, whoever he was. And don't forget about the vehicles. Just in case, check those two lodges too."

"On it."

"Hey, Nicky," Jason said, "wanna come down to check on your CSI with me? I need you to let me access there. Oscar may not be in."

"Sure, Sgt. Rivera."

Carter had called the *El Capitan Lodge*, but they couldn't find the record of Evalyn Roberts staying at their place with her boyfriend. He'd figured she'd stayed under a pseudonym but the problem was they didn't know her pseudonym. He'd desperately asked the Lodge if they could look for a Caucasian woman in her early twenties with a man, they'd said they'd had more than 1000 Caucasian young couples in the past six months and more than 600 couples had a white truck and more than 300 visitors in sedans and they didn't really keep the detailed log long, aside from their cash-only business ledger.

"What's wrong?" Sam paused the footage from the CCTV from a gas station.

"You gonna be up to check more than 1000 couples in six months to look for Eva? Or maybe at least 900 couples with a white truck or sedan when they might've used a different car? It's batshit insane, man."

"I got you…" Then Sam's personal phone on the desk began playing a distinctive ringtone, *Sister Golden Hair*. Carter snickering pointed at his phone, "Sam, it's for you."

He gestured with his index finger to come closer and sit next to him. Carter rolled his chair to him.

Then he touched the speaker mark. "Hey hon."

"Sam, I have good news for you."

"I'm using speaker. Carter's here."

"Hey, Alex," Carter greeted.

"Hey back Carter, long time no see."

"Sorry, Alex, I'm quite busy in here cuz your Sam's enslaving me." Sam punched his arm lightly. "Ow! Alex, arrest him for assault!"

She chuckled and said, "Okay, you boys, let me start with a clothes tag." Her voice turned serious. "Actually it's a new lead for you."

"Go on," Sam encouraged her, opening his notebook. A new lead?

"This is about John Doe, the fallen-from-the-sky guy."

"Okay." He nodded, jotting down a note.

"I asked Oscar to send John Doe's clothes to me after they were returned from the lab outside. I vaguely remembered I saw something odd when I'd first checked his clothes. It was a tiny piece of cloth in the seams of his top. I used my analyzer and consulted with Dr. Young at UCSF, a fiber specialist. We found it was the part of the thrift store's tag."

"His clothes were also from the thrift store on University?" Carter asked.

"Yes, but it isn't only that. The twist is the thrift store uses different color and kind of tags for each different batch of clothes so that they know when the clothes came in to the store since they want to sell earlier donations first."

"Oh, so if they could distinguish the tag, they could specify the clothes history and record?"

"Exactly," she concurred. "Oscar contacted the thrift store from my lab and took a statement from the manager. She said John Doe's clothes are from the same rack that had been stolen by the two robbers."

"What? You mean the same as ones in Evalyn's car trunk with Declan Kosarek?"

"Yes," she added. "Oh by the way, Declan was wearing the stolen sweats too."

"Huh. So, the clothes of John Doe, Declan, and the fillings of the trunk are from the same theft incident," Sam said.

"Yes, and I'm sure you can read it in Oscar's report."

"Okay, and hon, you told me you gonna look into the variants of hydrogen sulfide and thallium."

"Yes and guess what. Hydrogen sulfide and thallium in John Doe and Declan and the tire dirt of Evalyn's Camry are the same variant."

"So, in short," Carter needed to clarify, "all vics and dirt are exposed to exactly the same chemicals?"

"Correct," she confirmed. "From the same source."

"Connected. Alex darlin', you connected all three cases."

"Except for the case of Evalyn's death, hon," she admitted humbly.

"But her vehicle is connected with the other two cases, babe. It might've worked as a catalyst in this string of crimes. Anyway, well done, sweetheart."

"You remember I still have to do a familial DNA to find John Doe's relative, right?"

"Ah, yeah... Hope not much work for you?"

"The computer's doing the heavy lifting, hon," she snickered. "Okay, I'll let you know anything else coming up." She hung up.

Both detectives exhaled. Then, Carter said wholeheartedly, "Your woman rocks."

Sam just beamed at him, thinking of her, missing her.

*****

In the late afternoon that day, Sam had received a call from David Harp of the FBI. He'd told them how to access the recorded images of the satellite. For the images that David had judged relevant to the local investigation, he'd made an isolated loop of footage for them.

Nick, a self-proclaimed computer geek with a college degree to prove it, had decided to take care of the technical part that David had directed.

They kept looking for pertinent and viable images.

"I remember seeing something insane like this on TV, dudes," Carter said. "Could be some kind of facilities in a middle eastern country or something."

"Yeah, I remember that too," said Jason.

"Let's see, 160 miles east and flat terrain and dry. Can you get 'em?" Sam asked Nick.

"West of Yosemite so…around here?" He showed some of the satellite images.

"Goddamn huge area, ain't it?" Carter sounded pessimistic.

"Don't be a sissy; where're your balls at?" Jason chewed him out.

"Nick, don't go too far. Stick around CA-140 as the main road. And concentrate on the dates between Friday, the day before we'd found John Doe and Tuesday when Evalyn's vehicle was found near the Shore," Sam ordered. "And definitely daytime."

"Roger that." Nick started using David's instructions to find any of those times. "Guess we can put more keywords in the search."

"Put *structure*," Jason suggested.

"Good idea." Nick added it in the keywords along with the timeline and CA-140.

When they'd know their target, it would be a lot easier,

but this time they had no idea what they were looking for and where.

Nevertheless, after quite a few trial and error, they spotted something, a certain distance north from CA-140. It had appeared on the edge of one photo. "Hey, what's that?" Quick-eyed Sam spotted it first, placing a finger on the monitor. "This little thing."

"That…looks like the edge of some kind of man-made structure to me."

Nodding to Carter, Jason said, "Agreed. Nick, can you focus on it and zoom in?"

"Let's see… How does this thing work again?" he was mumbling but trying to maneuver the images. "Okay…here…goes…nothing…" But in fact it was something. When the satellite imaging suddenly zoomed in on one area, four detectives immediately stilled with astonishment.

It was overhead satellite images stitched together, so it wouldn't be able to tilt to show the angle of the structure. However, the resolution of the image was remarkable and they could clearly see a farmhouse-like structure with details of the roof, covered round pool or tank, many tire marks on the land, and there were two vehicles in front of the house. They could easily guess the vehicle models.

"Silver sedan like Camry and white…possibly Chevy…truck. I guess a vehicle expert can make out the models. I'ma contact him." Jason took notes. "Nick, when was this?"

"Late Sunday afternoon. The timestamp is…3:40pm."

"Evalyn's already expired at that time," Sam said. "Her TD was around early Sunday 1am."

"Who the hell is using her vehicle then?" Carter was exasperated. "And the truck? What's the connection?"

"Hey, Sam, what the hell do you think that is?" Jason asked, pointing at the covered round structure.

"Could be a septic tank or well, cuz this shed or farmhouse is sitting in a remote area?"

"Ah…yeah, plausible."

"Let's go to this place and investigate all the goddamn structure ripping inside out," Carter said heatedly. "'Nuff shit. Got three stiffs in a week already, in Berkeley, Berkeley, dammit."

"Wait, chill, Carter. Let me talk to Lt first. We need special preparations." Sam, being his boss, tried to calm him down.

"What for? We just drive up to…"

"Carter, don't you remember Eva's vehicle had contaminants? Hydrogen sulfide and thallium? Chemical that could kill?"

"Er…right," Carter resignedly acknowledged.

"I got you, you're frustrated and angry, cuz we all are," Sam said, "but no way we gonna create more casualties."

"Understood." He nodded, cooling down.

"So, do you think this could be a hideout?" Nick asked Jason sitting next to him.

"Dunno. But we gonna find out when we investigate it."

"Okay." Sam stood up. "Guess I'll see Lt." And he walked into the hallway.

Sam came back after meeting with Lt for half an hour and announced, "Lt said Berkeley hazmat crews gonna go there first thing tomorrow morning with specialists, and if they find those toxic substances, they're gonna deal with them. At that point, we gonna have probable cause to search and clean the structure without warrant. If they can clean up in a short time, they gonna do it right away. If they estimate a long time, the specialists and hazmat scientist gather evidence for us. So, we don't screw up anyone's lives."

*****

By the time Sam hit the road home it was way past

midnight. Again.

His team had still been combing through the security camera footage but this time for specific vehicles, Evalyn's Camry and the white Chevy Colorado – the conclusive response from the vehicle expert, to find more evidence, like who'd driven them.

It was his turn to go home for getting some rest and washing up.

He was bone-tired. He could drive to his own apartment since it was closer like four, five minutes away from the PD but he wanted to see Alex. He needed to snuggle up to her warm and soft body and doze off spooning and then make love to her when she'd wake up. She'd feed his heart and soul. So, he'd chosen to drive triple the time or more to go to the Berkeley Hills.

While he was driving to get to her, he was thinking of her, and why he hadn't, couldn't have said he loved her. He knew and felt she'd love to hear him say the words. It wasn't that he didn't love her. Of course, he loved her.

The elephant in the room was the fact that he didn't have any faith in those three words although it was due to his overuse of the words in the past.

He'd utilized the words to get laid on a daily basis when he'd been younger and those women who he'd dated had also easily said the words to get their own way. Having a cop or cop-to-be in their lives must've been something to brag about as their virile lover, strong bodyguard, attractive accessory to bring around…almost like the definition of a trophy boyfriend. Even recently whether or not they hadn't been okay with his scars, they'd used the words to get something out of him.

Consequently, he'd decided to show Alex what love was by his actions alone. Nonetheless, the words wanted to jump out of his mouth naturally. The ten years of his feelings for her were in fact none other than love, so, why had he restricted himself from saying the words to her, especially when it had been for his own egoistic illogical reasons? Idiot.

Still contemplating, he climbed up the hill. When he was upbeat, the serpentine roads were nothing. But when he was exhausted like tonight and somehow his thoughts became heavy in his mind, the roads were just so annoyingly long and twisting to reach his woman. He wished he had wings. He felt like he was crawling up the final stretch. He parked his car in front of her home and exhaled. Unbuckling the seatbelt impatiently, he got out of the car. When she was so close, the last few steps of the front stairs weren't any trouble. He hopped up two at a time.

Quietly opening the front door, he entered her house. The foyer was brightened by the streetlamps outside, the lights coming through the high window above the front door to the ceiling. He could easily see everything. He inhaled, smelling the familiar notes of scent, some flowers in the vase in the foyer, wood, metal and Alex. He was craving to see her. Then his feet stopped right there, when his eyes swung to see the living room.

Alex. He spotted her sleeping on the couch, tucked under a blanket.

Had she been watching a movie and fallen asleep?

He took his shoes off, and almost tiptoed to approach her.

The floor lamp was dimly lit, the tawny-amber hue casting soft glows on her and her fanned golden hair, as if he was in some kind of immortal's land. She was absolutely beautiful.

He bent over to kiss her. Her lips were so plump and soft that they were enticing him to kiss deeper, and his body immediately reacted, arousing, desire intensified. He gently lowered himself on her just to hold her, careful not to crush her. God, Alex.

Suddenly her eyes flared open, the glacial blue staring at him but not seeing him. He instantly knew she was dreaming and still between reality and dream.

And she asked, "What about you, Sam?" And again,

"Sam, what about *you*?" Tears welled up, spilling out of the corners of her eyes. She was reliving the night she'd been in the car crash. She was seeing him on her shielding her from the falling embers from her burning car. "No!"

"Alex, it's okay, I'm okay." He held her head, cradling her like a baby, stunned.

He'd known she was the one since their first night together. Not a single instant had he doubted it.

What shocked him was he hadn't had the slightest inkling that she'd been suffering from PTSD from the accident even now.

This was the first time he'd seen her suffer from nightmares, but she must've relived the accident many times in the past, in which he'd shielded her from the falling embers and received the burns. She must've felt sorrow and remorse for his burns in every single damn nightmare. How hard it'd been to deal with it all by herself for ten years? He wasn't the only person who'd been damaged in the aftermath of the crash.

He might've been physically hurt, but she'd been wounded in her heart, still going on. He could fight for her from now on to ease her pain.

"Sam?" She finally awakened in his arms. "You're home."

"Uh-huh, I'm *home*." He kissed her sweat-sheen forehead, wiping it with his thumb and smiled. "How was your evening? Did you miss me?"

"Yes." She hugged him tight. "Missed you a lot." Then her brow furrowed. She realized she was having *that* nightmare. "Did I say something in my dream?"

"I don't know, cuz I just got home," he said.

"Oh, okay…" she murmured, relieved.

Her soft voice and smell of shampoo, and the familiarity of his loving woman seeping into his soul, he couldn't hold back his overflowing emotions.

"Alex, I want you."

"Here?"

"Here. Now."

She pulled the blanket off of the couch. He quickly took his clothes off in economical fluid motions and started helping her take her PJs off. Her bare skin suddenly exposed to the cool air in the living room, it made goosebumps and her nipples erected.

"Will warm up soon," he whispered, embracing her. His body ablaze, her cool touch was pleasurable.

He took her mouth with his right away. And his lips were tracing on her skin from her jawline, neckline all the way to her breast. He tasted her nipples one at a time. She whimpered, holding his head.

He touched her. She was already wet and ready for him. He teased her sensitive bud with his wet finger. It'd quickly swollen and as he caressed more, her body started heaving, shuddering, and she came hard convulsing, calling his name, waves of ecstasy assailing her.

He held her in his arms until her paroxysm subsided.

"Like it, huh?" His lips curving, he looked into her eyes. Her eyes watery with heat looking up at him, she replied amusingly, "I thought I'd be the next on the autopsy bed." He laughed heartily.

Placing her on the couch, he gently grabbed her thighs; she spread her legs for him. His huge erection had been scary at first, but she'd gotten accustomed to it by now. He positioned and impaled her with one swift push and groaned as he thought how right and gratifying it felt. She sucked in her breath at the shock of his penetration and then sighed, feeling so filled, so complete with him.

His entire body plastering to hers, he supported himself on his elbows by her sides and his knees between her legs. She wrapped her legs around his waist. He held her head and looked at her. Their eyes locked. And he started moving in rhythm with her as if they were one.

Every move they made engraved in their bodies and memories, even stirring up old ones to the surface.

When their passion heated, igniting every tip of nerve

endings tingling their bodies, the speed of their motion became faster. The anticipation intensifying, their senses concentrated on only their sexual organs, then it happened, she thought it happened: She thought they were abruptly ten years ago, on I-80, dark in the night yet the flashing lights of the police cars, fire engines, EMT trucks, and yelling voices of the law, rescuers, medical personnel, and her car exploded. And in those reddish yellow embers falling, she saw him on top of her shielding her from them. Another nightmare. She didn't quite understand why but she was seeing, hearing, feeling her nightmare again.

But when her scared eyes met his and he kissed her hard as if he could take away her fear, she thought he was in the same place and the exact time, then and now with her. It must be her wishful thinking that he'd remembered her, but it didn't matter, because what mattered to her was she'd come to know the truth that she'd undoubtedly been in love with him since then, hoping someday she'd make her heart whole by meeting him again, knowing love sailed across place and time.

"Shh, shh, it's okay…" Comforting her, his motion faster, deeper, he touched her clit, pushing her closer, closer to the edge. Her thoughts muddled, eyes blurry, an aura forming around her, the scene of the accident was suddenly sucked into a bright hole disappearing quickly when she'd felt his presence with her. At that precise moment, she hit her climax hard again, taking him with her, while they were calling each other's name, echoing in the living room through the foyer.

They'd become limp.

But he came back to sanity first as she was still floating somewhere in seventh heaven. He didn't want to squash her, so he changed position on the couch, holding her on top of him. He tugged up the blanket from the floor to cover her. It seemed the temperature in the room had dropped.

He'd seen it. Okay, at least he'd thought he'd seen the

scene of ten years ago, reliving it with her. They'd been completely in sync, as if their hearts had been beating the same rhythm, reverberating, resonating, crossing time.

Perhaps it was caused by they'd made love on this small couch resembling a stretcher, making them feel like being trapped there. Or the floor lamp had a shade of orange, similar to the falling embers. Or she'd just had the dream of that night that had stirred his memory too. Either way, he felt both of them had run through the scene together again. And he'd grasped the truth that both believed the significance of the incident for years.

The specific time of the event that he'd met her had actually been right there at the same point in the past, looking at the back of them leaving the scene; they had walked away from the event going to the future. Yet, both of them had left something important on that spot. He hadn't noticed at that time since he'd just been shocked by the burns. Now he'd clearly perceived what they'd left at that point in the past.

A piece of their hearts.

Now they'd met again, picking up what they'd left. Their love was whole with their hearts integrated, for they were the event, they were the place, they were the time.

CHAPTER 11

Two days later, on Friday afternoon, all the detectives of the BPD and Jason from the OPD gathered in their main meeting room. Lt. Montfort and Captain Spinnar along with their CSI, Sgt. Oscar Silva and Officer Nash Bryce were among them.

Lt started. "Today I'm talking about new evidence. First, this is from our hazmat team and their specialists. The abandoned shed, actually a farmhouse, was found twenty minutes off-road north from the main road CA-140 and in between Mariposa and Merced County. They found hydrogen sulfide was actually from the old septic and sewage tank. The house looks built around 1970 so it's understandable. We haven't found the proper owner yet. Anyway, hazmat also found thallium from old rat poison scattered inside and outside the farmhouse. We asked their specialists to collect evidence since they need to clean it up. They discovered the remnants that some people lived in there recently, but since the conditions are not even remotely suitable for living, probably utilized for a hideout."

The detectives looked at each other, knowing their suspicion was getting more and more plausible.

Lt went on. "They first found a ledger under the bed

mattress, a bundle of clothes stolen from the thrift store, a small amount of old bloodstain and unknown body fluid. It contained our John Doe's and Declan's DNA and their fingerprints. They might've lived there. Also there are two more different male donors' DNA and a couple of unknown fingerprints found. And this is big: the standard tool kit and manual of Evalyn's Camry were there. And her vehicle registration paper, still attached to the manual."

Jason raised his hand and questioned, "Is there any evidence the toolbox was removed from Evalyn's vehicle trunk to make room for the body?"

"Yeah, Jase," Oscar replied instead. "The Camry has a place in the trunk for their toolbox. And the carpet inside the trunk had a clear indentation of it."

Lt nodded. "And we have more. Hazmat also retrieved a tiny loose gemstone on the floor; later we identified it as a loose diamond. It might connect to the ledger they found first. The ledger is in the hands of the forensic accountant."

"Maybe really a jewelry robbers' hideout," said Nick.

"Possible. We sent the loose diamond to GIA to scrutinize it. Yeah, they also reported they're still searching for the original source of Evalyn's diamond earrings. They ain't cheap stuff and they might've been from South Africa. They're still looking into it." He opened the bottle of water and gulped it and sighed.

Sam saw his boss quite exhausted. They couldn't always see him publicly, but when they needed him, he'd always be there for them. It was just that he trusted his men to let them work freely, yet, his eyes were always on them and he was working hard behind the scenes to support his detectives.

Lt resumed, "The scientists who participated in the investigation there mentioned John Doe breathed in hydrogen sulfide in a small amount for a long period of time but it shouldn't have killed him, but thallium in the rat killer definitely would. So, those are exactly what Alameda Coroner's *Sister G*…I mean, Dr. Alex had said in her report."

"See? Like I said, your woman rocks," Carter whispered to Sam. Glancing at him, he nodded.

Lt must've heard him and said, "Sam's woman who always rocks also sent us a report just now adding that Evalyn's nail had skin cells from Declan."

Everyone attending the meeting was surprised at the fact; especially Jason who'd been the lead detective of Evalyn's case was now half-standing. "Declan's? You mean, that Declan Kosarek? The one stuffed in Evalyn's vehicle trunk with a friggin' lead in the noggin?"

"Uh-huh, the one and only," Lt said, "and Dr. Alex also found a couple of scratch lines on his arm. She said she was sorry that she'd missed them in the first and second-time examination on Evalyn, but the amount of skin cells was so minute it was hard to find. Anyhow, I went down to the autopsy room and saw the scratch marks but it's also hard to see. Declan's skin is tanned and the lines are on the elbow." He shook his head.

"Huh…" Jason sank back into the chair, but his voice sounded excited, "So, now all the cases are officially connected on the victims' level."

"Yup," Lt affirmed, "not only her vehicle now. Her body has a connection to Declan."

"And since she had his skin cells in her nails, it's likely she was attacked by Declan at some point?" Nick asked.

"Highly likely," said Lt. "But we need more evidence to make Declan a killer. Just skin cells in her fingernails or scratches on his skin don't withstand a murder trial. Okay, now let's move on to CSI lab's results. Sgt. Silva."

"Thank you, Lt," Oscar began, "First, about the white paint found in a little dent on the Camry's passenger door: The FBI special lab said it was used only on Chevrolet trucks from 2007 to 2009. We know the truck was a Chevy Colorado. And the fiber scientist on a couple of tiny fibers on Evalyn's clothes confirmed one fiber belongs to a gray carpet lining of the floor of a 2008-2009 Chevy Colorado.

So we checked with Chevy and they confirmed."

The detectives clapped their hands. They'd need to search for only a 2008-2009 white Chevy Colorado with a gray carpet lining, starting from their county and then expanding.

Lt raised his hand to them. "Wait, there's more."

The detectives stopped talking and returned their attention to Oscar. So he carried on, "The other fiber on Evalyn's dress, the brown fiber is a carpet fiber made by a California carpet company. It's not generic but a very distinctive carpet. We're asking the company about it right now." He took a breath. "Okay now, let's move on to the results from the entomologist, geologist and environmental botanist we have asked for help. Nash. Your turn." Oscar cocked his head toward another CSI officer.

"All three scientists had checked Evalyn's vehicle's tire treads, some bug or pollen or anything, even dry grasses stuck on the windshield, radiator or air filter, etcetera, and of course, dirt particles. And most of the bugs and vegetation are very common in Northern California including Yosemite..."

"Dammit," someone cursed, frustrated; that was the collective feeling of all the detectives there for the disappointing results.

Nash kept reporting, "The geologist said the dust particle components are very similar to the soil between Merced and Mariposa and they also confirmed the particles are contaminated with the same chemical from the farmhouse."

"Is it the same chemical variant?" Captain asked quite an important question.

"Yes, sir," Nash confidently responded, "we have that confirmation too. In short, all contaminants are from the same source."

"We still don't know how Evalyn died." Jason wasn't happy about the evidence relevant to his case. "Yeah, okay, it looks more and more that she was killed by Declan but just still goddamn guessing. All we know so far is Evalyn and Declan got into some altercation at some point and she was drugged and then had contact with some brown carpet and the Colorado's floor. That's about it. We don't know where or how she was killed or even if she was killed or an accident. And where the hell two different water in her come from?"

*****

In this season, typical early summer of the Bay Area, it was often comfortable during mornings and evenings and a little hot midday to later afternoons.

The three girls' usual Saturday brunch had never failed to hold at Uncle Barry's comfortable corner.

Barry's place was basically open late afternoon till night on Saturdays, so they could have ample time to be there all for themselves.

He served them Barry's special waffle set coming with of course waffles, eggs, bacon/ham, salad, fruit and coffee or tea. After distributing the food, Uncle Barry was seated with them as usual.

Over the deliciousness of Barry's creations, Nora started, "How are you two's lives with those men?" She was the only member of the three musketeers whose life had been work-oriented sans a man. On her new online dating service, her batting average had been far from good. In fact, she couldn't have had anyone who'd made her date more than once. Yeah, meeting the right man was actually very hard, yet her two BFFs had successfully found the finest each. How unfair was that? "Let's hear about Sam."

"They're kinda domestic partners already. He even started paying half the rent to my hired landlord," Uncle Barry answered for his niece since her mouth was full of the waffle. "I'm waiting for the wedding bells."

"Uh-uh," swallowing the food quickly, Alex shook her head, refuting, "I don't think so. He's never said he loved me yet, so no engagement or marriage anytime soon." Her tone was flat and nonchalant.

In fact, although her epiphany had seemed so real about a week ago when they'd made love on the couch, it had turned out she must've had two nightmares that night, that was all, just that the second one had come in an unusual way. He'd seemed unaffected.

Her indifferent mood suddenly worried uncle Barry like hell. He frowned. "He still hasn't said *I love you*?"

"Nope." Alex also looked a bit disappointed. "I wish he had."

"I feel ya." Barry stroked her head lightly. "And I don't know why he hasn't yet."

"Maybe cuz he's still looking for."

"Looking for…?" puzzled, he had to ask her.

"The woman. I mean, his ideal woman. This is his trial phase with me, not definitive on his account." At that, Barry was agape with shock. Seriously?

"I have the same question too," Rae raised her fork. "Jason hasn't said the words, either."

"Er…is it some kind of *thing* that a man is not supposed to say he loves his woman?" Nora asked him. "Two out of three is quite high probability, Barry." She gestured to the other two.

"I didn't know such a stupid ritual's still alive." He cocked his head, thinking. "There was time a man shouldn't say *I love you* to his woman easily cuz it's kinda mushy. Men wanted to be strong and silent, but the fact is: what's the most significant difference being a human from just any other creature of earth?"

"Words," Rae said, of course, that was her thing.

"Precisely," he said. "Words are the sign of intellectuality. Do you think strong without words is really a good thing?"

"No," the three women simultaneously dismissed, with a snort.

"That's silly," Nora objected first. "If you wouldn't say

it aloud, how would we know our men love us? We're not psychic. And if they'd really think not telling *I love you* or staying silent makes them look strong, I'd prefer one of my thick academic books better cuz at least I could read AND throw it at his head to knock him out."

They all laughed at her analogy.

"But," Nora added, "according to my dating site, some men really believe showing his woman how much he cares in actions means saying to her he loves her. What do you two think?"

"Tell me, is this love," Alex started. "When: he always commutes with me. His Charger has more power to control so he can lead me the way downhill in the morning. And it has brighter headlights, he leads me the way during the late night. And he cooks meals whenever at home cuz,"

"You burn water," the three helped her.

"Yes, thank you, and we do dishes together; he washes my entire body in the shower and dries my hair; he cleans the house; he washes my little Leaf; he makes the bed; oh and he massages my feet and,"

"Shut the front door," Nora called out.

"Take the fifth." This one from Rae.

Uncle Barry was covering his eyes with his hand as if he could avoid seeing them intimately living.

"You think that's the same as saying *I love you*?"

"Yes!" the three immediately replied even before she'd finished uttering a whole sentence.

"Sheesh, thanks." Alex frowned.

"You're so loved," Nora said in a dreamy tone.

"But I still want to hear him say the words, though," she added softly, earning a little patting from the other three.

"If that's *I love you*, I don't know my case…" Suddenly Rae became apprehensive. "Jason doesn't commute with me; he never cooks meals; he doesn't clean the house; he doesn't…"

"Excuse me, excuse me." Nora raised her fork, appealing to Barry like she was facing her teacher in grade school.

"Yes, please, go ahead." He pointed at her.

"The statement just given by Ms. Rachel has complete flaws from the beginning, sir."

"I agree." Alex raised her fork too, dropping some waffle crumbs.

"What?" Rae held her hands up.

So, Nora stated, "First of all, of course, Jason doesn't commute with you cuz you don't own a car; you sold your Leaf to Alex. You commute by public transportation to the City (SF) and I know he takes you to the station and picks you up too. Liar, liar, skirt on fire!"

"And he told me you won't let him clean the house when you overnight with him, cuz you like the way you clean. We all know you're a cleaning freak for a long time," Alex reminded her of the truth. "And let me add you cook like a pro. Look, you help Uncle Barry prepare dishes here even now."

"I profoundly appreciate it." Barry bowed to Rae.

"So you guys think Jason…"

"Loves you very much," they replied for her.

"Look, ladies," Barry needed to give them peace of mind, although he didn't like the fact either. "They may not say *I love you*, but when guys say they're committed to you in public, that's a very big deal. Especially those guys like Sam and Jason, they're the epitome of honor, dignity, integrity, of men. I think you can believe them they love you and keep you."

Alex and Rae tilted their heads. But they shrugged and started eating waffles again, after Alex mumbled, "I'll believe you Uncle, if I could be at the altar wearing my wedding dress and Sam's my groom."

CHAPTER 12

A few days later, Jason walked into the BPD. Sam had given him a buzz to visit the Detective Bureau.

Yesterday, he and Rae had visited the hospital in the middle of the night to meet up with Sam and Alex after they'd received the telephone call from the BPD: Their BFF Dr. Nora Reed had been attacked by a predator on her way back from UC Berkeley, but luckily Detective Nick Montoya had been jogging in the vicinity. She'd been saved without serious injuries. Thank god. And they'd heard she'd said now she believed a live, good and strong man like Nick was in fact worth the same as her thick academic books.

As soon as he'd stepped into the office, he met with Lt standing in the hallway, just about finishing talking with a uniform.

"Hey Jase," Lt greeted him, "welcome back."

"I'm glad Nora and Nick are okay. He told me the bastard took out a screwdriver to attack him."

"I thought I was gonna get a heart attack when I first heard it."

"I bet."

"Rae is furious, isn't she?"

"You have no idea. Don't make your woman angry. My new mantra."

Lt snickered, but understood.

"Anyways, thanks for the invitation." Jason lightly cocked his head.

"Oh you're gonna love this. Like I said on the phone, this is relevant to your Evalyn Roberts' case. Nora's attacker's name is Lamont Priebe, a frequent flyer in the police record. He's been attacking women for a long time but couldn't be charged with rape cuz he only committed attempted. He's…you know, a kinky kind; attacking a woman, even unsuccessful, makes him excited, soiling his victim's clothes."

"Nutjob."

"Right? Not exactly rape by the book but it certainly is to me. This time he also attacked Nick with a deadly weapon so we can pin him for that, at least. Anyway he said he knows some info on Evalyn Roberts and wants to cut a deal with us."

"We never cut a deal with any sexual predator."

"No, we never. But our DA planned a scheme and Sam's executing it. We need one more good actor and Sam and I think you're the best. Anyway just get your ass into interrogation room #2; we gonna watch you work in the AV room."

"Yes, sir." He proceeded walking and stopped before reaching IR #2, finding Sam there.

"Yo, Sam,"

"Yo." He glanced at him over his shoulder. And he started reading the note for him, "You heard the suspect mentioned Evalyn Roberts' name?"

"Yeah, and what the hell does he have to do with Evalyn's case? Any connection?"

"No, not in any police record. But he said he'd heard she wasn't drowned in the Lake. Of course, anyone could say something like that, but what if he did know something?"

"And so whatcha gonna do? Lt said DA had a plan and you're playing it."

"She wanna hear what Lamont might know."

"So, what's her plan exactly?"

"Let him talk with the *distinctive* cops, the DA's favorite plot. So, you can be either cop. Which one you wanna be today, good or bad?"

"'Course, bad. Really, truly a badass bad, bad cop."

Sam laughed. "Deal."

Jason took his jacket and tie off and hung it on the back of a chair in the hallway, followed by unbuttoning the waistcoat and three of his shirt's front. He then rolled up his cuffs, showing part of his toned muscles and tattoos.

Carter came with a can of soda and a bag of potato chips. "Yo, bro."

"Ey, Carter. Yo a food vendor today huh?"

"Yeah, hire me if I got kicked outta the BPD."

"Where's Nick at?" looking around, Jason wondered. "He's okay, right?"

"Oh, he's fine. But went to the hospital with Shari," Sam replied.

"Shari?"

"Our SVU detective."

"Ah." Jason got it. Nora was still staying there to check for a light concussion. The BPD must really want this guy punished properly for sexual assault this time.

"Anyways, the Miranda's already recited, and he said he wanna talk. So, let's do it," Sam said.

Carter unlocked the door and stepped in, holding the heavy door for Sam and Jason.

In the AV room, Lt, Captain, other detectives were in front of the monitor and speakers, observing every move and conversation.

"Thanks for waiting, Mr. Priebe." Sam smiled and gave him soda and potato chips.

Eyeing those detectives, Lamont showed a thin smile almost arrogantly in triumph. The detectives knew he'd already believed he'd flashed a get-out-of-jail-free card effectively and he'd be either going home or staying in jail for a few nights.

Right away, Jason grabbed the chair, flipped it exaggeratedly and sat astraddle on it with 'tude. Watching him, Lamont's grin congealed and face grimaced a bit even though he'd tried to keep a poker face. Yeah, Jason was totally one or a hundred up on him, Sam thought, glancing at his buddy.

Sam extended his hand to Lamont and said, "I'm Detective Sgt. Crawford. This is Detective Halls, and that's Detective Sgt. Rivera of the Oakland Police; Ms. Evalyn is his case." Carter offered his hand to shake his, but Jason just lifted his chin for acknowledgement. That also made the suspect uncomfortable, his smirk disappearing.

"I gonna tell you a couple of good facts about Evalyn Roberts," sipping his soda, he began first, "if you cut a deal with me."

"A deal? What're you asking?" Carter cocked his head.

"Well, you either let me go, or book me for misdemeanor."

"It depends," Sam said casually.

"Depends what?" Lamont leaned forward to him over the table.

"Depends your story is credible or not," Sam answered.

"That's not even cutting a deal, Sarge, not fair, uh-uh." Then he leaned back and folded his arms behind the head. "You first and me next."

Suddenly Jason stood up, kicking another empty chair away and slammed his hand on the table in front of Lamont, scaring the hell out of him and yelled, "Shut the fuck up and tell what you know, sonofabitch! You think we're a bunch of idiots? If your goddamn stories are worth listening to, the Berkeley detectives here cut your sorry ass some fucking slack, dig it?"

Big applause filled the AV room, Lt and Captain laughing hard with the other detectives there.

"Sgt. Rivera, please, don't intimidate our witness." Holding up his hands toward him, Sam tried to pacify the detective from the OPD.

Jason sat back in the chair, folding his arms on his chest, squinting at Lamont. But his attention diverted to Sgt. Crawford, Lamont asked, puzzled, "Witness? Me?"

"Uh-huh," Sam nodded, calmly. "I thought that's what you wanna be?"

"Witness?" Okay he didn't get it, did he?

"Mr. Priebe, Ms. Evalyn Roberts' case is homicide. So, if you know something but withhold it from us, you might be charged with homicide as an accomplice."

"Whhaaa?"

"If it happened, Detective Halls, what'd his sentence be in case he's convicted?" Sam tilted his head to Carter and asked.

"Um…lessee…" He scowled as if he was solving the most difficult problem, tapping his pen, while Lamont was almost holding his breath. "Um…well, worst case, Mr. Priebe, you might carry 20 years," Carter told him.

"What? Why? I didn't kill her!"

"Well, in California, murder accomplice isn't lightly taken. Often as heavy as murderer. You see, our state law for aiding and abetting is severe. There are quite many cases where accomplice got long years."

Abruptly Lamont felt awkward. He wanted to use the info as his leverage not a chance to get arrested for murder accomplice. He started rubbing his hands, restlessly.

"But," Sam emphasized the word, "if you turn out to be a witness, then you'd be far from guilty; instead, you'd be appreciated by the prosecutors."

"Okay, okay so how can I be a witness?"

"Just tell us what you know about Ms. Evalyn Roberts. So you'd be a witness," Sam instructed him.

"What about me attacking a woman and the cop last night?" Frowning, he was still talking about the crime he'd committed last night. "Need to go to prison for that, right?"

"Oh I'd leave it as it is, cuz think about it, Mr. Priebe, which is heavier? Just serving a sentence for an assault or murder accomplice?" He opened both his hands palms up, as if they were a balance, weighing the two things. "Mr. Priebe, it's obvious, ain't it?" Smooth Operator Sam.

"Right. Okay, let me be a witness. Okay?" Lamont said insistently.

"Sure, be my guest." Sam lifted his arms welcoming.

"Good, let me start the story when I saw Evalyn and her man near my homie's apartment complex first."

According to Lamont, he and his friend had gone to the same high school Evalyn had. Lamont's buddy's apartment was next to her complex, obviously a different one than her parents had believed she had lived in. They'd often seen her there with a man. They'd looked like they were living together. Also, Lamont and his friend had seen they'd come through the gate in the Toyota Camry and Chevy Colorado on several separate occasions. They hadn't known who he was but he'd looked like G.I. Joe or Mad Max.

After he'd told them most of the information about Evalyn, they'd gone on to grill him with a lot of questions about last night's incident with Dr. Reed. Eventually Lamont confessed everything to them and was booked for attempted rape and various assaults.

The Detective Bureau suddenly became busier. First, they'd had to vet what Lamont had said and made sure he hadn't committed any crime related to Evalyn. Simultaneously they'd called the apartment management office and found out it'd been indeed rented by a man…Mad Max lookalike, but he'd used a fake name and address to rent it. The manager had said it was his staff who had let the rent contract through and the man had paid a year's worth of rent in cash plus a big tip for all the staff there. The detectives had told the manager not to touch anything until they investigated the unit.

The first team with Detective Tess Lou was sent for securing the scene and initial assessment of the apartment.

And the main team, Sam, Jason and Oscar and gang were prepared and right behind them.

*****

Evalyn's rented apartment was in a gated community. There was only one entry and exit point with a gate. And the gate had a security camera. However, the camera system was closed circuit and they only kept its footage for three weeks, not months. So, unfortunately this wouldn't help the police investigation.

The inside of the unit was clean.

"The management said no one came to clean it, but obviously someone did. We didn't find anything. Even in the kitchen. It's cleaned like my grandma's house. So clean that it made me uncomfortable every time I visited her," Oscar was complaining about it to his staff, Nash.

"Hey don't look at me. Not my fault." Nash stuck his head out of the kitchen sink. He was collecting swabs all over the house but so far there were no blood or any biological discharges found. "I bet the suspect cleaned it after the crime. Besides, Lamont said the rumor said Evalyn wasn't drowned in the Lake, right? She might've been killed here, and all we know the Lake was just a body dump."

"Good thinking, but we need evidence to support that," Oscar said.

"Evidence like brown fiber?" Jason came into the kitchen, asking, "Did anyone notice the floor of the hallway was covered with brown carpet?"

"Yup, Jase." Maria Serrano, ten-year veteran CSI mom who'd returned from her maternity leave raised her hand from the bathroom entrance.

"Hey Maria, welcome back." Jason gave her a fist bump.

"Hey, where's Carter at?" she asked. "Haven't seen him. Is he still alive or you and Sam killed him already with a barrage of preaching?"

Jason grinned. "Not yet. He's at the office right now.

We got another set of CCTV footage from a gas station chain just before we left. He decided to stay to check it if we can find Eva's vehicle."

"Holy crap, I heard you guys watching footage like a trillion hours' worth."

"Not me," he answered. "I'm just helping. Sam and his team mostly. Anyways, can you check the carpet?"

"I gonna cut a big piece out of it to bring back to the lab."

"Thanks, Maria." "No problem."

"Hey Jase," he heard Sam call him. "Yeah? Where're you at?"

"Bedroom." He stepped out of the bedroom and waved at Jason. "Take a look at the floor."

"Looks like someone vacuumed." Jason frowned. All the CSI and detectives were wearing shoe covers so that they wouldn't leave their own shoe impressions on the floors or bring in contaminants from outside. Among those unidentifiable faint footmarks left by the CSI personnel, he spotted typical vacuum lines on the carpet.

"CSI already checked the cleaner and it's shining clean. Someone vacuumed and then cleaned the cleaner too," Sam said.

"How considerate, less evidence for us," he spat out.

"But I want you to take a look at those lines there." Squatting on the spot, Sam signaled him. "Look, they were actually under the vacuum lines. See?"

"Whoa." Ducking next to him, Jason was taken aback.

"We're lucky to see this, Jase. The carpet is cut-pile, so it must've left impressions on its surface. Also someone didn't vacuum thoroughly to override those lines."

"You sound like a carpet salesman…, wait, hey, these lines beneath the cleaner's lines were almost like…"

"Dragging."

"Yeah, dragging a person. Made by two heels."

"Yup," Sam added, "this impression angle shows the dragger is definitely taller than the victim."

"I agree. And it's coming from the master bathroom."

They quickly leaped back to their feet. "But CSI already checked the bathroom and couldn't find any blood or bodily fluids."

"And the lines go out in the hallway," Jason told him.

Sam called out, "Hey, Oscar!"

"Hey, there you are." Oscar came back from the front of the apartment. "I just got a call from Tess. Her team had found a bunch of her personal effects in the walk-in closet including her Louis Vuitton purse we were looking for and brought 'em back to the PD, and they'd already scrutinized inside and out, almost ripping it apart figuratively."

"Great news," Sam said.

"No not really, cuz there ain't nothing that tells us about any crime or her boyfriend. Her team only found women's belongings, no men's stuff. She said it's almost like Evalyn tried hard to conceal the identity of her boyfriend. And no, no fingerprints either, if you're wonderin'."

"You know, either way, why hide? Why did her boyfriend need to rent another unit to let her stay?" Sam started. "It might've been not a legit relationship."

"Like adultery," said Oscar.

"Adul…okay, cheating on his wife, you mean."

"Generation gap or religious gap?" Oscar teased Jason.

"Language gap," Jason decided.

"Evalyn's boyfriend had to hide the relationship because he was either A. cheating on his wife, B. against his company's codes or C. a bad dude running away from the law," Sam enumerated.

"Do you think he killed her for that?" Oscar wondered. "I mean, she might've threatened him like she'd expose their relationship to the world if he hadn't given her money or something, something, blah, blah?"

"Possible." Jason nodded.

"Okay, so back to the original reason we called you," Sam had to cut in. "Snap photos of those dragging lines."

"Omigod."

And they realized the lines had continued to the door connected to the garage, although those marks were very faint and sometimes disappeared in certain spots, but they could see the continuation of them. Jason opened the door to the garage and turned the lights on. No car. Nothing, well, almost, here and there, small household items like some laundry detergent bottles, buckets, rags, etcetera. Oscar and four CSI staffers had right away started to check the garage, every nook and cranny.

"This looks more and more Evalyn was killed here and dragged to the garage, out to the Lake," Jason muttered.

"Hey, Jase." Sam turned around and said, "You remember Nora's report on the water in Evalyn's body, right?"

"Yup, her system had two different water sources, Lake Merritt and tap water simultaneously."

"Mm-hmm, and how she did have Lake water in her lungs and all over her system along with tap water? But still not enough Lake water in her system to drown in the Lake?"

"I can think of a couple of damn hypotheses but no friggin' evidence."

"Yeah, I know, Jase, we really ain't got 'nuff evidence."

Folding his arms, placing one foot casually on the wall, Jason stood leaning against the hallway wall, contemplating. Sam, his hands in his pockets, staring at nowhere, propped his shoulder against the wall, pondering.

"Oooh." Maria, passing by, grinned. "The image of *Tall, Dark and Dangerous*." And she took a pic of them. The strong flash hit them. "Oh, Maria," Sam complained.

Looking down at her digital camera image, she giggled. "You guys look sooo posh and…" but her words trailed off; so did her giggle. "Guys, look at this. What d'ya think this crap is?" She showed her digital camera display.

In the image, she pointed at a small sparkle near Jason's foot, on the floor near the wall. She grimaced. "I don't think it's my camera."

"No." They immediately crouched and tried to reach something shimmering in the image. Sam found a tiny part of a string sticking out of the carpet. He took out his Swiss Army knife, putting the knife into the edge of the carpet and wall. Jason was helping him pull the carpet. "Oh shit." Jason picked up a small loose stone, sparkling under the hallway lights.

"That looks like a loose diamond," Sam said to him. He picked it up from Jason's hand, "Yeah, it feels like real. The heaviness and the way it sparkles. Must be a diamond."

Now Sam yanked a palm-sized black velvet bag out of a hidden hole under the carpet near the bottom of the baseboard. He opened it by pulling the drawstrings, while Maria and Jason were observing.

"Damn," Maria muttered and began taking more photos. "I cannot believe what I'm looking at."

There was literally a bagful of seemingly loose diamonds. "Do you think they're real?" she asked Sam.

"Yeah they're heavy. And look at how it sparkles." He took one of them out of the bag and showed it to her. "See, under the light? Let's see…"

"Whatcha doin'?" Jason furrowed his brow.

"Testing," Sam said. He blew his own breath on one of them. "Ah, yeah, it must be real."

"How'd you know? Weight?"

"Well, yeah, diamonds are heavy, but some gems are heavier than diamond. So, I used another method."

"Blow your breath on it and if it's real, diamond blushes?"

Sam snickered, "If the stone's diamond, when it's misted up with human breath, the fog dissipates as quickly as it's fogged. Other diamond lookalikes don't clear up fast. I learned it to investigate the insane jewelry insurance fraud."

"Ah right, I remember. Anyways, let me put 'em in the bag and secure 'em," she said, collecting the one loose diamond and the velvet bag from the detectives.

"Maria, dust the baseboard and wall for fingerprints, will

ya?" Sam asked.

"Yes, sir."

When she was gone, Jason nudged him. "Lucky you; when you buy a diamond ring for Sister Golden Hair, no one would try to con you." In fact, he was half-joking.

But Sam smiled and replied, "I'm gonna do that as soon as we're done with these shitty cases."

Jason spun his head to gaze at him. "You serious?"

"Yeah, 'bout time. I don't wanna lose her."

"Don't you think…um…too soon?" He now was genuinely concerned.

"Nope," he just said one word. Jason glanced at him and just nodded.

Then he changed the subject. "Sam, da ya think this is part of the same damn game? The loose diamond found in the farmhouse and this case?"

"Yeah, I'm suspecting it. All the vics had a connection, more or less. It ain't hard to think it's the friggin' same name of the game."

"You're thinkin' a jewelry-heist-turned-out-to-be-a-fraud in Berkeley also? You guys arrested a couple of fucking idiots and I heard they sang good."

"Yeah, DA cut a deal. They sang like canaries in a late-night show. And we'd found it was actually a quite batshit insane insurance fraud case."

"The store owner bought good insurance for his store and inventory and asked those idiots to rob him, right?"

"Yup. The owner got copious money from his insurance. No one would doubt it was something more shit than robbery if the owner fixed his storefront broken by the robbers and reopened the store again."

"True, ain't it? Then what? I didn't read the BPD report in detail."

So Sam described a little more extensively, "Then the store closed. After the statement of those idiots, we investigated more and found the owner had sold his store and he and the insurance company disappeared. They were in friggin' cahoots. The insurance company was just a damn paper company for a one-time transaction with this dipshit owner. And we'd never know the details, cuz we ain't got evidence, the only name that came up was something like Jallal Renzo."

"I heard neither a search nor arrest warrant got through fast 'nuff," Jason recalled.

"Mm-hmm. By the time we had the warrants signed by a judge, all the major players, like the owner and insurance company, were gone, with all the evidence, jewelry and money, dammit. The judge told us he'd signed them as soon as he'd seen them on his desk. So, we figured some glitch had happened somewhere before they reached the judge. But, still, batshit, man."

"And diamond? What's the connection in Berkeley's fraud case?" Jason asked, returning to the original question.

"Well, cuz the pieces of jewelry that had sat in the showcase for the robbers to steal were friggin' fake copies of real ones. The idiot robbers were told that the real ones were for the owner to sell. The fake jewelry all used fake diamond like crystals or cubic zirconia."

"Okay, so the owner or fake insurance company had the real ones."

"Yup, if you imagine those in loose diamond, the value's off the chart. Jallal Renzo might know more but like I said, we have no fucking right to arrest him without evidence." Sam was furious.

"Huh."

"See the irony? If the search warrant had been issued ASAP, we could've gotten some concrete evidence in our hand and could arrest the real players and know what'd really happened."

"Either case, looks like some batcrap insane professional work to me," Jason suggested.

"Agreed, but need to investigate more; I ain't giving up," Sam said, taking mental stock, and he added, "Jase, I feel something hinky going on, but I just can't finger it. Yeah we did find evidence to connect all the vics in the morgue, but the truth is just that, connected our vics; no reasons why. They're all participants in a jewelry heist or fraud? Kinda like we're missing something big. Feel me?"

"Yeah." They were looking at the case as if through a frosted windowpane to elucidate what was going on inside, only knowing something evil.

"Like I said, we need more evidence anyways, Jase. Let's not interpret just yet."

"I concur. BTW anything about your John Doe? No new leads?"

"Nope. No one even claimed his body. Alex's familial DNA search is only our hope."

"Yo, don't you friggin' dare quote *Star Wars*," Jason warned him.

"Which one?" Sam pretended he didn't know.

"That one goes…something like… *You're my only hope*…that one and you know it, dammit."

"Ah lady Rae. You watched it together recently."

"Yeah, so?" He dared not say they'd ended up making love on the couch.

"Nothing." But Sam beamed at him, waggling his brows. Yeah, he knew.

"Smack the damn smile off your face." Jason showed his fist and Sam looked horrified.

Oscar appeared at the doorstep to the garage, calling the detectives, "You screwballs, come and take a look at this."

Both of them ran down to the garage.

CSI still working on gathering evidence, "I think these're significant," Oscar said and showed a bucket that had already been carefully wrapped in a big plastic bag. Sam and Jason looked into it. There was a small amount of water inside.

"That water ain't just tap water, fellas. Some biological material in it."

"Biological material…in what way?" Jason asked, hope in his tone.

"Not sure yet, sorry; but that means the water possibly contains human body fluids."

"Just some little creatures got into the bucket cuz it ain't closed with a lid? Or maybe rain got in?"

"Well Jason, then answer me. Why my swabs changed color?"

"Your swabs change color when they contact either blood or other body fluid."

"Uh-huh. And when'd we have rain? I wonder where you're at recently. Do you even live in the Bay Area now? It's early summer. It ain't frigging raining here in summers. Aaaaand the bucket's been in the garage for a long time under the utility desk. Can't you see the bucket impression in the dust, Sgt. Rivera? Aaaaand in case you're wondering, my swabs won't change color by dust."

"Okay, point taken. My bad."

But suddenly a detective instinct hit Sam. "Oscar, do me a favor."

"Sure, anything," Oscar quickly answered, noting Sarge had something important to know. "What you need?"

"Go back to the bathroom, will ya? I know you did like licking it all, but this time, concentrate on any places like a little dip or pocket or whatever you'd call it might collect water. Like the corner of the outside of the tub. And collect any swabs or water drops. ASAP please."

"Sure. What're you thinkin' tho?" Oscar cocked his head.

"I'm wondering if you can find any remnant of Lake water in the bathroom."

Jason's eyes glared. But he didn't say anything before evidence turned up.

"Alright. Nash," he called him, "you heard Sarge talk. Go back to the bathroom now and start collecting. Gonna be right behind you."

"Yes, sir." Nash disappeared inside with his kit.

But Oscar turned to the detectives. "Before I go…we got tire marks in the dirt left on the garage floor and took photos, but they look eerily similar to those marks in the photos taken by hazmat outside the farmhouse. I'll send the photo to our expert again but…"

"Do you think they belong to a mid-size sedan or truck or…"

"Definitely truck," Oscar asserted immediately. "They're too wide for a sedan, but let's wait until our expert has an answer."

CHAPTER 13

It'd taken another week to get good news from their experts and scientists. But early one morning, just about when Lt came into his office, it had started with CSI calling him with the lab result for the brown fiber. Lt heard the exciting news that the brown carpet fiber in the hallway of the apartment and the fiber on Evalyn's dress were a match. That meant she'd possibly been dragged on that brown carpet and her dress had picked up the fiber. The carpet maker had also confirmed both fibers were their products. The construction and interior design companies which had built the apartment complex had also verified they had installed the carpet from that maker and the product numbers were also a match. The evidence was conclusive.

Soon after that, he received another call from their CSI again reporting that the vehicle expert had confirmed the tire marks from the dirt in the garage were identical to the ones outside the farmhouse. Chevrolet had also corroborated those tires had been one of their choices for the Colorado. Since Evalyn's boyfriend had been seen driving the truck by Lamont and his friend, he must have owned it at that point.

The office of the Detective Bureau had become more

invigorated, when Dr. Alex had called Lt right after the CSI phone calls.

He gathered all the detectives in the conference room again and placed his phone down on the table. "Okay, Dr. Alex, thank you for waiting."

"Yes, Lt," her sweet yet stern voice came out of the phone speaker. Sam needed to hide his grin.

"About the liquid in the bucket found in the garage and the tiny amount from the bathroom collected by your CSI, I also consulted Dr. Reed…"

"Is she already working? Is she okay now?" Lt scowled, concerned.

"Yes, thank you. She said she preferred working."

"I see." Lt sighed, relieved.

"Let me proceed with the results. First of all, the liquid in the bucket and minuscule amount from the bathroom are a match, containing the water of Lake Merritt and the East Bay tap water, and Evalyn's DNA."

Alex heard some noises through the phone. Must be the detectives.

"Dr. Alex, so her blood was in both samples, that's what you mean by her DNA?" Lt asked.

"It turned out to be from three different types, her blood cells, mucus from her nasal cavity and a small amount of saliva. And I just sent the report to your desk and to the OPD."

"Thank you," Lt went on, "Do you think the two different waters, Lake water and the tap water, and her DNA got into the bucket about the same time?"

"Yes. It's usually hard to say but since chlorine in the tap water prevented bacteria or other microbes from contaminating the water in the bucket, it should be the same time."

"I see. Well, Dr. Alex, is it safe to say her blood, nasal mucus and saliva got into the bucket at the same time?"

When Lt asked that question, the detectives went silent almost eerily as if everyone forgot how to breathe.

"Yes, it is. From the level of degradation of cells, we can say all three, her blood, mucus and saliva came into the sample simultaneously."

At this moment, the detectives knew how Evalyn had been killed.

The BPD and OPD had just changed Evalyn's case to premeditated murder: So far, they knew that allegedly she'd been injected with the drugs and dragged on the carpet and drowned, possibly in the bathroom. The killer had collected water from Lake Merritt and used it as the murder weapon to confound the investigation hoping they'd believe she'd drowned in the Lake.

Still not enough evidence to make a statement who'd killed and dumped her, quite yet.

Soon after, a witness came forward on the thrift store robbery.

The store owner nearby had seen the white Chevy Colorado sitting in the back street. And two people had gotten out of the truck and disappeared into the store. Soon they had driven off with the bundles of clothes. He ID'd Declan as one of them. He couldn't have seen the other well.

*****

Late that afternoon, Carter's eyes were still glued to the monitor running the footage from the gas station chain's surveillance cameras. He'd figured they would be likely to have captured images of either the Camry or the Colorado if he'd chosen the gas station near the apartment rented for her. He'd been dedicating his day to search for those vehicles extensively. Sam, Jason and Nick had gone to canvass the area near the apartment complex. Sam had returned to bring him lunch. Nice boss. So, he'd had a sandwich and coke at his desk, staring at the screen.

His desk phone rang.

"Detective Halls," he answered half-heartedly, still his eyes on the footage. "Uh-huh..." While he was listening to the caller talk, his face abruptly changed and he hit the pause button of the monitor. "Wait, excuse me, could you repeat it again? Let me take notes too." He scoured his desk for a pen and took out his notebook. "Okay, let's start from the beginning. Your lodge name is...*El Capitan Lodge* in Yosemite. Okay, and you're... Mr. H. Walt... owner...yes, sir..."

The owner of *El Capitan Lodge* had said one of his employees, who'd left the lodge just before Jason had visited there had stayed with her mother and she'd said she'd remembered seeing a white truck, 2008 Chevy Colorado and two passengers. And she was willing to come to the BPD for an interview a few days later.

His face went blank for a while after he hung up the phone.

Wow.

Carter quickly gained his wits and exhaled. Okay, chill. Call his boss. Yeah. He speed-dialed Sam.

The three detectives had come back to the office empty-handed from canvassing the neighbors. So, Carter's big score was really helpful to ease their tired bones. When they were striding down the hallway to their office, they spotted CSI Oscar was talking to Lt.

Lt waved at them. "Got awesome news."

"What happened today?" Jason wondered.

"Maybe some mysterious power of the universe?" Nick tried.

"You boys, listen," Sam said, shaking his head. "We've been working and gathering evidence since about a month ago. So if you think of the time span, it's about time many results naturally come back to us. Statistically speaking, two weeks are an average length of the waiting period if not backlogged or sent out to an outside lab," ever-realistic down-to-earth Detective Crawford expounded impassively.

"You no fun." Jason didn't wait for him to dispute it and walked away to Lt. "So, what's the awesome news?"

Lt looked at Oscar, so he opened his mouth, "We ID'd Declan's left palmprint on the bucket."

"Well, if he visited the apartment, we found his fingerprints all over, right?"

"Nicky, we never found his fingerprints anywhere in the apartment except the baseboard where Sam and Jason found the diamond. Read the newest report, kiddo." Oscar scowled at him. "Anyways," he went on, gesturing what he meant, "he must've worn a latex glove on his left hand, usually both hands but we don't have evidence for that…but we know he wore one on his left, cuz we saw the latex's distinctive impression on the bucket too; and somehow the left latex got a little rolled up to expose the base of the left thumb and part of the center palm and the bottom of the left little finger, and it created the palmprint on the *rim*."

"Rim. Rim of the bucket! That's only possible when you placed your hand on the rim to hold the bucket down…"

"Now you're talkin', kiddo." Oscar grinned at Nick.

The rookie detective could imagine where Declan's right hand might've been when his left hand had been on the rim pushing the bucket down. "My god…" His right hand could've been holding down Evalyn's head…

"Goodness friggin' gracious." Carter also got stunned by the news when the three had told him. "So, Declan only visited her to kill and hide the diamonds?"

"Well, possible but not quite there yet for murder," Jason calmly stated.

"Why, Jase?" Carter was irritated a bit with his disagreement. "What else do we need to put the murder on that bastard?"

"Given that he'd killed her in that manner, we still ain't

got a damn connection that bastard dumped her body that night. We gotta get something even suggesting that as circumstantial evidence."

"Ugh…" Carter sagged in the chair. "You're right, Jason. We need that. Dammit."

*****

Alex's work was as busy as usual since she'd always been busy, wherever she'd been.

Taking care of all of Alameda County's unfortunate bodies every day, which was her main job, was quite a lot. In addition to that, now she was searching for John Doe's ancestor. That didn't hinder her from doing her own study. Nothing was making her life less hectic. Her habit of being a workaholic seemed still well and alive.

However, her life at home was far from hectic. Peaceful and fun, thanks to very dedicated partner Sam Crawford. He was still leading her way home even though the daylight was long and she could see the winding roads without headlights. Even when she'd complained she wasn't a kid, he hadn't given a damn about it. His woman's safety was always a priority to him no matter who'd said what. Then, he enjoyed cooking meals every night for two as long as he could get home that evening. Sometimes he had to work the night shift, or overnight to take care of his cases. If it happened, she just went to Uncle Barry's place to have a late dinner.

She'd started calling him 'my chef' when he was cooking at home, while she was sitting at the island watching him cook, sipping her wine or beer. His talent as a chef was high quality. She'd often told him he could quit being a detective anytime if he'd like to be a chef. He'd laughed and said, "I'm a chef exclusively for you." All women of the world would melt if their partner would say something like that.

They'd established their set routine: to have dinner, clean up, watch movies or go to the movies or gym or jog, foot massage by him, take a shower together, make love, or vice versa, sleep, make love again next morning followed by taking a shower and breakfast and off to work. Her only morning routine had been making them coffee, of course, for drinking in the morning, and preparing their smiley thermoses to take to their offices.

On that evening, they were sleeping, sated and pleasantly tired from their lovemaking. She was on her belly, one hand under the pillow, the other folded. Her golden hair was all over her face and the pillow, almost like she was wearing a golden veil; he was on his side, facing her, one arm under his head, the other stretched out to touch her bare butt possessively.

The huge windowpanes let the lights from the streetlamps and any celestial objects come through reaching inside, illuminating everything in the room. However, due to another slightly misty evening, the light from outside was softened as if it was behind white lace curtains. It was very noiseless outside, only their slow rhythms of breathing. And the faint humming of her laptop dedicated to run her program 24/7 to find familial DNA of their John Doe, a.k.a. the fallen-from-the-sky guy. It sat on the desk just below the big window, facing her, quietly processing, even during the night-mode, it wouldn't stop running.

In the dead of night, it abruptly started bleeping. It wasn't loud since she'd set it low in case it happened in the middle of the night…and she'd been right. Even though the sounds weren't loud, it was still high enough volume to wake her up. Well, hello, research was her life. Duh.

She immediately got up and quickly reached the desk and hit the mute button so that she wouldn't wake him up. Leaning over her laptop, her eyes were swiftly running through the display, reading what it said and why it bleeped.

Sam was awake as soon as she'd gotten up, just gazing at his woman seriously working on her program. She'd been bringing her computer home every single evening since she'd needed to babysit the laptop while it was running an enormous amount of data. He couldn't even guess how many people had emigrated back in the 1800s. Jeezus.

But his contemplation was soon distracted by her figure under the pale lights coming from outside through the panes. All the lights were as if directed at her hair. The golden threads were collecting every bit of glimmer, shining brighter. He felt he was looking at a meteor shower, billions of shooting stars falling onto him. One of them might be his wishing star. His wish that someday he'd meet her again had been granted. He kept gazing upon her, emotions overwhelming. She was his starry heaven. She was his universe. He loved her more than life itself. He'd never let her go again.

"Come back here," he called her with his hoarse voice.

"Just a sec. This is important." She was scrolling a cursor up and down, her eyes chasing wordings.

What else would be more important than holding his woman in his arms? Besides, look at her. Her bare back was exposed from the golden cascade, and her tiny waist was connected to a cute butt that extended down to become long, straight legs, and he knew he could bury himself where her two legs met and feel at home and safe.

He strode hastily; with only a few steps, he reached her and wrapped his arms around her from behind, enveloping her completely. He nuzzled her bundles of golden silk and her neck, licking it.

She immediately reacted and sighed, leaning against him. His pulsating hard shaft pressing her butt, her skin was cool to touch, feeling so good. "Ah…Alex…"

He could hear her breath pick up speed, the sounds of life that still reminded him of the night when he'd covered her body.

"Bend over." One word from him, she was transfixed. She'd been trapped in his enchantment, ever since they'd first met. He was still the same man, same good man, and she was fortunate to have met him again. And she'd realized his magic was in fact care, honor and integrity. She couldn't help loving him. Even if he hadn't loved, didn't love her. Sad, but still it was worth knowing this man.

He touched her. She was all wet again and ready for him.

She bent over on the desk, holding it like her life depended on it. He entered her from behind gingerly but steadily, once changing the angle a little, and the last strong push sheathing himself to the hilt. He heard she exhaled, relaxed. "Alex, look up."

She looked up and saw them in the reflection from the panes. The two looked fused, her back and his front, as one. He started moving. She was feeling ecstatic, but she couldn't hold on to him. She wanted to gaze at his warm eyes. She wanted to wrap her arms around his neck, his body and touch his scars on his back. They were not stigma; they were the symbol of honor.

When they hit the climax, utterly come undone, he was afraid that she might collapse on the floor. So, he put forth all his strength to scoop her up and brought her into the bed. She cuddled up to him in his arms. He held her tightly.

So peaceful. Safe. No pressure, no fear.

Home. He was home with her. At last. *I look at you…and I'm home.*

"Alex," he whispered in her hair.

"Mmm?" She was still drowsy from the afterglow.

"I love you."

There. It'd finally come out so naturally. He hadn't even thought not to say or to say it.

He'd let himself say the phrase. It was the truth. He'd say it to her over and over again.

There was a long moment that she held her breath.

In fact, he wasn't worried if she loved him, since he knew she did and probably she had. He felt it every single day. And he knew both were holding each other's heart to make it whole.

Maybe timing. Maybe she didn't know he'd loved her since they'd met, a long time ago.

But he couldn't have held back anymore. He knew she

was the love of his life.

He gently tipped her face up to see him. Tears were welling up in her eyes. The glistening made her eye color more translucent, mesmerizing him.

She wondered someday she wouldn't have nightmares at all, in which he still sacrificed himself that made her heart break every single time?

Tears rolling down her cheek because he'd finally said he loved her, because he still sacrificed himself in her dreams.

As if he'd known his love would absorb her pain and sorrow, he said, "I'll soothe you all night, sweetheart." And he kissed her tears off.

"Alex, I'm in love with you," he said, this time, looking into her eyes, articulately.

She smiled and said, "Sam, I'm in love with you too. I've been in love with you since I met you."

"*You had me at hello*?" he asked.

She smiled. "Yes, you did."

He brushed his lips on hers, drawing a light moan from her. "You know what?" he murmured on her lips, "I've been in love with you since I met you."

Her smile brilliant, she hurled herself at him, wrapping her arms around his neck. "I'm so happy to hear that."

As long as he loved her now, it was okay. Because she wanted him to love her of now, not of ten years ago. That was the main reason she hadn't told him she was his Connie.

Then she suddenly remembered and got up, startling him. "What the…?"

"My god, I totally forgot about it." She placed both her hands on her cheeks.

"What, babe?" His eyes full of concern, he grimaced.

"Oh no, no, you should be happy. I was standing in front of my laptop cuz it bleeped, before…" and she blushed.

"Before I fucked you?" Now his eyes darkened.

"Sam, watch your language."

"I rather fuck than watch."

"Sam."

"Okay, my bad. My apologies. So you were saying…?"

"I found his ancestor."

"Whoa, congratulations! So, we can get his kin soon."

She shook her head. "Not really. You know why right?"

"Um…okay, er…Dr. Alex, could you kindly explain to your sex-headed asinine boyfriend what's really going on?"

She chuckled and started, "The ancestor who was just found was his kin from Ireland in the 1800s."

"Oh, goodness fucking gracious."

"Sam."

"Um…I'm sorry."

She opened the nightstand drawer and took out a small empty box. And she put it under his nose.

"What's this?"

"Every time you use an F-bomb or S-word, you pay."

"Huh?"

"I'm not saying you shouldn't use the words ever, since many seem to use them on a daily basis. But at least, I want you to try not to use the words with me. Okay?"

"How much?"

"A buck a word."

"That's a rip-off."

"Sam."

"Okay, okay. My bad, again. I'm gonna pay, okay?" He flashed a smile and then became serious. "So, my understanding of your program is you found the first ancestor and now coming down toward recent years…but what are the criteria or denominators to decide which way to go? The program must have some algorithm to make a decision each time, right?"

"Yes, you're right. Now my program runs under the algorithm called 'proximity'."

"Wait, what exactly does 'proximity' mean in your program?"

"Any proximity to possible targets. For instance, proximity includes human habits, laws, policies, etcetera, from birth to death. But the easiest ones are where they were born and buried and where persons had resided."

"You mean, residential addresses and birth and death certificates are good specifications, then."

"Yes, you're correct. Any tangible evidence of life could show the identity of a person."

"Thank you for working hard for the BPD."

"Oh, you're welcome." She smiled. "Let's sleep for a while. We still have time till dawn."

"Great idea."

He pulled the cover over them. She snuggled up to him. He cocooned her in his arms.

CHAPTER 14

His phone on the nightstand buzzed when they were deep in sleep. But he was accustomed to that kind of abrupt wakeup call. His body reacted without him thinking. He snatched his phone and with one glance understood who it was from and answered, "Yeah, Carter. It's not even 4:00 and why're you at the PD? You ain't graveyard. Randy's supposed to… What? Where?"

His voice rising, he eyed Alex, stirring and waking. He tsked to himself. He hadn't wanted to wake her up. She blinked her eyes. And she was just observing him carefully.

"Alright, alright, calm down, Carter. Will be there in twenty." He hung up.

"You're going," she said.

"Yeah. Carter's been working on the footage all day and night and he said he found something."

"Okay, I'll make some coffee."

"Thanks." He kissed her lips tenderly but couldn't help but linger for a while.

Then, almost jumping up, he got out of the bed, trotted off to the master bathroom.

She also got up, pulling her robe from the foot of the bed. She went downstairs to make coffee for him.

He'd finished taking a shower in a flash, changed into his suit and tie.

"Here." She handed over coffee in his mug. "It's hot."

"Thanks," he said and quickly drank it up.

"Alright. Gotta go." Putting down his cup on the counter, he pulled her into his arms. "I cannot lead your way to the Coroner's today."

"I'll be fine." And she pushed her smiley thermos onto his chest.

The yellow smiley was staring at him smiling literally. His lips curved.

He touched her cheek. "Stay safe, love."

"I will, you stay safe, darling."

"It's my priority."

And he kissed her.

Yeah, he was completely, madly, hopelessly in love with her.

He gave Jason a buzz on his way to the BPD. He didn't know if Jason was sleeping alone tonight, but he must let him know about the news.

"Sorry man, but Carter found evidence for your case. Can you come?"

"No problem. It's my case and you guys are such huge help. Appreciate that. I'm on my way."

Hmm…the tone had been calm and very formal English dialogue, no vulgar wording. Must've been with his lady. When a man had a relationship with a woman with a college degree in English literature, his English must improve too. Oh wait, since Alex and Rae were BFFs, Jason must also pay a fine into a little box for saying a swearword or two? Sam had to smile.

*****

"Hey, Carter," Sam called out.

He was in the breakroom having a breakfast burrito and

coffee. It must've been from *Blue Café*. Tony the daytime manager always delivered their food to the BPD when they needed. God bless *Blue Café* and Tony.

Carter was in a wrinkled shirt and pants, no tie, along with his hair disheveled, eyes bloodshot, meaning he'd been staring at the monitor all night long. He looked rumpled but still energetic and sharp. Such determination and persistence. Those were very significant traits to be a good detective. And now it looked like his effort had paid off.

"Go home and get some rest or at least wash up and change."

"I will, after I show you kiddos a Christmas present from Santa in summer."

"You found a possible image of Declan, you said?"

"Yup. Let's watch it together. Where's Jason? He's coming? I know Nick is here already."

"Here, homie." Jason stuck his head into the room from the open door.

"Okay, then." Finishing up his burrito, Carter stood up.

Carter in the center, the other three detectives, Sam, Jason and Nick sat around his desk.

He started to control the desktop. "Declan appears around 1:53am that Sunday."

"Eva was killed around 1am," Jason muttered in a very low voice. Sam could feel his fury reverberating in the air around them. Well, the feeling was mutual. All the male detectives couldn't shake off the notion what if it was their mother, sister, daughter, wife, or girlfriend.

Especially Carter. He had a sister, Judy. He often trash-talked about her, but they were very close and cared about each other. And her age was about the same as Evalyn's. No wonder he'd stayed all night to scour the footage continuously for even a piece of an image of Declan or Evalyn's vehicle.

"Good work, Carter, good work," Sam said, patting his shoulder.

Jason seconded, "I agree. Thanks, homeboy."

Carter blinked his eyes several times. "You know, I just cannot get rid of the feeling what if it was my sister."

Then, he stopped the footage. "Okay so I go slo-mo from here, cuz this is about 1:50."

The camera was installed almost overhead with a tilted angle to observe cars and passengers before their customers drove out of the gas station parking lot. The images were very clearly recorded in HD. When a white Chevy Colorado approached from the front, it looked a lot like the truck they were looking for. "There. That's our truck. Wait for it." Then the young guy parked the truck in front of the camera and got out of the truck and stretched his body, rolling his head around, as if he'd done some kind of labor beforehand. "That's him." Carter paused the image.

The uncanny air had started filling the office. Had he just dragged Evalyn, killed her and carried her body?

The detectives now holding their breaths almost felt like they were looking at something very sinister, a devil on the move.

"Sonofabitch," Jason finally swore. Everyone could recognize the man standing by the white truck was Declan Kosarek at first glance. They also noticed his outfit was exactly the same one he was in when he'd been found in Evalyn's car trunk.

"So, he was killed after this before he had a chance to change clothes," Sam said. "Okay Carter, slo-mo."

He bobbed his head and started to run the image slo-mo again.

Declan got back into the driver's seat, keeping the door wide open, and he lowered the passenger seat window all the way. Possibly he wanted the air inside the truck to flow? Then, he took out a pack of cigarettes, pulled out one, put it between his lips. Next he took out a cigarette lighter from a pocket and he lit it for the cigarette. Carter paused the recoding and froze the scene.

"Holy shit!" Nick jumped off the chair first, placing his

palm on his forehead.

They were all paralyzed for an instant.

When he lit the lighter, the glow from the flame lightened the inside of the truck faintly.

And they saw a bundle of something looking familiar on the floor in the back seat.

"Carter, zoom in," Sam ordered.

"Yup."

Thank god for HD. The bundle they spotted was in fact part of a woman's dress and it was the same color and pattern of the one that Evalyn had worn when she'd been found in Lake Merritt.

It appeared to them that her body had been on the floor.

"On the way to dump job," Jason said. "Finally pinned him." He fist bumped with the rest.

"We also got quite curious notions from him." Sam was actually taking notes.

"What d'you mean?" Jason asked.

"Jase, we all saw him open the window and the door to smoke. When many people who drive want to smoke, they often open the driver's window. I hardly ever seen someone open the passenger side window all way down and driver's door full open."

"Huh," Jason understood what he meant. "The truck may not be his."

"Ahhh…" It seemed to hit the young detectives, Carter and Nick at the same time.

"He's nineteen, reckless, felon," Sam started to explain. "I read the report from Oscar about Declan's apartment. Our CSI ripped it open inside and out and they said it was awful. Friggin' filthy, messy and dangerous with used needles, syringes, drugs and a lot of cigarette butts and ashes in multiple ashtrays…anyways, do you think he cared if the nicotine color or smell stayed inside his damn truck? I don't friggin' think so. So, the truck might be someone else's."

"Her boyfriend G.I. Joe owns one," Carter remembered.

"That's one possibility. Also, I realized the apartment

where Evalyn had stayed had no stains or smell from cigarettes. In other words, heavy-smoker Declan hadn't stayed there long. Maybe never, we couldn't find any sign of a smoker or his fingerprints except one place, remember?"

"The possibility that he might've visited the apartment to kill her looks much more plausible," Jason said. "Maybe he hid the goddamn loose diamonds when he killed her."

"Or when he'd tried to hide the diamonds, she'd witnessed it and he'd killed her," Sam said.

"So, either he himself wanted to kill her or he was asked to kill her, possibly by her boyfriend since he allegedly used the boyfriend's Colorado," Jason suggested.

"We'll never know, will we?" Nick's voice was gloomy. "Declan's dead as a doornail. We cannot ask him."

"Nicky, sometimes dead bodies talk," Carter softly said. "We can study Declan's body again and find his killer and ask him why he killed him and shoved him in Evalyn's vehicle trunk. I feel his killer and Declan and Eva had some kind of connection."

"Good thinkin' Carter," Sam said, and he turned to Jason. "Okay so what d'you wanna do? It's your case. You ain't wanna close it yet, right?"

"Not yet, homie. First, I wanna hear from the ex-employee of the lodge in Yosemite. And we gotta find her boyfriend. And about Eva's diamond earrings. Where the hell they from and what for?"

Nodding at his remark, Sam stated, "Jase, I still feel like we're chasing something more than two cases…"

"Sure, of course, we gotta ID John Doe and Eva's boyfriend and Declan's killer…"

"Um…right. But what I mean is, like you said, we're still chasing multiple cases, but I feel like not seeing the forest for the trees, feel me?"

"Explain." Jason leaned toward him in his chair, his brow furrowed intensely.

Sam had to ponder for a short time. "Look, we got

basically three stiffs, starting from our John Doe, a.k.a. the fallen-from-the-sky guy, your Eva, and Declan, three cases in a week. We found they got some weird connections aside from the poisons…"

"Diamonds," Jason instantly answered. Carter and Nick glanced at each other.

"Mm-hmm," Sam went on, "what if all those cases and people are the trees? What if the diamonds we found are actually pointing to the forest?"

"Huh."

"Jase, you know Chimera?"

"A mythological hybrid monster, right? With small parts of various different animals. I think the main body's a lion or somethin'."

"Right. And we're looking at more or less smaller body parts of a Chimera."

"Ah… A good analogy. What'd Lt say about the diamonds? Did he get a response back from the Gemological people?" Jason asked.

"Not yet. Hopefully soon. Lt said he'd call them again today. So, stick around."

"Okay. Oh, what about Eva's phone? You found one in the purse, right?"

"Yeah, but that had nothing special on it. We even got the phone record from her carrier but she obviously used that phone for only conversations between parents, colleagues, her bank, you know, all those legit social relationships. No info about her boyfriend. Declan's phone too. Probably they used burner phones. And those are missing."

"Sammy, if Evalyn had it with her and Declan had dumped her in the Lake, the phone would never be found."

"I concur," Sam sighed.

The same day, as Jason had awaited, Aaron, one of the young detectives interviewed an ex-employee of the lodge in Yosemite with Lt sitting in as a supervisor.

All the detectives were watching the monitor in their AV room.

The witness, Joanie Gaffey, had met Evalyn Roberts and her boyfriend when she'd been still working at the lodge in the beginning of April, the first day they'd opened the lodge for this year.

They had stayed for a weekend under the pseudonyms, Mr. & Mrs. John Smith. Since the lodge was a cash-only business, they hadn't had any card record of them.

Ms. Gaffey said Evalyn had been very pretty and her boyfriend had looked very tough but tried to protect her all the time. However, he hadn't suppressed her or been controlling, rather he'd let her do whatever she'd liked to freely. She described him as 6'2" Caucasian man with brown hair, blue eyes Mad Max look-alike. They'd disliked smoke since Evalyn had been allergic to cigarettes and he had simply hated the smell. Ms. Gaffey said she'd actually talked with Evalyn quite a few times and she'd been very happy with him. So, she'd believed they'd been really in love with each other. Also she mentioned that the boyfriend had driven a 2008 white Chevy Colorado. On one occasion, she'd found out Evalyn had liked El Capitan from the balcony very much so he'd snapped the photo and he'd promised to create a framed photo for her.

"Oh shit." In the AV room, Sam cursed as soon as he'd heard what Ms. Gaffey had said about the photo of El Capitan.

He looked at Jason with keen eyes and asked, "When you asked Rae's friend to analyze the photo, did he take the photo out of the frame?"

"No, he didn't need to. And I didn't think of doing it either, cuz the frame glass's so frigging thin and delicate we didn't wanna break it."

Sam quickly grabbed his phone and called CSI. The other detectives were dumbfounded and just staring at him. Except Jason. He just realized what Sam was on to.

"Hey Oscar, you have Evalyn's El Capitan photo with

you now? You do? Oh great. Have you taken it out of the frame before? No? Oh okay, yeah, try not to break the glass, can you take it out from the frame now? Yeah, good. I'll wait…."

"What the hell are you doin'?" Carter asked.

"Wait till Oscar finishes his job," Sam replied. And he got back on the phone. "Okay, thanks, and any writing on the back? Can you read it for me? *Dearest my love Eva…*," Sam was dashing off the note in his notebook while repeating Oscar's words. "*I'm always your El Capitan. I love you and always will…*name? No name? No initial? Just *XO*? Oh shit. Okay, can you send me the image to my phone? Yeah, I didn't know that either." Sam hung up his phone and exhaled, "Dammit."

After Ms. Gaffey had positively ID'd Evalyn, all the detectives gathered in the meeting room and they discussed Evalyn's case from the beginning. They reevaluated the possibility of Evalyn's boyfriend being her killer: First, the boyfriend rented the unit for a year in cash for her. It was an expensive apartment to rent. And cash wouldn't be refunded more than half even if he'd cancel it. Thus, he wouldn't likely have done it if he'd planned to kill her soon. Second, he'd been really in love with her according to the statement by Ms. Gaffey and the writing on the back of the photo. Their Yosemite trip had been in the beginning of April and she'd been killed in mid-April. After all, there was no evidence to support he'd killed her.

Thus, the detectives had decided her boyfriend was unlikely to be her killer.

Sam and Jason knew if they'd build a certain hypothesis and it had so many conditions to prove beyond what the evidence provided for, then their hypothesis itself must have a flaw, a.k.a. *Occam's Razor*.

They'd consequently come to determine that Declan was the killer based on their findings. And they had enough circumstantial evidence to arrest and charge him with murder, if he was still alive. Too bad.

But there was one thing that had stuck like an old splinter in a finger… "Lt, I really need to discuss one thing I just cannot ignore," he raised his hand and called out to him.

"Go ahead, Sam."

"I think Declan and Evalyn's boyfriend knew each other, even John Doe too. John Doe and Declan had a connection in the farmhouse with a diamond. And everywhere Declan went, we saw Chevy Colorado, highly likely her boyfriend's truck. And everywhere we found Declan's movement, we found diamonds, like in the farmhouse and Evalyn's rented apartment and that's also where her boyfriend stayed with her. I think they might be in some kind of jewelry or diamond business."

"Declan was using her boyfriend's truck even when he went to dump his girlfriend's body. That tells us they must be so close that it was natural to borrow the truck all the time…" Lt also pitched in.

"Yes, exactly my point," and Sam continued, "And one more thing, Lt. Jason and I feel like we're looking at the trees and missing the forest. Like looking at smaller body parts of a Chimera."

"Chimera, huh?" said Lt. "That's a very interesting implication. The problem is we have no evidence we had a diamond heist involved with those three men anywhere in the Bay Area."

"Yeah, I know. Understand. But it may not be just stealing loose diamonds from the jewelers. Maybe more complex. Like our Berkeley jewelry insurance fraud. Isn't it another twisted scheme for the suspect and cohorts to steal diamonds?" Sam sighed, "Okay, I know we didn't get 'nuff evidence cuz our warrants had a snag and we lost chances to get evidence. But can't it be seen as possible diamond-related crime since it's too intricate and meticulous to be a regular crime?"

Lt thought, *Sam thinks like I do.* But the bottom line: they didn't have evidence. "I get it, Sam. But like you said yourself, we're lacking evidence to continue the investigation. I know you're frustrated, hell, so am I. Just because these goddamn warrants hadn't gone through fast 'nuff, we'd lost almost all evidence, at least we got those two idiot robbers, thank goodness."

Then an idea fell into Lt's mind. If Sam and he were right, they must've had a string of diamond related crimes somewhere, especially in California, since they'd had a suspicious one in Berkeley. And the truth was no matter what they didn't have, all the evidence they'd gathered on John Doe, Declan, the farmhouse, and Evalyn's hidden apartment were still the facts. Then, where had they come from? He must check statewide.

And the same day, one of the uniform officers had brought in a male construction worker residing in Berkeley.

The uniform had said he'd come in and asked for a detective working on John Doe, a.k.a. the fallen-from-the-sky guy.

Sam and Carter had volunteered to see the man in the small meeting room.

"I'm Detective Sgt. Crawford and this is Detective Halls. Uniform officer told us your name is Mr. Martin Lopes and showed him your driver's license."

He bobbled his head nervously, crumpling his hat on the table.

"Mr. Lopes, you're okay in here. No matter what you'd say, you'll never be arrested or detained, okay?"

"Yes, Sgt."

"So, you said you have some information on John Doe, who was found below the University overpass in mid-April. You saw him fall?"

"No, um…" he muttered incoherently at first but soon decisively started, "That morning 7:20-ish, I was driving on University to get to the overpass ramp. But my lane was blocked by a white Chevy Colorado parking in the far right lane just before the ramp and…" Lopes took a breath. "Then, suddenly the passenger door was open and a man was pushed out of the truck and then driver closed the door and drove off to San Fran."

Sam asked, "Mr. Lopes, so you recognized the man pushed out of the car?"

"No, detective. I don't know who the poor guy is, but I know the man driving the Colorado. It's Declan Kosarek."

Carter dropped his pen and it rolled on the table until Sam picked it up before hit the floor.

"I worked with him on the construction site a couple of times. So I know him well."

"You didn't see the man fall off the overpass?"

"No, but he looked so weak and wobbling all over near the edges, walking up the overpass barefoot."

As soon as Carter took out his phone to show him a mugshot of Declan, he pointed at him, "Yup, this is Kosarek, bastard. The driver I saw!" Lopes quickly added, "and he was the mean guy who dumped the sick man on the road."

Hell yeah, mean, alright, he'd killed a woman who'd been in love and lived quietly, Sam thought.

*****

Another week passed, the detectives were just spinning their wheels as if some sort of drag was holding them back, while looking for Declan's killer and the whereabouts of Evalyn's boyfriend and his Chevy Colorado.

Nonetheless, Lt had been working behind the scenes in close cooperation with other law enforcement agencies, especially with the Alameda County Sheriff's Office and the CHP Investigations Division. It was unobtrusively yet steadily developing:

After scrutinizing any jewelry related crimes in California in the past three years, Lt and Captain had come to know there were six cases of related fake insurance fraud in

Southern Cal, very similar to Berkeley's fraud scheme, starting from three in LA County, then two in San Diego County, one in Orange County. If they added their own as the last one, in Berkeley, Alameda, it would be seven cases. Much to their surprise, a familiar name had been in one of the San Diego cases, Jallal Renzo. And he'd also been the owner of the store that had been robbed…in pretense. Lt and Captain looked at each other.

This evidence had to be shared with their detectives, so Lt gathered them and imparted the news. But what they'd wanted wasn't just another complicated bit of news but evidence to solve their cases, which was to find Declan's killer and Evalyn's boyfriend.

Then, Oscar walked into the meeting. "Can I have time?"

"Any good news?" Lt asked him.

"Kind of."

"We'll take it."

"Okay, have it, friends. Our forensic firearm analyst just ran the computer again. Within a few minutes, boom! The spent slugs in Declan's murder case and in Orange County's larceny are a match."

"You mean, the jewelry insurance fraud case in Orange County?" Lt verified.

"Yes, sirree," Oscar confirmed. "In the fake larceny, the idiot robber shot out the front door and a bullet was embedded in the wall. Thankfully, both were intact. Anyways, the same gun was used to have committed both crimes."

All the detectives cheering gave each other high fives to fist bumps. They knew now whoever had killed Declan was likely part of the insurance fraud scheme done in Orange County.

"Oh Lt, one more thing. We don't know exactly which pistol shot this bullet, but our analyst who seriously knows about firearms said this bullet has a characteristic of a Sig Sauer. We might need to look for a Sig Sauer pistol 9mm or can shoot 9mm bullets."

"Ain't Sig Sauer used by the Army?" Lt asked, getting a shiver running down his spine.

G.I. Joe, Mad Max…an Army operative? An Army operative was part of the fraud scheme? That was very scary. The Army operatives were firearms experts. "Hey Oscar, keep tabs on the bullet and pistol for a while, okay?"

"Yes, sir."

CHAPTER 15

Lt had dug up all the similar insurance fraud schemes in a longer time span than three years, and they'd discovered the first two had actually occurred in Sacramento County long before it had happened in LA County. However, those two had looked a lot like small test cases and the effect of the statute of limitations had already kicked in. Since after those two, there had been a time gap between those and the spree that had started in LA County. Maybe that was why no one until now had realized the first two had been connected with the others, and also the owner of one of the stores in Sacramento had been Jallal Renzo.

Something fishy going on around Jallal and where the hell was he now? Lt wondered.

Then, the CHP Investigations Division had sent him a message on a joint DAs' operation to catch the suspects committing all the fraud statewide and the Berkeley PD was one of the forces since they'd also had the same kind of jewelry fraud. Also their DA had given them a call to elucidate what the outline of the operation looked like.

All of a sudden, Lt and Captain's territory, the BPD Detective Bureau had become one workforce of the joint operation. Now Lt must ask help from his detectives to start setting a smokescreen, a precursor to the prosecutors' operation. Even Lt didn't really know what it was yet, but when the prosecutors of LA, San Diego, Orange and Alameda County had gotten together and planned it, Lt and Captain naturally followed the orders.

Lt came into the detectives' office and found Sam.

"Hey Sam, I want you and your team to investigate this guy on your computer. I mean, by using the desktop stationed at your desk." He gave him a piece of paper that had a name scribbled on it. *Jallal Renzo*

He looked baffled. "This guy is…"

"Yup, one of the cohorts with the insurance fraud in Berkeley," Lt said it for him. "He might be in the registration list of state-certified jewelers or other criminal records in other counties. Just search in Alameda or statewide records for anything about him."

"Okay, Lt." Sam first sent a text to Carter and Nick outside, then started looking for *Jallal Renzo* in the criminal record on his desktop computer. Lt sat next to him, observing his work.

"Lt, I have a question."

"Yeah, go right ahead." Lt looked into his face. "Anything related to the fraud?"

"Um…yeah, Jallal Renzo was the very first Sacramento jeweler, San Diego Jeweler and of course fraud suspect in Berkeley, from the record. In other words, he is one of the main players, correct?"

"Correct."

"Don't you think we can make out a search warrant form for Mr. Renzo of his home and business maybe even his vehicles? I know he's on the lam now but we still have a couple of his properties here in the East Bay. We couldn't do it with our Berkeley case, cuz the warrant didn't come swiftly and he fled with his stash. Maybe this time we could smoke him out with a warrant? That's more efficient than just looking, poking around?"

"Er…" He'd known Sam was sharp, but he was extremely quick.

"I ain't talking about an arrest warrant, just a search warrant. This time, I gonna make sure our judge…"

Lt held his arm and stared at his eyes, judiciously gleaming. "Sam. The key is to *stir up around him.* Be patient. No warrant yet. Cuz it's gonna be our ace card. Tell your team to just *poke around.*" And then he whispered at him, "Intel and instruction from DAs' offices of the multiple counties. The intel says *they* seemed to watch us via police network."

He blinked at first, but soon Lt saw understanding run his face. He *is* sharp.

Sam nodded silently; Lt wanted them to send smoke to Jallal and someone who might be protecting him.

"Using our desktop and check his background deep. Smoke 'em out."

"Yes, sir."

In the afternoon, Lt had finally received a call all the detectives had been waiting for: a proper response from the GIA, Gemological Institute of America.

First, about Evalyn's diamond earrings: They'd been bought from a consignment store in San Diego County. The detectives knew the previous owner/suspect of the store was Jallal Renzo. He must've forgotten to retrieve the pair when he'd committed the fraud. According to the new owner who had acquired Jallal's old store, the earrings had been paid for in cash by a tall, strong-looking man with a military haircut and sharp blue eyes in a suit, who'd mentioned they were for his fiancée. Of course, the detectives could suspect who that man had been.

Next, the GIA researchers had discovered that all the loose diamonds that the BPD had found had been originally set in merch like rings, earrings, bracelets, and necklaces. Some diamonds still even had microscopic metal remnants attached, including platinum, silver, and gold.

Those loose diamonds were valuable and the most convenient form for worldwide diamond dealers, sold at a higher price in any deal as assets.

Now the forensic accountant who'd analyzed the ledger had proved the loose diamond plot:

The ledger was essentially a log of procedures and methods of the diamond business plot. Whoever had created this ledger had been the brain of the scheme and had kept records of their diamond deals, a log and maps to lay out their plans and results.

The scheme had been double, triple-layered to get profit out of it as well as hiding from law enforcement. Based on the analysis of the ledger:

First, it'd started by making the pretense of an insurance fraud case: A shady owner, short on cash and/or his business sinking, was asked to buy theft insurance for cash return. Jallal Renzo established the insurance company for a one-time transaction for this owner. And the insurance company told the owner to hide all expensive merch with diamonds and helped them leave copies of those items in the showcase. Jallal hired some criminals to rob the jeweler and stole everything from the showcase.

Now, afterwards, the insurance company paid whatever the owner claimed and then the company was dissolved. However, behind the scene, Jallal bought all of the expensive diamond merch in the safe at a knockdown price from the owner and even sometimes the store itself to resell. All of the deals with the owner were in cash only so no trace or proof of their deals existed.

Then, Jallal and cohorts took all the diamonds out of any setting. They melted metals to sell, and loose diamonds were their main products sold internationally in person or on the dark web to create their wealth. Their profits were sent to off-shore accounts, or kept in cash for another scheme.

The ledger entries had included how the group worked and how it'd profited out of every single transaction and the structure of the group. And the ledger had started back with the Sacramento County cases.

The good news was after careful iterative swabbing and dusting, their CSI had found the ledger contained mostly the DNA and fingerprints of John Doe, the fallen-from-sky guy, and around the time he'd gotten sick, the ledger's log had become confused and then suddenly had no entry just before he'd fallen from the overpass. Consequently John Doe was determined to be the author of the ledger.

The detectives also learned of six main members in the group. Although the ledger author hadn't mentioned exactly who those people were, the FBI profilers had concluded there had been two as brawn to lead the robbery. Those had looked like Declan and one other person who'd provided a truck and power, probably Evalyn's boyfriend. Definitely Jallal Renzo had been the main executor of the scheme planned by John Doe and a person called Big One. However, Big One's real role in the group was still unknown.

Even though all those cases were getting clearer to see, Sam had begun feeling very uneasy, almost jittery. His gut feeling had been ringing a warning bell ever since. He could sense one more layer that had been hidden under all those flashy stories of the diamond scheme.

Of all the six jeweler robbery cases in Southern California, why hadn't Southern Cal's agencies been able to seize the evidence and stop them from increasing the damage when they'd already suspected the fraud? For one, they'd been unable to execute search warrants fast or effectively enough to confiscate the evidence. The suspects had time to run with it including cash and gems.

Sam saw the similarity of the cases in Southern Cal and the one in Berkeley. The mention of a warrant delayed, an ineffective warrant…and the judges had signed them as soon as each had reached their desk. Something had happened in the course from the police to the judge.

He'd read the police inside reports from Southern Cal

over and over, and still it couldn't quite have sunk in. They'd sensed there had been someone or something that had hindered law enforcement from arresting suspects or investigating the cases, so they'd suspected a mole at first. They'd re-vetted each personnel. They'd found none.

In other words, the mysterious obstacle hadn't been inside the police.

Some kind of power from outside that could cut through the strongest fort of all, law enforcement, the last line of defense.

Chimera.

The same word had come back into his mind like a pendulum that swung back when he hadn't been watching it.

Where the hell was the forest, the main body of the Chimera?

*****

While the detectives were cataloging evidence daily, they were compiling the report on the case of Evalyn's murder and the deceased suspect nightly.

Then, one evening, Sam's ringtone played *Sister Golden Hair.*

Every single detective's face brightened. Yeah, they needed something like that.

"Sam, could you use speaker? I need everyone to hear me out."

"Okay." He turned the function on.

"Have you ever heard the name *Tyrone O'Keefe*?" Who? Everyone's face said it. "Is he in your police or even in the DMV record? He's the one, the closest kin to your John Doe."

"What? Congrats, babe. Let us search in our records," Sam said, and the detectives were suddenly scurrying around to look up the name in their files or records.

"Alex, I cannot find him in our criminal record. He

must be a law-abiding citizen," Nick said to the phone.

"Alex, do you know anything about his appearance? We can search for him in other records by the keywords," Carter suggested.

"Let's see," she said, "he's ethnically mix of Irish, Italian, French, English, etcetera and I don't think that helps you but he possibly has brown hair and blue eyes. His height is like at least 6'1" but no data for his weight since I don't know if he was in physical labor or a librarian with no muscles." Sam and other detectives had to snicker at her last sentence. They needed a little witty, funny wording from Alex.

Lt came out of his room and stood by him. "Hey, Alex, congratulations. So this is our John Doe's kin?"

"I think so, Lt. He is a brother."

"That close, huh?"

"Yes, the name came up because he once sent DNA to a special site to check if he had a genetic disease. People often do those things when they want to get married so…"

"What? He might want to marry?" The detectives remembered Evalyn's boyfriend G.I. Joe or Mad Max lookalike. He'd also allegedly bought the pair of earrings in San Diego County, mentioning that those were for his fiancée.

"Ooh!" Suddenly Nick shot up from the chair and pointed his finger at the computer monitor. "It's, it's the DMV driver's license site."

Everybody's head came together and stared at his driver's license.

"Whoa." His photo was staring down at whoever looked at his face. He had brown hair and blue eyes with height 6'3" and weight 200lb, according to the license.

"Yeah, definitely Mad Max," someone declared.

"Well, he is in the Army. Look. That's a special license," Lt said.

Sam picked up his phone, "Hon, thanks. Now we can check the Army to see if he has a brother."

"Okay, Sam, see you later. Drive safe."

After reading the data, Lt mumbled, "He's a Captain in the Army."

Sam glanced at his driver's license and abruptly opened his phone's photo app.

"Lt, look at this." He showed him the image of the message written on the back of Evalyn's El Capitan photo. "Mr. O'Keefe is an Army Captain right? That's why there's a special connection to Yosemite El Capitan."

"Oh Jeezus," Lt groaned.

"Yeah, hence this writing on the back of the photo. *I'm always your El Capitan.* And see the last line, Lt? After *I love you and always will, XO…* That ain't XO as in hugs and kisses. It was his signature. I just saw it on the driver's license. His first name T and y in Tyrone became almost like an X in his signature. O as in his surname. He really signed his name on the photo. He's Evalyn's boyfriend."

They printed out his driver's license.

All witnesses who'd seen him before, Ms. Joanie Gaffey, a former Yosemite lodge employee, the gate security guard of his rented apartment, Lamont Priebe in the penitentiary, Lamont's friend, the jeweler in San Diego who'd sold those earrings had successfully ID'd Captain Tyrone O'Keefe from the photo lineups.

The Army had confirmed that Captain O'Keefe had written his brother's name in their paper. His name was Xeno O'Keefe. They'd also mentioned he'd been taking an extended leave.

The detectives had discovered his driver's license existing in the DMV. The medical examiners, Dr. Barry Taylor who'd given the initial assessment, and Dr. Alex Wallace who'd performed his autopsy had confirmed his ID.

The author of the ledger, John Doe, a.k.a. the fallen-from-the-sky guy now had a name, Xeno O'Keefe.

Since Captain O'Keefe was the only known family

member of Xeno, the BPD must find him to let him know his brother had passed.

Later, the Army had sent the list of their issued firearms that Captain O'Keefe owned. Among his handguns, shotguns, assault rifles, they'd found a military version of the Sig Sauer P320, 9mm pistol.

Okay, Lt thought, had he shot Declan? No Captain O'Keefe's fingerprints or any other evidence that he'd killed him. He issued a BOLO for Captain Tyrone O'Keefe as a person of interest, his weapon and truck.

Now he ordered CSI to check the Camry's trunk again and also gave a call to the Coroner's Bureau to reexamine Declan's body, hoping to find any evidence Captain O'Keefe had killed him.

*****

Next day, Captain Spinnar called Lt into his office and locked the door, after a discreet meeting with their DA.

"What did the DA say?" Lt asked.

"Well, she said we didn't have any concrete evidence to arrest the main players of the diamond scheme group, but if we succeed in this special operation, we could get evidence to arrest them."

"Okay, I get that. Can I have more details?"

"Let me start from the beginning," Captain started, "she said several months ago, the CHP Investigations Division (I/D) found someone had left digital footprints in the police record. Turned out it was Crawford's accident file and his HR record."

Lt was jarred. "Someone checked Sam? Why him?"

"He's the lead detective of the jewelry fraud in Berkeley and we know about Jallal and we're still investigating him, and at the end of the day Crawford will be the one to write the arrest warrant form for Jallal. Jallal Renzo is the most important player to run the diamond scheme business, so they'd need to get close to him to gather intel and prevent him from bringing the warrant form to a judge."

"Okay, so how exactly are they going to use his accident?"

"FBI analyst said Big One's planning to exploit his accident with his sister who has a little fascination with his incident especially since her data are very close to the real Connie. Remember, not many people know who the real Connie is?"

"Yeah,"

"I think they don't know either. Anyway, the CHP I/D said Big One touched his sister's birthdate. Now he thinks his sister's driver's license is identical with the real Connie's, based upon the old plastic she'd had ten years ago. The CHP issued that fake birthdate driver's license intentionally, so they believe we didn't notice anything."

"Jeezus," Lt pinched the bridge of his nose. "They're targeting Sam with a honeytrap scheme to get intel and stop Jallal's arrest."

"And we're going to utilize that to do our operation."

"Okay, exactly how?" Lt was very nervous for his best detective.

"We have to attend the mission planning with the DAs in detail, Dan. It's still a bit over our payroll level." Captain puffed out his breath. "But we know the analyst said the suspects decided to change the venue from Southern Cal to the East Bay."

"Ah, the East Bay is familiar to Jallal since he has properties."

"Uh-huh," Captain continued, "Look, after all, we couldn't arrest any of them because we had no evidence. Therefore, the sting operation. The first step, *smoke 'em out* plot worked well. We definitely freaked them out for Jallal. We also leaked we're going to investigate Jallal and draw up the form for his warrant."

"But that puts Crawford in danger." Lt gazed at his boss.

"Not necessarily. It's supposed to be just a honeytrap

counterplot and, Dan, it's a cops' sting operation not some spy agencies'," he said defensively.

Easy to say, Lt thought, he hated the unknown.

"And don't worry, they'll never, ever find out who the real Connie is."

"Better not."

"Oh, Dan, don't forget to tell Sam to attend the mission planning."

*****

Sam arrived at the office of the Santa Clara Police. As he'd been directed, he parked his Charger behind the building. Lt hadn't told him much about anything, but he'd said two things: the SCPD was the safer location to gather behind the suspects' watchful eyes according to the FBI analyst, and he'd been chosen to slay the Chimera at all costs, a nice way to express something not so nice. He knew the feeling of getting into the battle. Been there, done that. He knew what he was expected to do. That was what he'd signed up for. No regrets.

The mission planning had prolonged for about two hours.

The attendees aside from Sam himself were mostly familiar faces, his Captain and Lieutenant, some Asst. Sheriffs, their DA and Asst. DA from their County, Judge Duncan who'd agreed to help law enforcement, a couple of Captains from the CHP, David Harp of the FBI, and two Deputies from LA County, and their DA.

They were ultimately part of the strike team to covertly execute the sting operation. They must lure the main suspect out into the sunlight with evidence. And Sam would play a role in the main undercover operation, the counterplot-honeytrap.

It was already past 11pm. By the time he got to Alex, it would probably be way past midnight. But still she'd be up waiting for him. He knew it.

And tonight he'd really have to see her to tell her not to worry because it was just their sting op.

When most of the members had left and only Alameda County's Asst. DA, who had long experience in the field of espionage and sting operations, and Lt. Dan Montfort were in the room, ADA immediately said to him, "Sam, I'm sorry that we have to utilize your case to counterattack their ploy. But like I said to all, they picked you first to exploit your incident to set up a honeytrap to get you. In short, we're utilizing you being victimized as part of the counterattack in the sting operation."

"Understand. I know I have to do it cuz they're exploiting my incident. But we sure they don't know anything about the real Connie?" he needed to know.

ADA nodded. "They have researched it but couldn't get the intel. The fact that Dr. Alex moved to the East Coast and Europe helped a lot. And now we have a special firewall to protect the real Connie's intel. Anyway, Sam, it's started already. They're moving fast after they picked up our bait. So, our strike teams are all standing by. Now, you'll stay at the place we planned from tonight on with your Lt and our staff. Don't go home until all resolved."

"What?" He lost his color. "But Alex doesn't know anything about it. I got to explain to her. Can I call her then?"

"No, send her two texts, that you'll work the graveyard shift and then stakeout ops for a while. And after that, stop using your own phones. They could track you." ADA sighed. "Look, if you stay with her, we put Dr. Alex in possible danger, because she is an obstacle for them to get to you. Need-to-know basis to protect her. You know that, right?"

Sam closed his eyes. She needed to have it explained. But he had to protect her too.

"If you'd need help, ask Lt for anything. Remember, if

we fail, we'll miss the last opportunity to apprehend the worst kind of criminals. It might not surface as tangible damage right away, but this kind of crime always has serious repercussions for entire communities."

Not telling her anything and lying to her when he'd always tried to be truthful, honorable, faithful…

"After everything finishes, we'll get you back your reputation," then ADA sternly asked, "Do you understand?"

"Yes, sir."

"*Chimera.* I like your analogy. You stand strong and slay the monster."

"Yes, sir." Or *fuck it all.* And he needed to pay Alex a buck in her cute box for swearing.

"Sam, meet you downstairs." Lt squeezed his shoulder lightly in the hallway, giving him space.

He'd left the conference room dismayed. How would he ever convey the message to her?

While he was in the elevator going down, an idea sparked in his mind. When the elevator door opened, he asked Lt in a hurry, "Lt, can you get me a piece of letter paper, an envelope, preferably no mark on it, just regular kind, and a stamp if possible?"

"You wanna write a letter? To Alex, presumably?"

"Yeah, one time, now is okay, right?"

"Of course. But try to explain in your own way that only Alex can get it, in case it's intercepted by our enemy."

"Got it."

"Wait here, I think I might know where I can get 'em." Lt jogged away.

He returned with the stationery and a stamp. "Here you go. A graveyard uniform gave 'em. Got a pen?"

"Yeah, thanks." He sat at the table in the elevator hall and started dashing off a letter.

"There's a mailbox near the back door. Can throw 'em in on our way out."

"Lt, do me another favor?"

"Sure."

"Do you remember David Harp explained about *steganography*?"

"Ah, concealing real intel within other data, right?" Yeah, Sam almost forgot Lt was quite tech-savvy.

"I need you to talk to David, and I wanna him to tweak it for me. Have an idea."

"No problem. Just explain to me."

*****

The Detective Bureau at the Berkeley PD

It was three days after Sam had secretly attended the planning with Lt at the SCPD. Nothing seemed to have changed except he couldn't see Alex. He missed her so much.

Sam was thinking about her on and on. He was facing his desktop typing the report, but he just couldn't concentrate on anything. He wanted to see her. Period.

He'd met her in the middle of April for the first time at the Coroner's Bureau as Alex Wallace. And now it was in summer already. About two months but it felt like a lot longer… Well, yeah, ten years plus.

"Hey Sam, you have a visitor in meeting room A," Lt stepped into the detectives' office and announced. The office was still quiet since it was around 7am.

"Who is it?" Sam asked.

Lt gave him a long gaze and added, "A very beautiful woman."

"Alex?" He truly hoped it was her, his heartbeat leaping.

"Um…Sam, if it was her, she'd just walk in to your desk."

Uh-oh.

Sam shivered. This was it. Part of the Chimera. He had responsibility to carry out his part in the operation and it was vital.

A huge lump the size of a meteor in his throat and a knife stuck in his heart: He was leaving his beloved woman all alone in the dark. A speck of hope was his letter. Hope she'd read it by now and understood what really was going on. He was sure she could get the meaning of the letter.

"Alright." He stood up. Lt squeezed his shoulder several times in silence.

Then Carter walked into the office. "Mornin', Lt, Sam, 'Sup?" He put his laptop bag on the desk, kicking in his duffel under it.

"Sam got a pretty female visitor and she's in meeting room A." Lt thumbed in the direction of the room.

"Oooh, Sister Golden…"

"Nope, unfortunately not her," Lt said.

"Aw…shoot." Carter made a moping face intentionally.

"I know right?" Sam wholeheartedly agreed.

Opening his laptop, Carter grimaced. "Who then?"

"Carter, come, I'll keep the door open so you can hear what we're talkin'." Sam cocked his head toward the room. "Go on, Carter," even Lt vouched. They needed a witness.

"I think I can make ten copies of this…whatever shit it is…" Carter said, picking up a random paper from the paper trash. The copy machine was set right next to meeting room A, so he could pretend to copy something while he was listening to what the mysterious woman was talking about. Also, meeting room A's upper part of the walls were tempered panes so he could see what she looked like.

Over the windows, Sam studied. She was indeed very pretty. Brunette and blue eyes. And she was part of the criminal ploy.

Alex, my love, stay safe, until I come home, he breathed a prayer, closing his eyes for a quick moment.

Lt nodded. He grinned. And he marched out of the office, followed by Carter.

Sam leisurely walked into the meeting room and kept the

door open so Carter could hear.

From the next room, Carter was staring at them, still pretending to copy the paper, with his ears flapping like Dumbo's, catching every single word from them.

"I'm Detective Sgt. Crawford. What can I do for you?" He stretched out his hand to shake hands with her.

"Sgt, I know you very well. At that time, you weren't a Sergeant or Detective yet. You were just a rookie officer. My name is Connie Morgan. I'm working as a clerk at Alameda County's public defender's office."

Sam looked perplexed.

"Sam, I'm Connie. You saved my life ten years ago on I-80."

CHAPTER 16

Carter dropped all the paper that he was placing in the paper cassette. He forgot to pick them up, just watching them petrified, gaping. Connie Morgan? *The* Connie Morgan?

She opened her purse and took out her driver's license. "Here. My driver's license. Hope it stirs up your memory."

Sam picked it up and checked front and back, along with the data, her name, address, b-day, biometrics and photo. It was a legit California driver's license, of course. And she quite looked like his Connie on the driver's license at that time. Except for…

"So, you're Connie Morgan that I saved ten years ago?" Sam asked, smiling, returning the driver's license to her.

"Yes, yes, I'm so happy we finally met again. I wanted to say thank you in person cuz I didn't know if you had received my thank you card."

"Yeah, I did get the card, but it was four months after the accident so I couldn't track you down."

"Here I am!" She looked so happy and genuine.

Oh shit…shit, shit. Carter was in panic. Sam had finally been happy with Sister Golden Hair. All his friends were waiting for their engagement. And now his long lost dream girl had suddenly appeared in his life and looked like she was willing to get involved with him.

What the hell? Omigod, they were hugging…

What if Sam would change his mind from Alex to this…Connie? He'd been in love with Alex head over heels. Was it even possible that he'd choose Connie over Sister Golden Hair? But it wasn't just another woman, it was Connie. Not unthinkable, cuz he'd had a long history of infatuation for her image. He knew how he'd been obsessed with her for a long time as he'd been on his team.

Jase. Yeah, Jason must know this. He wanted to let him know about this fact right away, but he was out of the state, taking special seminars for young leaders of the police. For three weeks. And Carter just remembered he couldn't use his phone during the seminars.

After Sam had sent her a text message that he'd had to clear all the graveyard shift requirements for a week or more, due to some glitch on the computer and mix-ups in his schedule, he'd sent another text telling her that he had some stakeouts for a month so he and a small number of his colleagues would be staying at an undisclosed place provided by the BPD.

So, it was logical for him to stop visiting the Coroner's Bureau to talk with her or Barry or coming home. And she hadn't even had an iota of doubt about any of his messages. She'd been just hoping for his safety as always and praying for it.

Until she'd realized she couldn't get hold of him by any means, phone call, text, email…

At first she'd thought he'd been too busy or concentrating on his work. But soon it had started making her concerned. Was he okay? His phone had been set to voicemail 24/7 but he'd never responded to her messages. She'd called Sam's boss, Lt. Montfort. He'd apologized to her that he'd been in serious stakeouts and it would be very hard to get hold of him. She'd been relieved Sam was fine.

Then, suddenly the air in the Coroner's Bureau had changed a little, like the wind had shifted. She just couldn't put her finger on what had been wrong or different.

On the eighth day after Sam had started working like hell without coming back home, she'd got a text from Tony at the *Blue Café.* She was actually at her desk in her office, working on her laptop.

"*Hi Alex, hope you're doing fine, but what's with you and Sam?*" With a glance at it, she frowned. That was a strange wording.

"*Hi Tony, we're fine.*" Sent.

"*You two still an item?*" What? Silly. Must be some misunderstanding.

"*Yes.*" Sent.

"*Have you ever heard story of Sam and Connie?*"

Huh? Tony and most people didn't know Alex was that Connie. But why the story now? "*Yes.*" Sent.

"*Sam and Connie often dine at Café. I thought you guys broke up.*"

What? She almost jumped out of her chair with a shock. Then her logical cerebral cortex brought her back to calmness. "*Maybe part of stakeouts he's working on?*" Sent.

"*Stakeout includes a hot date?*" Er... Maybe not. Then Tony sent her another.

"*She showed me her driver's license. I asked her ID when they ordered beer.*"

They ordered beer. That didn't sound like stakeouts. Or maybe undercover op? Must be.

"*Maybe a fake?*" Sent.

"*I screenshot and showed Lt when I delivered lunch. Lt said she was the Connie on 80 accident 10 yrs. ago.*"

Lt. said she was... That knocked the air out of her. "*Lt said that?*" Sent.

"*Yup.*" Seriously? Lt didn't know Alex was Connie either? So, no one knew it except her uncle and BFFs?

All of them had fallen for the fake Connie including Sam. Omigod.

"*They come BF or L and Dinner since 7 days ago.*"

A couple of days after he'd sent her text about his work.

No. Her Sam wouldn't cheat on her. Never. Er… Um…

"*I attached four images.*"

And she saw them, whether she liked it or not. Dammit, text message.

Connie had beautiful shoulder-length brunette hair with sapphire blue eyes. Pretty, petite.

It still amazed her no one, even Sam, had ever deciphered her hair at that time had been just dyed.

The images attached to the text were brutal.

Their foreheads almost touching, the girl was laughing with him, over some food, in one image. In the other, he was holding her hand and smiling as if he was assuring her; in a different image, they were walking down to the parking lot his arm around her shoulders and her hand on his back. And the last one, he was tucking a few strands of her brown hair behind her ear…his habit he'd always done to Alex. Thanks to Live Photos. Holy crap.

That didn't look work-related at all. Besides, she'd never heard of police stakeouts or sting operations involving romance.

"*I'm telling you this cuz you don't know while all the town is talking about it.*"

"*What talk?*" Sent.

"*Sam has finally met his long-lost dream girl, Connie, again.*"

"*Didn't know.*" Sent.

"*I'm sorry. I cannot forgive him for dumping you.*"

Dumping her… Ah, so she'd been dumped. And she was the only person who hadn't known it.

Now she got it. The reason why she'd felt some wind shifts behind her in here.

Everyone must've been talking about her being dumped by Sam Crawford. And she hadn't known. Stupid. Nope, it was beyond stupid. Ludicrous.

"*Thanx. Gotta run. Autopsy. Talk to you later!*" Sent.

"*Take care, dear!*" Tony said.

Hadn't seen it coming. She was an idiot. Hadn't thought of the possibility that someone could've claimed him, since Connie Morgan wasn't a rare name and there must be many women with that name, birthdate and appearance in brunette, especially when he hadn't known what she'd really looked like due to the accident and dyed hair.

It was purely her fault. She was the one who'd adamantly never told him she was his Connie…

One other thing she'd learned: Although he'd told her he was in love with her, he hadn't really loved her in the way she'd wanted him to love her.

No matter how much he'd done for her, all were his characteristic to be attentive to detail. It'd had nothing to do with love but been just his nature to be unstinting. TC not TLC.

Another thing she'd found: He'd never really discarded his obsession for Connie. He hadn't been able to find her, so he'd settled for Alex.

Now Connie had appeared in his life again and he'd believed she was the real one from her driver's license. He was a cop so he could tell if it was a real driver's license. Must be the real deal.

Of course, Alex was ditched, replaced by the *real* Connie. He hadn't needed a substitute named Alex anymore.

She felt dizzy and nauseous.

She didn't think she could keep working today. She called Barry, her boss in the on-call van today and asked for the afternoon off. "No worries Uncle, I'm having a severe headache. Can I go home now?"

Nonetheless, her home in the Berkeley Hills had suddenly become too big and empty. Most of all, her bed was too huge to sleep in by herself. Strange. Before he'd started living with her, she'd slept in the bed by herself and hadn't felt it too big. Now it had become humongous as if it had grown in size. She'd begun feeling like freezing in the bed as it had never warmed up. When he'd slept in the bed, it had gotten warm quickly not only they'd made love before sleeping but also his body had radiated heat, which had always kept her warm.

The memories in the master bedroom had been too much to bear.

How they'd made love the first time and every night and day afterwards.

How they'd talked about everything together looking down at the amazing view of Berkeley and the Bay.

And he'd left his belongings behind in her place as if they were mementos.

She could recall when he'd decided to stay in her house right after the first lovemaking, she'd felt it could be his trial period. And it looked like it had come to an end. His trial period had finished and he had no intention of renewing the period. Yeah, she had to remember. He'd never said he'd stay forever. Or marry her. Now she knew why. His heart had been always with Brunette Connie back in time ten years ago. She'd missed her chance to tell him the truth.

After he'd stopped living with her for Connie, she'd moved out from the house into the upstairs of Uncle Barry's residence, *EZ Poppas*. He'd always kept one extra bedroom with a bathroom for her. He was happily taking care of his beloved niece/daughter again. He'd still regretted he should've adopted her as a real daughter a long time ago.

Since Sam and Connie looked more and more intimate all over town not bothered by other people's eyes, they'd completely become the main talk of the town gossips and so had Alex unfortunately. She was called a woman scorned. Dumped and left. *Hell hath no fury like a woman scorned.* But she just couldn't get furious when she must. She'd resigned herself and started thinking as long as he was happy, she shouldn't complain.

Because it was her own fault she'd lost him for *that* Connie and she still loved him.

However, the rumor had gradually taken a toll on her, so

she'd decided to take a week vacay that she had to kill within six months.

The first two days she'd cried a lot like a broken faucet. She hadn't known how much water her body could retain for tears. She'd felt like she might drown in her own tears like Alice in Wonderland.

Even though her BFFs wanted to see her, she just couldn't see them, especially when Jason and Rae were doing awesome and Nora was dating a new guy.

Fourth day, Uncle Barry sat on the bed next to her. "Don't you think you should tell him you're the real Connie?"

"It's too late, Uncle. He's chosen her over me when he knows me well. He thinks she's his real Connie. And I don't think I can change his mind."

Her uncle knew once she'd decided, it was hard to change *her* mind either. He sighed and asked another question, "Have you seen him at home after the incident?"

"Uh-uh." She shook her head. "He never came back."

He asked, "His clothes still there?"

"Yes. All of his stuff is still in my place. Well, that's before I moved out, though. He might've visited there and picked them up while I'm here."

"Huh…" Barry's brow furrowed. "That doesn't make sense."

"What doesn't?" She grimaced also.

"Alex, men…even women, generally if they break up with someone, they tend to pick up everything ASAP from their ex's house, trying not to leave any of their stuff. So, when he didn't pick up his from your house if his intention is to break up with you, it puzzles me. On top of that, he didn't even say goodbye to you not even in a text message."

"Probably too busy. Or he's hoping that I'll clean up his stuff for him…" And she started crying again. He passed the tissues to her and held her until her tears dried up this time around.

Next day early in the morning, Uncle Barry drove up to his Berkeley Hills house on his way to work.

He must check if Sam had come to pick up his stuff. If he'd done that, then Barry would be sure he'd really broken up with her.

He entered the house after collecting letters from the mailbox. The inside was almost in the same condition as usual. Only the surfaces of the furniture had collected a little layer of dust. He checked all the rooms. Sure enough, he'd found Sam's clothes, shoes, etcetera in the house, and some personal grooming items in the master bathroom. Then he started to check all the letters. None of them were personal. Mostly advertisements or flyers. None were for her.

"Huh…" His first odd feelings about this whole ado came back again. And stronger, more suspicious. He didn't believe this was his way of leaving his woman, any woman. Intentionally leaving his stuff as if he'd still make his woman long for him. No, he didn't think so. It wasn't Sam. He'd never do such things.

Barry had known him for years. He'd observed him as Alex's CI and his colleague. He liked him a lot for his great disposition, courageous yet levelheaded, honorable, humble, compassionate… He'd never changed. Always a good cop, better man.

Hence, dishonorably dumping a woman, without telling her anything, leaving his stuff for her to clean up, didn't fit his profile. On the contrary, this must be the sign he'd left for her to understand that he hadn't dumped her or stopped loving her. His goal was to come back to her later.

In other words, the whole thing that was happening around them in their eyes was not even close to the truth.

Barry had been a good soldier in a reconnaissance unit and he'd had an incredibly trustworthy gut feeling. And it was telling him this was too problematic to take it as it seemed. It looked more like a ruse.

Abruptly he was stirred by the notion that he'd seen

many times from the experiences of having worked with intelligence agencies in his past. But they'd been trained agents. Sam was a local cop, but he also knew the local law enforcement agencies conducted sting operations and that sometimes included an intricate plot. Was Sam involved in that? Even if he was, it wouldn't be right to hurt an innocent person, in this case, his niece. So, what had gone wrong against Sam's will and hope and what had been happening?

He locked the door and left, alarmed by his new theory why Sam had left his personal effects in the house.

*****

Three days later, after finishing the three weeks of seminars, around 6pm.

As soon as Jason landed at Oakland Airport, he turned off airplane mode, and he received a bunch of messages. But among all the messages, there were two important texts that attracted his attention.

One was from Carter:

We have a situation.

The other from his lady, Rae:

Do something about your imbecile BEST friend or I'll kill him!

He wiped his face in one stroke with his palm. Okay. What was happening in the East Bay now? And what had Sam done?

Carter's message was disturbing. A situation? He was BPD and Jason was OPD so not work-related batshit or wut?

And why hadn't everyone fucking behaved themselves while he'd been away?

First Carter. He called him up. Carter picked up right away. "Jeezus Jase, welcome back home and I cannot be happier."

"What the fuck happened?" He had no decorum or qualms spared for his dude after being canned sardine-ish on a long flight home.

"Sam's gone off on a fucking tangent."

He closed his eyes and tried slow breathing. What the hell had he done this time? Got shot? Or burned again to protect Sister Golden Hair? Well, in that case, he'd be happy to go to see him at the hospital. Shielding his own woman from any harm was one of the most honorable things to do.

"What shit happened? Burned again?" He was half-joking.

But Carter replied, "Wish he was."

"Wut's that supposed to mean?"

"Jason, no joke. He found Connie Morgan and he's chosen her over Alex."

"Huh?" That was moronically redundant. Connie *is* Alex. Alex *is* Connie.

He'd figured it out as a fact. The keyword had been *hero-worship syndrome.* He'd become interested in it and investigated it himself. Okay, not many people knew who Connie was, because she'd left California after the accident. Unless someone had diligently dug up the facts and known where to look, like Jason had.

Carter went on, "Okay, so, a girl named Connie Morgan had come to us three weeks ago, and introduced herself that she was the one saved on 80 by Officer Crawford ten years ago and now they're dating…"

"Wait, you're fucking confusing me, homie." And he'd pay Rae several bucks for swearing with the F-word, if she was with him.

"Sorry, I'm also damn confused for three weeks, Jason."

"I should talk to Sam, then."

"Good luck with that."

"Say it again?"

"Nick and I tried hard to talk him out of it but nope. He's as stubborn as a screwup mule. We now diss him."

Carter's story muddled his fine mind more. So, he stepped back in his story and asked again, "Carter, what do you mean he chose *her* over Alex?"

"Ah, this Connie girl is brunette with blue eyes, and like I said, she revealed she's the girl that he saved. He's infatuated with her, dumping Alex, they're dating so fucking intimately appearing at our *Blue Café* and all over town. Together."

"He dumped Alex?" No, that was impossible. He was convinced that Sam had identified Alex as Connie on their first intimate night if not their first kiss. He'd believed that was only reason why he'd decided to make a commitment to her so fast so that he wouldn't lose her again. But now this? What had happened to him?

He'd secretly kept seeking his dream girl Connie and now he'd thought he'd found her?

Wasn't he really as smart as Jason had hoped for? At the end of the day, Sam had fallen for this Connie who was an impostor. In conclusion, Sam had no fucking clue who the real Connie was. Oh shit.

Carter went on, "Yeah, Alex's now called *a woman scorned* by gossips."

"What the…?" His blood pressure shot up, losing his temper at the waiting area for his rideshare.

"So, Jason, he was actually still looking for Connie behind our back even when he was with Alex? And he finally found *her* so he dumped Alex? She ain't disposable, for fuck's sake."

But he asked him back, "Carter, you sure this Connie was the girl that he'd really saved back then?"

"I was worried about that too, so I made sure she was telling the truth. I found her driver's license at the DMV site and it's legit. Oh actually, Sam saw her driver's license the first day and he was staring down at it for a while. And her old residence record proved she was at UC Berkeley when Sam got the burns, and she's now working as a clerk at the Alameda County public defender's office, a credible workplace and…"

Wait a minute. "Hey Carter, tell me why you believed

this girl ain't a fake Connie?"

"Well, cuz all the official records support her that she's the one. Everything like her plastic issued by the DMV…"

"Carter, listen, why did you believe *this* Connie Morgan and Connie Morgan in our official accident records are the same person?"

"Well, cuz the data of the girl who came to the BPD is…" Carter suddenly lost his voice and burst out next moment, "Oh shit! 'Course, anyone can claim if every data on the driver's license is identical."

Bingo. There must be gazillions of Connie Morgan with the same data existing. Of course, except for the address, but that was not a critical point since people moved around.

"Carter, you know Sister Golden Hair is the real Connie, right?"

No words for a few seconds. Then a little sigh. "Really? How'd ya know?"

Alright. He got to explain to him, then. "Ey where're you at?"

"Home. Me and Nick worked all night and Lt gave us afternoon off today."

"Can you dudes come to my apartment?"

*****

Monday morning had broken. Alex had still been dwelling at her uncle's place. It'd been just so hard to move on or move out. However, gradually her ever-logical mind had started adjusting to her calamity and taking it as rationally as possible.

She returned to work after a week vacay. Thanks to her methodical brain, she didn't care that much about whatever gossip she'd encountered like *did you know Sam is dating a brunette?* on the fact that she'd been dumped. And always they concluded with *I'm so sorry*.

She'd heard them all. And seen some.

She was at her desk, just staring at the thermos. The

smiley was glancing at her. One of many that evoked the memories of him in her.

Waves of warmth were rolling in, undulating her, intoxicating her; it felt so good like being wrapped up in a soft cashmere blanket. She recognized the feeling. It was Sam. His presence had always given her protective cover. Just like when he'd thrown his life for her ten years ago or tried to ease her pain in everyday life. He'd never changed; he was a shield, a guardian. Probably he saw she was strong enough that he wasn't required to protect her anymore, although she still needed him.

When that Connie had appeared so quickly, he'd immediately had to fly away from her to take care of the woman. That was the only reason she could finally deduce why he'd left her abruptly. Otherwise, it didn't make any sense. Sam was an honorable protector. He wouldn't dump her like this unless it was an emergency. An emergency named Connie Morgan, his forever love.

She should've known this was the consequence of loving a guardian angel.

Angels were known to land and fly away unexpectedly.

CHAPTER 17

She wasn't only working for Berkeley or Oakland; she and other medical examiners and scientists had duties to support law enforcement and the prosecutor for all Alameda County. So, her job wasn't just staying in the Bureau performing autopsies or analyzing biological materials and so on. She often had to testify at a trial for the County DA also.

She'd had to appear in court that morning, so she'd headed to the Alameda County Superior Courthouse. The case was manslaughter, but the defendant's side was planning to claim self-defense. How had they thought they'd been able to stand against the evidence that the defendant had shot the victim in the back three times even though after a very serious altercation?

Alex had finished her duty including cross-examination smoothly and left the courtroom. She sat on the bench just outside the room and sorted out the paper file she used for her testimony, putting it in her bag then hanging it from her shoulder as she stood up. Gee, her business purse seemed heavier every time she came here. Either she was getting old and losing muscles or the gravity in this Courthouse somehow increased like Planet Krypton.

She started walking in the hallway into the atrium.

And she spotted Sam and Connie coming in at the front glass doors.

Oh crap.

They were walking hand in hand…more like arm in arm. Connie was small in stature almost as Alex was. Her brown hair bouncing around her shoulders, she was laughing at whatever Sam said to her. Yeah, she was prettier in person than in the photos.

Sam looked as good as ever. Tall and handsome as usual. She felt a sudden sharp pang in her heart. She looked around if she could escape from this situation. Nope. Their only doors were in front, which the two had just used. Okay, she could walk naturally, say hi naturally, chat naturally, and out she'd go naturally.

Sam noticed her first. He stilled, gazing at her. Connie looked at him. Her laughter faded and she stared at her as well. Alex was clad in a dark gray suit and a white blouse, with pumps, hair up, no accessories except her iconic men's Rolex. Her steps were confident. She was professional. Should never waver.

"Hey, Sam." She smiled at him. Her smile came naturally, as planned. Good.

"Hey." He cleared his throat. "Um, Alex, this is Connie Morgan." Strange to hear him say her old name. "Hi."

"Connie, this is Dr. Alex Wallace."

"Hi." The two women shook hands.

Alex noticed she had beautiful sapphire blue eyes, different hues as her blue. Brunette and blue gem eyes. She didn't look like an impostor. Understandable that he'd fallen for her. Only if she'd told him she was the one…again, too late for that.

And then she heard him say, "Connie, she's my ex."

She thought her heart stopped. She was his ex, former. And he'd said it effortlessly.

So, Uncle was wrong after all; she'd been dumped but he'd just never bothered to pick up his stuff or tell her they'd broken up. She was already somewhere buried in the graveyard of trashed memories in Sam's life. His new history had begun with Connie and Alex wasn't in the picture. Of course not. A very straightforward ultimatum from him. The strongest goodbye ever.

Alex tried to be amicable and courteous. She could cry later. "You guys are here for…?"

"Just to pick up some paperwork from the DA," Sam answered. Connie added, "My public defender's office's next door. We decided to have lunch together."

"Oh, ah…I see. That's…nice." The memory that they'd used to have done the same rushed into her mind. But she held her ground.

"You here to testify for the DA?" he unexpectedly asked this time.

"Yeah," she replied in one word. She hoped he wouldn't talk to her anymore.

But he didn't seem to get the memo. "The manslaughter case outside of San Leandro?"

"Yes." *Please, Sam, stop talking to me.* She didn't want to hear his voice. Smooth and warm that it caressed her body and soul just like before.

"The vic got three leads in the back but the defendant insists self-defense?"

"Yes."

"How did it go?"

"As usual."

"Cross-examination?"

"Okay. Not much logical rebuttal."

"Sheriff's deputy was complaining about him when…"

He was trying to keep talking to her. Maybe he was appealing they were still friends.

But the truth was he didn't really need her, because he'd found the ideal girl, his Connie. Even if she wasn't the real one, he believed she was his Connie and that was the whole point.

"Honey," Connie put her hand on his chest. "I'm so

sorry to interrupt you but I have a limited lunchbreak time."

"Sorry, darling."

Honey, darling… Jeezus. Let's pretend she hadn't heard them.

"Alex…" he wanted to add something, but Connie stretched her hand out and said, "Nice to see you, Dr. Wallace. Sorry that we don't have enough time to chat. Maybe next time around three of us can have lunch or something."

"Oh I'd like that." Alex succeeded in smiling more at her and even hugged her. Then she'd turned to him. "Sam, I'm so glad you've finally found the one and only," she said almost tenderly, her eyelashes casting shadows on her blue eyes.

"Alex," his expression changed. But she went on, as it was getting harder to talk. "Be happy, Sam. Life is short so enjoy each other as much as you can."

Connie nodded. "I know what you mean, Dr. Wallace. When he told me he loved me, I just knew we're meant to be."

What? She desperately eyed him. His mouth curved up a bit, so she asked bravely or stupidly, "You said you love her?"

"Uh-huh."

"You love her."

"Yeah, that's what I said I said. Didnnai?" He sounded irritated. And he pulled Connie in and kissed her forehead. She looked up at him, and their eyes met. They kissed again, this time on each other's lips. And intimately.

He'd said he loved her, probably making love with her every night and… Wow. She'd thought being called his ex was the ultimatum but compared with the fact that he loved her and they had their own life together somewhere, it was nothing.

She felt dizzy and couldn't breathe with pain, like when her airbag had deployed on her ten years ago. And this time there would be no Sam to rescue her.

She looked at her watch deliberately. "Oops, alright, sorry gotta go. Nice to meet you, stay safe and be happy!" She smiled and waved at them, turning her heels toward the front doors, walking away from them in a hurry. *Bye, Sam; it's been wonderful to have shared my life with you.*

She heard him call her name once again, but just couldn't stop scurrying away. She got to get out of the Courthouse right now.

She'd be okay. No. She'd never be okay or the same. She'd lost the love of her life. Oh wait, she wasn't the love of *his* life from the get-go. She just hadn't known his *I love you* was different from hers. Or maybe the same. Just that he'd made a mistake saying it to her but this time with his Connie, it was true. She was totally in love with him and she'd been in euphoria not seeing the reality.

My god. How stupid she'd been.

She hurried to the parking garage and climbed up into her Leaf. As soon as she was in the confined safe space, droplets rolled down her cheeks. She covered her face and held back tears, biting her teeth hard. But her sob came out between her lips, as if it was a scream from her soul.

*****

Jason was called by Lt. Montfort to come to the Bureau this afternoon. He'd just said he needed to pass new evidence on Evalyn's homicide case and also told him nonchalantly that Sam had been staying with Lt at an undisclosed location for some trouble with the BPD since he'd had a romantic conflict with two women. Huh. Fucking idiot.

When Jason stepped into the Detective Bureau, most of them weren't in the office but he found familiar faces, Carter and Nick sitting at their desks, talking in a low voice.

"Yo, homies." Jason appeared between the partitions.

"Hey Jase, Lt called you?" Carter looked up at him.

"Yeah." He sat on one of the empty chairs and wheeled

to them. "Where the hell's everyone at?"

"Lt said they all went to recanvass." Nick raised his hand, circling it.

"Again?" Jason scowled. "I thought we closed Eva's case," then he just remembered, "Oh he said something like new evidence on her case."

"Right." Carter nodded. "He said unexpected."

"Unexpected, huh?" Jason crossed his arm behind his head, leaning against the chair, his legs up on Sam's desk. "Speaking of which"—he jutted his chin out motioning to that desk—"where the hell's the man-ho at?"

Nick was drinking a bottle of water, but he shot it out of his mouth at his remark, chortling hard, totally throwing his head back.

Carter, also laughing, expressed his sentiments. "When you put it that way, dude, it sounds incredibly credible." And then he informed Jason, "Sam's coming with her and introduce her to us."

"No thanks. I have no intention to meet the girl."

"Oh you *will* meet Connie." Lt came into the office. Jason quickly put his long legs down from the desk. "Lt, why? You know the story. He dumped Dr. Alex when he was talking about marrying her."

Putting his hands on the partition, he said, "Jason, I need you to meet her."

Jason grimaced like an old dog stuck in thorny bushes, the highest, strongest level of his grievance and accusation on his face.

"Please?"

When Lt said please, who'd say no? "Yes, sir. But I might punch his face with my fist like a couple of hundred times."

Much to everyone's surprise, Lt smiled and said, "Be my guest."

Within a few minutes, Sam came in with his new woman.

Jason's eyes popped out. Well, figuratively. In fact, not because she was pretty, okay she was pretty but she was almost the exact copy of the girl from Sam's incident ten years ago. Almost.

The impostor Connie was small and dainty, had shoulder-length brunette hair, nearly straight only curly on the ends, with beautiful sapphire blue eyes and little lips on an oval face. She was a pretty woman. Any hot-blooded man could easily fall for her, if only appearance would count.

And Sam was awesome looking as usual. His beige suit and thin-striped dark purple tie looked so great on him. They were nicely ironed. Didn't look like a lovestruck douchebag to him.

But in fact, at this moment, Jason really wanted to punch his face a million times. He'd learned the story that Sam had just done the fucking dishonorable business in public this morning.

Sam casually took off his jacket, and hung it on the back of his chair.

"Okay, Connie, meet my buddies." He gently pushed her back to step closer to the detectives' desk.

"Sgt. Jason Rivera of the Oakland PD." He extended his hand to shake hers, without a smile.

"Hi Sgt. Rivera, Connie Morgan, nice to meet you." She charmingly smiled at him, even though he was adamantly not smiling at her. Because he didn't trust her.

"Jase, give it up. Be nice to my woman." Jason's brow shot up, and he mouthed just to let Sam notice, *your woman?* And he nodded to him, mouthing, *oh yeah.* So, Jason added, mouthing, *go to hell.* But he just shrugged, pushing all sorts of Jason's buttons. He gonna punch his face later.

"Carter, Detective Carter Halls." He also shook her hands lightly.

"Nick Montoya." He just waved over the partition.

And Lt walked to her. "Hey, you must be Connie Morgan."

"Yes, sir,"

"I'm Lt. Dan Montfort."

"Nice to meet you." She radiantly smiled and they shook hands.

"Sorry, Connie, most of them are out canvassing. Can't introduce you," Lt said.

"Why canvassing again?" Sam wondered.

"We have a couple of new leads," Lt explained to him, "but first, Declan's murder case. A new name. We can finally ask the judge to issue an arrest warrant putting murder on him."

"What's the name?" Sam took out his detective notebook and pen. The other detectives followed.

Lt took out the note. "Ready? Captain Tyrone O'Keefe for one count of murder."

"Got the new evidence?" Carter asked Lt.

"Yeah, CSI found his fingerprints inside the Camry's trunk where the toolbox used to be. One was hidden under the blood spatter and the other was with Declan's blood. And a couple on Declan's body," Lt explained then he added, "Hey Sam, by the way, as for the jewelry fraud, CSI is cataloging the evidence for charge. You're the lead detective of this Jallal's mess. You'll submit an affidavit for his warrant after the DA gives us a go."

"Got it."

"Connie," Lt turned to face her, who was standing by Sam's desk quietly. "I didn't mean to scare you or bore you. We just have quite complicated cases and we really need to put them together ASAP. I hope you don't hate us." Lt smiled at her.

"Oh no problem, Lieutenant. We appreciate the police work making society safer."

"Good. Just because your boyfriend is a detective, it ain't always a bad thing," Lt said, patting Sam's shoulders.

She looked at her watch and said, "Oh, wow, almost three. I took a half-day off, but I have a meeting with my colleagues at four."

"I'll take you and drop you off there, sweetheart."

"Oh thanks, Sam, darling, but I'm going to meet the

team first at the library for prep. So no worries. Besides, it looks like you'll have a busy day."

She turned around. "Nice to meet you all. And Lieutenant." She tilted her head.

"C'mon, hon, at least I can take you to the elevator hall." He stood up and placed his hand on the small of her back.

"Oh, let me take you downstairs," Lt said.

"You?" Sam frowned but didn't argue.

"Thank you, Sammy." Lt grinned. And he said to her, "You see, Connie, I'd actually love to hear about the public defender's office. My nephew graduating college in a year wants to be part of it. Could you tell me a bit about it? I mean, even a little general information would be helpful."

"Gladly." She smiled at him.

She looked up at Sam. "Okay, sweetest, see you soon."

"See you, love."

Connie tiptoed, putting her hands on his chest. Supporting the back of her head, he lowered his head to kiss her.

"Don't you dare suck in her whole face, you dickhead," Jason voiced like thunder booming.

So, she quickly separated her lips and kissed his chin. "Bye, hon."

Lt ushered her out the office.

As soon as they left there, Jason grabbed Sam's shirt collar.

"You fucking dipshit sonofabitch, a sheriff's deputy called me he saw you make Alex almost cry, you bastard. You said you love the new chick now and you shoved your damn tongue into her throat in front of Alex, of all the friggin' places in all Alameda, you shithead done it at the Superior Courthouse's atrium!"

"What?" Carter jumped off the chair. "No respect, man."

Nick dropped his water bottle, his mouth wide open.

"Cuz I love Connie," he declared loud at Jason's face.

"Damn you Sam, what about Alex? Didn't you love her?

You said you wanna marry her! It's only fucking a month ago." Jason was also yelling at him.

"I don't love Alex anymore. I love my Connie now. I wanna marry my Connie," Sam shouted back at him.

That was it. Jason pushed him all the way to the wall near to the office door, clutching his collar almost squeezing his throat, pounding him on it. The banging sound along with the vibrations of the tempered panes of the door echoed in the office. Nick stiffened, his face draining of color, thinking how to react in case they started killing each other.

Although Jason was taller, both were quite tall and toned men. Carter was now worried about the office wall and glass. "Hey Jase, go easy on…the wall and office door, will you? Our office is more important than Sam at this point but we have a tight budget."

"My lady Rae wanted to kill you and I understand. Might as well I take care of the wet job for her," his low yet booming voice scared the hell out of the people walking down the elevator hall.

Sam didn't say or do anything, just trying not to hit his head directly on the wall or panes. Then, he peeked at the elevator hall. He saw Connie and Lt get on one of the elevators, soon the door closed and the lights on top of the elevator box designating floor numbers were going down.

Jason grimaced, sensing something not quite right. He was studying Sam's face closely. Then the realization struck him. Sam grinned. "She was within earshot."

Jason let him go. Then, he bent down, placing both his hands on his knees, and breathed with his shoulders. "Jeezus…"

Fixing his shirt collar and sleeves, adjusting the fit, Sam uttered quietly to his best friend, "Sorry, couldn't tell you."

Jason thought he must learn to trust his homie more. He should've been able to speculate the mission he was on. He'd thought something was not right, yet he'd lost his temper. He grabbed Sam's arm, giving him a man hug.

"Sorry, Sam my man. Should've trusted you more." And he questioned him, when they were still in close proximity in the man hug, "Are we safe talking open in this office? No bugs possible?"

"Lt said FBI checked it and they also planted bug detection device and micro surveillance cameras. We're well protected," he assured him.

"What the hell just happened?" Carter came around to them. His mouth finally shut, Nick also approached cautiously.

"Turned out to be your bosses, Lt and Sam Crawford, are such hams."

"What? You mean acting?"

"Correct. And we were just kept in the dark…like a doormat in the basement."

"Cuz the more people close to me believed it real, the better outcome we could get," Sam said a little defensively. "You know, *need-to-know*?" In fact it was true, strategically speaking.

"Yeah, understand; but I ain't sure of Alex, though," Jason was concerned about her. "Something ain't right, according to the Sheriff's deputy guarding the Courthouse there."

"About that… I think I screwed up."

"Sammy, that's the one and only place you shouldn't screw up, you dumbass." Jason lightly punched his arm.

"Well, I thought everything was working the way it should be…but today when I met her at the Superior Courthouse, I realized she really truly believed I dumped her."

"Alameda Sheriff's must be in the loop to send you a message via me; otherwise, they'd already have filed a complaint alleging police misconduct against you and the BPD."

"Right," Sam looked down, sighing. "I never cross my woman."

"That's what you thought, Sam. You gotta do

something."

"I think I need help from Lt."

"Okay, so we didn't know nothing about nothing even a shit bit?" Carter rolled his eyes.

"Nope, it's a honeytrap, man," Jason said, beaming with relief, knowing his best friend wasn't a real jackass.

"I thought honeytrappin' was only in spy movies." Carter crossed his arms on his chest. "Guess not. So my question is…" when Carter started, Jason took a white cotton square out of his pocket. Carter's eyes becoming tripled, he was staring at him, while he wiped his sweat off his face and put it back in his pocket.

"Wut?" Jason narrowed his eyes at him.

"Er…your…your white stuff." Carter kept a serious face, but his lips were trembling.

"It's called a handkerchief, you idiot sea hare."

"Sea hare?" The new word baffled him. "What's that?"

"A large sea slug in Lake Merritt," Jason described with a hand gesture. Nick burst out laughing.

Sam's lips curved upward. "A classy white handkerchief. Must be Rae," he said. "Who else?" Jason smirked proudly.

"Nicky, your laugh was heard even in the elevator hall." Lt came back to the office after he'd locked the outer front door.

"How far did you hear me yelling, Lt?" Sam asked.

"Until the elevator closed…. So let's see…*I wanna marry my Connie*," Lt mimicked him.

"Cool." A smile was breaking on his face.

"She was happily giggling at your love confession all the way downstairs, and I ushered her to the front door and opened it for her. I really gotta make sure she was out of the building. She was waving goodbye to me," Lt said.

"I didn't know you had a nephew," Carter said to Lt.

"Me neither," Lt replied assertively. "Okay, you guys, come to my office. You too Jason."

"Aye, aye." Jason quickly followed his friends.

The four detectives entered Lt's office.

"Um…Lt, before everything." Sam raised his hand. Lt noticed a very disturbed expression on his face. "What's wrong? Talk to me." His brow furrowed tensely, Lt urged him to speak up.

"I think she didn't get that letter."

"You sure?" he asked, growing concern in his voice.

"Affirmative." Sam started pacing in the room. That kind of perturbation was contagious and before too long it had soon infected the other detectives. "Lt, you might hear I had a big play in the atrium of the Courthouse today. And I thought she got my letter already so I didn't worry at first. But then…she sounded different…I mean…I felt she was saying a real goodbye cuz she thinks I found my real love and dumped her…so I believe my play backfired… Lt, please, I need your help."

"Holy shit, it's an emergency. I think I'm gonna talk to her Uncle."

"Yes please, Lt. I know we cannot directly contact her but maybe Uncle at work? I just cannot forgive myself knowing that I hurt her."

"I'll do that, Sam, rest assured." Lt nodded firmly, taking his phone out of his pocket.

"Who's her uncle?" Carter asked.

"Dr. Taylor, Carter," Lt replied. "Ah." Carter bobbed his head.

"Your other detectives ain't canvassing again, right?" Jason asked, after Lt had done conversing with Barry.

"Nope. They're at the Santa Clara PD, listening to the explanation of our sting op in detail. The FBI is also helping this case and they analyzed and chose Santa Clara City. It's safer there especially since Alameda County is a target right now," Lt said, "and why're only you guys here? Cuz you guys started digging where we didn't want you to dig. So I volunteered to stop you doing it."

"What?" bewildered, Jason asked.

"You tried to pull out Connie Morgan's intel just a couple of days ago, Jase." Sam poked him.

"The FBI electronic intelligence team has built a firewall around the real Connie Morgan's intel to protect her, so they don't want you breaking in." Lt said, smirking. "Cops break in never sounds damn good."

Jason stared at Sam. Then, understanding flashed on his face, "You really knew Alex *is* your Connie; that's why you agreed to do this ploy."

"Mm-hmm." Sam felt so relieved that his face looked a lot younger. He wouldn't need to hide it from them anymore.

"Huh, so whichever bad guys thought they set you up don't know Alex is your Connie. That's dumb," Jason said, "but maybe safer for Alex."

"Yup." Sam felt safe for her too.

"The enemy got no friggin' clue about her and they cannot dig now." Lt added.

"Lt, question," Nick asked, "Why we need to do this sting op?"

"Yeah, and who the hell is our enemy? Relating to the diamond things?" Jason also questioned.

"Let me explain everything step by step." Lt walked to the corner of the room and pulled out the whiteboard and flipped it.

On the other side, he'd written their operation's name on top, *Op: Chimera*, and then the suspects and their committed criminal acts and roles in the group.

Suspects of Chimera criminal ring:

1. Xeno O'Keefe (ex John Doe): brain, planner, ledger keeper (deceased)

2. Declan Kosarek: brawn, shooter in OC, jewelry welder, Evalyn's murder suspect (deceased)

3. Jallal Renzo: Insurance fraud planner, main executor, jeweler (owned some stores), jewelry welder

4. Tyrone O'Keefe: brawn, (Army Captain, on leave), Evalyn's boyfriend, murder suspect of Declan, owner of the

gun used in OC and murder

5. Connie Morgan-Stone: legal clerk, legal paper expert, Gary's asst. honeytrap main player

6. Gary Morgan-Stone: a.k.a. Big One, law/judicial clerk (DC), Staff Attorney (CA) of Judge's office, computer expert, Chimera main body

"Alright." Standing by the board, Lt said, "Note that all suspects are siblings or half-siblings, except Declan Kosarek. The information on the board is collective intel gathered by all the law enforcement agencies that have been affected by this criminal ring. We got to take down the ringleader, number 6, Gary Stone, Big One in the ledger. He works for a couple of judges all over California wherever his pack goes to commit crime. His mission is only one. To protect his siblings from law enforcement. He's the reason often search or arrest warrants weren't issued quick enough or even never issued. In some cases, he succeeded in changing part of the judge's paper. Without him, nothing had been done. Those people are all part of the Chimera named Gary Morgan-Stone."

Lt continued, "You remember how this ring works. How they get good diamond cheap and get max value out of it. Basically, Gary and Xeno are planners, Jallal and Connie executors, Declan and Tyrone led the heist, Jallal prepared the loose diamonds and sold them. Gary protects them from the law. Wash, rinse, repeat."

Nick raised his hand. "Lt, question." Lt nodded. "When we know all those facts, why can't we arrest him? What kind of evidence we lack?"

"We later discovered that the judge-issued warrants had slightly different wording from the forms we submitted. Also timing of the judge signing them was much later than it should be. We investigated and found it always happened when Gary was staff attorney for the judge. But we don't have enough evidence that Gary really committed all that. So we need good evidence."

"Ah that's why the sting op."

"Yup. We know Jallal Renzo is the most important player in the diamond business and also the weakest link. He's seen easily to cut a deal with the DA to avoid a long incarceration. If he gets charged, it'd give ultimate damage to them. So, if we try to submit the warrant form for his arrest to the judge, Gary must intercept it and alter it to save Jallal."

"A chain is only as strong as its weakest link," Jason muttered.

"Gary's friggin' good at computers and the FBI learned our police network has been hacked by him so we decided to use it to distribute the news that Jallal is under investigation."

"Oh." Carter remembered now that Lt had ordered Sam and his team to use the desktop since the desktop was hooked up to the police network 24/7.

"Then we got the inside intel that Gary saw his sister Connie's obsession with Sam exploitable and set up a honeytrap to get closer to Sam, thus, our sting op to utilize their honeytrap to counter. Gary now thinks his sister is inside the BPD to get info for Jallal. Soon, Sam writes a form for the warrant…and we all move."

Just because she had *blue eyes*, it didn't make her his Connie, Sam knew. Alex's eye color wasn't just rare blue. When she looked at him, her eyes sparkled with love. They'd never imagine such color.

CHAPTER 18

"A letter…? Letter with only her initials? Where the hell?"

Uncle Barry had been scouring inside and outside his house in the Berkeley Hills after he'd received a call from Lt. Montfort.

Why had he missed it if it'd really been delivered? He'd checked the mailbox from time to time while she still lived above his Café with him. But no letter to her ever. Lt had said it was a very important letter for her to read but it was not a goodbye letter from Sam. Good news.

So where the hell was it now? Where the hell had it been sitting for a month?

He'd gone outside around his house many times if the letter might possibly have been blown away by the wind and landed somewhere unexpected in his driveway or side yard, or even backyard. No letter found. It'd been a month already so he wasn't sure if he could even find it.

His heart sank. If he couldn't find the letter, she'd never know what Sam really thought of her until he came back and explained. And he didn't know if he could make her understand either. Although everything was just a sting op and counterplot-honeytrap, he wasn't so sure that she'd be persuaded by that kind of story. She'd been hurt so brutally that he didn't know if anything or anyone would mend her heart.

It was almost like an MIA soldier coming back to his platoon or even home. No one could predict what would happen after the soldier arrived.

He decided to look for the letter outside around his house one more time.

"Barry," the next-door neighbor Ms. Sonya Litton called out when he went outside. He'd known her for quite a while as a good friend. She was a nice middle-aged lady working at a stock brokerage in San Francisco. She came down the stairs to meet him.

"Hey Sonya, long time no see. How've you been?"

"I had a month vacay and went to Toronto to see my folks."

"That's nice."

"Here, I came to see you for this." Sonya presented a plain white envelope to him.

"Oh my god," he muttered breathlessly.

"I think it belongs to Alex, ACW? Barry, I'd notified the USPS to hold my letters for a month…but I surmised either a temporary mailman made a mistake or someone picked it up to put in my mailbox when the letter was blown by the wind. Anyway it was sitting in my mailbox for a month. Hope it's not an important letter."

"Oh Sonya, thank you, thank you for telling me and bringing me this letter. Alex was waiting for this letter to arrive…" The back of his eyes suddenly stinging, he hugged her.

"I'm glad. Tell Alex don't be a stranger; text me when she needs anything." She smiled.

"Thanks, Sonya."

After he saw her leave, he took his phone out and quickly called Alex.

"Hey, sweetheart, wherever you are, whatever you're doing, just drop everything and come to the house in the

Hills right now. Right now, this moment. I don't care what you're doing."

"Uncle?"

"Come inside." When she arrived in front of the house, he urged her to get in the house.

"Alex, here." He gave her the envelope. "Sonya next door had this letter for a month since she was on a month's vacation."

"Ah, okay, thanks." She was about to put it in her purse, so he said, "No, open it right now. I'll be in my study. Let me know if you need any help."

"Alright, thanks." He walked away leaving her alone.

She sat down in the armchair in the living room and studied the envelope. Just a plain white envelope sold anywhere. No sender name. Just her initials and address, written in uppercase. The postmark said City of Santa Clara. She didn't know anybody who lived in that city. She was baffled.

But she opened the envelope anyway. A piece of plain letter paper. She tilted her head and unfolded it.

It read:

ACW,
"I wanted it to be you; I wanted it to be you so badly."
"I promise I'll come back for you. I promise I'll never leave you."
4evr,
SBC

"ACW, Alexandra Constance Wallace," again her initials, and "SBC… My god." It didn't take her long to realize who'd sent the letter. "Sam Brayden Crawford…" Apparently he must've dashed off the letter.

"Oh Sam…" Her lips trembled. Clutching the letter on her chest, she started weeping.

Now she knew whatever he was doing wasn't the real thing. It must've been his work that he couldn't tell her.

That was why he hadn't been able to use his own phone to send her messages. Ergo, the beautiful paper mail, a.k.a. the letter.

She knew both quotes, of course. The first one was from *You've Got Mail* and the other from *The English Patient.*

What Sam was trying to tell her was obvious: He knew she was the real Connie and he'd come back to her after his mission was complete; that was the reason why neither had he picked up his stuff nor told her they'd broken up. Because they hadn't.

He was still in love with her and forever. Not with that fake Connie but Alex Connie.

His act that had broken her heart today at the Courthouse had been acting. Part of his mission.

The date of the stamp said it was sent a month ago. He'd sent it right away so that she wouldn't worry…too bad it hadn't reached her sooner…

But now nothing would matter. He loved her, and she loved him. She'd need to be calm and wait until everything would be settled.

Relief flooded her heart. Happiness overwhelmed her soul. She burst into tears. She just couldn't stop sobbing.

"Alex sweetheart? You okay?" Concerned, Barry ran to her.

She gave him the letter and jumped onto him, crying like a baby.

He held her with one hand, the other flapping the letter to unfold it, and ran his eyes through it.

It wasn't difficult for him to know where those quotes came from. And he realized this was actually Sam's way of saying *I love you, my Alex Connie.* As he'd suspected, he'd really been in a covert operation. He'd been careful about what he'd written in the letter in case his enemy had chanced to see it. Hence the initials and quotes.

"Sam…" He was just like a soldier with a mission, carrying responsibility and protecting the country and its people, even though his heart was always apprehensive for his loved ones. Maybe that was why all wore the same color, regarding the purpose of their ultimate mission. To protect their people and country. The color named honor.

"I'm happy for you, Alex, sweetie." He hugged her and patted her head.

"I am too, Uncle. Now I can live." She smiled at him, looking up.

The purely happy smile that he hadn't seen for quite a while.

And he heard her tummy growl. "You hungry?"

"Mm-hmm, so funny. Suddenly I feel hungry."

"Let's go back to the Café then. I'll make you anything you'd like."

*****

Connie Morgan had regularly visited Sam and his team. She'd often brought them some snacks, sometimes donuts, pastries, cookies, etcetera, reminding them of Alex. But Sam felt a void on his desk without her black thermos with the big yellow smiley face. Whatever she was doing now was in his mind all the time. He'd heard from Jason who'd visited her at the Coroner's Bureau that she'd finally received the letter and now she'd looked much more settled and happier. Also she'd started eating more just like before. Thank heavens.

Now, Jason, Carter and Nick had been frequent visitors checking on her for him, under the pretense of '*Gee, we got another body today; goin' to the Coroner's.*'

Due to the sensitivity of the operation, Lt must shield Sam from really getting into a serious honeytrap situation, which was of course a deeper relationship with this fake Connie.

Sam had had to declare he'd loved her and would marry her yet he hadn't moved on to a sexual relationship, which had created awkwardness between them. Lt had kept insisting to her he was the lead detective in this complicated case and crazily busy. However, he couldn't keep saying it since the detective's work wasn't really 24/7.

He was at his wits' end. He just couldn't let it happen. Sam was doing this through his good will and honorable responsibility as a police officer who had sworn to protect and serve the public; saying I love you or kissing in public might be forgivable but he wasn't sure it would be okay if he had sex with her due to the mission. It would hurt Alex, for sure. He was neither a trained intelligence agent nor an unfaithful boyfriend. He'd never cheat on Alex. He'd quit the BPD if he was pushed to do it.

"Um…what ammi supposed to do to avoid having sex with her, or making out for that matter?"

Okay, at least he hadn't done it yet. So far so good. But that time had come. Lt breathed out. "She wants to live together?"

"Well, that too, but just regular dating."

Lt groaned. "Regular dating requires sex too?"

"I don't know what you're thinking, but if you're in love with someone passionately, you'd often end up in bed at the end of a date?"

"Um…okay… Oh dammit."

"Or she might think having sex makes a better connection with me, which she could exploit later." Sam circumspectly described, his eyes sharp.

Oh yeah, he was an excellent detective, very smart and dependable, Lt thought of him. He got to keep his good reputation intact. "Oh wait, I got an idea," Lt began. "I think I can use the codes of ethics and conduct in our *Law Enforcement Services Manual*."

Sam was quietly listening. Or he must be racking his brain trying to find which wordings they could use.

"Don't you remember the part, in *Conflicting Relationships? Restricted Duties and Assignments*?" Lt opened the PDF file on his computer and turned his monitor toward Sam and even recited for him.

"You see, vics and witnesses always got a special status

that can never be violated. The police officers would be penalized if we had an inappropriate relationship with them. Hey, remember that she's pretending to be the victim you protected ten years ago? So, at least she cannot say she ain't a victim or an individual you'd contacted at the event when it had occurred. We can use her own claim. And that you gonna tell her you don't wanna jeopardize your case or Jallal's warrant. She gonna definitely get it, cuz that's what she's working for, to get the intel on Jallal's warrant."

"I see."

"And tell her, I, Lt has been personally processing your relationship to be lawful. Send her my way if she'd still complain."

"That works. She gonna want me to stay the lead detective so I gonna be the one to write a request for his warrant."

"Exactly. And hopefully we can finish the damn honeytrap ploy soon before this shit gets any deeper. Look, we ain't trained as spies; we ain't cut out for goddamn sexpionage, especially you, you're a paragon of honor and cleanness at this PD. Yeah, it's a goddamn sting operation and we the cops do that, I get that, but not on this level of depth. Don't push yourself to be something you ain't."

"Yes, Lt."

"And Sam, don't you friggin' dare drop your damn pants for Fake Connie, no matter what. That's not her department. That's Alex's, and she got 'nuff of the batshit she never signed up for."

About a week later, on Saturday morning, the order from their DA to draw up the form for an arrest warrant for Jallal Renzo had finally reached Sam's desk. Saturday was always a good choice as most roads around the public offices were less crowded in case they had to move fast.

He'd first given Connie a buzz. She'd said she'd been working today too since her boss had a defendant who'd need to come in today after lunchtime.

He'd asked her to meet him at the Bureau for lunch. He'd casually passed the information that he would be writing a warrant form for Jallal Renzo before noon and bringing it to the Courthouse after lunch.

While he was at that, Lt sent a signal to all personnel. Everyone must be ready now.

Relief had finally begun flooding into him. This would be the last phase of the operation. And soon he could go home. To Alex, the love of his life. She'd been alone holding strong the entire time. He'd heard she was now back to the house in the Berkeley Hills from her uncle's Café, waiting for him to come home.

The thoughts of coming home to her raised his morale. He opened the template of the special form for the arrest warrant on his laptop as he'd been instructed to use it. His lips were curving upwards.

A few hours later, he spotted Connie coming from the elevator hall into the Detective Bureau.

Game on.

"Hey Sam." She approached his desk and smiled. "How're you doing?" She bent over a little to kiss his forehead.

"Hey." He gave her a kiss on her lips lightly. "It's already lunchtime?"

"Yeah, duh, it's noon." She laughed. "You didn't even realize it?"

"I was too busy to look at the time. Can you wait for a sec? I'm about to finish this."

"This?"

"A warrant form for our suspect. Jallal Renzo."

"Okay, I can wait in the breakroom."

"Thanks."

She stood straight and looked around. "Huh, I didn't realize… Where's everyone?"

"It's Saturday, Connie."

"Yeah, but you're working."

"So are you, no?"

"Well, that's true, but…"

"Lt is in today, too."

"Hard workers." She caressed his shoulder.

"Someone gotta hold the fort, right?"

"Ain't that so true?" Connie giggled. Looking up at her, he also smiled, showing his white teeth and a little dimple. He was such a gorgeous guy.

She quietly walked into the breakroom and sat on a chair at the table.

She'd always wanted to be in the romantic story of Connie and Sam. She had everything the UC Berkeley student had, brunette, blue eyes, the same name, age and figure and even birthdate now. And when she and her brother had checked Sam, he hadn't been married yet. Some other intel had said he was still searching for Connie Morgan. He was now having a relationship with a blond bombshell. Well, yeah, a man like him needed a woman even though he was looking for Connie, but her? Okay, she was pretty when she'd met her at the courthouse, and she was a famous forensic scientist according to Alameda County's personnel file, but she was a coroner, for god's sake. She dealt with dead people, cutting them up into pieces like in horror movies. Didn't she smell like corpse? She still didn't understand why the hot-blooded Sam had dated her. But it was all in the past.

"Hey Connie, sweetheart." He stuck his head in the breakroom through the open door. "Finished with the warrant form, but I gotta talk to Lt about Jallal's arrest, so…" and then he added apologetically, "So, can you wait for ten, fifteen more minutes or wanna go ahead to *Blue Café*? I can catch up with you there."

"Hon, don't be ridic. Of course, I can wait. Take your time, baby. Say hi to Lt for me."

"Okay, thanks, love." He lightly gave a knock at the doorframe and disappeared back into the office area.

Hmm…ten, fifteen, minutes. She stood leaning against

the doorframe and crossed her arms.

She heard the door close in the hallway, right after the words, *Lt, I need to talk about the arrest.*

He'd just said he'd finished the warrant form. She'd need to download it for Gary right away before he'd take it to a judge himself.

She asked her brother what if she'd electronically send it to him and he'd said he wouldn't want to create digital footprints heading his way on the file or Sam's computer, so to create a flash drive physically, as it could be a lot safer.

He'd left her in the breakroom alone and she had time. And she carefully walked back to his desk. His laptop was open showing the warrant on the display. How careless. He must really trust her. Thank you very much.

A warrant form was useless unless a judge signed it to become a warrant. No one in law enforcement had ever discovered what Gary had been doing for his siblings. He'd worked on the East Coast to West and so far they hadn't been caught. Thanks to her brother.

Jallal was practically the factual linchpin of their diamond business if Gary was the boss. If he was apprehended, it would be a big problem for them, especially when they were thinking to expand their operation.

Oh, and she was worried about another brother, Tyrone. But he had one murder on him and the warrant had already been issued by a judge. So, it wasn't just 'changing wordings on a warrant form' level anymore. The fastest and probably only way of escaping from a murder charge was to destroy evidence. The main evidence.

Wearing latex gloves, she inserted her own USB flash drive into the USB port of Sam's laptop and skillfully downloaded the warrant form. Then she retrieved the flash drive and double-checked to erase all possible traces and footprints that she might've left on his laptop.

When Sam came out of the Lt's office, Connie was standing in the hallway a few steps away from the office door.

"Hey, sweetie, thanks for waiting. Ready to go?"

"Sam, I got an urgent text from my office. Our defendant arrived at the office early. See?" She showed her phone. Sam read it and the order was from the Alameda County Public Defender's Office.

"Oh, damn." He grimaced. "No lunchtime for you?"

"Usually my boss prepares some light lunch and water for all the staff."

"Oh, okay so at least you gonna have something in your tummy."

She laughed. "Yes, my tummy."

"What? Tummy is funny?" He pulled her into his arms. But the office door opened, and Lt stepped out.

"Hey, Connie." She jumped up and stood straight, knowing they weren't cleared yet from the strict process whether or not their relationship was lawful.

"Hi Lieutenant. I was about to leave for my office. Our defendant came too early so lunch with Sam is out."

"Aw, I'm sorry. I'm sure he'll make it up to you."

"Sure, what about tomorrow lunch?" he asked, taking her hand.

"Okay, tomorrow lunch. Let me know the time, okay?" Connie smiled. "Gotta go."

"I'll see you off."

"Oh, no need, Sam. I really need to run. If you come with me downstairs, I'll be late."

"Oooh." He waggled his brows, sending her a chuckle.

"Okay Sam honey, talk to you later."

She hurriedly walked the hallway into the elevator hall. One descending elevator was about closing the door. Connie quickly squeezed herself into the door as it closed.

Lt and Sam, standing side by side, looked at the elevator's lights above the door. It went down.

And then their arms raised, they fist bumped sideways while still staring at the elevator.

*****

Connie parked her car in the parking lot designated for the office personnel.

And she walked hastily to the Courthouse where Gary's office was situated. Fortunately it was the weekend so the roads around the Courthouse weren't crowded.

Gary had instructed her to ride the elevator #3, no camera inside the box, and press one through ten for the floors.

While the elevator was ascending, one stop at each floor, on the fourth floor, he stepped in, startling her a bit.

"Thanks for the texts."

"No problem. We needed that ASAP." He gave her a sidelong look and said, "Flash drive."

She handed it to him.

"Connie, well done. I'll take it from here. If you wanna break up with him, you can do that now."

"Can I keep him?" She looked up at him with those sapphire eyes that must've attracted Crawford from the beginning.

He laughed. "You really do like him."

"We love each other."

"Well hell, why not? But mind you, he's the lead detective of this case. You should be careful."

"Oh no worries. He's head over heels in love with me."

He chuckled again. "Whatcha gonna do today?"

"Probably stay home."

"Good idea. Okay, I'll get off on ten. You go straight down to the first."

"Got it."

As soon as the elevator arrived on the tenth floor, he dropped a kiss on the top of her head, "Take care now, Connie."

"You too." The elevator door closed at the same speed of its open, giving ample time for him to step out and raise his hand to wave at her.

Gary was a very handsome brother. And his brain was

superb. He'd studied diligently to have earned several law degrees and passed multiple bar exams to have become an attorney in a couple of states.

She'd followed him and acquired her JD. But they hadn't been able to stay in the lawful world themselves. They liked money too much and their other brothers were too smart to just stay in the ordinary world. The siblings had believed they'd been destined to rule the world, well at least a certain world.

It'd be a good time to leave California or the country after this case. Maybe she could bring Sam into their family affair.

Gary rushed back to Judge Marvin Duncan's office. He had his Staff Attorney's desk there along with his laptop that was connected to Judge's work computer so he could take care of most of the office work for him. All staff attorneys worked like that. They were essentially high ranking clerks for the judge.

He sat at his desk, opened his computer, inserted the flash drive and opened the file.

A warrant form for Jallal Renzo appeared.

He sighed, long. He'd made it. All he needed was half an hour or so to alter the warrant. Now Jallal would remain free to keep them affluent and their business would also stay intact no matter where they'd go. Relieved, his mind had unwound a little bit. And that had also brought some unfamiliar emotions to him. Sadness to have lost his half-brother Xeno.

It'd been all because of Declan Kosarek, an asshole. Xeno had wanted Declan not only for his jewelry welding skills but for taking care of him since he'd had to hide and plan another diamond ploy somewhere quiet without the eyes of the California law. But Declan had been just a lazy dumbass. He hadn't used his brain to do anything right. Intention to kill rodents and other vermin had eventually made Xeno sick, according to his ledger entries. Who'd used that old rodenticide manufactured in the 70s? It must've been there for a long time, because the farmhouse had been built by Xeno and Tyrone's great-grandparents eons ago.

Declan had abandoned Xeno as he'd been dying. And he'd heard from Tyrone that Declan had taken Xeno's stash, a bag of loose diamonds and hid it in Tyrone's apartment. Son of a bitch.

The BPD had eventually gathered enough evidence, interpreted accurately for each case of Xeno, Evalyn and Declan.

However, he'd never given a damn about small steps and struggles of the cops to seek truth.

The law enforcers' ethics and conduct seemed to him generally foreign, often remote, as it was so illogical.

They'd sworn to protect and serve the public. The public were basically strangers. How could they risk their lives for strangers?

Like his sister Connie's crush, Crawford. He'd almost died from the burns to have saved a stranger from the falling embers. Then, a nutjob had fired a couple of bullets at him while he'd been protecting the college kids, again strangers.

Gary just couldn't fathom those cops' sacrificial, selfless minds.

His eyes restarted scanning the warrant form. Then, abruptly he noticed a peculiarity of the wording.

Jallal was in fact charged with seven counts of insurance fraud of the jewelry stores in California, three in LA County, two in San Diego County, one in Orange County and one in Berkeley, Alameda County including his own store in San Diego by the joint investigation team. Holy shit, he hadn't realized the team had gotten evidence to arrest Jallal for those fraud. Where had they obtained evidence? He'd helped Jallal and other siblings get ample time to run with evidence and he'd known they'd cleaned each scene good. What the fuck was going on? And why had Crawford drawn up this form? He hadn't been on the joint investigation team, according to Connie or their inside intel.

The seal of the District Court on top of the warrant form was authentic. It didn't look anything like a fake. Besides, why did the local police have any reason to write a fake warrant form? For what?

A very thin veil of uncertainty and suspicion had started forming, steadily advancing from the edge to the nucleus of his mind, but his self-assured disposition called for more audacity and calmness. Relax, he'd always had a way to handle anything.

So, back to the form. The truth here was all the counties were hoping to charge Jallal with even one fraud investigated by the joint investigation team in view of the evidence adduced.

At the end of the day, no matter how the warrant form looked if it was issued, Jallal would be charged with and likely to be convicted of one or more hard fraud. Then, he'd be fined, pay restitution to his victims and serve time.

Money wasn't a problem. What concerned him about his baby brother was his trait of weakness to face adversity. For fear of incarceration, Jallal would definitely cut a deal with the DA and tell them about the other siblings and the crimes they'd committed in detail. He was chicken, so it would likely happen.

In that sense, this warrant might accomplish exactly that: To intimidate Jallal into confession with the list of all the charges he would face. And also, it would be a huge appeal to judge and jury if the cases would be presented by the joint investigation team at his trial. Cross-examination would be hell.

He'd have to save Jallal's sorry ass.

What would be the best way to do it in this case?

He should alter the list of the cases and make it look like a lighter charge.

Rather, if he could turn off the wording 'Joint Investigation Team,' the warrant, if issued, would only cover the jewelry fraud in Berkeley, where the BPD had jurisdiction.

The main thing was he shouldn't have this warrant returned to the BPD to rewrite, the risk they'd take increased as Crawford and the BPD might realize the honeytrap ploy.

Let's see how it'd look... Gary started tweaking the warrant.

Then, the door to Judge Marvin Duncan's office suddenly opened and Judge himself stepped in.

"Oh, hi Gary, I didn't know you're working on Saturdays. Conscientious, uncommon, but conscientious."

CHAPTER 19

"Judge." Gary stood up from the chair at the desk. "Why are you here? I mean, it's Saturday. You should be off today."

"Well, I remembered I have some unfinished work due next week. Besides, my wife is on her way to see our newborn grandson. So might as well work today." He took off his iconic bowler hat and hung it on one of the hooks of the coat rack standing in the corner of his office.

Judge Duncan was a tall and solid man originally from the East Coast. He was in his late sixties, yet his strong legs and respiratory system made it possible for him to run for a few miles daily after work. He had very sharp hazel eyes, glaring often to see criminals, with a stubborn looking nose and jaw and high cheekbones. This judge would be one of those people that criminals wouldn't like to encounter in the hallway of the Courthouse. But he was in fact known for fair judgment and compassion.

Hanging his jacket on the back of the chair, he asked him, "What are you doing now? Anything beguiling?"

"This is just another warrant that came through now."

"What is it?" He came around to look over the laptop.

"This one looks simple enough, so just checking

wording, terminology, and if it's fine…"

"Ah, Jallal Renzo case…okay. But I thought Judge Shiller was today's warrant signer."

"Yes, but sometimes mix-ups happen to a certain PD."

"I see," Judge said. "Even the police are human."

"Yes, indeed, sir." Gary laughed with Judge.

Judge Duncan eyed him and his laptop quickly again. "Maybe I can sign it instead of Judge Shiller."

Then he went to the other corner of the room where he kept his favorite espresso/coffee machine on the sideboard. He turned it on and poured espresso in a demitasse. "Would you like one too?"

"Well, yes, but I can do it myself."

"No, let me do it since I'm standing right here." He made one more cup of espresso. "Would you care for sugar and cream?"

"No, thank you."

"Have a seat, Gary, let's enjoy coffee."

"Thank you, Judge." So, he sat back on his chair and started nursing his espresso.

Standing near the fireplace, leaning against the frame of it, Judge enjoyed his.

"I don't know why, but I like to drink espresso even when it's summer."

"I understand, Judge. I like to drink coffee hot even in summer too."

"Some things never change." Judge glanced at him. "Indeed, sir," Gary agreed.

"What about people?" Judge cocked his head to glance at him for an instant.

"What about them?"

"I mean, do people change?"

Gary didn't answer that. In his opinion, yes, of course, especially easier in a deteriorative way.

He hadn't formed his fraud/diamond scheme ring with Xeno and Jallal in his youth. But he had ultimately established the criminal group. Because it had given them an enormous amount of return more than they'd imagined from their investment.

"I have a very good friend and great judge in D.C., and he once told me his best judicial clerk had suddenly disappeared from his office without any trace. It looked like he might've done some suspicious acts at his office, not to mention dereliction of duty, though it was hard to trace at that time."

"That's very unfortunate." He drank down the last sip of his espresso. The bitterness suddenly came to the fore, rolling down his throat, pricking inside, calling forth the memories that he'd hurt many who had cared about him. But... He persistently maintained that it was simply a necessary evil and part of human nature in a sense. To acknowledge the presence of light, we all need darkness. Night and day, shadow and glow, despair and hope, secrecy and awareness, therefore, good and evil.

"Do you think he could change again, supposing he did commit a crime, back to when he'd been different?"

"Judge, if you're talking about the recidivism rate, you know felons are mostly repeat offenders, even if sometimes given a chance by the government or public volunteers. What does that tell you, Judge? Besides, in my opinion, once they tasted evil, it requires a lot of guts to get out of it."

"What do you mean?" disturbed, Judge asked.

"Well, basically, it's lotta easier to be evil, I surmise," he said, rolling the empty demitasse in his hand. "Being good is harder than being evil. Need to do work that often gives you back nothing. Or worse, it takes away more from you."

"Really? Gives us nothing?"

"Well, Judge, can you think of any tangible and acquisitive personal effects or possessions when you chose to be good over evil, like giving up something for someone? In short, when you're hungry, you'd like to eat not do some charity."

"That's true."

"Sure, you take some when you work hard, like your salary, but you often give more than you take, that's why some people are still poor. Working hard and doing the right thing won't necessarily give you what you want easily, so you'd be better off if you'd do something creative to get what you want, although it may not be the right thing to do."

"You sound like almost affirming larceny or any criminal act was okay."

"Oh no, I'm not saying such an outrageous thing, Judge. I'm just saying doing the right thing needs a lot of hard work, grit and sacrifice."

"You're right about that. Take law enforcement for instance, they do put people's lives before theirs. Even if paid, life cannot be valued as monetary worth. But at the end of the day, they'd just say imperturbably *I'm just doing my job*."

That, Gary would never comprehend, and he even detested it the most.

"Gary, you and I do too. We don't risk our lives on our ordinary job here, unlike the kids in blue. But we all are on the same page, aren't we? We live our life by the law. I think to do the right thing means basically live honorably. And I believe it's part of our moral obligation as human beings. Look, like I do, you also work hard for the public by the laws, don't you?"

"Yes, sir, I'm trying to do the right thing all the time," and Gary added in his mind, '*by us*.'

Judge's keen eyes gazed at him for a moment. "I really hoped so."

Hoped so? What the hell is that supposed to mean?

He quietly walked to the door. Gary's eyes followed him. The cloak of unknown suspicion that he'd felt before Judge came into the office appeared again in his mind.

Judge's office was connected to the admin room where his guests could sit and wait to see him. He opened the door and called out rather softly, "Gentlemen." Then he was out of the office.

A group of law enforcement rushed in. The Special Response Unit (SRU) and Warrant Team were at the head of the pack, followed by the police in multiple jurisdictions' uniforms under bulletproof vests since they'd had knowledge that Gary kept guns near him.

No sooner had he spotted them than he snatched the flash drive and stomped on it, destroying it and opened the drawer attempting to take out his gun. But in the middle of that action, he froze.

"I wouldn't do that if I were you," Cmdr. Ramos of the SRU of the Alameda County Sheriff's Office holding his gun on him, warned in a menacing tone. Another member swiftly seized his pistol.

"Hey, Sam." The Captain of the deputy team from LA County Sheriff's tossed his cuffs at him. "Do the honors."

Sam caught them in midair. "Appreciate it."

He approached the man who looked as white as a wax doll from fear of being shot.

"Turn around," Sam said.

Sam Crawford. Gary recognized him. "You still love my sister, don't you? She's innocent."

He didn't reply to that. It was over. Finally. He had no obligation to respond if he wasn't up to it.

Watching his deadpan expression, Gary was abruptly touched by the truth and angrily spat out, "You deceived her, bastard!" He tried to charge at him, but as both his arms were held by strong deputies, struggling to move at first, he soon stopped resisting. "You duped my sister!"

"No, you and your sister tried to deceive me," calmly Sam countered. "You two exploited the car crash vic and my injury."

"But you believed my sister is the real Connie Morgan and you…" It belatedly dawned on him they'd been wrong about Sam Crawford from the beginning. "Dammit, Crawford, you know the ID of the real Connie Morgan."

"Uh-huh."

"But we couldn't find her anywhere. We searched for her all over. Where did you hide her?"

"I didn't hide her anywhere."

"Bullshit."

"No shit. Turned out she's been here all along."

"Here? Berkeley?"

He didn't utter, but he meant *she's been in my soul all along.*

"Alright, turn around," he ordered, holding his wrist and twisting it around behind him.

He couldn't disobey but just yipped, "Ow!' and turned.

"Gary Morgan-Stone, you're under arrest for Obstruction of Justice."

"I won't say anything without my attorney present. Besides, you cannot find any evidence from this laptop. And that's just an arrest warrant form from you."

Sam snorted. "Probably you need to see what this warrant form holds, then."

"You can't threaten me, Crawford," he blatantly defied. "You have nothing on me. Do you think I'm that stupid? I'm an attorney. Chosen staff attorney. I know the laws and I'm also good at computers. That's why you couldn't catch any trace of my acts for years."

"Till now," the Captain from the LA County Sheriff's growled. "Now you have left extensive evidence for us."

"No. It's impossible."

"Guess he never heard of something like a *sting operation*," one of the deputies from San Diego County grunted.

"What?" Gary frowned.

"I think you need to see what a real computer expert is." Lt. Montfort intentionally scowled, standing by Sam, assisting him.

"Asst. Director," Lt called out to the back of the room. Threading through all the local police forces, a very tall man clad in a blue suit and tie approached.

"Hey, Sam, congratulations." David smiled. "Thanks." He just nodded. He'd caught the ringleader and all, but the sacrifices he'd made had been too extensive. He even didn't have any good strategy to fix everything with Alex afterwards. Would she be able to forgive him? Could he possibly mend her broken heart and wounded soul ever? He'd hurt her, even though it hadn't been his intention, but the cold truth was staring down at him. He'd hurt her good.

"I'm from the FBI in electronic intelligence."

"So?" Gary looked up at him but didn't feel threatened.

"Well, you know not all heroes wear capes, right?" David put on latex gloves and pulled Gary's laptop close. "You have no idea how much information you can hide in one image, you know." He typed in some codes.

"You see, we know this warrant form is from the flash drive that your sister gave to you."

"No, you cannot prove that."

"Well, we can," he said. That attracted attention from Gary, squinting at him. "You're bluffing."

"Oh no, we at the FBI don't bluff. Here we go. Lo and behold, angel has landed." And he turned the laptop around to show it to him.

While Gary and all others near the laptop were watching, the image of the insignia of the District Court in the warrant started transforming into tiny bits of pixel squares.

"What the…" His brow furrowed. But David just said, "Wait for it."

And then the audience saw the hidden image start taking shape. It appeared to be something yellow and round. Soon they burst into happy giggles and chuckles.

Gary's eyes open wide, he muttered, "Steganography…"

"Oh, you know the technology," David grinned. "We were quite serious making this for you."

Most law enforcement personnel in Alameda County knew that a smiley was the symbol on the thermos belonging to their best medical examiner.

"You see, this warrant form was specifically made to be your evidence since this is only found on Sgt. Crawford's laptop, and on your laptop and on the flash drive that your sister delivered to you."

"You cannot pin it on her cuz you have no evidence that my sister delivered it to me."

"Sure we can. Not only the delivery service part but also the stealing part. Very bad lady."

"What?"

"We installed a micro surveillance camera near Sgt. Crawford's desk. Very clear HD quality. And in the Courthouse elevator #3. We figured you guys were going to use it since it doesn't have a surveillance camera installed yet. Oh, and one above you. See near the light just above you?" David pointed up at the LED light fixture over his desk.

Gary's face turned pale. This time, he realized he and his siblings were in big trouble.

David snickered mockingly. "You just smashed the flash drive with your foot, and by the way, now you committed a federal offense since the evidence of this electronic information belongs to the FBI. Also, if you think you could destroy a flash drive in that manner, think again; you just created more evidence." And he jutted his chin toward a person who had been collecting the broken flash drive in a plastic bag. "The FBI lab will happily be all over the flash drive as well as this laptop," and retrieving it, he added, "Oh, and you're also being investigated now by us for your international diamond operation, and lucky you, the IRS is now very much interested in your case too. You've become so popular. Anyway, my team and I'll meet you at both your local and federal trials, Gary Stone."

Sam pushed him toward the door. Lt was standing by him, holding his other arm. "BTW Gary, your accomplices are all under arrest already," Lt said behind him.

"Accomplices?"

"Yeah, your siblings."

"My siblings…"

"Yeah, Connie was arrested in her apartment in Oakland, and Jallal was in one of his residences in Berkeley,"

Lt answered. In fact, Jason and the OPD had gotten her soon after she'd given the flash drive to her brother and got back home. She'd been caught live stealing the electronic information from the BPD on the FBI's security camera at Sam's desk. Carter, Nick and the BPD had arrested Jallal just before he escaped in his car. He'd been found with a stash of diamonds, cash and a one-way ticket to Morocco. Gary was listening to the process of his two siblings' arrests from Lt. Then he gave a glance at him.

"What?" Lt scowled, unpleasingly. He knew something wasn't quite right from his eyes.

"Nothing." He started walking again, indifferently.

"Captain O'Keefe," Sam muttered. "Gary has one more brother, Tyrone. And we're trying to find him."

"Where's he at?"

"No idea," Gary replied to Lt, shrugging.

"He knows he'll be charged with one count of murder of Declan Kosarek. That's why he's running." Sam's gut feeling was giving him unshakable discomfort that he'd missed something significant.

David overheard their conversation. "Do you have a warrant for that murder?"

"Yeah, but it's in the warrant team's hands now," Sam replied.

"Okay," David quickly considered. "What about evidence? He'd surely wanna destroy it."

"All in the evidence locker. Locked."

"Any material evidence not in the locker he could destroy?"

"His evidence…um, the bullet from Declan's body is in the locker. His clothes and related materials are also in the locker. Evalyn's vehicle's in our vehicle evidence garage, locked… Everything's in the locker. Locked and guarded," he said, enumerating.

"What about reports?" he asked. "You have all reports from your specialists and experts in your electronic storage?"

"Hmm…reports. Well…all the expert's reports're in electronic storage already."

"Sam!" Lt almost yelled at him, remembering a grave fact. "Autopsy report! Barry said it needed to be rewritten after the new evidence was discovered on his body. They still have the report and all related evidence electronically there."

"What?" The final medical examiner's report was usually sent electronically to the top of the Detective Bureau, Lt. Montfort, and he'd let the detectives read it when they needed.

"Sam, she's working at the Bureau today, did you know that?" one of the deputies of the Alameda County Sheriff's also barked at him. "I saw her name on today's roster."

The color in Sam's face drained. He hadn't known her schedule. They didn't live together now, and he'd been prohibited to make any contact with her until the operation was completed.

"It's Saturday, so officers and deputies were just a few, mostly riding the on-call coroner's vehicle. Practically no one's there," another deputy warned him. "Better hurry!"

"Shit." Sam's brain was rapidly running.

"It's too late, Crawford, go to hell." Gary laughed out loud, but Sam didn't give a damn about it and dashed, calling out, "Commander!" He was looking for the top of the SRU from the Alameda County Sheriff's Office.

They'd been already in the hallway out of the rooms.

"Cmdr. Ramos!"

"Here! Sam, 'sup?" He was at the head of the team farthest from the rooms.

"Captain O'Keefe's heading to the Coroner's Bureau to destroy Declan's autopsy reports. My fiancée is working today, possibly alone."

"Your fiancée? *Sister Golden Hair*?" He wanted to ask when they got engaged, but it wasn't important now. "Dammit." And he pulled out his radio.

"All available units, to Alameda County Coroner's

Bureau. Murder suspect Tyrone O'Keefe possibly at scene, possible hostage situation. Suspect drives 2008 white Chevy Colorado, tag is… Code ten on channel one. Suspect is armed and dangerous. Repeat, suspect is armed and dangerous."

*****

Alex was as busy as she could be to finish up multiple reports on the autopsies in her formal office. Not all autopsies were homicides or other violent deaths, but when the Alameda County Coroner's Bureau took care of about 4,000 bodies per year, anyone could see all medical examiners always had a handful.

In addition to all those reports, she'd been requested to finish rewriting Declan's case ASAP by Uncle Barry. Lt…not Sam, had come to see her for information on it even yesterday. Why hadn't Sam come for inquiry? It wasn't personal. It was work-related. And he'd yet refuse to see her…okay, maybe not refusing as he'd still been on the Connie thing.

Recently she'd come back to the house in the Berkeley Hills to wait for him. But she didn't know when he'd be able to come back to her. Even Carter hadn't known, or he couldn't tell her.

It'd been more than a month. The longest, crappiest one month that she'd ever had. Felt like ten years.

Ten years. That long time ago, she'd first met him. Place and time weren't so important anymore after she'd reconnected with him.

And he'd given her a fun time and *I love you.*

But she wasn't sure what their future together held. She was still unstable after she'd seen him tell Connie *I love you* and kiss her intimately. It was so confusing.

According to his simple letter, she could guess he'd been on some kind of covert mission. She could believe that.

She was a movie buff and watched spy movies too. But

movies weren't reality or fact. And fact was stranger than fiction.

She was getting more and more disturbed, even antsy.

What had really been bothering her was she didn't know whether or not his mission had involved sex. She still remembered Connie's expression at the Courthouse not long ago: *When he told me he loved me, I just knew we're meant to be…*

So, when a lover said he loved her, didn't they make love at some point?

She knew there were spy missions that involved sex, sexpionage or honeytrapping from the movies she'd seen. Had Sam also been required to do the same? It didn't look natural not to make love when they were in love, did it? And the extended question was: Was it plausible just another mission could become a serious fact after sleeping together?

Fact was stranger than fiction.

According to Jason and Carter, she must trust him. Oh duh, easy for them to say, especially when they were his dudes. Homies protected homies.

She grudgingly returned to her work and realized she needed a book reference in the report. She stood up to fetch the book. People would think it must be easy to use eBooks, but academic books were hard to convert into eBooks. And/or extraordinarily expensive. Not all books were created equal.

Her book collection was far from perfect, but at least enough books to cover writing any reports in her field. She picked up one book, opened it, her finger on the glossary and looked for the information she needed.

Even though it was Saturday, many machines were humming in the background. And she was listening to music streaming.

It took a while to realize she had company.

She jumped, dropping the book, when she spotted Tyrone, leisurely standing by the frame. Yes, the door was always open so anyone could come in. Even a murder suspect who was running away from the cops. Where was the warrant team when she needed it?

He didn't look worn out or like being hidden in a shed or anything like that and didn't look like a murder fugitive whatsoever, tall stature, military-cut brown hair and blue eyes, clean, sharp, wearing black clothing. Except a handgun. Oh, dear. Why did bad guys always come with a gun?

"You're Dr. Wallace?"

He knew her name? She swallowed, just staring up at him.

"Whoa, you do have some scary blue eyes." He looked purely shaken. "Along with that golden hair. Wow. Are you really a human living in the human world? No fairy or something?"

She was in a pale blue summer dress with sandals. *Regular human outfit.* And she still looked like some inhuman form of some magic land? Seriously?

When she was small, some kids and adults alike had called her a creature with a monster's blue eyes and golden fibers, a scary fairy. Very much bitter memories that had resulted in her hatred for Halloween. She believed blue-eyed Siberian Huskies could do better than she could.

"Hey, I came here to ask you a favor," wielding his gun as if it was just part of his hand, he told her. He was accustomed to using firearms and had administered an accurate shot to Declan. Yup, he was an Army captain.

"A favor?"

"More like a demand. If you don't want to die, you accept my demand."

A bad guy's logic. All bad guys assumed using some excessive force could get them whatever they wanted.

"What kind of demand would it be?"

"Destroy Declan's autopsy report."

"What?" Jeezus, another bad guy's logic. Tampering with or destroying evidence was just another criminal offense to add to his charge.

"Autopsy report and any evidence related to his murder," he rephrased.

"Do you think that lets you get away with murder?"

"At least it'll help increase the doubt,"

"Besides, even if I destroy my report, other doctors have written other reports on him and I cannot access all of them. You cannot destroy them all." Hey, look at her! She was so calm in front of the killer.

He snorted. "I know you're the performer of his autopsy. You have responsibility for all the autopsy related evidence. They need your signature to be admissible evidence. So, in other words, Dr. Wallace, you destroy your autopsy reports and evidence means you destroy all the reports with your signature on them."

She couldn't refute that fact but could reject his demand. "What if I say no?"

"That's not very smart." He aimed his gun at her. She sucked in her breath. That was the one that probably had killed Declan.

"If you shoot and kill me, you cannot get your file deleted."

"I can shoot you not killing you soon and make you work until you die."

"Mr. O'Keefe, your hypothesis would be correct if the subject to be shot was as big as yourself, but not in my case. I'm small. You see, your bullet is too big. No matter how you try not to kill me, you'll end up killing me if not instantly but within several minutes. If you penetrate me in the torso or even part of the extremities, I won't survive."

He gazed at her and said, "Dr. Wallace, Declan had killed my brother and Eva. He deserved the slug in his head."

"I'm sorry for your loss and pain, but it doesn't justify murder."

He looked a bit stunned at her. It occurred to him that no one had ever had the guts to tell him that straightforwardly. "Yeah, you're right," he self-mockingly scoffed, "fundamentally we aren't…weren't killers. Murder wasn't in our playbook. Declan made everything hell."

If Declan hadn't been part of their activities, Xeno and Evalyn would've been still alive. It wasn't too hard if someone knew how to put two and two together.

He looked down at his gun, fondling it. "We'd met in San Diego."

She hadn't understood what he'd begun talking about at first, but it soon registered with her.

Evalyn. He was talking about her, his lost love.

"She was attending her bank conference. I was there just killing my vacay. She was young and pretty and so delicate, elegant."

She felt odd, listening to him talk about her. She hadn't known her personally before, but she'd become the closest human being to Evalyn after her death. And she did understand what he'd just expressed how she'd looked when he'd met her… Even on an autopsy bed, she'd been exactly a young, beautiful woman.

She looked at him. His eyes sad, he gazed back at her. Some woeful yet serene air, as if it was an elegy for the young woman whose life had unreasonably been cut short, filled the room for an instant. The feelings for Evalyn were shared at that moment even though they stood on totally different ground.

"Even when Eva's gone, I cannot stop loving her."

Oh. That, she did understand. So, she nodded at him.

"I needed to kill Declan for that."

That, she couldn't agree with him. She shook her head.

"She saw him hiding Xeno's diamond stash when he came to our apartment to pick up my truck, so he killed her, dumped her like a dead fish. And you think I was wrong to kill the fucking bastard?"

"Murder is wrong," she adamantly insisted. Because it was her code of ethics, and of course, her workplace also had the similar code. The Coroner's Bureau was under the Alameda County Sheriff's Office, so, hello? Of course, murder was not only ethically wrong but unequivocally illegal.

"You're worried about that dipshit rat? You'd say like other cops say, *he doesn't deserve to die like that,* or *you have no right to take someone's life*?"

"Yes."

"What about Eva's right, then? She didn't deserve to die like that either."

"You're correct." She agreed with him unreservedly. Then she asked, "Did she know you are part of…er…"

"The diamond sale ops? Fraud and stuff? No, she didn't. She thought I was in Special Ops in the Army and I needed to be covert. That's why she tried to help me stay secretive."

"Ah, I see." Well, really. She in fact doubted that. Women were relatively sensitive to their partners. She believed it was almost impossible for Evalyn not to know what kind of man she was in love with. She'd known the truth about her boyfriend but she just hadn't said anything to him. If Alex was her, she'd do the same. If she was in love, she'd tried to understand him, even his bottom line.

Oh, wait, not *if*, she *was* still in love with Sam Crawford and still trying to believe in him, trust him. Was it an answer to all the questions she had?

He raised his head and looked at her. Somehow her small stature reminded him of Eva.

"After I found out what he did to her," he began recollecting. "I tied up Declan and threw him in the Camry's trunk. I asked Jallal to drive my truck up to the farmhouse while I was driving her Camry. I told Jallal to go to the next town to wait for me, cuz I didn't want him to be part of my revenge. I drugged Declan good and left him in the farmhouse. I drove the Camry to meet up with Jallal. Spent night in the RV Park, we drove back next day hoping Declan was dead. But he was still alive. Weak but regaining consciousness."

Alex had realized he was practically confessing murder

to her. He might've decided to kill her. Well, then let him talk.

Eyeing her occasionally, staring at his gun often, he kept talking, "While Jallal was waiting, I drugged him again good to subdue him. I shoved him in the trunk and I shot him. It was for Eva, so I made her car trunk his coffin." Her car trunk was his coffin…such a powerful statement of revenge for his love.

"Why did you steal the clothes?" she needed to ask.

"Cuz Declan said he and Xeno needed the clothes in the farmhouse. I stuffed some in the trunk later."

"I see."

"So, I took her Camry back to Berkeley."

"You wanted it to be discovered fast?" she asked.

"Yeah. It was Eva's car. I couldn't just leave it like that."

She just nodded. It was clear he'd loved her so very much that it had made her heart squeeze with sorrow.

He decisively said, "You gonna destroy the evidence, for Eva's sake?"

She shook her head. "I can't. I'm the same as a sworn officer. I cannot violate the law or go astray of the Sheriff's manual."

"Don't make me kill you." Gazing at the gun in his hand, stroking it for a while, he then aimed it at her.

She was petrified, her back against the bookshelf wall.

What should she do? What was she supposed to do? No one had taught her that, even Uncle or Sam or Lt. It wasn't in any textbook or research reference either.

If she'd destroy the autopsy reports or any evidence for that matter, it would be obstruction of justice. She might be able to use *duress* in defense, even though *duress* is not justification to commit a crime. And he might get away with murder for lack of evidence. She didn't want that. Even when her life was threatened? Totally. She'd rather die than do illegal activities. She'd want Sam to be proud of her even if she'd be under six feet of earth. She'd never want him to visit jails or the penitentiary to see her.

She saw him move his thumb and cock the gun.

Okay, that was it. She breathed slow to calm herself down. It would be a shock for an instant, then she wouldn't feel anything since she'd be dead. Even though he'd try to make her live by controlling the place to shoot, 9mm in her small body wouldn't leave her alive that long.

Just one little sting in her heart. She wished she could see Sam.

She shut her eyes tight, hoping not to see the gun fired at her.

"Dr. Wallace, look at me!"

CHAPTER 20

The SRU and other police vehicles parked one block north of the Coroner's Bureau. Uniforms cordoned all the roads in the vicinity.

"Ayden, I wanna go in," Sam implored.

Cmdr. Ayden Ramos, who'd known him for a long time, stared at him.

When he'd protected the girl ten years ago, Ayden had been a five-year veteran deputy on the special tactics team. He remembered when Sam had still been in the SRT, he'd gotten shot by a terrorist-wannabe nutcase who'd effectively had one college locked down. But even though he'd been plugged with three slugs, thanks to the vest, he'd also shot back at the suspect. The suspect had been stopped yet survived as he hadn't been critically injured. Sam had only aimed at his arm that had held the assault rifle. But the case today, his wife-to-be was with the suspect. And the suspect desperately wanted to destroy the evidence to get away with murder. And he was an Army soldier who knew how to kill.

"Hey, Sammy, any idea?" he asked.

"Yeah, got one, hear me out."

His brow furrowed. "No way if you might get shot like before."

"Not my plan, the shithead ambushed me, remember?" he refuted exasperatedly.

"Ain't it the truth."

"Ayden, the thing is I gotta protect Alex. That's my only priority."

"Okay, let me hear you out."

After the last short meeting, only the SRU and Warrant Team moved to the back of the parking lot protected by the SRU armored truck rolling slow.

And Cmdr. Ramos spotted a matte black pickup in the east end of the parking lot.

"Yo, I thought it's *white* Chevy Colorado," he said to Sam.

"Shit," he swore under a breath. No wonder they couldn't have found the truck.

He'd had it repainted in matte black. If it parked somewhere in the shade or dark, even in the daytime, it was almost impossible to spot.

"Look at the tag. He partially hides it with some sort of dry leaves."

Sam now knew the reasons why they'd had difficulty finding the suspect's truck.

Then they sighted Dr. Alex's Leaf in its parking space, near the front, where no other car was around.

Leaf, in fact, suited her, cute like her, clean like her, self-sufficient like her. But in that parking lot, it was almost literally a lone leaf floating on the still water of a remote lake. All alone, like Alex in the Berkeley Hills without him looking over her. In the California king bed, by herself, like a leaf floating on the pond. The notion squeezed his heart. How lonely had she been?

Because he'd left her for his mission. Because he'd hoped his mission had also protected her along with the public.

His throat constricted, making him feel like suffocating.

He shouldn't have accepted the order to execute the

undercover operation.

He should've found Tyrone's truck much earlier, so they might've already arrested him and she wouldn't have been trapped with him in the Coroner's Bureau…

Should haves, shouldn't haves…

Everything, e.v.e.r.y.thing that he'd been doing for this case including the goddamn covert operation had been to the detriment of his personal life with Alex. Fucking huge blow.

Even fate hadn't been on his side.

The letter.

His letter should've been delivered to her more than a month ago before he'd started carrying out the undercover assignment. But the fact was it hadn't. She'd had no way of knowing he'd been acting undercover for the sting operation, and he hadn't realized she hadn't received his letter yet.

He'd hurt her so much that he doubted he could fix it in his lifetime, and he couldn't forgive himself for that.

Even though his regret had been eating at him, he knew he must save her from the situation. She was his woman. His love.

Then, they heard a gunshot, muffled yet reverberating in the building in actuality, a more distinctively metallic sound in the Alameda County's gunshot detection device in the truck.

"Shot fired!" One of the SRU deputies radioed. One shot, but one was too many.

Sam froze. With Tyrone's Army SIG, petite Alex had no chance of surviving. He was too late.

With all the images conjuring up one after another, haunting him, his eyes turned glassy with no mettle, no flames of life. The image of Alex lying in a pool of her own blood almost pushed him over the edge, too much to bear.

Another clear epiphany. He couldn't live without her.

"Sam!" Ayden lightly slapped his face first, then he

covered his cheeks with both his hands, staring into his empty eyes. "It's just a blank. Our gunfire detection analysis."

"A blank…"

"Affirmative. Tyrone might've needed to scare the shit outta her. Cuz I'm sure she stubbornly rejects destroying the evidence. Your woman got more cojones than us. So, Sam, get a grip. No need to be a hero, but just be a man who can save his woman. You'd done it ten years ago; you sure can do it now. Get it?"

Just like ten years ago. He'd known right then, he knew right now. Sam blinked and nodded. "Hell yeah." His cheeks regained color, his eyes showing determination. Good ol' badass protector Sam Crawford was back. "Damn right." Ayden sighed with relief.

No other sounds came afterwards, so Cmdr. Ramos quickly gave orders, "Okay, last time we checked from our sound and infrared detection, we know Dr. Alex and the suspect are in her formal office in the belly of the building. We proceed up to the lab. Let's move. Go, go, go."

All the team started moving toward the building clandestinely.

"EMT is ready. Waiting for Code four. Just in case," one of the Warrant Team sent out the message to the SRU, and Sam heard it at the back of his head, thinking, of course, no one would be hurt.

They entered the building and quietly kept proceeding gradually to her office.

Ayden pulled Sam aside. "It's your move. Sam, keep your chill, okay?"

"Roger that."

"Alrighty, flash team go first and you. I'm right behind," Ayden assured him.

"I trust you. As always," he returned. Ayden just nodded, and his fingers gestured behind him. Two men advanced in front of the unit. Then he gave the last order to the flash team, waving his hand once.

"Looked like I scared you good," Tyrone laughed. "It's just a blank for intimidation. But next time isn't the same," said he.

Whatever it had been, a blank or not, her shock was indescribable. At the same time, she'd realized he was really serious. He'd shoot her and kill her without qualms. He was Army. He'd been well trained. He wouldn't miss a shot.

"I said if you'd help me, I won't shoot you; especially a doctor like yourself," he went on, "Yeah, I really respect doctors and scientists. They're the farthest from violence and contributing to the world."

She'd decided to go along with him to buy time. She wanted to believe Sam and the police force wouldn't be too far away to get her out of the situation…well, at least she was hoping so.

"Alright. You win," she sighed, purposefully. "I'll do it. Just don't shoot me or anything else here. Everything in here has nothing to do with homicide or police thingies. It's mostly for my pro bono research for patients." She'd tried to appeal to him since he'd said he respected doctors and scientists.

"I'll promise I won't shoot you or anything here from now on. My apologies," he said.

Really? Yeah, right, and she had land on Mars to sell him.

The configuration of her official office was two walls of bookshelves, one side of a regular wall with a counter/sideboard with a fridge next to the incubator, and one side made with huge tempered windows. He was standing in the corner of one of the bookshelf walls and the window wall so that he could see anything that might happen outside her office through the window. Her position was diagonal to him, in front of the other bookshelf wall.

When she was about to walk to her desk, they heard a

huge noise, a short burst of a bang, outside the office a bit far away. She was startled. But not him. He wasn't affected by the sound of a bang.

"What's that?" he'd immediately reacted as a soldier; his body behind the bookshelf wall, he gradually moved his face toward the window, trying to observe if it was anything he could see from his vantage point. Then, a small version of a flash grenade exploded just below him on the other side of the window. "Shit!"

The flash had been so strong, temporarily blinding her too. But it seemed he'd been trained to cope with a flash grenade. He could still see partially.

However, Sam in his tactical suit and gear didn't hesitate to dash into the room, closely followed by Cmdr. Ramos. Tyrone shot once, aiming at Sam, as he'd known him as the lead detective of his case, but missed two inches over his Kevlar-covered shoulder. He must've still not seen him well from the effective flash. But he wouldn't give up now. He wanted to shoot Sam.

Without flinching, Sam jumped to grab Alex into his arms, diving to the floor, when she heard another shot hitting the bookshelf again although she couldn't see anything in his arms tightly covering her head. Just before she was about to hit the floor, he turned his body around so that he hit the floor first, skidding. He extended his arm to prevent their heads from smashing at the bottom of the sideboard.

"Okay, okay, don't shoot, don't shoot!" When he saw the SRU coming in, he raised his hands.

"Put the gun down!" Commander ordered, aiming at him with his pistol.

"Put it on the floor now!" another SRU deputy shouted, also aiming his gun at him, "Right now!"

"Okay, don't shoot!" As he put down his gun on the floor, a deputy picked it up and took it outside the office, locking it and taking out the magazine. A few deputies pushing him on the ground frisked him. "Tyrone O'Keefe, you're under arrest for one count of murder, abduction, and assault with a firearm." And one of them cuffed him and then together with the others pulling him up, pushed him outside the office.

Good, Ayden thought, exhaling, since he hadn't wanted to have a shootout with him in a small confined room risking Dr. Alex's life. He glanced at them and left the room, grinning wide.

The hustle and bustle of the arrest hadn't reached Alex and Sam.

The tossed helmet by his side, still holding her on him, they were just staring at each other.

He quickly chucked his gloves, picking up the wild hair from her forehead, smoothing down her golden cascade, feeling the familiarity all over again, and he asked, "You okay?"

"Yes," she said. "You saved my life again."

His lips curved, "I'll do it over and over to protect you."

"Oh Sam…" she murmured, her voice breaking.

"And it's Saturday again."

She blinked at his statement, baffled. "Saturday…"

"Don't you know all the events happened on Saturdays?"

"Oh," awareness turning up in her expression, she muttered, "Omigod…Saturdays."

"Uh-huh, on that night ten years ago and when we reconnected over the fallen-from-the-sky guy and…well, I never counted, but today when I saved you again…"

"Saturday."

"Yeah,' Sam nodded. Then he said, "*I wanted it to be you, I wanted it to be you so badly.*"

"You knew all along."

"Yeah, for quite a long time."

"When? How?" Her eyes widened.

He asked, smiling, "Does it matter?"

"No," she shook her head.

"Nope, cuz you're you no matter where we go, when we

go."

She smiled then softly uttered another quote from a movie to him, "*I have crossed oceans of time to find you.*"

It was from *Bram Stoker's Dracula*, but it told him the truth he'd never known. She'd been actually watching over him, seeking the chance to meet him again, from Europe.

"Oh, Alex, I never knew." The warm emotions surged into his heart, the back of his eyes burning.

Her face closer, the golden silk coming over him, she asked, "What's your name?"

He batted his eyes at first, but another smile touched his mouth. "I'm Sam."

She went on, "*Hello*, Sam. I'm Alex. Nice to meet you. No worries. I'll protect you."

You had me at hello… He closed his eyes for a brief moment. Ten years ago, that Saturday night when all the stars had been aligned and every event leading to the accident had been destined to have happened under the promising shooting star…

He opened his eyes. Her strikingly beautiful eyes that were exactly the same hues as on that night were gazing down at him. He could drown in her glacial blue and love. The thought almost sent him to orgasmic rapture.

He propped up his upper torso against the sideboard, pulling her up. She naturally straddled his thighs. Then, bracing the back of her head with one hand, holding her tight with his other, he kissed her, kissed her hard.

The real kiss, the true love's kiss that he'd been dreaming of.

Her lips tasting so familiar, he knew he was home. Her same soft lips apart, accepting his tongue. He enjoyed kissing her so much that he almost forgot to let her breathe. She panted, her face burying in his neck. His whole body shivered, the hair standing up. Yeah, that was one of the signs. Only happened when he was aroused by her.

"I thought I'd lost you," she said, wiping sweat off his forehead with her fingers, giving him another shudder. "I didn't receive your letter for a month. So…I thought you and Connie were…and you said you loved her…and kissed her and…" she trailed off. For a month of torture, she'd thought her heart had been torn to cut open. The pain still raw, the tears rolled down her cheek.

He kissed her cheek to wipe the tears away, sucking some of them gently. He had to remember the taste of her tears forever, he thought, so that he'd never forget the fact that he'd hurt the love of his life. "I'm so sorry I hurt you. Please forgive me." Although it was his mission, there was no excuse to hurt his woman. "Even if it might take forever for you to forgive me, will you please try to forgive me?"

She kissed back his cheek. "Sam, it wasn't exactly your fault. You had a mission to accomplish. Part of to protect and to serve, right?"

"But I couldn't protect you or serve you, babe. It won't happen again, and I won't do such a mission ever again. Ever."

Clinging onto him tightly, she murmured, "I like it when you come home every night."

"Yeah, me too." Then he remembered there was one silver lining she might like to hear out of this awful event.

"Hon, I never slept with her."

"Really?"

"Really. Lt helped me out of it. I'd decided if I was ever required and ordered, I'd leave the BPD. But my Lt pulled up the BPD manual and found some legal issues we could utilize to stop her putting the make on me."

Relief appeared on her face. Her tears welled up again. "I'm so glad to hear that."

And he held her cheeks with his hands and said, "But you'll never lose me. '*If we're meant to meet again, then we'll meet again.*' Remember, *Serendipity*? We met again on Saturdays."

She lightly nodded, a small smile coming back onto her face.

"The truth is we're really meant to be; the universe cannot separate us, baby. Nothing can defeat us."

"We've come full circle and will always. I like it."

He grinned. She snuggled up to him, inhaling him.

He sucked in her scent, another shiver pleasurably assailing him. "Alex, sweetheart, I'm coming home to you tonight and every night from now on," he whispered in her hair. He felt her nod. "I can start cooking for you again, making love to you all the time, taking a bath together every day, and having a family with you." Her head shot up to look at him.

"Alex sweetest, I've loved you since that night ten years ago." His eyes never averting from her face, his hands enveloping her cheeks gently, he said, "Ten years ago, I'd met you and left my heart there. We met again here and you made my heart whole. Now I just can't live without you. Alexandra Constance darling, marry me, have a family with me, and make me a man you can be proud of."

"Sam, my love, when you saved me that night, you were already a man of honor and dignity. You don't need me for you to be a man I can be proud of, but I think you need me for you to be a father. So, yes, I'll marry you."

Sam laughed softly in a low tone, reverberating in his chest. He was aroused. She could feel it even under his tactical suit. He raised his butt to press his hard-on to her thigh. "Sam." He finally heard her special way of calling his name in that scolding tone, making him harder, dammit.

"Alright, tonight, hon."

"That's better." But she smiled and kissed his jaw. He dropped a kiss on her forehead.

"Alex, let's go to the jewelry store tomorrow. Wanna buy you a ring you like."

"I'd love that."

Sam helped her get up and kissed her one more time before they left holding on to each other.

*****

Next afternoon, the joint law enforcement operation

team held a press conference for the series of crimes and the police sting operation, with a display of the suspects' mugshots.

First and foremost, they had to clear Sgt. Sam Crawford's name as ADA had promised; the public had believed he'd dumped Dr. Alex Wallace over his infatuation of ten years, Connie Morgan. It'd actually been the counterplot of their sting operation against the honeytrap ploy. And Dr. Alex was the real Connie herself.

Then, Lt. Montfort explained each case separately, and he concluded the efforts by the detectives and uniform officers as well as CSI, medical examiners, analysts, and private companies had made it possible to close this intricate case, not to mention the helpful witnesses and understanding of the communities.

Alex was watching Sam also speak to the press on the monitor in the Detective Bureau with other detectives congratulating her on their engagement enthusiastically. She was proudly wearing her engagement ring they'd just purchased, a blue diamond with the color like her eyes that they'd eventually ended up choosing.

*****

Uncle Barry's *EZ Poppas* opened for the celebration of closing the case and the engagement of his niece and Sam after the press conference.

He had help from several cooks who were veterans and, of course, the band *EZ Poppas* playing for them, sans Barry, since he was busy serving and chatting and babying his niece.

In addition, Tony Novato had also sent out some help and their supply of drinks to them. He felt bad about the incident.

And he clearly stated, "I practically hurt Alex by texting her. Yeah, sure, I did worry about her and didn't know it was Sam's undercover op, but hello? I once was in the military and knew such honeytrap ops in reality, goddammit. And I trusted Sam for a long time… Jeezus, feel so dumb and sorry for them. Anyway, Alex will eat as much as she likes at our Café for the rest of her life. Anytime. Day or night or even holidays. What? Sam? 'Course NOT. He's the one who screwed up and hurt her so bad."

Uncle Barry had separated the tables between the girls and boys among their friends. The reason was obvious: If Alex and Sam, Rae and Jason would be seated together, he was sure the tables would be close to R-rated. He was right at least about Sam, who craned his neck every five minutes to look for Alex at the girls' table. Even after a short absence, if she wasn't within his arm's reach or eyeshot, he felt deprived of part of himself. Frustration and lament of not seeing her for a month had finally come back to bite him in the ass. Or it was just who Sam had always been.

His beloved fiancée was laughing and giggling with her BFFs Rae and Nora, her gorgeous eyes dancing with joy. He was reassured by just watching her how much he loved her and quietly promised that he'd do anything to make her happy.

"You met her where?" At the boys' table, Jason asked for the third time when Carter disclosed he'd started dating a girl.

"I said at *Blue Café*," he answered defiantly while munching on his chicken enchilada.

"Who is she?" asked Nick again, after asking about three hundred times.

"Okay, for the last time, her name is Shelly and she's a librarian at UC Berkeley, alright?"

"Librarian?" Jason asked.

"Librarian," Sam nodded.

"Ain't it only me librarian sound so fucking sexy?" Jason wanted to mess with him, but he was caught even before Carter said anything.

"Jase," Rae's calm voice came from the next table.

"Shit…" "Jason."

"Here goes my two bucks," he mumbled and tried to make the case turn around. "But Rae, my lady, I thought the rule should only be applied in our chamber."

"Chamber?" his eyes wide, Carter blinked, his lips twitching.

"Chamber," Sam confirmed, keeping his face serious, "Jase, just don't say anything. With guy talk, you cannot escape from the swearword police."

"Who's the swearword police, Sam?" sweet but stern voice from Alex reached him.

"Oh shit."

"Sam."

Even with her calling his name in the tone like that, the sound gave him a shiver, the taste of her crawling up and down his spine, arousing him. She'd always taken him down singlehandedly just with her voice. He was helpless, helplessly in love with her.

He stood up, coming around to her and hugged her from behind, nuzzling her hair and neck. "'K, a buck and flowers for you babe, and I'm sorry for the swearword police part. Hope you're still in love with me and marrying me, sweetheart."

"Yes, I am; remember, *you had me at hello*?" Hugging his arms, she smiled, as Rae and Nora giggled.

And then Nick, having been quiet all along, looking around at his buddies, asked, "What's chamber?"

*****

The amazing love story of ten years + of Alex and Sam had made them local celebrities.

Some press had begun telling their story in serial form, spearheaded by the local journalist Tom Parson, Sam and Jason's college buddy. His first episode started like this:

Serendipity in Berkeley: *Love story of an officer and a student.*

It turns out ten years of time have no meaning before the phenomenon called serendipity. It seems to travel through place and time; be prepared, be alert, as it might tap you today for something unexpectedly life-changing.

'If we're meant to meet again, then we'll meet again.' --- Serendipity, Film, 2001

The End

About the author

Kay C. Beerman is an author of Romantic Mystery/Suspense.

She writes stories about detectives, agents and medical examiners who are dedicated to protect and to serve in the San Francisco Bay Area.

She resides in Northern California with her husband who works in the geeky world.

Website: https://www.kaycbeerman.com

Made in the USA
Las Vegas, NV
24 June 2021